Vivian & Wendy
It's been so much
fun traveling with you
gals. I hope you'll enjoy so
of my fun adventures. An
please you've been email
experience. Happy Trails.
Winnie

Wish You Were Here

by

Winnie Bowen

Table of Contents

Dedicated to my children,
John and Shirley,
who sometimes unnecessarily worried
but willingly, albeit sometimes skeptically,
supported my travel adventures.

Author's Note

As a Navy wife for many years, we traveled across country, coast to coast, many times, always choosing a different route. By adding leave days to travel time, we turned those trips into vacations. Since my husband was a history buff, we made many detours to see a place of interest or historical significance.

Travel is a passion of mine, and after I retired I indulged in earnest. Because I had seen so much of the U.S., I concentrated on overseas. I've tried to do the active trips and destinations while I still had my health and stamina to participate in those activities.

Wiser now, I always have a pad of paper and pen in my pocket. I take notes all day, transcribe them at night into my diary-- while I can still read my handwriting.

I love to and am always willing to share my experiences with others who are interested, fully realizing not everyone gives a diddly squat about anywhere other than home. In such cases, I choose not to bore, and definitely soft pedal any and all experiences.

Although I, in turn, love to hear about other's travels and view their pictures, I do find it boring to see Susie in front of the Eiffel Tower, Susie in front of the Louve, Susie in front of the bridge— you get the picture. This also translates into I, I, I, I, so you'll soon discover within these covers, I relay information I found interesting rather than I did this, I did that.

What follows is a compilation from my travel books that I've written for my family over the years. I've tried to glean the highlights from those books into this one volume for friends who always want to read about my "adventures."

As I put this book together, I found a recurring theme—nature and wildlife. Interestingly enough, that was completely unconscious. I know if I had been born any time after when girls grew up to be nurses, teachers, or secretaries, I no doubt would have been an environmentalist, park ranger, or something along those lines. In my fifties, I was not looking for a career change and had long ago decided any further studies would be in areas that truly interested me, not something required for whatever purpose or degree.

Occasionally, someone asks me if some organization sponsors my travels or if I'm a travel agent, and the answer to both questions is no. I pay all my own expenses and feel very fortunate that I'm able to do so.

Although I travel all ways, I prefer small groups and in-depth exploration. I enjoy meeting and interacting with local people, and learning their customs. Small groups allow for detours, longer stays, less rush, no lines, and no waiting.

I still have that curiosity of learning something new and different. Most times when I ask younger friends if they've been to a certain place, they almost always answer, "No, we should, but there just isn't time," or "We didn't get around to it." To me, this is a shame, as travel is great way to grow closer to the family as well as enjoy our country.

It's been a great adventure, and fun to relive my trips as I've put this book together. I hope you'll enjoy traveling with me and sharing my adventures.

Winnie Bowen

Chapter 1

Panama Canal: The Big Ditch

The big ditch, as the Panama Canal was often called, claimed up to 20,000 lives before the United States took over construction in 1903. Besides the many accidents, malaria, yellow fever, and the plague claimed those lives. It would take the conquering of those diseases, and the work of 75,000 men over ten years, before the canal was operational and able to save ships and their crews thousands of miles by avoiding sailing around South America.

This manmade wonder had always intrigued me, so it was in 1988 that I attempted my first canal transit and the most unforgettable cruise of my life. It is only because I documented daily our trials and tribulations in a letter to my folks, who fortunately kept it, that I am able to reconstruct this incredible story many years after the fact.

The First Attempt
A Real Adventure Called A Mutiny

Golden Cruise Lines in San Antonio, Texas ran a national advertising blitz with a slick multi page brochure. The ship, *Galaxie*, was small in comparison to luxury cruise ships, and the idea that she carried only 200 passengers, and had an unusual itinerary is what attracted us to her. A couple of weeks before we sailed, I talked to the office in San Antonio and asked, "Since it's February, what happens if we're delayed because of weather?"

They informed me that they would consider us "no shows" and we wouldn't be able to get a refund. To avoid such an outcome, we made arrangements to fly into Acapulco a couple of days early to sightsee and have a little fun. The ship was scheduled to leave from Acapulco, visit Guatemala, Jamaica, Costa Rica, transit the canal, visit Columbia, and return to Cancun.

The literature stated that *Galaxie* had made many canal transits. They also promised all the usual amenities of pool, three lounges, duty-free gift shop, beauty shop, casino, and air-conditioned cabins.

Arriving at the port at noon for boarding, as directed, we were surprised to find nearly 200 tired, hungry, and irritable people who had been in a holding area several hours that morning. Most had flown in from colder climes.

Spying the empty five-gallon water bottle, I remarked to my husband, "Boy, I'd be mad too." However, we were all forced to wait another two hours for the "tour director" to arrive and organize a little game of cabin key bingo.

A little red flag should have gone up in my head. On previous cruises our luggage was waiting for us in our cabin as well as the key. All we had to do was arrive. But on this day we surrendered our Mexican Tourista Card in exchange for our cabin key. It was a slow, laborious process, and when all was said and done there were about eight of us who had no key at all, but we were allowed to board anyway. As it turned out, it didn't matter because all the keys were master keys and fit all the locks!

As we boarded we picked up our luggage, which had been sitting in the sun on the pier for three hours, and struggled aboard. Having studied and being familiar with the ship schematic, we headed directly to our cabin, where we were met by a steward who said, "No good. No can use. No light, see no good."

The cabin we had paid for, #222, was actually a storeroom! And the steward was absolutely right; it was *no good.*

The hot ship attested to the fact that the A/C was not working.

Back on the main deck we were reassigned cabin #126. After putting our luggage inside, we discovered the cabin had no running water, no light bulbs, a non-functioning toilet and a porthole that had been painted shut. The room was as hot as a sauna! It is not hard to imagine the passenger outrage! Because of the heat, I opened my luggage so I could put on a pair of shorts before heading to the lounge for a meeting with the Swedish captain.

We were all delighted to hear, "I've only been aboard three weeks and cannot answer any questions regarding anything that happened prior to that time." He continued to tell us the ship had passed a Coast Guard inspection and had a Lloyd's of London certification. When I questioned him about the certification he, showed me a certificate dated 2/29. Since it was only 2/11, I questioned him farther.

He replied, "Oh this is the wrong one," and flipped to another dated 1/31/88.

I wondered who had been playing with the whiteout and the copy machine!

Late that afternoon we smelled the unmistakable odor of an electrical fire followed by a strong insecticide smell that soon camouflaged the electrical odor. Watching the foam residue being pumped from the bilges confirmed the denied fire. Maybe we were just lucky the ship didn't blow up!

While on deck witnessing that procedure we casually walked over to one of the fireboxes and discovered it contained only a hose nozzle, but no fire hose. Checking farther, we found this was the case with every fire hose box. When we confronted the captain, he denied our accusations, but when I offered to physically show him, he said he would check on the situation.

The crew's forward deck was dirty and cluttered. Half of the deck chairs and cushions were thrown in a heap down a stairwell. Two of the three lounges were dirty and unusable. One of the port doors could not be opened from the outside deck, so all week every time I found it closed I lashed it open again.

Before dinner I went to the cabin to wash and met a late arrival who stated cabin #126 was his. Inquiring about our luggage, I learned it had been moved to cabin #86. That cabin did have light, running water and a functioning toilet. How lucky could we get!

About 8:00 PM we were told that the A/C was now working, but that it would take 24 hours for the ship to cool down, so we were being sent to a hotel for the night. We would sail when the ship was ready, which was anticipated to be 5:00 PM the following day. We were given $20 in food vouchers for breakfast and dinner at the hotel. Later we learned the catch was that we had to pay for our meals and the vouchers would be bar credit on the ship. A sly maneuver indeed! A bus would come to the hotel to pick us up at 2:00PM.

Before loading the bus for the hotel we packed an overnight bag with nightclothes, bathing suit and other essentials. How we enjoyed the cool water in the big hotel swimming pool!

The next day we had to check out of the hotel by 1:00PM. The 2:00PM bus did not arrive, nor had it arrived by 2:30. I figured that we had just been stood up, so about 3:00 I called the hotel that we had stayed in on our own and booked a room for that night, learning they would hold the room until 5:00 that afternoon. Just as I returned from the phone booth, the ship's rep arrived, but not on a bus. She told us the ship A/C was running in *most* cabins, the ship would sail at 6:00 PM with 60 people, and was booked as an *adventure* cruise. The rest of the people would remain in the hotel, be flown home, and given refunds.

We had had long discussions about the pros and cons of sailing or returning home. In hindsight I don't know why there was *any* discussion, we should have just taken our lumps and flown home! However, we did decide to return to the ship and see what improvements had been made before making a final decision.

With no bus in sight, we hailed a cab to return to the pier. Our luggage was still on the ship, so we had to return anyway. On

4

reboarding we found a much cleaner ship. Fire hoses were in place. Of course we had no way of knowing if they actually were functional. The upper edge of the pool had been painted— however, it never did contain any water! The A/C seemed like the major inconvenience, so we decided to go.

We were moved out of our hot box cabin to cabin #51—our fourth cabin in 24 hours! It was large, completely functional, and in a perfect location, only one doorway, approximately 15-20 feet, from the ladder that led to the upper deck. The fact that my husband knew how to release the lifeboats gave me some comfort It's always dark when something happens, so I then disembarked briefly to walk a couple blocks to Woolworth's to purchase a flashlight.

I had a terrible time with my almost non-existent Spanish being understood. Maybe if I had asked for a torch rather than a flashlight I might have made out better. Finally I found a fellow who spoke a *wee* bit of English and managed to understand me. I made my purchase and headed back to the ship.

About 65 of us sailed close to 7:00 PM leaving 150 people in the Acapulco hotel. The ship's agent/owner had arrived from San Antonio and sailed with us, so I often speculated who made homeward arrangements for all those people. I'm sure everyone was on their own to cope the best way they could.

Weeks later we learned the agent had just left his home, his children were taken out of school, and they and their mother just vanished into thin air. No doubt they all met up in Italy where the ship eventually docked permanently.

Our gastronomical delight that evening was rice with beef so tough we could not cut it with a knife. Unknowingly then, we were to be served this same meal three more times! Dessert was always pears or apples. Teatime brought us boxed cookies, which lasted three days. Breakfast was half a grapefruit, scrambled eggs with bacon or Vienna sausage. The second morning the bacon was raw and the eggs inedible, so our dining steward cooked breakfast for us. Bless his heart, he had been brought from Carnival Lines and was most embarrassed over our conditions.

The original cook left after one day, so I guess the one on board was pretty much kidnapped. He certainly wasn't a chef. He quit after two days and refused to cook. A couple of days later we learned that one stove out of four worked, but wasn't overly reliable. The smallest of four coffeepots was the only one working. There was no A/C, and not even a fan, in the galley. There was no broiler or toaster. On this small ship we did not expect gourmet meals, but we did expect three decent meals a day with fruit and coffee available throughout the day.

After a couple of days at sea, one of the passengers bit into a piece of spoiled chicken. He hit the ceiling, and that's when the captain appeared, checked the chicken, and ordered it all dumped overboard. He was furious. We then learned all the refrigerators had gone out. We stood on deck aghast watching cartons of good food that had spoiled be dumped over the side to feed the fish.

The first night our cabin was too hot to sleep in, so we and several others slept up on deck. We pulled the chaise lounge cushions on to the deck and really were relatively comfortable. The people who had sailed were pretty seasoned travelers, as all the novices immediately decided to return home. The next morning our cabin was at least cool, or I should say cooler.

In actuality it probably was a blessing in disguise that the A/C did not function to capacity. Several people picked up coughs and several, including my husband, got quite ill. Who knows what spores and bacteria we inhaled coming out of those dirty, dusty vents.

The purser quit before the ship sailed, as did the operators of the barber and beauty shops. There was no photographer, and the casino never opened. It probably wasn't even equipped! Oh yes, I do remember we could see two black jack tables through the glass door. The PA system was broken for two days, sputtered on the third day, and worked reasonably well after that. The ice machine broke down the second day.

With the intermittent water/toilet situation I told the "doctor" she was irresponsible to let the ship sail without adequate sanitary conditions. She just looked at me with a shocked expression. She was Spanish, trained in Spain, and even after careful questioning I still did not know what her credentials were. She seemed to be a *middle* doctor, whatever that is. I guessed it was about the equivalent to a medical student or Physician's Assistant, although I've seen better. She spoke very limited English and the best any of we passengers could do was some pidgin Spanish.

I do know from personal experience that she did not keep records of any kind, nor did she keep any office hours. I secured antibiotics for my husband and was given a one-day supply! When I went the second day she gave me Dramamine! She seemed very confused when I insisted he take at least five days, preferably seven, of antibiotics. So much for faith and confidence in the doctor who was supposed to be on every cruise!

The second day at sea, as required by law, we had a farce of a lifeboat drill. The assistant tour director knew nothing so was unable to provide any instruction or to answer any question! We all wrestled with old WWII life jackets. Fortunately my husband, who was familiar with this type of life jacket, provided instruction, help, and safety precautions to many.

It was obvious that the crew were pretty frustrated and unhappy campers. Rumor was that they had not been paid, and of course unhappy passengers tend not to tip well. I really felt sorry for the crew as they had been sweet-talked into leaving several of the big cruise lines to sail on *Galaxie*. We couldn't help but wonder what they had been promised. They were young and anxious to please, but had so little to work with. There was talk of them jumping ship in Guatemala. It didn't happen though.

The first full day of sailing, at a meeting, we were told that we were two days late and that we would be bypassing Jamaica. We were following the coastline and making about ten knots as the engines kept chugging along.

Really rough seas while crossing some channel resulted in 90 percent of us being sick, but the next morning we were rewarded with a large school of dolphins playing for several hours off the bow of the ship. Ever graceful, dolphins are always so much fun to watch when they ride the bow of a vessel.

About 10:00 PM, a couple of days after leaving Acapulco we put into Puerto Quazlas, a lovely new sheltered harbor in Guatemala. We were only a day-and-a-half late! Floodlights illuminated the area and we could see armed guards surrounding the perimeter. We were told we could go ashore *if* we stayed within the lighted areas. We decided that was not a very good idea and would wait until daylight to look around.

The ship took on ice in Guatemala. Some of the blocks were tinted a pale yellow, and looked dubious indeed. Later some of the ice was used in the dining room, and it was not unusual to see little insects floating in the glass as the ice melted! Most people know block ice is never purified.

The following day we were scheduled for an 8:00AM tour of Guatemala City and Antigua, a good two-hour trip from the coast. We passed the morning speculating on *when* the buses would arrive. As noon approached we wondered what they would serve for lunch. Somehow this all had become a joke, and amazingly enough no one was in a twit. Finally at 3:00 PM our 8:00 AM bus arrived! Since no one had had lunch, we all decided to go to a restaurant in the small fishing village of San Jose, four miles away. Someone remarked that if we'd known it was only four miles, we could have walked to the village for lunch, and still been back to the ship in time to catch the bus!

I don't remember much about the lunch, except that the food was good. We ate outside at picnic tables with chickens running all around the area. Of course these country folk spoke only Spanish, but we managed okay. I do remember that we all drank warm sodas instead of trusting the water.

At 4:30 PM the tour was ready to leave for the highlands. Since we knew it would be dark by 6:00, my husband and I determined it would be a long ride in the dark, and that we'd see very little. We and three other couples decided to return to the ship and bypass the darkened tour. The ship's owner, who had accompanied us, managed to get a couple of cars to return us to the ship. Late that evening when the bus returned to the ship, no one thought it had been a worthwhile excursion.

Money for that tour was *not* refundable, but applied to the next tour scheduled in San Jose, Costa Rica. We later learned that the money we had paid had been used to pay the restaurant and the bus! Talk about a shoestring operation!

The next morning in Guatemala the dining room didn't open until very late because of a late dinner the night before. All the dishes were still dirty! This really gets more laughable all the time! They didn't even have milk, so we all had dry cereal for breakfast. Maybe we didn't need any dishes for breakfast. We could have just eaten the cereal out of the box like wild kids. We sailed for Costa Rica at about noon ready to face another day of *adventure*.

I had slept in my clothes, at least a pair of shorts and a blouse. My glasses were on the table beside the flashlight, and all our documents, money, and tickets were in a plastic bag secured in my fanny pack, which was on the bed with me. In an emergency we could have abandoned ship in a timely manner with at least the important things.

One evening we struck up a conversation with the engineering officer who told us the engines were literally held together with bailing wire and chewing gum! He deserved a lot of credit for just keeping the engines running and getting us to port.

We hit rough nighttime seas, but the days were nice as we chugged along to Costa Rica, arriving only eight hours late. But the exciting thing that happened on that leg of the trip was that one evening an irate crewmember went after the captain with a knife. The word was that the first mate and radioman intervened and subdued the man before putting him in handcuffs. Now the rumors were rampant that the crew was about to jump ship, so when we arrived in Caldera, Costa Rica, the captain dropped an anchor instead of going along side the pier. That little maneuver not only kept the crew aboard, it also prevented any passenger from disembarking and going to the U. S. Consulate.

That very morning all the passengers had banded together and elected a committee to go to the captain with all of our grievances.

Immigration boarded the ship, and after clearing it, the captain and doctor accompanied them ashore in their launch. They were gone all the rest of the day. About 10:00 PM the ship was moved alongside the pier. When it was obvious that no information would be forthcoming that evening, we went to bed.

The next morning eight couples decided to disembark and head home. Most of the rest of us went on a delightful eight-hour tour of the countryside and the capitol, San Jose. It was a positively delightful day that ended up being the highlight of the trip.

When we returned at about 5:00 PM, we found the ship under armed guard and the naval attaché on the pier. A good half of the crew was under guard in a holding area on the pier. They were to be held until the ship sailed, then returned to their own country.

A meeting was to take place immediately in the lounge. The tour guide, who was most inept and rude, informed us that the A/C was still not working, the food would not get any better, the ship was sailing at 6:00 PM, but no ETA could be given. However, eventually the ship would reach Cancun after going though the Panama Canal. *Absolutely no more complaints would be heard!* If we chose to leave now, a bus would return us to a hotel in San Jose.

We looked at each other, and both agreed we'd had enough of cheese and cracker meals.

My husband said, "I'll go start packing."

"I'll get us on the list to disembark," I responded.

The steward who helped us off the ship was practically in

tears. Shaking our hand he said how sorry he was.

We and another couple were delivered to the Racquet Club in San Jose. It was a lovely facility and we enjoyed a fantastic meal that evening in their restaurant.

The next morning we saw the local papers and I'll never forget the headlines: *Captain gives orders to shoot to kill.* I still have a copy of the paper. The desk clerk was most helpful in translating the story. Apparently the captain had gone to the government for help with the mutiny on his ship. Because it had occurred on the high seas the government was hesitant. He then called on the American Consulate because, except for eight Canadians, we were all Americans. It was the high tourist season, but the American Counsel had secured rooms for us, although it was one here and one or two there. We were most grateful.

In San Jose, I put my husband to bed with a fever along with other symptoms. I then set out to try to communicate at the farmácia for antibiotics for him and Imodium for myself.

Then the other gal and I started nagging the Costa Rican land agent for airline tickets to Cancún. The hotel reception clerk was most helpful in placing calls for us and in translating.

In between phone calls I did a little sightseeing. Eventually three days later, about dinnertime, airline tickets arrived for the next day. Our flight was an hour late leaving, but did get us to Mexico City in time to get through Mexican immigration and change airlines, for the milk run to Cancún. We arrived at 8:00PM. It had only taken us ten hours to make a three-hour flight—if it had been direct!

Arriving in Cancún we went to the hotel that I had booked and paid for through my local travel agent, before leaving home. I had paid vouchers. Unfortunately, when it was obvious that we would never be in Cancún on the proper dates, I had placed a call in San Jose, Costa Rica (before the mutiny) to the States asking a friend to have the travel agent cancel our reservations.

There was no arguing with the hotel. They would not honor

the vouchers, but they did give us a room. We had a restful time for a couple of days in Cancún. The airline was helpful in allowing us to fly home a day early without penalty.

We ended up paying for the hotel twice. It was that or land in jail. I certainly didn't want any jail time, and definitely not in Mexico! At the airport we were stunned to find several passengers who had toughed it out and gotten though the canal.

We learned that they had existed on cheese and fruit for the last few days. They did transit the canal, but when they got to Colón, the ship was declared unsafe, and all the passengers were put off —dumped is a better word—and were on their own to do whatever. Most had managed to get to Cancún where they could at least use their original tickets to get back to the States. Most of the people had gotten ill during those horrific last three days.

I was feeling very lucky to be back in the good old U.S.! When I saw our daughter at the Dallas airport, I gave her a bear hug and burst into tears.

After we got home we heard the story on the TV national news. Many of us contacted the Texas Attorney General, but the long and short of it was that they could never find anyone to prosecute. In addition, the whole event had taken place on the high seas. That alone deterred legal action. Eventually we received a letter stating that nothing could be done. Case closed.

Years later, a crewmember spotted the *Galaxie* moored somewhere in Italy, apparently being used as living quarters. The whole exercise just had been a big scam to get the ship back home to Italy at the public's expense. It was a nightmare no one wants to live.

A Successful Passage

Seven years later I again was on my way to transit the canal. I had intended to meet a friend from New Jersey for lunch in Miami, but because of delays I almost missed my flight for Panama City out of Miami. Ah, the best laid plans of mice and men! By the time

I made it to the gate of our South American airlines, COPA, my friend was pacing the floor. I made it just about the time they were ready to release my seat. A flashback to seven years ago: was this some kind of an omen?

Since both my friend and I preferred small ships, we chose to sail on American Canadian Caribbean Lines' *Mayan Prince.* At that time this was the only truly American cruise line. I had sailed on this line in the late 70s and really liked their format.

First of all, life is informal and the atmosphere friendly. There just was no waiting in line for anything! Because the ships carry only about 100 passengers, meals are served in one seating. The open seating gave us the opportunity to visit with many different people by rotating dining partners. The food was extremely good. Coffee, rolls, and fruit were always available and because of the absence of absolute gluttony, it was easy to maintain one's weight and not go home with an extra ten pounds on the hips.

Because of a late evening arrival, we spent the night along side the pier in Balboa. Early the next morning as we were getting underway for Contadora, we learned that "Mr. Panama" was aboard. This native Iowan had lived in Panama for 35 years, at times among the Indians. He was a walking encyclopedia of Panama's customs and history, and was always available to talk to on a one-to-one basis. His lectures were fascinating. What a bonus!

We were on the Pacific side of the canal where we played for several days. We lived in bathing suits. For the evening meal we did put on a pair of shorts and a shirt.

Leaving the harbor and passing Ancon Hill we learned that wind damage necessitates changing the tennis court-size American flag flying there every six months. Balboa was the chief city of the Canal Zone, and its semblance of a manicured American suburb was a marked contrast of the rather typical Latin disorder bordering it. I wonder what has happened to all the military housing now that American troops have withdrawn from the Canal Zone.

Mosquito breeding grounds were eliminated decades ago, so malaria, plague, and yellow fever are no longer a problem. In fact, no shots are needed to visit Panama, unless one intends to go into the jungle or the interior of the country.

The mile-long Bridge of the Americas spans the Pacific end of the canal serving as an important link between east and west sections of the country.

In 1815 Vasco Nunez de Balboa discovered the Pearl Islands. The sparsely populated chain contains 35 large islands and numerous small islands. Pearls were plentiful in the islands, and Indians used them to decorate their canoes and paddles. Eventually the development of cultured pearls put an end to that local industry.

All that morning we spotted dolphins and whales. Lucky us! Shortly after lunch we dropped anchor and ferried ashore at Contadora Island. The Pacific side of the canal has a 22-foot tide, so anchoring is always used instead of docking alongside a pier. With that much of a tide, one can literally see the water come in and go out. We had the sheltered, sandy beach nearly to ourselves and enjoyed swimming in the calm, clear, warm water.

During WW II the military built an airstrip on Contadora that still is used today for small planes. The small island has a fair amount of recent history. The Shah of Iran stayed on Contadora while in exile. Costa Rica's President Arias and the negotiators of the Panama Canal Treaty found respite there in 1977. The "Contadora Group" retreated there during the trying times between Nicaragua and El Salvador.

We enjoyed a couple of highlights on this restful, relaxed vacation. One was a ride in a cayuca (*kai u coo* —a dug out canoe) up the Sambu River, through the Darien Jungle to Chunga, a Choco Indian village. In spite of the ship's shallow draft, it still had to anchor two miles from the mouth of the river because of the water depth.

Very few people are able to make this trip, because large

cruise ships would run aground, and there aren't many small cruise ships. The village, situated in the dense jungle, is ten to twelve miles up the river.

We had an early wake up call because we needed to load the cayucas at 5:00 AM, just at daybreak. One has no choice on when to go up the river. It is *imperative* to go up on the tide and back out on the ebbing tide. At high tide, the river depth is 22 feet, but at low tide it is only six inches!

I never could figure out why there was no bug problem on this little jaunt. The morning air was warm and humid. We were serenaded all the way up the river by many varieties of birds. What a delight!

The village had only been receiving visitors for five years. Arriving at the village, we were met by the children and escorted the half-mile into the village. Otella was the little girl who walked me over the path. Like all the females, she wore a waist to knee sarong with her upper body and arms covered in designs made with a black vegetable paint obtained from one of the native trees. Many long strands of seed necklaces hung around her neck. Females wore their black hair long and loose over their bronze bodies. The men wore a rendition of a Prince Valiant haircut. The Choco are small in stature.

As this 13-year-old held my hand, we managed to converse a bit. At that time they spoke only Spanish (plus their own dialect), but I bet now, a few years later, they are picking up English.

The children put on a dance demonstration for us. The beat of their simple dances is kept with flute and drum. The women weave baskets from black palm fronds. The tightly woven baskets are capable of holding water. The men do rather good woodcarvings from rosewood, known locally as cocobolo. They also carve animals from the vegetable ivory nut, tagua. This nut is *very* hard, and when polished the carvings look like ivory.

These people are very individualistic, and one deals with them individually, not as a group. They live deep in the jungle separately, not in a village. Their buildings are set on wooden pilings six to ten feet off the ground. The home contains nothing but a floor with a cooking sandbox, elevated on six-inch legs, in the center of the single room. They sleep on the floor. They are a farming tribe and both men and women work in the fields.

It was a pleasant and fascinating visit. The noon return down the river was hot, hot, hot! The *only* shade was that from our hats.

The day before our canal passage we anchored off Taboga, the *Isle of Flowers*. We enjoyed the peace and quiet of this small island while the Panama skyline was visible only twelve miles away. Taboga, home to 700 residents, has two roads, the high road and the low road, each little wider than a sidewalk.

There is never a traffic jam on the island as there are only a couple of small, open trucks used to transport goods from the floating dock in the harbor. The high road led us to the second oldest church in the hemisphere, and the low road led us to the hotel where we could enjoy a cold drink, overlooking the ocean from a large, sweep-around veranda. Walking around the island we noted the cozy houses painted in quaint pastel colors. Gauguin lived and painted here at one time. We stopped to read a memorial plaque in front of the ruins of his old house.

The hilly island is a nice laid back get-away where nearly all the homes have a lovely ocean view.

Transit day had arrived! I was about to be "lifted up and over Central America." When I went on deck early that morning I counted 26 ships in line waiting for passage through the canal. All passenger ships have a narrator accompany them for the passage. Our narrator started on the loud speaker at 7:15 AM. He would keep us informed and educated with stories and history all along the 50-mile passage. Annually 13,000 ships from 79 countries transit the canal.

The fact that the area is geographically stable was a big consideration for the canal location nearly a century ago. Fees are based on tonnage. Today arrangements and payment must be made in advance, and ships are required to stay in the immediate canal area for about 24 hours before passage.

The six locks are split with three on each end of the canal. They are 110 feet wide and 1050 feet long. Each lock has two chambers, side by side, so ships can go in either direction at the same time. Four and a half million cubic yards of concrete were used to construct the locks and dam. The gates are seven feet thick. Water drops 39 inches a minute through 18-inch culverts. All the water in the locks and lakes is fresh fed by the mighty Chagras and two other rivers. If all the excavated dirt from the canal were put on a train it would circle the earth four times!

The ship's captain must surrender control of his ship to one of the 250 pilots working the canal. Canal linesmen also board the ship. At the mouth of the lock, they heave lines to two men in hard hats in a rowboat, who row the lines to the edge. Here a fellow takes the lines and attaches them to an electric mule. From then on the operations through the lock is controlled by the lockmaster sitting in a small lookout tower. Each electric mule has an engineer in its cab. Interestingly, the original 39 mules were built by General Electric for a *total* price of $528,680. Mitsubishi was building the new mules for a cost of $2 million *each*!

One sails across rather small Miraflores Lake and through the Pedro Miguel lock before entering the Gaillard Cut. The cut crosses the Continental Divide and has been widened to 500' from its original 300 feet. Water depth throughout the cut is 40 feet.

Eventually the ship entered Gatun Lake, which, before Lake Meade was dammed, was the largest manmade lake in the world. The Smithsonian has a research center on Barrocaro Island, one of the larger islands in the lake. This island has 150 miles of trails, and it takes three to four months to obtain permission to land on the island.

In 1914 a mile long dam was built on the north end of the lake. The dam, 105 feet above sea level, and 20 feet higher than the normal lake level, is a half-mile wide at the base tapering to 100 feet at the crest.

Exiting the lake through the three Gatun locks opens the way to the Atlantic Ocean, 22 ½ miles west of the Pacific entrance. The cost to build the canal was $400 million. It was a long, hot, but exciting and informative day! The cook had a BBQ lunch for us on deck so we wouldn't miss seeing anything. The canal transit probably becomes old hat to crewmembers, but the passengers find it an exciting experience.

Columbus described the Atlantic along the Panama coast as having contrary weather. That night we experienced seven-foot seas on the breach.

The next day we were ready to play in the San Blas Islands for a few days. San Blas, one of Panama's ten provinces, is also an archipelago of 365 incredibly beautiful islands that are home to the Kuna (also Cuna) Indians.

A gently arched barrier reef extends 110 miles to Columbia in the south. Visualize a three-color rainbow with the outside blue containing 250 small, uninhabited islands with coconut palm trees and beautiful deserted white beaches. There is no tillable land or fresh water, but great fishing, swimming, and snorkeling.

The center yellow strip is one mile wide with a cluster of small islands inhabited by large Kuna families/clans. This area is population dense with 50,000 Kuna living in 50 large villages.

The inside three to five-mile wide green strip is jungle. Kuna men tend to their fields here using a slash and burn farming technique. However, they clear only three to five acres at a time, are not involved in commercial farming, have no animals, do not irrigate, and use no pesticides or chain saws. Their farming is strictly for survival and when they rotate their fields the jungle takes over again.

The Kuna live in large extended family groups in thatched huts with dirt floors. They sleep in hammocks and hang their clothes from the hut rafters. They are a well-organized people and commercially aggressive, but not pesky. The women own the home, property, and wealth, and make it desirable for the man to maintain it. The women are strictly domestic. The men are hard working, traveling daily to the mainland jungle to tend their crops.

The Kuna are physically small, women barely reaching five feet tall. The men dress European style with long or short pants and tee shirt. The women wear mola decorated blouses with either a long or short sarong. Their black hair is short and always covered with a small red and gold headscarf. They wear multi-seed necklaces and adorn their wrists and ankles with many seed strands. Women all wear a gold ring through the end of their nose.

It is the custom to pay a dollar to take pictures of individuals, a rather common convention in many parts of the world I have visited. However, tourists can snap general village scenes without payment. The women, creative and artistic, spend many hours making molas, which is a reverse appliqué technique. They buy the cotton material and perfectly matched threads from either Columbia or China.

For centuries the Kuna and Choco tribes, with very different lifestyles and beliefs, have lived near each other without conflict and with respect for each other. The Kuna dance is very complicated and really a sport in which they have competitions.

The Kuna build a separate cookhouse because they cook in large quantities, in five-gallon pots, over large fires, for their large extended families. Mangrove, being a smokeless wood, is the favored fuel. The fire is laid out like a spoked wheel with seven-foot long logs!

Fresh water comes from the rivers. Besides their dialect, they speak Spanish. Infant mortality is high, but if a child survives the first couple of years, he has a good chance of living to 70. Eye problems are common at a young age, and they have an extremely high incidence of albinism.

Kuna cemeteries are on the mainland and near a river. Funerals are family affairs and take place one or two days after death. They are buried in their hammock with all their personal possessions.

Over the centuries, the Kuna have maintained their traditions, legends, beliefs, and myths, and today continue to use a witch doctor for the treatment of ills. Practicing monogamy, adultery is a felony. The Shahila is the leader and has authority over the community.

Every day the captain cruised to another beautiful small island, often just running the ship up on the sandy beach and tossing a line around a coconut tree! The clear water was warm and calm and the snorkeling was good. It was fun to just lollygag in the water.

The ACCL ships are of a special design where the bow of the boat opens dropping a ladder/gangway to the beach. One could walk most of the islands while hunting shells in less than an hour. All too soon these fun, relaxing, lazy days came to an end and we had to motor back up to Colon where we disembarked.

Our bus, with police escort, took us over a paved road, following the old mule canal trail, to our hotel in Panama City. We chose to spend a couple of days seeing and learning about Panama City before flying home.

It was a delightful, restful, and exciting vacation, very different from my first attempt to traverse the canal!

Chapter 2

Peta and Belize

Reading in the literature that we would be swimming close enough to the dolphins to determine their sex, I thought to myself, "Boy since I don't see anything without my glasses, I'm in big trouble!"

When I relayed this information to my adult children in 1994, they said, "Mom, buy yourself a prescription mask."

"What do you mean a prescription mask?" I asked.

Then they proceeded to tell me that I could have my eyeglass prescription built into a facemask, for about $35 or $40 and when in the water, it would be just like wearing my glasses.

I did peruse that option, but it cost more like a $150. But as it turned out, it was a good investment. I have taken that mask all over the world with me, and it has allowed me to see some wonderful underwater seascapes.

This was my first trip alone since retiring. Previously I had gone with a friend. When I told people where I was going they, without exception, responded, "You're going where?" Once I told them that Belize used to be British Honduras they nodded in recognition of the name anyway.

This also was my first travel service project. We stayed on an atoll 32 miles out in the ocean from Belize City and found ourselves living in individual thatched roof cabanas. Anything you forgot, you would end up doing without for the two weeks, as there was no store on the tiny atoll. The facility did have complete plumbing, and a reverse osmosis system for all drinking water. They also employed a great cook!

The weather was warm. After all it's the tropics. I didn't want anything hot to drink, and after a glass of fresh fruit juice I wanted my ice tea! I asked the cook if she had a jug I could borrow to make some sun tea. After all, ice tea is the national drink of Texas.

After breakfast the next day I picked up my jug from the kitchen, put three to four tea bags in it, screwed the cover on loosely, set it in the sun, and when we came in off the boat at noon the tea was ready for drinking. Ice wasn't a problem, so many of us enjoyed the tea, and before long the jug was empty. After that, it became a daily ritual for me to make sun tea while on the atoll. Everyone enjoyed it.

We spent half of each day on the research boat looking for and following bottlenose dolphins up and down bayous among the mangroves and spent the other half of the day snorkeling. Each day we would be taken to a different reef. The snorkeling remains the best I've ever done.

In the evening we had either a lecture, or spent time on the very difficult task of trying to identify dolphin slides. Bottlenose dolphins live in temperate and tropical waters throughout the world. There are two ecotypes: an off shore and a coastal form, and they can be identified by skull and teeth structure and blood characteristics. Coastal groups vary in size up to 30 animals with off-shore groups often larger. Twenty of the 32 species of dolphins have been found in waters around the United States.

One day near the end of the second week, we all got in the big motorboat and motored over miles of the Caribbean Sea to Lighthouse Reef where Peta was often seen. Peta used to be called Peter, until one day someone discovered he was a she, so her name was changed to Peta. She was a lone dolphin living among the atolls of Belize. Dolphins are very social animals and generally seen in schools.

No one knew much about Peta, except that she liked to

socialize with humans and was always seen alone. At that time no one had ever fitted her with a transmitter to learn where she went during the day or where she spent the night.

When we arrived at Lighthouse Reef the captain dropped the anchor in an area where it would not harm the reef. The water was so clear, you could see the bottom with the naked eye, so it was easy for the captain to find a sandy area to anchor. The reefs are protected in Belize.

We all went swimming for about an hour and in the clear water it was like swimming in an aquarium where the fish were plentiful, different, and colorful. I'm not very good at identifying fish, but I did know the barracuda when I saw it. Both of us remained suspended in the water just looking at each other. Eventually, I wanted to see other things so I just eased off. I saw corals I had never seen before. It was truly an amazing experience! But there was no Peta. No dolphins at all.

We all got back on the boat and were just beginning to take off our gear when someone yelled excited, "There she is. There's Peta!" And sure enough, there she was swimming toward us.

The researcher calmed us all down saying, "When you go back in the water, enjoy Peta, but please don't try to pet her. If you splash and kick a lot she'll think you want to play, but remember she's a wild animal of good size and you could get injured."

What a thrill it was to swim with her. She circled by me close enough to brush my leg a couple of times. I just wanted to reach out and hug her, but all I did was mostly float on top of the water with my hands at my side watching her. She frequently went down to nose around the anchor and eat whatever she found there. I stayed in the water until I got cold, then reluctantly got back on the boat.

The last swimmer to get out of the water was not the strongest swimmer among us, and Peta decided she wanted to continue to play, so she positioned herself *between* the swimmer and the ladder cutting off the swimmer's access to the boat. Peta seemed to be

23

saying, *Stay awhile longer; I still want to play.* Eventually the swimmer became tired of treading water and trying to gain access to the ladder, so the researcher jumped in the water to distract Peta and the swimmer climbed back aboard the boat.

We were all happy and excited on our way back across the ocean to our own private little atoll. Then what do you suppose happened? A large school of dolphins decided to bow ride our boat. It was the perfect finish to a perfect day!

Postscript:

The battery in my camera had died and I thought it would not be a problem to replace when back in Belize City. Wrong. After scouring the city, I ended up buying a disposable camera. It was not my brand of choice, but I didn't have a choice! I had to have a camera for the next couple of days in the rain forest. The lesson learned here was that I now *always* travel with a spare camera battery *and* one disposable camera, which many times has substituted as an extra roll of film.

We traveled about 20 miles through the rural countryside. Although the road was paved it had no dividing lines. After five miles there was very little traffic. Then it was onto a dirt road for another 20 miles. Our four-wheel van progressed slowly dodging ruts and holes in the road, up the gentle climb to 2000 feet.

In the valley we passed huge citrus farms. The pine trees, covering 300 square miles of steep hillsides in the foothills of the Mayan Mountains, were tall and straight, slightly smaller than a telephone pole. The Mountain Pine Ridge, in the southwestern part of Belize, has some of the most diverse scenery in the country. We learned that along the edges of the pine ridge are limestone caves, whitewater rivers, hardwood forest, and sharp escarpments with sweeping views.

Approaching Blancanceaux Lodge, which at that time happened to be owned by Francis Ford Coppola, I was surprised to see the beautiful tropical landscaping.

We were housed in lovely thatched roof cabanas. Mine had a

small screened veranda with a view of a waterfall in the Privassion River beyond. Life couldn't get much better than this! The river provided water for a hydroelectric plant, which supplied all the power for the lodge.

At dinner that evening we learned that recent rains made it questionable if we'd be able to make it to the Mayan ruins of Caracol the next day. We'd have to wait until morning to see what the weather was like. The rainy season normally starts the end of May, but that year the archaeologists had left the area in mid May, two weeks earlier than normal. That was not a good sign!

Since this was the main purpose for my venture into this area, I whispered a silent prayer. That evening, sleep swept over me quickly while I listened to the sound of running water from the river.

Waking to a sunny day we learned the trip was a thumbs up! The road, and I use the term *very* loosely, through the jungle was clay-like and very slippery. We did our share of slipping and sliding but managed to stay on the road, as there was nowhere else to go. There were no shoulders and the narrow thoroughfare had no gutters to fall into!

The young driver kept the four wheel-drive vehicle from getting stuck, although at times we wondered how. As we inched along on this, my first jaunt into a jungle, I tried to visualize what it must have been like to cut a path through the jungle during wartime. The jungle does not stay at bay long and grows back very quickly.

It took us nearly three hours to travel the 18-20 miles. Suddenly we sighted a ruin and then we were in a large clearing— the entrance to Caracol! A five square mile clearing in the thick jungle comprised a classic period complex including pyramids and an astronomical observatory. Caracol is the most extensive known Mayan ceremonial center in Belize. The most visually striking structure was Caana (sky palace), a temple towering 136 feet above the plaza floor. Of course several of us had to climb the *sky house,* and although it wasn't all that far to the top, the steps were *very* steep.

Only a small portion of those ruins had been excavated, but the site tour with a very knowledgeable guide still took over three hours. When fully excavated, Caracol will be one of the largest discovered Mayan ruins. The capitol of the Mayan civilization for many years, it is estimated that 180,000 people lived there reaching its cultural zenith between 500-600AD.

It was very hot, humid, and breezeless in the ruins causing us all to consume large quantities of water.

On the return trip to the lodge, our nice driver detoured to the Frío No where we went swimming in the cool pools. Some of us just *had* to bounce down a waterfall or two. The cool clear water was so refreshing after the sticky humidity of the jungle. We just played like a bunch of kids.

The next day it was necessary to pack up all the fun and relaxation, as it was time to head home and back to familiar routines. It had been an interesting, educational, and delightful vacation!

Chapter 3

Munich to Vienna on a Bike

In 1995, everyone, relative, friend, neighbor, thought I had completely lost my mind, when in my mid 60s, I informed them that I was going overseas to bike from Munich to Vienna. No one thought that would be fun. But the joke was on them because it was one of my favorite and most fabulous trips!

I rode my bike everywhere until our last move when we lived off a dirt road that was off a very narrow, winding country road. My bike sat under a tree for nearly two years before I could emotionally give it away.

Between two trips, this one and one I had just returned from, I moved from the country to the city. This bike trip was coming up in six weeks, and suddenly I realized I hadn't been on a bike for nearly seventeen years! After purchasing a new bike, I left it at my new house in the city with the intent of riding every day after I arrived with a carload of belongings. The problem was it was summer time, and when I arrived in the city early afternoon it was hot, and all good intentions disappeared.

When a worried daughter left her excited, optimistic mother at the airport, I had managed to get about ten miles on that bike during my moving exercise.

The literature said we'd be biking 35-40 miles a day, but that didn't concern me. Having a very logical mind, I reasoned that I walked about three-and-a-half miles an hour, surely I could bike at least twice that fast, and seven miles per hour times six hours equaled 42 miles a day, and that shouldn't be too hard. WRONG!

Little did I know that we'd be stopping for morning and afternoon coffee, plus stopping frequently to visit some place of interest, a church, monastery, historic building or village.

Being strictly a recreational biker I knew *nothing* about biking equipment, shorts, gloves, seat covers —or saddle sores. I was about to learn a lot! A helmet was a requirement for the program, so I had bought one. It was not as fancy as the ones others had, and I'm sure not as good, because I knew nothing about helmets when I went to buy it.

I didn't tell anyone that I had never ridden anything but a one-speed bike with plain old foot brakes. I listened carefully to instructions and mastered shifting gears and braking with the hand brakes. I was issued bike #10.

The peddling was easy, but no matter where I started, I was always the last one to arrive at the designated stop. That didn't bother me a bit though, except it meant I literally had no rest period. To my disadvantage 19 of the 23 of us were avid bikers and members of biking clubs. How lucky could I get! And there I was, just a relaxed recreational biker having the time of her life!

On the afternoon of arrival, we were fitted to our bikes and had to demonstrate to our guide, Achim, that we could mount and dismount without falling off. Could we stop without falling? Could we ride single file and signal our intentions properly?

After a short run to test out the bikes and our skills we had a lecture on some unique rules of the country, procedures for the trip, and the next day's itinerary.

We had bused for about an hour from the Munich airport to the small town of Deggendorf in a light rain. We stayed, with a couple of exceptions, in quaint small hotels. Breakfast was at the hotel, where we were lucky enough everywhere to have large coffee urns, which provided us with the bottomless cup of coffee. A really rare occurrence in Europe!

Mid-morning each day we stopped in some little village to buy lunch fixings, and then we'd find a park to eat and relax around noontime. One day we ate beside a pristine lake. I loved the lunches because I could indulge in the wonderful hard rolls and breads, great cheeses, and yogurts. Only one day did it rain hard enough to force us into a restaurant for lunch.

Dinner was always a big meal in the hotel. We indulged in lots of good wines, but after we were off the bikes. No drinking while riding!

Our first day was a trial run of about ten miles into the village of Michaelbach. That twenty-mile day gave me no problem, but the second day when we rode to Passau, on the German-Austrian border, I thought I was going to die. I discovered 43 miles made for a *very long* day. However, after that first day each 40-mile day became easier, and at the end it was a breeze.

Most of the time we rode on good bike paths. They are very common in Europe as nearly everyone rides a bike. Annually 200,000 bikers make the trip from Passau, Germany to Vienna, Austria. Because it had been a rainy year, the Danube River was over its banks in a few places, which meant some of the bike paths were under water, requiring us to detour onto the road. The drivers were considerate though, but again they're used to seeing bikers all the time.

While the temperature remained nice the whole trip, it did rain on and off nearly every day, but it didn't dampen my enthusiasm or my spirit. The scenery was beautiful with a photo op around every curve.

This trip provided me with many highlights. One was in Passau. Besides a city tour, a history lesson, and visiting a castle, I ate lunch in a 600-year-old restaurant.

After learning that monks established the restaurant across the street from our hotel, several of us just had to eat lunch there. Although no longer run by monks, this establishment has been in *continuous* service ever since 1358! The wine was excellent, the food was only fair but expensive. We really didn't mind paying for the ambience and history. Sometimes there are things that one just *must* do.

We visited several monasteries, castles, plus many churches, mostly baroque. Baroque architecture is very ornate and busy with lots of gold. St. Stephens's church in Passau houses the largest organ in the world, with over 17,000 pipes on 600 organs, taking *80 miles* of electrical wire to connect it all.

We biked through small picturesque Austrian villages, in mountain foothills, through wheat fields, farmland, forests, vineyards, and outside Grein over a horse footpath, where horses used to pull barges up and down the river.

We crossed the river several times. The Danube is called the Donau in Austria. The water was muddy and dirty with a strong current, far from blue in the "Blue Danube" by Strauss. There were many locks on the river, which also served as electrical generating plants. We crossed over many locks, on grated bridges with heavy traffic, and by ferry, one time by a pull ferry.

Apparently, I hunch over my handlebars because the muscles between my shoulders burned like the dickens. I even made a conscious effort to drop and relax my shoulders. We never could figure out the reason for it but suspected the position of the handlebars, which we adjusted several times.

The terrain was just hilly enough to make it interesting, but one day, when we hit totally flat terrain, we found it quite boring. Another day we bucked a good head wind. Although only a 30-mile day, it was tiring because I could never coast. If I stopped peddling, the wind simply brought me to a standstill!

One day it rained so hard all day we all got soaked, no matter what kind of raingear we were wearing. Late afternoon we ferried across the river to Donauschlinge at Schlogen, (love to say that!) where we stayed in a large, modern hotel. Although it only had been a 30-mile day, the rain had made it a tough one.

While my roommate was in the shower I opened the room fridge and retrieved a small bottle of wine. I was enjoying it when one of the other gals came in the room asking where I had gotten the wine.

When I told her she asked, "Do you know how much that costs?"

I answered, "I don't give a tinker's dam what it costs!"

After my shower we utilized the hair dryer in the bathroom to dry out our shoes. The small heater coils in that room took care of the wet clothing. We were all glad that was the only soaking rainy day we had on the whole trip. After all that rain, we were happy to be in a large new modern hotel with all the amenities.

Achim had a real sweet tooth and twice a day when we'd stop for coffee he'd indulge. I abstained most of the time, except for the afternoon we detoured into Eizendorf for apple strudel. It was warm, fresh out of the oven, and without a doubt the best strudel I've ever eaten. We had a choice of with or without schlag, (whipped cream), the real stuff! That strudel was soooo good, and I'm sure I'll never have any that tastes that good again.

Whenever we did stop, we lined all the bikes up together, and usually Luke, the driver, stood watch over them. We covered the seats with shower caps to keep them dry. Many of our group had sheepskin seat covers. I happily bought one in Grein at a sporting goods store close to the hotel. I've used it ever since.

The only really hairy day of biking was the final approach into Linz. We stopped so Achim could caution us to be very alert and to be sure to keep our distance in single file. We were traveling an elevated sidewalk of sorts with cars passing on our right about 30" below on a very busy four-lane highway. Bikers going in the opposite direction were passing us on our left. It was the end of a long day that became a bit stressful, because of the potential danger, but we all concentrated on the exercise at hand, and all went well.

After we got into our room I told my roommate, I didn't want any more juice or soda, and that I would wait for my wine until dinner, but right then I sure wanted a nice big glass of ice tea. She

31

asked just how I thought I was going to accomplish that. I went down stairs to the bar, and asked the bartender for a cup of hot tea. After I paid him, I asked if I could have the largest container he had full of ice.

He looked at me like I had three heads, but indulged my strange request with a large plastic bowl full of ice cubes. I then stated I was taking it all up to my room, and that I would return the container and the cup when I came down to dinner. A glass of ice tea never tasted so good! I was lucky to get the ice because in much of Europe ice is a pretty rare commodity. Drinks are most often drunk at room temperature. Soft drinks are often kept in a cooler, but are chilled and never really cold.

One activity I'd never voluntarily choose to do would be to visit a concentration camp. The second day in Linz we were all bused up a very long steep hill, I was mighty glad we were not biking, to Maunthausen. The name means "mother camp," and it was the first concentration camp built in Austria.

Prisoners were sent from Dachau to build Maunthausen. The camp sits high on a hill near a rock quarry below. Thirty-four Americans were among the 159,000 prisoners who died there. Each country that lost citizens at Maunthausen has erected a memorial. They were all different, and all powerful. There was no Austria between 1938-1945 because Germany's Third Reich occupied that country.

We saw many young people visiting. Everyone was very quiet, speaking only in hushed tones. When we reached the gas chamber, we all stepped inside. It gave us all the chills, and it took every bit of willpower I had to remain calm while looking up at the pipes that people thought were water pipes. A very spooky feeling indeed! We all emerged from the chamber with tears in our eyes. It was a very sobering experience, one I shall *never* forget! In the end, I was glad I had made the visit.

Achim, a retired German Army Officer, was a very sweet man. It was so hard for him when we visited the concentration camp, but he told us it was part of history, and the story must be told. He spoke extremely good English and was a world of information. He was always willing to answer questions. Could he ride a bike!

Vienna is a wonderful city, full of history and culture, and beautiful massive architecture. St. Stephen's towers can be seen from nearly anywhere in the central city and is an easy landmark. Traffic is very heavy, and the streets one-way. Although Vienna is easy to walk, it is a bear to drive, and would have been a nightmare on a bicycle, to say nothing of trying to keep 23 people from getting lost.

It really was a sad day when we had to surrender our bikes just outside Vienna. Number 10 had taken me safely over 250 miles of the beautiful Austrian countryside, and it was like saying good-bye to a good friend.

Chapter 4

Peru and the Inca Trail

The Inca Trail, although only 40 kilometers (25 miles) long and a four-day hike, was without a doubt the most physically challenging exercise I've ever undertaken. The uneven footing of the rock trail and the steep steps would have been bad enough, but adding altitude of twelve to thirteen thousand feet made it a bear. Breathing became an aerobic exercise 24 hours a day for the entire two weeks!

Arriving at the airport in Cuzco, everyone deplaned and started walking at their normal pace into the terminal. It was only about a minute before *everyone* noticeably slowed down. We all knew we were now at 11,500 feet. Stopping to listen to the local Quechua entertainment gave us a chance to catch our breath and mentally adjust our pace and attitude to the altitude.

Before leaving home people who realized I would be in the Andes Mountains asked what I'd do if I experienced altitude sickness. My sometimes flippant answer was that I would drink coca tea. So you can imagine my surprise when on arrival at the hotel we all were offered and accepted a cup of mate de coca, better known simply as coca tea.

We soon learned that the hotels always had a large thermos full of hot coca tea in the lounge. It was on all restaurant menus and everyone drank it everywhere. The Andean people often chew coca leaves. Our local trail guide told me that it aids in digestion and is also an appetite suppressant. The leaves look very much like a bay leaf, and the tea tastes much like any herbal tea. I drank many cups of mate de cocoa while in Peru, and I did not suffer from the soroche (altitude sickness).

On arrival while we were sipping our coca tea, we were cautioned to drink lots of fluids because altitude can easily cause dehydration. Symptoms of soroche include headache, shortness of breath, dry cough, feeling faint, fatigue, weakness, nausea, and generally just feeling lousy. It was suggested that we take it easy for a day or so, to eat lightly, and that it was also advisable to abstain from alcohol and cigarettes.

Quickly one learns that all the streets in Cuzco are cobblestone and very narrow. Fortunately most are one way. Vehicles are small, so they drive the narrow streets without difficulty. Most streets have narrow, stepped sidewalks. Nothing in Cuzco is very far, and the city is very walkable, but the altitude and the hilly terrain tires one very easily. I *never* did make it up to our hotel without starting to huff and puff about a third of the way up the hill. My son would always ask if I wanted to stop and rest.

I'd always answer, "No, I'm okay, just one foot in front of the other." Then I'd stagger through the hotel door and lean against the wall gasping for air. I always received concerned looks from the hotel staff and questions regarding my well-being. After a few minutes I'd make it up the few stairs to our room.

Nestled high in the Andes Cuzco boasts some magnificent scenery. Once the center of the Inca Empire, the city had a sophisticated water system, thousands of miles of roads, and a total lack of poverty.

The Incas believed Cuzco was the source of all life, and therefore the city is often referred to as *the belly button of the world*. Inca myth says children of the gods settled there to provide light and culture to a dark world. Cuzco remained the supreme city of the Inca Empire for over 200 years. Today it is the archaeological capitol of South America, a cultural treasure of humanity.

This city, rich in history, tradition, and legend has woven the native Quechua Indian, the conquering colonial Spanish, and the modern Mestizo cultures into a rich tapestry. The majority of the city's 330,000 people are Quechua.

The Plaza was, and I guess always is, full of hawkers selling their wares. Some of them are pretty young children. They really are very pesky, and won't take *gracias, no* for an answer, but continue to follow you a good way.

Peru's plazas are very much like our Texas courthouse squares, a place of business, entertainment and activity. During out first visit to the Plaza we visited a grocery store to buy water and a package of Oreo cookies. Leaving the store we headed across the plaza when a couple of shoeshine boys approached us. They were cute youngsters, about 10 or 11, so we stopped and talked to them awhile giving them a chance to practice their English. They knew many of our state capitols, our president, and several other things about America. We gave them an Oreo cookie, which seemed to be rather unfamiliar to them.

During our time in Cuzco we visited the Sacred Valley, the home of several easily accessible Inca ruins. Sacsahuaman in Quechua means "satisfied falcon." The name is more easily remembered by saying sexy woman. The site is massive, and perhaps the most important Inca monument after Machu Picchu.

The skill of Inca builders was incredible. These stones were so accurately cut that a knife blade cannot slip between them, even today! No mortar was used; the stones were precisely cut and fitted together. Some of the stones weighed up to 300 tons. What an amazing feat!

Covering an area of six square kilometers, this once huge structure was cannibalized for years for building material for Cuzco's homes and 22 colonial churches. Only 20 percent of the ruins remain.

It is said that if one stands in front of a certain stone with his belly button on the marked spot, with arms extended to the handholds, positive energy can be absorbed from the stone. Likewise, at another stone one can rid himself of negative energy.

Quechua women dress in vibrant colors. Traditional dress of Quechua women is a combination of pre-Spanish and Spanish colonial. Skirts are full and gathered, and worn in layers giving the hips a broad dimension. Hats may be a Panama-type woven from palm fibers, but the most common hat we saw was a brown woolen rounded top-hat that sat on top of the woman's head. I tried in vain to figure out how they kept those hats on their head. Women wear their dark hair long in two braids fastened in back with a ribbon.

The women are short, generally a little less than 5 feet tall, and physically small. Babies and supplies are carried on their back held by a large colorful woven cloth. At Sacsahuaman we saw Quechua women with their babies leading llamas across the fields. They were most cooperative posing for us to take pictures, and grateful for the couple of Sols we gave them.

Men wear traditional western clothing including a vest and brimmed hat. Sandals are either leather or made from tire rubber.

The 90 mile-long Urubamba Valley was sacred to the Incas. The Sacred Valley was so named because it had a good climate, fertile soil, and a river. The terraced hillsides of the valley are cultivated, producing one crop a year. But in the valley, which is irrigated via mountain water, three crops a year are grown.

Diagonal flagstone stairs set into the terraced walls join the many agricultural terraces at the Pisac site. At the top of all the sites sits the usual sun and religious rooms. Ollantaytambo, a *massive* Inca fortress, had huge *steep* terraces guarding it. From this site in 1536 Pizarro, the Spanish conqueror, was unable to fend off the barrage of Inca arrows, stones, spears, and boulders, and made a hasty retreat.

I figured all the climbing around the ancient ruins in the Cuzco area, and getting acclimatized to the altitude was just good practice for the trail that lay ahead. We left our excess luggage at the hotel in Cuzco, and only took essentials on the trail.

My son and I were the only Americans in our group of twelve. Everyone else was in their late 20s and early 30s, making me the old, old grandma of the group, and even my son the old man. Eighteen local porters supported our group.

We were individually responsible for our daypacks with rain gear, camera, sunscreen, water, first aid kit, and jacket. We packed everything else, sleeping bag, clothes, cosmetic kit, pjs, and other essentials into a large, heavy canvas bag, which the porters carried. One canvas bag per couple.

We rode about an hour and a half over a very rough road. Actually I'm not sure that we were really on a road. I think we were mostly riding over pastureland to K 82 where most people start the Inca Trail Trek. After checking and signing in with the Parks Service, we immediately crossed over the Urubamba River via a swinging bridge.

Excitement ran high as we started up the trail. This four-day trail winds over 25 miles, so we mistakenly though it would be easy. It didn't take long for me to fall to the end of the line, often falling farther and farther behind. Marsiel, a guide-in-training, brought up the rear. Reality started setting in when we stopped for lunch, or rather when my son and I were the last to stagger in to lunch.

Mountains always have seemed awesome and beautiful to me. The lunch stop was very picturesque. I could have stayed there all afternoon absorbing the scenery, but after lunch we had to trek on. I found I could walk *or* I could enjoy the scenery. But I could not do both at the same time, because, when walking over the rough rocky path, I had to watch my feet every step of the way. Be assured I stopped frequently to gaze about. Besides, stopping gave me a chance to catch my breath and slow my gasping to mere panting.

As we left the lunch site I spotted an older Quechua woman, across the trail, weaving on her unique loom. One end was tied around her waist as she sat on the ground, and the other end of the loom was tied around a tree stump.

The first couple of days we saw many waterfalls and listened to water flowing most of the time. The first day we crossed the river four times on different kinds of footbridges.

I had expected to be walking over a dirt trail, but the trail turned out to be all rock making for uneven footing, requiring all of our attention when walking. As we climbed higher breathing became harder, something I never thought possible! Of course we were in the mountains so the trail wove up and down, often steeply. Thank goodness for my comfortable hiking boots and trusty sturdy walking stick! I was most grateful I had taken it. I'm certain I would never have made it in one piece without it.

The hike was rugged, and the last hour and a half I really pooped out. We reached the campsite at 9000 feet about 45 minutes behind the rest. When we finally stopped about dusk, I was really tired.

I thought, *why am I doing this*? But the thought of turning back and repeating that tough terrain was not at all appealing. I was sort of at the point of no return.

I slept poorly on the trail. The tents were very small with room for just two sleeping bags. Then we had to find room for our packs and all our stuff besides. It was pretty cool at night. And of course the baños (bathrooms) were just a hole in the ground. With no hand supports or way to get any leverage, getting up was the hard part.

We were on the trail at 7:00 AM each day. The second day we started out on a steady climb to the highest pass called *Warmiwanusca* or Dead Woman's Pass, at 13,775 feet above sea level. Let me tell you it was one tough climb up! After the pass it was straight downhill over many very steep steps that often were narrow and uneven. The steps were so steep that they had to be taken one at a time like a small child would do who was just learning to maneuver steps. I gave a totally new meaning to the words slow and snail! The stairs and hills made my thighs ache.

When I stood on a step, the next one up was at my knee. My mind and body were definitely out of sync!

I'm not talking about just a couple of steps. We'd hit areas with 50-200 steps. It didn't make any difference if you were going up or down, there was no easy way and they were very tough on the knees and hips. In many areas, the trail was narrow with drop offs to our left of hundreds of feet. If you ever fell into that lush growth, you'd never be found. Besides you'd never survive the fall. I hugged the mountain. The same was true of all those steps, if you ever fell at the top, you'd kill yourself rolling down all those steep rocky steps. It was a very stressful day!

If I thought I was tired the first day I was even more tired at the end of second day. I was exhausted when we wandered into camp at 6:00 PM on wobbly legs.

That day I perspired like never before and when we got off the trail, my head was soaking wet. I pulled a wool cap out of my pack and ended up wearing it for two straight days. As soon as the sun went down it turned cold.

The bonus that day, besides the gorgeous scenery, was seeing several varieties of hummingbirds. I saw nothing that was familiar. Peru has 125 varieties of hummers.

The first day we hiked through a eucalyptus forest, and the second day we passed through cloud forest and saw herds of llamas grazing in the valley hillsides below.

The weather was nice. The hike was strenuous and I was soaking wet most of the time. If it had been raining or the trail wet, it really would have been hazardous!

The second night I was too exhausted to eat much dinner, but I forced myself to eat some. I had been drinking lots of water all day, as I did not want to dehydrate. At this point we were half way and I kept thinking, *I've made it this far, I certainly can finish!*

The third day we had two more passes to travel over, and it was more of the same. We went through a tunnel in a huge rock and tried to imagine what it must have been like for the Incas to

41

carve those steps.

The third pass was long and wound around the mountain. I hugged the inside most of the time, as the path was narrow and the drop off steep. You couldn't even see the bottom of the valley.

Lunch was near some ruins. Our guide talked to us about the Incas. Toward the end of his talk I took advantage of a head start to walk down the steps of the ruins.

Smiling he said, "It's all down hill now."

He just forgot to tell us it was 1000 feet straight down over 1824 steep steps! It was a tough afternoon and I didn't think we'd ever reach the campsite. We walked in exhausted just as darkness approached. That evening everyone complained of aches and pains. Thigh muscles were especially sore from all the steps.

That evening I asked the porters for a pan of hot water, as I wanted to wash my hair. We were due in Machu Picchu the next day, and I was ready to shed that wool cap. It felt so good to have a clean head of hair! My son and I were laying down our sleeping bags in the tent and conversing when we heard, "Are you Americans?"

Poking my head out of the tent I answered, "Yes, we are."

A couple of medical students from Galveston asked, "Have you heard about what happened in the States?"

My son said, "No, we've been on the trail three days and haven't heard any news at all."

Then they told us about the planes running into the World Trade Towers in New York and the Pentagon in Washington, D.C. The news stunned us.

My son asked, "Where did you get this information?"

Then they told us, "One of our porters had a radio, heard it, and translated for us."

Like the day JFK was shot, we'll always remember where we were and what we were doing on September 11, 2001!

That campsite was crowded and noisy with a lot of other hikers also camping in the same area. Sleep just kept evading me all night.

The wake up call the next morning came at four. At breakfast our trip guide asked me if I'd like to start on the trail with him a bit early. Even though it was still dark, that sounded like a good idea.

The previous evening I had told my son I wanted him to go on ahead with the rest of the group as it was important for him to be at the Sungate when the sun came up. It was just important for me to get there. If I make it before the sun, great; if not, no big deal.

I couldn't believe the torture was almost over. This really was the most physically challenging undertaking of my nearly 70 years.

So we started down the trail at 4:50 that morning, each with a flashlight in hand. I wasn't sure how smart it was to hike in the dark, but apparently it was the routine, for all trekkers did it. We arrived at the trail gate, only to find it still closed. We were just a couple of minutes early.

The park people arrived, opened the gate sharply at 5:00 AM, and we continued on our way. A few others followed right behind us. The trail was of packed earth, finally the kind of trail I had expected all along. I certainly was cautious in the dark. Eventually everyone passed us, and that was okay. Almost without exception, everyone passing was moaning about aches and pains.

I was glad when it was light enough to turn off the flashlights, and it was after that that I stumbled and fell to my knees. The only damage was a slightly scraped knee through my long pants. It just made me angry that I had done such a stupid thing when the trail was relatively flat! But if I had to fall I couldn't have done it in a better place!

We ran into a few places with rocks and one area of steps so steep and narrow that we had to literally crawl up like a monkey, on all fours.

We were the first on the trail, but we shared being the last ones off with a young French couple. *And* we made it in time to see the sun come up!

It was just 6:45. As we walked through the Sungate many of

the people who had passed me on the trail were milling around. The whole area was covered with mist, a common thing in the early morning. After taking in the scene I started a slow, wall hugging decent down into Machu Picchu. The cliff drop offs were steep and there were no barriers. About an hour later, just as I was arriving at the center of Machu Picchu, the mist cleared and the most magnificent sight opened up before me. It took my breath away, and suddenly all the torture of the past three days faded. It had been worth the trek and misery!

It was too early for the site to open, so we were the only people in those massive Inca ruins. It is something I shall always remember, and although I'd never do it again, I'm glad I did it once. By the end of the day I learned that most of the guides quit trekking the road after they reach 40!

In Inca times the *only* way into Machu Picchu was via the trail we had just traveled, and in those days it was an eight-day trek from Cuzco to Machu Picchu. That day we had entered the site via the back door and had to walk *down* to the main visitor entrance to log into the site.

The people on the trail were very friendly, but there were few Americans. Even though I was huffing and puffing, it was a bit reassuring to me every time we passed young people who had also stopped to rest and catch their breath.

We played catch-up-tag with a couple from California and their 13-year-old daughter. Considerably younger than I, but probably about my son's age, they did not labor as hard, but they did stop frequently. We chit chatted for brief moments as we caught up with each other, first them to us, then we to them.

We always at least said hello and asked how they were doing to everyone on the trail. There were a couple of sweet Kiwi ladies on the trail. Being New Zealanders and rather avid hikers, they faired a bit better than I, but we met up with each other several times a day. Each time we passed each other we exchanged a few friendly words.

On one pass on the third day, one of the ladies remarked, "Seven decades sure catches up with one, doesn't it?"

Oh yes it does!

They were traveling by themselves and had their own local guide. We ran into each other for the last time in the center of Machu Picchu.

All smiles, the Kiwis said to me, "Well hello, we made it didn't we!" And then we gave each other a high-five and congratulated ourselves and wished each other a safe journey home.

Our group gathered at the café. My son headed for the bank of phones to call his wife, before she left for work. I headed straight for the bathroom. What heaven to find a clean bathroom and to actually sit on a toilet seat! I didn't want to get up.

I had tucked my toothbrush and paste in my daypack, from my porter pack, so afterward I leisurely brushed my teeth using my bottled water. Then I was ready for our trail guide to walk us all over the site, while explaining everything to us. We had just finished before the crowds arrived from Aguas Calientes.

Machu means "ancient," and Picchu means "summit," in Quechua: "ancient peak." Machu Picchu is the name of a mountain peak as well as the ancient Inca site. The *sacred, ancient city of light* is at an elevation of 8500 feet. This lost city nestled in the Andes Mountains was never completed, and was never discovered by the Spanish. Actually the Incas had abandoned the city before the Spanish invasion.

A local Peruvian, Agustín Lizarraga, discovered Machu Picchu in 1901. But it was not until 1911 when Yale archaeologist, Hiram Bingham, guided by a local campensino, following a crude mule trail through the treacherous Urubamba River Gorge on a "National Geographic" expedition looking for another city, happened upon the ancient city Machu Picchu. The site he found looked nothing like it does today, as it was covered with dense vegetation. It took ten years to uncover the site, with Bingham returning in 1912 and 1915. However, Machu Picchu remained inaccessible until the 1940s when another archaeological expedition discovered the ancient Inca Road. The pre-Colombian fortress, and the wellspring of one of the world's greatest cultures has fascinated the world ever since.

It is estimated that 1200-1500 people lived there. It was a major town and the largest city in the rain forest. It is strange that archaeologists have found no household items, and they speculate that Machu Picchu was abandoned, probably because of disease.

Below the Temple of the Sun, the only round building on the site, is a series of 16 ceremonial baths. The Temple of the Sun sits over a huge rock and had an outside altar for offerings. The site is divided into several sections: agricultural, religious, social, astronomical, and residential.

The llama was the only animal known to the Incas. Gold and silver were used for religious purposes only and never used for barter or in jewelry.

At certain areas in the site the Urubamba River can be seen in the valley below. The Urubamba flows directly to the Amazon.

It was late afternoon before we were ready to take the bus down over the dusty switchback road to the town of Aguas Calientes. Walking past numerous street vendors we found the restaurant designated as the meeting place.

Sitting at an outside table with others from our group we enjoyed a sandwich and Inca Cola, a yellow carbonated drink that tasted a lot like a crème soda.

It didn't take the shoeshine boys long to find us. We splurged by spending the equivalent of 60 cents on a shoeshine and getting all of the trail dirt off of our boots. There's nothing like clean, shiny boots on your feet!

Early evening we walked to the train station for the hour long train ride back to Ollantayambo, where we picked up a bus for the ride back to the hotel in Cuzco.

While my son retrieved our luggage, left at the hotel four days earlier, I jumped into the shower. I wanted to stand under that hot water forever, but of course I didn't. I hopped out just as he brought up the last bag. Then I flopped into bed and was sound asleep before he ever finished his shower. Being rather sleep deprived, I slept like a baby until morning!

Because of an old Little League injury, occasionally my son's knee gives him a bit of trouble. As we awoke in Cuzco the next morning, I learned that his knee was pretty swollen, but he never said anything to me on the trail.

He spent the better part of the next two days propped up in bed with ice packs on his knee, ingesting anti-inflammatories, and reading his book. I went sightseeing as well as taking care of such necessities as exchanging money and buying bottled water. One of the young Irish gals had asked our guide about the possibility of securing a masseuse. He made arrangements for one to come to the hotel. She did a great job on the leg and thigh muscles, and we both agreed it was an hour well spent!

During those couple days of recuperating in Cuzco we listened to the BBC on the lounge TV. The terrorist attack on the World Trade Center towers was the constant topic of conversation.

The morning of the day we were leaving Cuzco for Puno we were awakened at 2:00 AM by blasting sirens. They sounded forever, and it seemed they would never stop, making both of us rather nervous. The Andes are rather unstable. Was this an earthquake warning? The last severe quake in Cuzco was in 1951. We had no idea what was going on.

My son got up and went outside to see if he could see anything unusual. The hotel, located up the hill, provided a good view of the city below. He saw nothing. Returning to the room he got dressed and headed to the lounge to see if there might be any information on TV.

Then at 5:00 the church bells rang, but not normally. They rang and rang and rang. Was that a warning of some sort?

When he returned to the room, I asked, "What do you think

47

about flying home from Puno? We can visit Lake Titicaca, the Eros Islands, and by-pass La Paz?"

He immediately agreed. With all the events that had happened, and in spite of making phone contact with loved ones, we were still both anxious to get home to our families.

At 7:15 that morning our regular mini-bus picked us up to take us to the main bus station. After checking all our luggage, except for our daypacks, we had about a half hour wait before boarding the bus.

I don't know what it is with the toilets in Peru. Except for the hotels, toilets never seemed to have a seat, just the bowl. Everywhere, including the hotels, one is asked to put nothing in the toilet. A plastic lined wastebasket is provided for all paper. Personally this drove me crazy, but I complied, as I understood the toilets clogged easily and then would overflow. With the exception of Machu Picchu and one restroom in a plush shopping mall in Lima, where the bathroom was clean and had an attendant, I found public bathrooms generally dirty.

At home, the travel people had told me we would be driving over the altiplano by local bus. After seeing the local buses in Lima, I was somewhat concerned. So I was happy to board a large Greyhound-type air-conditioned bus, where we were assigned specific seats. The bus stopped only once, at the halfway point to change drivers and stewardess. Of course at that point, there were local vendors with more of the same merchandise.

The bus ride was a smooth, uneventful one. We ignored the lousy movie displayed on the TV monitor and read our books. The scenery was like any high plain anywhere, rather desolate with an occasional village. Every once in awhile we'd see a Quechua woman tending her livestock.

Arriving at the Puno bus station at 3:00 PM we were in the midst of complete chaos. People were everywhere, while taxis clogged the streets. Eventually we managed to retrieve our luggage and make it safely across the street to a waiting mini-bus.

It felt good to stretch and stand after the seven-hour bus ride, so we just deposited the luggage in our room and went out walking around town to see what we could see.

Puno, located at the southeastern highlands on the shores of Lake Titicaca with a population of 80,000 turned out to be a rather uninteresting town. The business part of the city is on level ground, albeit at 12,500 feet. The residential areas run up the hillsides all the way around the town. Puno, capitol of the province of the same name, is the folklore capitol of Peru. Inhabitants call themselves "children of the sacred lake."

Puno, the major port on the Peru side of the lake, was founded in 1668 near the now defunct silver mine called Layakota. Except for the cathedral, there are few colonial buildings. The sun is very strong by day, and the nights are very cold. We were glad our room had a portable electric heater!

Although at 12,500 feet, I finally had little trouble breathing, probably because I was on level ground and my body was beginning to compensate by making more red blood cells. I managed two flights of stairs in the hotel without huffing and puffing, but walking up four flights of stairs to the rooftop restaurant in the morning was another story!

Getting airline tickets from Puno to Lima was a bit of a hassle, but eventually we succeeded. The airport located in Juliaca was about an hour's drive from Puno.

After an early breakfast the next morning, we made our way to the waterfront. Our boat slowly motored through the bright green algae covering the entire harbor area, then through a cut in the reeds to the open mirror-like calm lake.

The guide on the boat told us *titi* means "puma," and *caca* means "stone." The Incas thought the lake was shaped somewhat like a puma. Looking at the map, I thought that took a bit of imagination. The lake covers over 3200 square miles. The depth ranges from 15-20 feet deep to 900 feet in the northern part of the lake, which is over 100 miles long.

49

There is a tremendous amount of evaporation that takes place on the lake because of the altitude and the hot sun. The lake is fed from 22 rivers flowing into it. The areas around the lake have been inhabited since 1300 BC.

Lake Titicaca, located between Peru and Bolivia, is the largest lake in South America. It is also the largest lake in the world, over 6500 feet, and the highest navigable lake in the world. Because of the altitude those arriving here from sea level stand a good chance of experiencing soroche.

Needless to say the air was clear, and the lake water was the deepest blue. The sunlight shining on the altiplano (high plain) was luminescent, and the horizon seemed endless.

On a perfectly gorgeous sunny day, the famed floating islands, five to fifteen miles offshore, was our first stop. The Uros people and their Floating Islands are the major attraction in Puno. Even though a bit over commercialized, it is popular because of its uniqueness.

Because the Uros have intermarried with Aymara-speaking Indians, there are no pure blooded Uros left. They now speak Aymara, as their original language has been lost. Always a small tribe, the Uros began their unusual floating existence centuries ago. About 160 people live on the islands today, with 1600 more living in Puno, as the attractions of shore life beckon to the young.

Heavy rains that year caused some arthritic-like problems, so the Uros people arrived on the islands early morning with their wares and left for Puno about 4:00 in the afternoon. This very different life style now is pretty much a commercial venture. Only three or four people actually stay on the islands at night.

The lives of the Uros are totally interwoven with the totora reeds growing in the shallow waters of Lake Titicaca. The floating islands are made of many layers of reeds. As the reeds on the bottom rot, new reeds are added to the top layer, so the islands are a bit soft and spongy. Walking on the islands was sort of like walking on a waterbed. The biggest of the islands contained several buildings including a small school. Another island had a small one-room museum.

Since 1445 the totora reeds also have been used to build a canoe-type boat. These boats last a family about six months for transportation and fishing. We couldn't resist riding in one of these boats, but we all sat very still as we rode from one island to another. I'm sure the boats were much more stable than we thought. However, the water was very cold, and none of us wanted to land in it.

Taquile, a real island, lies 21 miles from Puno. Here the people speak Quechua rather than Aymara. The people have a strong sense of identity, rarely marrying non-Taquile people.

There are no roads on the island, thus no vehicles, not even bicycles, and for some reason, no dogs. Electricity came to the island in 1990, but is not available everywhere. The islanders own all the boats for transport, therefore keeping tight control on tourism.

I thought I was finished climbing, but as we disembarked we faced a long winding rocky path half way around the island to get up to the main square. It took about an hour to navigate the path, but I was able to manage without too much panting and breathlessness, remembering that we were still at 12,500 feet.

On the island women wear many layered skirts and intricately embroidered blouses. The men wear tightly woven woolen caps, and are often seen walking around the island knitting. A red hat signals the man is single, a red and white one that he is married. The women weave the elegant waistcoats the men wear. Under the waistcoat they wear a rough spun white shirt, all of which tops thick calf-length black pants. These people continue to live the cooperative lifestyle of their ancestors.

It seems they are never idle. The men knit, the women spin yarn from wool carried on the hip in a cloth sack. Each seemed to have a different color wool, so it must be dyed raw, before spinning. It was a fascinating sight. The island, about three-and-a-half miles long, has several hills with Inca terracing and small ruins at the top. The scenery was beautiful with the deep earthy hills contrasting with the intense blue of the lake water. Add the backdrop of the mountains and the result was breathtaking!

After lunch getting back to the bottom of the island and the boat was a trek down 550 steps. I didn't count them, but we were told there were that many, and I believe there were! They were not as steep as those on the trail, but it still provided a lot of good exercise. I counted my blessings that these were the very last steps of this type I would have to maneuver.

It was a long three-hour boat ride from Taquile back to Puno. The calm, mirrored lake of the morning was covered with white caps, apparently a normal late day event.

Back in Puno, passing the square, we saw many people chanting, "Strike tomorrow!" referring to a possible transportation strike the next day. Locals told us that meant all means of transportation, bus, train, and cabs. I said a little prayer that night for normalcy the next day.

I have never been so happy to wake and hear road noise. Ah, the welcome sound of cab's horns blowing! That meant the strike did not take place that day, so we'd be able to get to Juliaca to catch our late afternoon plane. We were ready to go home!

Author's note: Cuzco is also spelled Cusco, and Qosqo, depending on the map or piece of literature.

Chapter 5

Buttercup and other Safari Animals

Jambo, jambo, with a meaning similar to aloha, was a greeting we often heard in Kenya in 1994.

While in Nairobi we did and saw many things, but the sweetest memory is of feeding Buttercup, an adult female Rothschild giraffe. Living at Giraffe Manor, a wildlife preserve, she was very used to people. Her six-month-old baby was always near, and we were allowed to feed them both.

Standing on the elevated wrap-around porch we were able to feed the giraffes while they stood tall and erect. The food pellets were about the size of my little finger and looked a lot like dry dog food. Buttercup ate right out of my hand, her tongue was *very long* and she could curl it around doing all kinds of tongue calisthenics! I envied her big, expressive eyes and wished for such long eyelashes.

She was beautiful! Giraffes are one of my favorite animals, and I considered myself very lucky to see her before even getting out into the bush.

A Rothschild giraffe is easily identified because he has white stockings up to his knees. This species was nearly extinct, with only eight animals known to be alive when the park opened. The numbers have now increased beyond the danger point and many of these animals have been returned to their natural habitat.

Two other giraffe varieties live in Kenya. The Masai giraffe is found only in the Serengeti. The other specie is the reticulated giraffe, probably most familiar to us because we see it in zoos.

Male giraffes grow 18-20 feet tall and can weigh 4200 pounds. In the wild they live about 28 years. Giraffes are browsers, and their only natural enemies are the hyena and the big cats. To kill a giraffe, the predator needs to go for the neck and the giraffe is most vulnerable when his head is down while drinking. He can run 35 miles an hour and can kill with a kick from his powerful legs.

A baby weighs 100 pounds at birth, is six feet tall, and literally is dropped into the world. Within an hour he can stand, and within two hours can run with his mother.

School children visit the park daily and are being taught to respect wildlife. While in the park they attend lectures gathering information to take home to their parents. Most Kenyans never get out to the game preserves. Kenya believes that its future lies in the education and conservation efforts of its youth, so a few school children are now going on safari each year.

Food was good all during this trip, but one night in Nairobi we had an exceptionally memorable evening. Five of us set out to walk to an Indian restaurant a couple of blocks from the hotel, but the Askari insisted on accompanying us. Askari were the uniformed guards, armed with Billy clubs, found on every floor of the hotel, and at all business establishments and banks within the tourist district of the city.

Arriving just before opening we spent a few minutes in the reception area. While conversing, a young man from England arrived. I asked if he was alone, then invited him to join us.

Just as he accepted our invitation we were ushered to a round table for six. While researching the extensive menu, Michael approached our table asking how he could help us. He then told us he owned the restaurant.

After a bit of discussion we asked him to choose a pork, beef, chicken, and fish dish he thought we would enjoy. He probably was the best judge anyway.

There was a lot of lively conversation that evening. In Nairobi on business, the young man from the UK was a delight. Michael had a wonderful sense of humor and kept us entertained with stories each time he came to the table. At one point he told us he used to cut sisal in the field for a living, but that is was very hard work, so after a few years he decided to go into the restaurant business.

When the dishes had been cleared from the table Michael reappeared telling us he had a special surprise for us, as his special guests. Then he showed us a bottle he had been holding behind his back.

"This is very smooth, very special," he said. The beautiful glossy black bottle was in the shape of a woman's bottom. The bottle provoked comments from us all as well as our curiosity regarding its contents.

As soon as we all had a sip we immediately knew Michael was so right. The *Coco d' Amour* was sooooo smooth. It was wonderful!

The first bottle was only partially full so when it was empty Michael produced and opened a new bottle. I asked if he was going to throw the empty bottle away.

"Why?" he asked.

I said if he were going to throw it away, I'd like to have it. He said he'd sell it to me. I repeated I didn't want to *buy* it. But if he were going to throw it away I'd like to have it.

We continued to enjoy the smooth refreshment. When we were finally ready to leave Michael appeared with the check—which we simply split — and handed me a clean washed out bottle, saying, "For a special guest."

I thanked him profusely. After studying the bill I suspect we somehow paid for that bottle even though it didn't show up as an itemized item. Nonetheless it had been a wonderful, fun filled, memorable evening. I packed that bottle all over Kenya, managed to get it home in one piece, and gave it to my delighted son-in-law.

Ever since that trip whenever I'm in a foreign airport I wander into the liquor store looking for that wonderful Coca 'd Amor. Made in the Seychelles Islands, I have never been able to find it, but still continue to look.

While in Kenya we traveled nearly 1600 miles in Nissan vans equipped with special pop top roofs. These vans also had special guards to protect their undersides. Nearly all tour companies in Kenya use the Nissan. After this trip, I surely had a lot of respect for those vehicles. I doubt we drove on 500 miles of decent pavement.

Most of the old roads had never seen any repair. The dirt paths were almost better than the pot holed roads where the pot holes were so close together there was no way to avoid them. At times we were literally bounced out of our seats. We bounced over riverbeds, over the Mara, and often zigzagged like a drunken sailor down a road. One time we were on such an angle we all instinctively hi-sided and were amazed that we did not tip over.

To reach Amboseli we traveled over Masai land for 80 kilometers (50 miles) on a rutted, sandy, eroded road. Amboseli sits among the foothills of majestic Mount Kilimanjaro. Part of the foothills are in Kenya, but all of Kilimanjaro is in Tanzania (locally pronounced Tans-zane-e-ah).

After riding over the arid areas it was a surprise to find our hotel located in an oasis in the middle of the desert. We had comfortable accommodations in quaint cottages. The grounds with tropical landscaping, complete with waterfalls, were gorgeous. We enjoyed cooling off in the full size swimming pool.

After checking in, I rounded the corner of the lodge veranda and nearly tripped over a yellow-faced monkey! Later in the day I observed him going into the coffee room and stealing a packet of sugar, then scampering off with his treat.

When on safari, game runs are done early in the morning before breakfast and in late afternoon. The animals are most active at those times, and tend to rest during the heat of the day.

On our first afternoon game run we saw hundreds of wildebeest followed by as many zebra. Both species were migrating south to the Serengeti. There are 1.7 million wildebeest in Kenya and this migration is the largest animal migration in the world. We also viewed many Grant's gazelles, Thompson gazelles, elephants, giraffes, impalas, warthogs, buffalo, ostrich, a jackal, and many colorful birds, some small and some very large. A swampy watering hole revealed many egrets and flamingos.

Just as we were getting ready to head back to the lodge, and just before a big dust storm blew up, a large herd of wildebeest did a classic movie stampede right in front of our van. What a bonus!

With a grin, our terrific driver told us, "The wildebeest is a combination of many animals. He has the face of a grasshopper, the chin and beard of a goat, the horns of a buffalo, and the tail of a horse. When it came time for a brain there was only room for an insect brain, which is why the wildebeest runs sideways, stumbles, and gets easily confused."

Although we kept our voices muted, you should have heard the oohs and ahs. What a thrill! Each night we marveled at all that we had seen, but every day seemed to be better than the previous one.

Monkeys playing outside the window woke me the next morning. I lay in bed listening to what sounded like barking dogs, wondering what dogs were doing here in the wild. My son had been up early to photograph Kilimanjaro at first light and returned saying there were a bunch of zebras down in the marsh just beyond the path outside our cabin. I didn't know zebras barked!

One afternoon while in Amboseli we visited the Elephant Research Center. In 1972 Cynthia Moss established the Center to conduct the most comprehensive study of elephants ever done. Her palm tree oasis included four sleeping tents, a dining tent, kitchen, shower, and outhouse. Two maintenance men and three research aids were employed as full time residents in this oasis.

During a lecture we learned that droughts in 1976 and 1984 killed many elephants. At the time of my visit the reserve had a population of 830 elephants who were identified and named. About fifteen elephant babies are born each year.

At birth, a baby weighs on average 260 pounds and stands three feet tall. The gestation period is 22 months. A baby elephant is born with two sets of teeth. Over its lifetime the elephant has several sets of teeth, the sixth set coming in at about age 40 will last 20-25 years. Eventually when the elephant can no longer eat, he dies. The average life span is 60-65 years.

Male elephants mature at about 14 years and at that point leaves the family. Tusks appear between two and two-and-a-half years. A family is led by the matriarch of the herd, not by a male, as is commonly believed.

Males socialize together. Babies stay with the mother. When one sees a lone elephant it is usually a male who has left the family but who has not yet linked up with others.

A female elephant goes into estrus and is fertile only four to six days every four years! A male comes into musth once a year, but not all males are in musth at the same time. However, a male may be sexually active even at times when he is not is musth. He is fertile when in musth and the time is definitely marked, as he dribbles urine and secretes a smelly secretion from a gland behind the ear. Hormonal changes also give him a distinctive walk.

Adult elephants eat 300 pounds of food a day and often travel as many as 20 kilometers (12 miles). Adult males can weigh 12,000 pounds, a female half of that. Elephants walk in a straight line like playing follow the leader, as many animals do, especially when migrating.

The animals leave paths across the plains 12-14 inches wide that some people think are tire tracks.

When in Kenya, I found the Masai of almost as much interest as the animals. They live a simple and primitive lifestyle in arid desert areas, much of it in the rift valley. Masai men wear typical tribal garb of red blankets and tend their goats and cattle on the plains. None of the local tribes eat wild game. Goats are a staple of the Masai diet, eating it like we eat chicken. Their simple diet consists of goat, beef, milk, and cheese. I still wonder how they stay healthy on such a limited diet.

Typically a Masai village is made up of a circle of small mud huts surrounding a large open area. A fence of thorny branches, similar to tumbleweed, surrounds the outside of the village to keep wild animals from entering.

The nomadic Masai follow green pastures for their livestock. They live and walk among the wild animals. Our driver told us the many tribes in Kenya get along with each other respecting each other's differences. Except in the large cities, crime is very low. Daycare centers and nursing homes are almost non-existent in Kenya as families take care of their own. All of the children belong to the whole village.

Our driver was a Kikuyu. The Kikuyu, the largest tribe in Kenya, are farmers. He told us he no longer lives in his village but with his wife in Nairobi. He was fluent in English, French, Spanish, Italian, Swahili and nine dialects.

Living between two cultures, he returns to his village for ceremonies and other important events. His dad lives in the village where life is very traditional, and sometimes it is hard for him to understand his son's non-traditional ways. He said he had, and only wanted, one wife and that he played with his children, also non-traditional. Men normally leave all the childcare to the mother.

In spite of popular belief, the Mau Mau was not a tribe. They were people who believed in independence. Actually the first Mau is Swahili meaning *white man go home* and the second Mau means *independence for Kenya.* Of course the Mau Mau no longer exist because Kenya gained independence in 1963.

The views of Mount Kenya were spectacular. The Aberdare National Forest is in the hills of Kenya. We spent an interesting night in The Ark, but first we needed to check our luggage, except for a small overnight bag. The only way to reach the Ark was over a long elevated trestle leading directly to reception. Taking our time walking over the forest floor we saw a lot of birds.

The Ark, a unique structure, had a large elevated deck overlooking a salt lick and watering hole. It was a great place for viewing animals when they came to drink from the pond and to lick the salt. On the observation deck everyone was asked to be extremely quiet.

All the rooms were on the second and third level. Each room was equipped with a buzzer. All night the buzzers went off when animals wandered into the area. Two rings meant large animals, such as rhino or elephant were feeding. Three rings meant big cats had arrived.

It was too cold to sleep on deck that night although my son and another hardy photographer made it until 4AM when a little fog rolled in. The rest of us slept in our clothes and when the buzzers went off grabbed a jacket or wrapped up in a blanket and quietly and quickly made it to the observation deck. It was an interesting experience, resembling an old fashioned slumber party.

The next morning driving out from the Ark a beautiful spotted leopard crossed right in front of our van on his way home to rest after a night's hunt. He was beautiful. This was another bonus, particularly because leopards are nocturnal and many visitors never see one.

On our way to Samburu Game Preserve we crossed the equator where the vans stopped for anyone who wanted to shop the multitude of vendors. It also was a pit stop for those who had to go, but after realizing it was just a hole in the ground, most of us gals elected to pass up the squat.

Standing with one foot on each side of the equator we watched a demonstration of water going down a drain, clockwise on one side and counter-clockwise on the other side. Fascinating!

Samburu is noted not only for elephant, leopard, and lion, but also for species of wildlife seldom seen elsewhere such as the Grevy zebra, reticulated giraffe, oryx, and gerenuk, (giraffe-necked antelope).

The Samburu tribe, living in the arid desert of the Rift Valley, is related to the Masai, speaks the same language, and observes the same customs.

Our driver told us the locals refer to the general area as Somaliland because of the Somali bandits who roam the area.

Going through a security checkpoint was a little unsettling. At that time I noticed a subtle change in our driver. After all, what could be more attractive than a van full of tourists with cameras and money? However, we trusted his instincts and abilities, and had been assured that safety was top priority.

Walking the grounds of another lovely oasis lodge we wandered over to a fence at the edge of a cliff above the muddy Uaso Nyiro River, which bordered the grounds of the lodge.

Spotting a huge crocodile sunning himself at the river's edge and several more in the water, my son got a bit too close to the fence, which he quickly learned was electric. Recovering from a pretty good jolt, he decided a telephoto lens would have to do, as he wasn't going to get any closer to the river.

That was "Born Free" country, and we were hoping to see Elsa. Instead we spotted a beautiful male lion, many oryx, Grevy zebras, Grant's gazelles, and Somali ostriches with the blue neck and legs.

A family of at least 30 elephants, with many small ones, was traveling along in an area where we could follow them for some time. Once they moved onto the roadway, we gave up the right-of-way. They were too big to argue with, and besides this was *their* territory, not ours. It was exciting!

Lake Nakuru is home to over a million flamingos. They were everywhere, and there were always some flying overhead. The lake is quite large, but very shallow. Wildlife along the shore was abundant. Seeing the Rothschild giraffes in their natural habitat was neat.

We spent one night in a quaint English cottage lodge along the Naro Moru River. Located on the gentle lower slopes of Mount Kenya, this area offered us a good opportunity for nature walks and bird watching. The river, with several small waterfalls, was relatively clear, but the water was very cold.

Checking into our cozy little cottage, I spotted a fire laid in the fireplace. That night we lit the fire and fell asleep in our cabin to the cracking logs burning. It was delightful!

Papyrus-lined Lake Naivasha is one of Kenya's most beautiful fresh water lakes. Our boat ride took us close to many huge hippos. Among the many species of birds, we saw the beautiful and rare fish eagle.

It was a 240-kilometer (144 mile) ride to our tented camp in the Masai Mara. The first 50 kilometers was over the old rutted, nearly non-existent road built by Italian POWs during World War II. It was not much fun, and I truly believe no repairs had ever been made on that so-called road. Kenya had recently created a badly needed road and gasoline tax that was supposed to go to road repair. I wonder if it ever did.

The Masai Mara, one of Kenya's best known game reserves, is famous for its black mane lions and huge herds of wildebeest, zebra, and gazelle.

Our lodging changed dramatically when we reached the Mara. Although tenting it for the next few nights, we really were not roughing it.

Our rather comfortable tent, approximately 10 x 14 feet, sat over a concrete slab and had a permanent, sturdy roof. It was equipped with two single beds with linens and small bedside tables. No sleeping on the ground here!

Unzipping the back of the tent revealed a bath complete with toilet, shower, and running water. The outside walls were concrete block. It sure beat an outhouse! The water was solar heated. Showering at night provided plenty of warm water. In the morning the water was a bit on the cool side.

The tents were arranged among the foliage so all we could see from our tent was the tiny corner of the one next door. Away from the pathway in front, the tents were quite well hidden. A large permanent lodge housed the reception, dining areas, bar, and gift shop.

The Masai Mara, in the northern Serengeti, is only 1510 square kilometers (900 square miles). Smaller than some of Kenya's other parks, it is animal dense, but there is enough water to support the animal population. The Mara River runs across the area and there are numerous watering holes. The Mara runs across the border into Tanzania. Mara means spotted. From a plane one sees spots of treetops (giraffes graze the bottoms of the trees) and spots of mud. Take your pick of interpretation.

The Masai Mara is probably the most popular spot to visit in Kenya. Of the eighteen lodges in the park/preserve, the first was built in 1962. Our first safari run provided us with hartebeest (kongoni), topi, (only seen there) jackal, cheetah, and several lions.

A ranger told us the black rhino population had increased from two to 38 animals. There were 1500-2000 elephants in the area as well as 700 lions. He stated it was difficult to count, as sometimes the animals wander in and out of the preserve because of the absence of mechanical barriers.

Twenty percent of park fees now go to the local people living in the area, allowing the Masai to be a little less dependent on their goats and cattle. All employees in the lodges are local people, and as a result the Masai culture is slowly changing.

While in the Masai Mara we awakened each morning to the black-faced monkeys squabbling outside our tent. It was as if they were saying, "Okay, it's daylight now, it's time to get up."

It is hard to see leopards, as they do their roaming at night. One afternoon on a game run the radio suddenly crackled with information that a pair of leopards had been spotted on a hillside. We hurried to the designated area. What a sight! The leopards were half way up the hill, camouflaged by rocky bush-covered terrain, but the sun shining on their gorgeous coats afforded us a good view and a great photo op.

As we watched in awe, the male suddenly mounted the female, and we knew we were watching a mating pair. Afterwards the female rolled over on her back like a contented playful cat. Then, suddenly they disappeared into the bush!

Heading back to our original location, we spotted a beautiful golden lioness, then saw that there were two! I never thought about them blending into their environment, but in the tall golden grass, they do. When one is lying down resting, it's easy to miss him.

Before the excitement died down, we spotted four, year-old cubs. Mamas had brought their children together to play. They were darling and appeared oblivious to our presence.

We thought our day was complete, but the excitement continued when we noticed a mating lion pair under the shade of a tree. She appeared to be sleeping soundly, but he was sleeping with one eye on their surroundings. They were so beautiful, we couldn't take our eyes off of them. What an afternoon. In all we had spotted eleven lions!

On our last day of safari, we counted our blessings at the multitude of animals we had seen. When we thought it couldn't get any better, our driver spotted a pair of cheetahs resting in the shade of a tree. Our cameras were clicking away when suddenly the cheetahs sat up with the hair on their neck standing up stiff. A quick glance revealed a lion walking across the field. We immediately backed up the van to allow the animals plenty of maneuvering room. The cheetahs were so fat, we thought they were pregnant.

Cheetahs travel in pairs, and these two were both males. Obviously they had just finished a big meal. Suddenly the cheetahs split, each running in a different direction. The lion chased one. Then both the lion and cheetah stopped in a standoff. Suddenly the chase was on again.

The cheetah outran the lion that soon sat down, despaired, and then slowly got up and wandered off. The cheetahs were safe for another day. Together the cheetahs ambled off to the shade of a tree on the opposite side of the field.

What a fantastic finish to two wonderful, very exciting weeks!

Chapter 6

Down Under-- Australia

It seems Australia and New Zealand go together like bread and butter. Maybe because it's such a long trip. However, because I've made two trips, one in 1995 and the second in 2000, and seen a great deal of the countries. I'm going to treat them separately.

Both times I flew Qantas Airline. Qantas is spelled without a U, because Qantas is an acronym for Queensland And Northern Territory Air Service.

Most flights leave the U.S. in the evening, arriving Down Under at daybreak. When going overseas I often go 36 hours or so without sleep, however I broke that record in the new century on my second trip. At 10 PM, after having been up 47 hours, and having lost a day crossing the International Date Line, I put my weary body to bed in Sydney. I envy people who are able to sleep on planes. Unfortunately, I'm not one of them.

We landed in Sydney, a giant city stretching 60 miles north to south and 35 miles east to west. Complete with subway and monorail systems, the city also has a downtown monorail that loops the area every six minutes. The combination of narrow streets and many vehicles makes traffic gridlock almost a constant. Sydney, home to 3.5 million people, is the capitol of New South Wales. Natives call themselves Sydneysiders.

The harbor divides the city into its north and south sections. The north side of the bridge includes Sydney's commercial center and its suburbs. Visitors frequent the south side of the city, which is bordered by Darling Harbor, Chinatown, Kings Cross, and the Harbor Bridge.

The famous Harbor Bridge, built in 1932-34, is the longest single span steel bridge in the world. Paul Hogan was working on the Sydney Harbor Bridge when he was discovered. The Bridge was a monumental engineering feat when completed. The arch spans over 1600 feet. It is 434 feet up to the top of the 3735-foot-long, 160-foot wide arch. There were no openings to climb to the top of the bridge, which has now become a very popular activity. After seeing how steep the steps were, we agreed it would have been a really tough climb. From harbor level it's 200 steps up to the bridge level. Walking to the second pylon we had a wonderful view of Sydney Harbor and the city.

Historically, after 1776, the English could no longer send their prisoners to the United States, so they sent them to barren and isolated Australia. Sydney was established as a penal colony in 1788 when Captain Arthur Phillip arrived, after an eight-month voyage from England, with a flotilla of eleven ships and a thousand convicts. Forty of the original passengers died during the 250-day voyage. They landed on a sandstone peninsular known as the Rocks.

The Nurses Walk was only a block from our hotel. We learned the colony's first hospital was established in that area. Many of the first settlers suffered dysentery, smallpox, scurvy, and typhoid after the long voyage. A few days after landing, Governor Phillip set up a tent hospital to care for the worst cases.

When the second fleet arrived in 1790, a quarter of its convicts had died, and many others were critically ill on arrival. The Second Fleet carried a prefabricated hospital, which was quickly erected, and immediately filled with patients. The first free settlers did not arrive in Australia until 1830.

The first crude wood huts erected by the convicts were followed with simple houses made of mud bricks cemented together with a mixture of sheep's wool and mud. Rain soon washed the mortar away and no buildings in The Rocks survived the earliest period of convict settlement. There were no permanent buildings before 1816. The Rocks was burned to the ground in 1838 because of the plague, and then rebuilt. Much restoration on historic colonial buildings has taken place in the last few years.

New South Wales has little timber for building and as a result most homes were brick or stucco with tile roofs. Apparently there is a big termite problem so these construction materials serve their owners well.

The city's largest Catholic Church was burned twice, and it was vowed that it would be burned whenever it was finished. Today the church stands with its two towers unfinished!

The oldest surviving house in Sydney is Cadman's Cottage. John Cadman was sentenced for stealing a horse. He eventually married a woman named Elizabeth who had stolen a hairbrush and a knife. This cottage, built in 1816, is of yellow sandstone. The Cadman cottage was a small two-story building. Cadman became superintendent of government boats and was allowed to live in the upper story of the cottage. Originally the cottage was at the waters edge. Because a fair amount of land in the harbor has been reclaimed, the cottage now sits back approximately 100 feet from the water. Part of the original seawall still stands in front of the cottage.

The waterfront of this thriving port was once lined with warehouses backed by a row of tradesmen's shops, banks, and taverns. Above, cobblestone alleyways led to the cottages of seamen and wharf laborers. The original Campbell warehouses, 1838, have been restored and now many cafes and restaurants occupy the ground level with homes occupying the upper levels. Robert Campbell was a Scottish merchant sometimes referred to as the father of Australian commerce.

Holy Trinity Church (also known as the Garrison church), built in 1840, is the oldest church in the country. It was the place of worship for British and Colonial Regiments. The church houses a distinctive "wine glass" shaped pulpit.

The Sydney Sailors' Home, 1859, is now the Visitor Center. The Argyle stores date to the 1800s, and Susannah Place, an example of a typical dwelling occupied by working class families from the mid 1840s, is now a museum.

Sydney Tower, top of the Centerpoint shopping complex is the highest vantage point in the city and is actually the highest public building in the Southern Hemisphere. Besides the viewing area, it houses two revolving restaurants and provides a spectacular view at any time of day! One day after shopping, we rested there awhile with a cup of coffee thoroughly enjoying the view on a very clear day.

QVC is short for Queen Victoria Building, a beautiful sandstone structure, built in 1893, that occupies a whole city block. The building has been restored and now houses 150 specialty shops. The tile on each of the three floors is different. Stained glass windows tower above the large marble stairways. A large clock dangles from the ceiling in the atrium in the center of the building, and the basement level, under the street, is full of eateries.

Once a town of soldiers, sailors, whalers, and merchants, Sydney now is Australia's largest city, surrounded by sprawling suburbs. By 1840 there were more free settlers than convicts in Sydney. With 75 percent of the country desert, 86 percent of the population lives in urban areas, with the majority of those in Sydney and Melbourne. In fact Australia has the highest rate of urbanization in the world. All of the large cities, except for Canberra, the capitol, are on the coast. The harbor officially titled Port Jackson, but commonly called Sydney Harbor, has 150 miles of waterfront, and is situated downtown. Ferry usage is increasing as traffic grows and it becomes more difficult for the bridge to handle the increased traffic.

The rolling parkland of the Royal Botanical Gardens forms the eastern boundary of the city. Originally a farm garden in 1816, the Gardens now have duck ponds, groves of palm trees, a cactus garden, and acres of lawn and pathways. One pathway leads to the point and Mrs. Macquarie's chair. The wife of the governor used to sit in her chair, carved out of stone by convicts, and yearn for her English homeland and contemplate how she could help her husband. Governor Lachlan Macquarie was an accomplished soldier as well as a man of vision. He was the first governor to foresee New South Wales as a free society as opposed to an open prison. He laid the foundation for the plan of the city by constructing public buildings and advocating that reformed convicts be readmitted to society. This radical thinking in the 19th century blurred the distinction between soldiers, free settlers, and convicts. He was forced to resign in 1821 and died three years later. Buried on his Scottish estate, his gravestone reads *Father of Australia*. The park is lovely and what a view of the harbor! Of course I had to sit in Mrs. Macquarie's chair each visit.

The white sails of the opera house are a symbol of the city and a visit to this famous landmark was absolutely fascinating. Pictures just don't do it justice and what a history! The four and a half acre building stands facing the harbor on Bennelong Point.

A docent was a world of information as she toured us through the facility. I've made three visits to this fabulous place and was in awe each time. The opera house has ten "sails" and stands 22 stories high.

There was enormous controversy and debate from the inception of the idea for an opera house in 1959. An international competition resulted in 233 submissions. The dazzling and dramatic design of the Danish architect Joern Utzon fired the imagination of the judges. But the technology did not exist in the 50s to build the sails that formed the roof and walls.

Original cost estimates were seven million dollars with a projected construction time of four years. The actual cost was 102 million and construction took 15 years. However, a special opera lottery paid the additional bills, and the opera house was completely paid for by mid 1975, just two years after its opening!

The criterion was for a multi purpose hall and minor hall. The first of a three-stage construction plan started in 1959. Stage I involved the foundation and base, to the podium level. Stage II was the construction of the roof vaults. One day, while peeling an orange, Utzon had the inspiration to construct the shells from rib sections of a complete sphere. And so the 2194 concrete ribs, forming the skeleton of the building, were prefabricated and joined together with 217 miles of tension steel. Each section weighs 15 tons. These ribs are clearly visible in the foyers and staircase areas of the concert hall.

The "roof" is covered with 1,056,000 white Swedish tiles, which appear as a mosaic. Any one section of the sails can be removed without compromising the entire structure. This is also true of the ribs and the tile coverings.

Shortly before completion of Stage II, in 1966, Utzon resigned from the project. A team of Australian architects took over the project and completed this stage in about a year.

Stage III involved the glass walls, interior rooms, and all the interiors, promenades and approaches. The Opera House is actually an arts center. Besides the 1547 seat opera theater there is a 2690 seat concert hall, a 544 seat drama theater, and a 398 seat playhouse.

The building houses 1000 rooms including a reception hall, five rehearsal studios, four restaurants, six theater bars, extensive foyers and lounge area, sixty dressing rooms, library, artist lounge, administrative offices, and extensive plant and machinery areas.

The concert hall roof vault is the highest at 221 feet. The roofs are supported by 32 eight-foot square columns sunk 82 feet below sea level.

Brushbox and white birch plywood, both obtained from northern New South Wales, are used extensively throughout. The 67,000 square feet of two-layer glass was manufactured in France. One layer of 2000 panes in 700 sizes is tinted, and the glass wall acts as soundproofing. The four hundred miles of electrical cable runs from 120 distribution boards and supplies enough power for a city of 25,000. Twelve miles of air conditioning duct run from 26 air conditioning rooms/areas. Wouldn't that be fun to troubleshoot? It is a fabulous building.

Darling Harbor is lined with shops and eateries, and small pockets of green are everywhere. Street performers are always in residence. We watched a couple of very good mimes. On a beautiful sunny day we enjoyed a Harbor Cruise and got a different perspective of the city.

In Sydney we used leg power to get around. However one afternoon we took a bus into the Blue Mountains. We followed the first road built out of the city over the new $3 million Anzac Bridge, built in 1995, which replaced the old bridge built by convicts.

The Blue Mountains are a barrier between Sydney and the rest of the country, and are part of the Great Divide Range, which originates in Melbourne and stretches some 1500 miles to Cairns. The range varies from 12 to 36 miles in width. All the eucalyptus trees in the mountains give off a vapor giving the mountains a blue tinge, thus the name, Blue Mountains. There are 1000 eucalyptus varieties, and they all belong to the gum family, however, not all gum trees are eucalyptus.

Pastureland lies on the other side of the Divide where apples grow well. The Granny Smith apple is said to have originated there when it sprouted in a compost pile. I suspect Granny Smith owned that compost pile! Parramatta was the first agricultural area. For many years, all produce was sent down river by barge to Sydney. Some variety of flowering tree is in bloom every month in Sydney. There are no native deciduous trees in Australia.

Our first stop when we got to the mountains was at an overlook where we could look straight down to the valley floor through a large crevice between the rocks. It was also a spectacular view of the mountains beyond.

Along the way, the driver had pointed out the blooming

jacaranda trees, the flame trees and pines. Azaleas, jasmines, and rhododendrons were all in prolific bloom. Now in the mountains he pointed out the banksia tree, saying, "This tree has a hard seed and needs heat to split open to germinate. So a forest fire actually helps this tree."

Approaching a small clearing we spotted our first kangaroo in the wild. Suddenly there were many of them feeding. They were relatively tame, or at least paid us little attention. Cameras clicked away.

We saw several mamas with a Joey, baby kangaroo, in their pouches. A female kangaroo becomes fertile at 18 months, the male at three years. These were eastern gray kangaroos, which grow four to five feet tall. There are 27 species of kangaroos from the smallest nine-inch kangaroo rat to the red kangaroo, the largest of them all that can cover 47 feet in a good jump/leap.

The kangaroo is sensitive to its environment. If food is scarce, mama can delay development of her baby until conditions improve. Kangaroos are marsupials, meaning that mama carries her young in an abdominal pouch. The fetus is born after only a few days, then claws and climbs its way into the pouch where it develops. Mama has two teats in the pouch making it possible for her to have two babies at different stages of development in the pouch at the same time. In such a case she produces a different kind of milk for each baby!

The strong muscular tail is used to balance when hopping and as a prop when resting. Hind legs are long and strong and forelegs short.

The dominant male can live to 12-15 years. He spends his life checking on his females, as they are not synchronous breeders. Their thick, strong claws often claw their opponent's abdomen when fighting. A dominant male only remains so for three or four years before a younger, stronger male takes over.

The poor female spends most of her life pregnant and raising children. Mama can determine the sex of her child, and usually waits to have a male until her later years, as she is the one responsible for raising him and teaching him to fight. Kangaroos, have no herding instinct, each reacts in his or her own way.

When European explorers first saw the strange jumping animal, they asked an aborigine what they were called. He answered, "Kangaroo" meaning "I do not understand your question," and that is how the kangaroo got its name.

We enjoyed tea and cake on this lovely day at this gorgeous spot. As we watched the kangaroos feed, one lone kookaburra up in a tree watched us in return.

In 1901, when all the states joined as one federation, even though each state had a capitol, it was apparent that the country also needed a capitol. Stiff competition developed between Sydney and Melbourne for the honor, but Canberra was chosen for its inland location, its clean air and water, for security reasons, and to put an end to the bickering between the two large cities.

The 900 square miles of prime sheep country is in a valley known as the plains of Yass, and is about equal distance from both Melbourne and Sydney. It is known as the Australian Capitol Territory or A.C.T. for short. The Aboriginal word *canberry* meaning "meeting place," was changed to Canberra. The city is referred to as the bush capitol, city of the gray flannel suit, monument valley, or the garden city of the commonwealth, depending on the view of the speaker. And the inhabitants say, "To know Canberra is to love it."

The city is a totally planned one. After an international competition, Walter Burley Griffin from Chicago was chosen as the architect to design the city. Griffin arrived in Canberra in 1913 to supervise construction. Two World Wars and the depression slowed progress and by 1947 Canberra still was a country town of 15,000.

Griffin envisioned a spacious city, a city that could breathe. Development was rapid in the 1950s and the city built for 50,000 is now home to 300,000, with surrounding suburbs. Lake Burley

Griffin was originally planned as three small lakes, but was built as one larger lake with three bridges dividing it. The impression of the city is one of spaciousness, calm, and order. The streets are wide. Because the city was built on the plains originally there were no trees. Thousands of trees were planted every year for many years and now the city boasts of 11-15 million trees, all planted by hand! Normal rainfall is 64 inches a year.

Major public buildings were built on low knolls around the lake. There were no billboards. All the colors were muted and generally all buildings were low. Canberra is a one-company town and the government owns all the land. The government employs sixty-five percent of the city's workforce. The rest work in service industries.

One exception to land ownership is the ten acres the U.S. embassy sits on. Australia deeded this land to the U.S. for its help in World War II. The U.S. Embassy is the largest and sits on the highest knoll. The red brick in the colonial building was imported from the United States. It is a beautiful building!

There are numerous embassies and high commissions of traditional and unusual design in this capitol city. Countries related to the Motherland have high commissions instead of embassies.

The new Parliament building cost the country a billion dollars to build. Opposition to tearing down the old parliament was so fierce, it remains standing intact in front of the new building making a nice contrast.

The new Parliament actually consists of five buildings joined together with glass link-ways, 23,000 granite slabs cover the curved areas. We walked some of the 20 kilometers (12 miles) of hallways.

The 260-foot flagpole is a central landmark of the city. The foyer of the parliament building with its wide curved stairways is a show place. The masonry and timber used throughout is beautiful.

The great hall houses one of the world's largest tapestries. Measuring 30 x 9 meters, it weighs 400 kilos, used 360 colors and took two and a half years to complete. It appears to be an oil painting. Only on close inspection is it evident that it is truly a magnificent tapestry.

The contributing factors to my choosing the second trip was the fact that Tasmania, Kangaroo Island, and the Outback were included on the itinerary.

The flight to Tasmania was an early one but our driver was waiting for us when we arrived in Hobart at 8:40 AM. Abel Tasman discovered Tasmania in 1642. Actually he sailed the island's southwest coast. Called Van Dieman's land, it was not until 1798 that the landmass was actually thought to be an island. And it was not until 1803 that a settlement was established at Risdon Cove on the bank of the Derwent River. The island was named Tasmania in 1856.

Tasmania is Australia's only island state. The island, no larger than Scotland, covers 68,300 square kilometers, runs 175 miles north to south and 189 miles east to west. This unspoiled island has only four major cities and a population of less than a half million, 40 percent of whom live in Hobart. The lush lowland farms and villages with their Georgian cottages look very English.

The west and southwest coast of the island is still unexplored, its access barred by the impenetrable rain forest. The island provides vast expanses of space, as a large amount of land has been designated as National Park and 27 percent of the land is used for agricultural purposes. Mount Ossa at 5303 feet is the highest peak.

The island's entire aboriginal population was wiped out 73 years after the first Europeans arrived. The last of the 6000 full-blooded aborigines died in 1876. She was a female whose husband had died in 1869.

Tasmania Botanical Gardens was our first stop. Early in the morning there were few people about. The gardens were beautiful, restful, and peaceful with a view of the sea. In true English tradition, the gardens were well kept, spacious, and filled with both native and imported plants. The park just got prettier and prettier as we walked along. There were ponds, bridges, specialty gardens, flower gardens in bloom, and green lawns. There were many benches where one could sit and rest, or contemplate. We saw some of the most gorgeous birds, we later identified as Eastern Rosellas.

Hobart, Tasmania's capitol, located at the foot of 4160 feet Mount Wellington, is a blend of heritage, beautiful scenery, and a relaxed island lifestyle, but with all the amenities of a thriving city. Graceful old trees cover the manicured lawns of the city's many small heritage parks and gardens.

In 1804 Colonel David Collins settled the city with 262 people, naming it for Lord Hobart. The same distance south of the equator as Boston is north, Hobart is Australia's second oldest city (after Sydney).

Once a whaling base, the city of 139,000 has one of the finest deep-water harbors in the world, and is now a busy port. The Derwent River runs through the city.

Hobart is the center of the state's government. Ship movements in and out of the Derwent River have been watched over by 1105 feet Mount Nelson since 1811.

Governor Macquarie established the 1818 signal station at Battery Point after a visit to the island. Twelve relay stations made full communication available between Hobart and Port Arthur. Battery Point was named for the guns that once protected the area.

Some of the old buildings in Hobart include St. David's Church, 1868, a Regency Egyptian style synagogue 1843 (the oldest in the country), Parliament House, built by convicts in 1840 as a Customs House, and turned into its present function in 1856, and the Cascade Brewery, the country's oldest. The oldest theater in Australia is located in Hobart. The city also houses a maritime museum and a folk museum. The main street in the city is Liverpool. The expressway out of town was built in 1954. The harbor contains much reclaimed land. Convicts spent 60 years reclaiming it.

Apples grow well in Tasmania. Many of the 250 varieties are exported to Japan.

Salamanca, a series of old warehouses, was built in 1930 to store apples, corn, and wheat for export. At one time there was a jam factory in one of the buildings. Now trendy restaurants, sidewalk cafes, stores, and art studios occupy those warm sandstone buildings lining the uncrowded waterfront.

At our lovely old hotel, previously a mansion, we climbed up to the widow's walk. I've seen many widow's walks over the years, but had never been in one. What a view! The sun was very warm shining through all the windows.

On the way to Port Arthur we rode through rolling hills and farmland. Passing a field of opium poppies we were told Tasmania is the only state allowed to grow the opium poppy for morphine. It is the bulb of the poppy that is harvested, because that is where the seeds are. Poppies take so many nutrients from the soil, the area cannot be replanted for four years.

For security reasons the entire area was fenced, and unmarked cars patrolled the area. The farmer also has authority to police. The farmer is allowed to prepare the soil, plant, tend, and water his crop, but is *not* allowed to harvest it. A special company does that. The farmer is paid by the ton. The seed harvest is then sent to a drug company.

Tasmania Devil Park was a delightful little park. We watched three or four Tasmanian devils run around and play in an enclosure. A wolverine-like animal, it is extinct on the Australia mainland and is found only in Tasmania. The devil is a carnivorous marsupial, the size of a small dog, black in color, and has a spine tingling screech.

Its powerful jaws can crack bones so when feeding it devours the entire animal. It is fearful rather than aggressive. A picture showing its teeth is usually a yawn rather than an aggressive act. Making loud noises shows aggression.

These synchronous breeders mate in March, and the babies are born in the spring, about April or May. A female can have six to eight pups, but only has four nipples in the pouch, so only four survive. The gestation period is only four weeks, however the pups suckle in the pouch for another six months. The life span is about five years. Inhabiting virtually all of Tasmania, they survive any and all climates. They sleep by day and eat at night.

Devils were a nuisance to early settlers, raiding poultry yards. At one time the authorities offered a bounty for them, driving them to more remote areas. When finally protected in 1941, they had already been hunted almost to extinction. The population has survived, and today is healthy. Although they have a reputation for killing sheep, they are rather inept killers, preying on small animals when they do kill. They prefer to scavenge and are very good at it. When under stress they produce a rather unpleasant odor, but otherwise are clean and tidy animals.

Walking around we saw several wallabies, emus, and birds in an aviary. Then we came upon a park guide who was holding an animal neither of us had ever seen before. It turned out to be Lilly, a baby wombat who was just as cute as can be. About 18 months old she was still small enough to be held in the caretaker's arms.

Wombats grow to about the size of a pig, and they can do a lot of damage to a car if one is unlucky enough to hit one on the road. This burrowing animal is another marsupial. They suckle in the pouch for six months then stick around with mom for twelve more months. Related to the koala, wombats are vegetarians, and are nocturnal.

Port Arthur, located on the isolated Tasman peninsula, was just as much a natural prison as Alcatraz. The peninsula was surrounded by hungry sharks, and was connected to the mainland only by 100-yard wide Eaglehawk Neck that was guarded by angry chained dogs. Escape was nearly impossible. There were only two successful escapes in the history of the prison.

Chain gang convicts built a causeway in 1872-74. All

deliveries to the prison were by boat, as the overland road from Hobart to Port Arthur was not built until 1893.

In 1830 Colonel George Arthur with 68 men established Port Arthur as a timber station. The first three years 1.5 million cubic feet of lumber were cut and sent to England. There were no permanent buildings for three years. Over the next eleven years Port Arthur housed 6002 convicts in the settlement. Although the prison generally held 600 to 700 prisoners at any time, at its peak in 1840, the prison held 2000 plus a complement of soldiers and supporting personnel.

Of the 73,000 English convicts sent to Australia, 12,500, mostly second offenders or violent criminals, found themselves in Port Arthur. Those worst offenders also included women and juveniles. Males and females were separated. The young boys were sent to Puer Island, (abandoned in 1849) and were required to attend school. This was a progressive concept, as school was not yet required for the general youth population.

Although the conditions at Port Arthur were brutal, the prison also was progressive. All convicts were gainfully employed in one of 47 trades. The trades all evolved with a commercial bias. Included in the complex were a sawmill, granary and flourmill, railroad, shipbuilding workshop, tannery, coopers, gardeners and shoe making shop. The brickyard produced 50,000 bricks a month. The blacksmith made all the nails and fasteners used. Between 1834-49, the shipyard produced over 200 long and whale boats. The largest boat was the size of the Mayflower. When the shipyard was closed, a lime kiln was built to produce lime for mortar. Seashells were collected and crushed as a limestone source. The bakery produced 1000 loaves of bread a day.

A docent accompanied us about the grounds of the old prison. Original punishment was whipping with a cat 'o nine tails—nine leather straps, each knotted nine times and dipped in salt water. Then the punishment was carried out in front of all prisoners. Solitary confinement replaced that punishment in 1849.

We went into the old solitary cell, and once the lights were turned off, it wasn't 30 seconds before I wanted out!

There was a lovely church, hospital, and personnel housing on the grounds. Today the site radiates a peaceful atmosphere. The ivy-covered ruins and restored buildings really make a lovely historic site. What would we hear if those walls could talk?

Port Arthur was definitely worth the visit. Tasmania was a beautiful island with a feel of spaciousness, and a slower lifestyle.

Without a doubt Melbourne is my favorite Australian city. I simply adore it. Known as the garden city, it was established by merchants for trade, and therefore the city is planned and orderly. The city boomed in 1850 during the gold rush. The first Parliament was seated in 1851. With a population of 3.5 million, Melbourne is Australia's second largest city, and is the financial, cultural, and intellectual capitol of the state of Victoria, Australia's smallest state. The city is the site for the nation's most prestigious schools and universities.

Melbourne is an ethnic melting pot with dozens of nationalities. With its elegance and calm the city is charming rather than dazzling. Public transportation is fast, efficient, and reasonable. A free tram runs around the city center during the day. The city has one of the world's largest tram systems that include 227 miles of track in the city and suburbs. The system is reliable, fast, and convenient. The streets, originally built to run sheep, are wide enough to accommodate the tram system. The city's lack of traffic problems is the envy of many a large city.

Nearly one quarter of the center city is set-aside for recreational purposes. This added to the multitude of flowers and trees creates an atmosphere of rural tranquility in a busy city. The Yarra River, bordered by parks, runs on the south side of town. The western part of the city is the business district. Melbourne is the third largest city in the Empire, following London and Sydney. Natives call themselves Melbournians. Great rivalry between Melbourne and Sydney has existed for decades.

Beautiful Fitzroy Park and Gardens, covering 65 acres, were named after Sir Charles Fitzroy, Governor of New South Wales in the mid 1840s. The gardens are over 150 years old. Located in the park was a conservatory full of gorgeous flowers, many of which were new to most of us. It takes 7500 plants to keep Melbourne's stunning floral clock, in another park, in its beautiful colors.

Captain Cook's cottage was disassembled in England, shipped to Australia, and reassembled in the park in 1934. A small garden with a statue of its owner is behind the cottage.

The fairy tree is nearby. Many years ago a large tree had to be cut down. A local lady requested the stump be left, as she wanted to do something to delight children. Between 1933-35 she carved little fairy figures all around the tree stump. It is still a sweet delight.

Queen Victoria Market covers 17 acres and contains 1000 stalls selling everything imaginable. Originally, in 1837, the area was a cemetery. In 1877 part of the cemetery was converted to the market, requiring the relocation of only three graves. In 1917 Parliament authorized the relocation of 10,000 remains, razed the cemetery, and by 1922 the market was in its full glory.

Accents do sometimes get in the way. One of our fellows was talking to some chap and was asked if he had a *merble fern.* He was totally puzzled, until he finally figured out the gentleman was talking about a *mobile phone*!

All directions radiate from the post office which was built in 1836. Parking signs in the city are a bit different. A P 5 means one can park for five minutes; P 1 mean one-hour parking. Parking maids in the city are diligent.

The Old Treasury, a neoclassical brick and bluestone building built in 1857, is near the lovely old Windsor Hotel on the opposite side of the street. Flinders Street Station, a grand Edwardian building, is the hub of Melbourne's suburban rail network.

St. Patrick's Cathedral, a gothic church, is made of sandstone. The church started in 1850 has undergone two expansions. The sanctuary's bluestone altar is an island at the end of the nave and pews. Surrounding the sanctuary were seven small chapels whose walls were painted to resemble tile. The capacity of the church is 1800-2000. The magnificent stain glass windows were made in Birmingham, England in the late 1800s. The wooden pillars and woodwork were truly beautiful. How unusual to have the hammer-beam ceiling decorated with angels, 32 of them. The grounds surrounding the church were lovely.

A visit to the Old Melbourne Gaol showed us what jails used to be like, very austere and stark. The restored jail is located in the center of the city. Defying all law and order Ned Kelly, Australia's Jesse James, was probably the most famous bushranger. Wearing a suit of armor, he escaped authorities for some time. Eventually he was captured after being shot in first one knee and then the other, vulnerable spots in his armor. Hung in 1880, his gear and death head mask are displayed at the Gaol.

During World War II, Australia lost 62,000 men, 19,000 of them from Victoria. The Shrine of Remembrance is a memorial to all who served in all wars.

This memorial, costing $470,000, required a great deal of effort. The main part of the memorial is built so that on the eleventh hour of the eleventh day of the eleventh month a shaft of light shines through the ceiling to illuminate and move across the heart in the center of the floor. Due to popular demand, the light is now mechanically reproduced each day. A hush fell over the crowd as we watched this most spectacular sight! It was a very moving experience.

The name of every serviceman who has died defending his country is engraved on the foyer walls. The names, in alphabetical order, are grouped by conflict. The interesting museum covered two floors in the memorial.

Serendip Sanctuary located at the foot of the YooYang Mountains was established in 1970 to breed endangered water birds. A lagoon is included in the one square mile of natural land.

Driving around the perimeter we stopped a couple of times to take a short walk.

We saw lots of kangaroos, some in rather large groups. Many water birds were in the lagoon, and more birds were in an aviary. Rock wallabies and an occasional emu were also seen.

One day, on the first trip, we rode out of the city to see kangaroos at a museum/farm. It was exciting to walk among them and to be able to pet them. Little did I know then that I would have the opportunity many more times to see kangaroos!

On another afternoon we rode out of town again to visit koalas in a zoo. Koalas, also marsupials have very sharp claws so at the zoo they were weaned onto a stuffed koala pillow. They could cuddle with the toy, and in captivity could be handled without the handlers getting too many nasty scratches.

Koala is an aboriginal word meaning "does not drink." The koala rarely drinks, deriving all of its fluid from their exclusive diet of eucalyptus leaves. Very susceptible to human illness, virtually all of the koalas on Phillip Island are infected with chlamydia and are dying out. Living on a preserve, when they are all gone, healthy koalas will be reintroduced to the island.

These nocturnal animals can travel as far as five miles in search of food. They are small animals, not much bigger than a good size teddy bear.

New South Wales and Queensland climates are warm so the koalas are gray with white on the inner ears and chest. Victoria is cooler, and the koalas are larger and have a darker fur, more of a charcoal gray. Babies spend six months in the pouch and then cling to mama's back until they reach full maturity. Koalas seldom have more than one baby and if they do only one survives, as the pouch is only big enough to accommodate one baby. The furless newborn looks like a pink jellybean. The normal life span is 16-18 years.

On the way to Phillip Island we stopped at a restaurant and had an excellent lobster dinner. Fairy penguins live only in southern Australia. Every evening shortly after sunset the penguin parade starts when hundreds of penguins march across Summerland Beach to their nesting area.

Because people would trample the beaches, a visitor center was built to protect the penguins. Bleachers line the beach for spectators to watch this evening ritual. If the pathways leading home through the sand are destroyed the penguins get lost. Flash pictures are not allowed because the flash hurts the penguins' eyes.

Over a half million people visit the center each year. You can imagine how quickly that many people can destroy the nesting area. The penguins live in homes burrowed in the sand.

These tiny animals, smallest of the 18 species, often swim 20 miles off shore seeking food. They can dive 33 feet and have been clocked swimming 24 miles per hour. Mating season is July-September and penguins mate for life. Each couple raises two chicks, and the parents take turns feeding the youngsters. After six-eight weeks the little ones leave the nest and learn to swim, The fairy penguin is, on average about a foot long and has an ink blue coat. Watching the penguins walk across the beach was an experience! They were so tiny, just precious.

After the parade one can walk on the boardwalk through the nesting area listening to the sounds of the penguins talking. Do you suppose they are asking, "Did you have a good dinner?" Pretty fantastic to be so close to them.

The center had a lovely museum, a restaurant, and a nice gift shop. It was a fabulous evening that wasn't too cold at the ocean's edge.

Leaving Melbourne for Adelaide, the capitol of South Australia, our flight was delayed a couple of hours. Arriving in Adelaide we set our watches ahead another half hour.

After checking into the hotel we immediately left for the Barossa Valley to visit a winery. It was misty going over the mountains, but when we stopped at Mengler's Hill, it was clear as could be giving us a fantastic view of the valley below. The driver explained that the valley was a hung valley, because one end of the valley was 600 feet above sea level while the other end only 150 feet.

Sixteen varieties of grapes grow in the valley, and there are many small wineries. We had dinner at the winery where we had the choice of kangaroo or chicken. I chose chicken, as I just couldn't suppress visions of the roos jumping around. My roommate bravely chose the kangaroo. She let me have a couple of bites, and it wasn't too bad. She said it got better after the first couple of bites, but that it wouldn't be her first choice again. Kangaroo is a very lean meat with only ten percent fat content compared to beef's 25 percent. Because it is so lean it can quickly become tough, so is best marinated and undercooked.

The next morning the driver said he was going to take the scenic route to Cape Jarvis to give us a change of scenery and for him to avoid 37 traffic lights. The hour and a half drive through rolling farmland and dairy farms was delightful on a cold windy day.

The 50-minute ferry ride to Kangaroo Island on the *Matilda* was rough, rough, rough! People on my left and people on my right were sick and using the barf bags. We apparently crossed over some channel.

Kangaroo Island, Australia's third largest island, is 90 miles long, 20 miles wide, and about the size of Long Island. The English explorer, Matthew Flinders, discovered the island in 1802.

The population of 4500 is located mostly in four cities, the largest of which is Kingscote with its population of 1800. The island is home to 20,000 kangaroos, so there are about five kangaroos for every person! The island was hilly, covered with trees, and had no public transportation. The island had 19 national park/conservation areas.

Norfolk Pine trees grew along the coastline. Because they grow tall and straight, if a ship, in days of old, lost a mast, the pine was ready and waiting to be cut to make a new mast.

Only pockets of land on the island are fertile enough for

agriculture. Crops include canola, olive oil, honey, and eucalyptus oil. Vineyards are in their infancy on the island. Fish farming is growing. Fishing includes crayfish, oysters, and mussels. There are two cheese factories on the island.

The narrow leaf eucalyptus grows only on the east side of the island. American Beach was the site of an 1803 shipwreck.

A visit to Emu Ridge Eucalyptus Oil Distillery was an interesting stop. The owner's wife showed us around saying 90 percent of all eucalyptus oil comes from Japan, ten percent from Australia, and three percent from Emu Ridge. At one time there were 48 distilleries on Kangaroo Island, now the only one left is Emu Ridge. Sheep raising replaced the industry as it is easier work and the money is better.

A ton of leaves is put into a large caldron of boiling water. Depending on the season, the ton of leaves produces five-30 liters of oil. At that point the oil is light amber in color, but after a second distillation the oil is colorless. Trees can be re-harvested every three years. By holding a leaf up to the light we could see the small oil seeds.

In the show room we spotted a baby kangaroo hanging in a sling from a hat tree. Mama had been killed, so the people at the Ridge were raising it. The sack confined her like she was in mama's pouch. We all took turns holding the baby and loving it while cameras clicked away!

After lunch we stopped at Seal Bay Conservation Center where a National Park naturalist took us to the beach.

This area is home to a colony of 600 Australian sea lions. The population has remained pretty constant for several years, and it is thought that the environment cannot sustain any larger numbers. These are opportunistic feeders, loners and not at all family oriented.

Hunted for their skin and blubber the sea lions were almost extinct. A reef protects the bay, and the sanctuary extends one mile out from shore and extends five miles along the coast. Being deep divers, an adult female with an unweaned pup will consume eight to ten kilos of food a day.

The gestation period is 18 months. The female goes into heat again 17 days after birthing! They are not synchronized breeders. A female has four teats. Sea lions are mammals and have hair and ears. The large front flippers allow the animal to walk, where seals cannot. These animals go to sea for three days at a time, then return to rest and sleep on the beach. A bull often stays a month at a time on the beach.

Living up to 25 years, males can weigh up to 600 kilos, and are brown to yellow in color, where the female is more cream colored. Forty bulls live in the bay. Pups stay on the beach 12-18 months to suckle from mom. Mortality rates are high with only about 30 percent of pups making it to maturity.

It was very windy and very cold on the beach. Though a long walk, it was worth it. There must have been three-dozen sea lions sleeping on the beach in the immediate area.

Riding along, the driver detoured off the road where we spotted many koalas up in the trees. A couple of moms had a baby in the pouch. Since they are nocturnal animals it is a bit unusual to see them during the day. Daytime is when they usually curl up in the fork of the tree branches and sleep.

Suddenly a baby started climbing down out of a tree. When on the ground that baby walked several feet to where one of the gals was standing and started to climb up her leg!

Her pants were almost the exact color of the tree trunks, and she figured the little koala thought her white shoes were rocks. The driver wiggled the koala off her leg, but not before he left a puncture wound in her lower leg. They do have sharp claws!

Koalas are often referred to as koala bears, which is incorrect. They are not bears and have no relation to bears. Correctly, they are simply koalas.

Driving along the rugged rock-bound coast we stopped at the Remarkable Rocks, a cluster of granite boulders sculptured by the weather and perched on a granite dome high above the ocean. Centuries of wind and rain have sculptured many weird shapes. We walked the catwalk out to the rocks and took some pictures. Talk about windy!

Late afternoon we headed to the airport, for our return to Adelaide. We each were weighed with our packs. Looking out the airport window we saw a lot of little planes with EMU painted on the tails. One of the gals with a quick wit said, "Who would ever name an airline after a flightless bird!"

When we reached the little plane, the pilot took our packs and stuffed them into the end of the wing. We were all seated and buckled up when we watched the pilot crawl up over the wing into the cockpit. This seemed like a good alternative to the ferry. What was I thinking?

A good part of the short flight was above the clouds. When I could see the water, the whitecaps looked like wiggly little viruses under a microscope. When over land the sheep in the pasture looked like little golf balls.

I was happy to be on the ground. It was still foggy over Mount Lofty, but we'd had a wonderful day!

It had been a long day, and we all heeded the guide's advice to enjoy the dining experience at the hotel. We were not in an area where cabs were available and the hotel did not run any shuttle service. Besides there really wasn't any place close to dine.

We really didn't dress, but we did clean up a bit for dinner. Our dining experience occupied a good two hours. The presentation of all the meals was exquisite and the food was scrumptious.

Driving down off the mountain the next day we stopped in Hahndorf to wander the town and do a bit of shopping. Hahndorf was a small town with a current population of 800. Settled in 1839, it was the first German settlement in Australia. In the mid 1800s women took their produce 18 miles to market in Adelaide. A determined, hard working lot, they started the long day's journey at

3 AM.

There was one traffic light in that delightful little town. We poked around in several shops and I did a bit more Christmas shopping.

We almost forgot to buy a bottle of wine for the train ride. A woman I met at Admiral's Arch on Kangaroo Island, who had just come back from Alice Springs on the train, said to drink lots of wine and to keep remembering it was only for one night.

We found a local winery, did a little tasting with explanations by the lady holding the bottle. When we found one that satisfied both of us, we bought it.

The train was going to be a bit late, so we had a bus tour of Adelaide. Adelaide's flat one square mile is laid out in a grid.

Colonel William Light surveyed the town in 1836, taking two and a half months to complete the task. He created a green buffer zone all around the city. By firing off a cannon he was able to determine at what distance the green zone must be placed. This small city of one million people lies between the Lofty Mountains and the Southern Ocean.

Germans settled the area in 1842 as a free colony, when land cost one pound an acre. Many of the emigrants seeking religious freedom, were non-conformists, so there has always been a tradition of tolerance there.

King William Street is in the center of town. All the cross streets change names as they intersect there, because it is improper to cross royalty with commoners. The streets were wide, and traffic congestion never a problem.

The fountain in the center of the square was erected in 1963. The tallest building is 21 stories. The annual rainfall is 24 inches. Crops include grapes, apples, cherries, wheat, strawberries, beef, and sheep.

Building construction was of brick instead of sandstone. Colonel Light died in 1839. A brush fire in 1983 in the Lofty Mountains raised the temperature in Adelaide to 110 degrees!

Another check with the train station revealed the train would be delayed a bit longer so we visited the Adelaide Botanical Gardens. We all agreed there was no point in just sitting around the station.

The bicentennial conservatory has created a rain forest with 900 misters and more than 2000 panes of glass. There is a weird glass sculpture within the gardens. It was a pleasant respite to wander the lovely grounds.

Eventually it was time to head to the station to board the Ghan train for the 970-mile overnight ride through the Australian outback to Alice Springs.

We arrived at the train station just about the same time the train pulled in, but there was still a bit of a wait before we could board. It was a surprise to see the stewards washing the windows before we started the trip. Nice clean windows to look out onto nothingness!

We were all assigned to the N car. I was in #15, while my roommate was in #13 across the hall. The cabins were compact so we were happy with the extra room of a single, as neither of us had to climb into a top bunk. The train finally got underway at 4:30 PM.

Checking out our environment, we learned our sleepers were about midway in the car with toilets on each end. The dining car was about four cars forward, right behind the lounge car.

After a few minutes a voice on the loud speaker said, "We have one locomotive pulling 26 cars and the train is nearly 360 meters long. Afghani camel trains, carrying supplies, made the long 970-mile trek between Adelaide and Alice Springs for many years, thus the name Ghan Train."

A paved road between the two cities did not exist until 1980. The train traveled over level ground in the center of the country. After the wheat fields of the Flinders Range, it was flat expanses of saltbush. Flat, flat, flat!

Before dinner we opened the bottle of wine we bought in

Hahndorf. When I had told my son about the tug of war we had with the cork in Warsaw, he showed me how to use the opener on my key ring as leverage for the corkscrew. It worked like a charm, and I couldn't believe how easily the bottle opened!

With a laugh I said, "I have to tell you though this is the first time I've ever drunk wine from a paper cup!"

My roommate reminded me it all was part of the adventure. And we certainly were having a great time in the comfortable, air-conditioned car.

Before dinner we learned from our little booklets that the 1929 steam driven train traveled over track laid in a flood plain. Rains often washed away the track. The jolting ride over meandering tracks was not much fun, and long delays were common. The original tracks were narrow gauge; the present tracks are standard size.

The evening on the train was a good time to learn a bit more about The Land Down Under. We agreed Australia is a land of awesome natural wonders, vibrant contrasts, friendly people, sophisticated cities, exotic and unique wildlife and has a short but interesting history as a nation.

The county's bush ballads and folk tales tell the story of the perseverance of farmhands, miners, and sheep shearers to build a nation in a challenging environment. It is the only nation in the world that covers an entire continent, and is the world's sixth largest country in land mass. It is the flattest, smallest and second driest continent, after Antarctica.

The country, known as the Commonwealth of Australia, won its Independence on January 1, 1901. Geographically Australia is the size of the United States. The country's seven states are Victoria, Queensland, New South Wales, South Australia, Western Australia, Northern Territory, and Tasmania.

The country is bordered on the west by the Indian Ocean, on the south by the Southern Ocean, on the east by the Pacific Ocean, and on the north by the Coral Sea. The Tasman Sea is between

Australia and Tasmania in the southeast corner of the country. The country is surrounded by 23,000 miles of coastline.

Until the 20th century, Australia remained a collection of distinct colonies with greater ties to England than to each other. It was not until after World Wars I and II that a true national identity evolved.

Most of the population lives near the coast, leaving the interior of the country basically unpopulated. All major cities are located on the coast.

Leaving South Australia and crossing the boundary into the Northern Territory meant another hour change on our watches.

Arriving in Alice Springs at 9:40 in the morning, we off loaded, found our bus and driver, but had a bit of a wait for the regular luggage to be off loaded from the special car. All we had carried aboard was an overnight bag.

We branded the Alice Springs motel as a nothing motel, which really wasn't fair. It was just like any motel, but it was a let down after the wonderful quaint small accommodations we'd had.

After studying a map of the city we headed for the Todd Mall, which wasn't very big, but held our interest for a short while. We then wandered around the city, all five blocks of it. We studied some aboriginal art, talked and visited with a couple of shop owners, and then met the rest of the group for lunch. Aborigines make up 20 percent of the city's population.

The city, originally named Stuart after an explorer, was renamed Alice Springs after Alice Todd, the wife of the telegraph station project foreman. In 1939 the population was 700, today it is 26,000, and the center for Aboriginal artworks, and base camp for Outback travelers.

Alice Springs started out as a cattle town, and as late as the 1970s the city still had a wild west image. It now survives on the tourist trade. In the Northern Territory, twice the size of Texas, the 178,000 people are out numbered by sheep and rivaled by kangaroos, dingoes and Afghan camels.

Alice Springs is home to 1600 Americans most of whom work at the NASA Pine Gap tracking station.

A visit to the School of the Air was fascinating. Established in 1951 it has a broadcast area of 1.3 million square kilometers to reach school children living in isolated areas of the outback. At that time 120 children were enrolled, ranging in age from four and a half to 12 or 13. The average enrollment is 150. At its peak, 180 children were enrolled. A third of the children are aboriginal. There are several such schools in the country's vast expanses.

After age 12 or 13 children go to Alice Springs to attend boarding school, which consists of four ten-week sessions costing $10-15,000 a year. The program and facility was most impressive! But the next stop positively fascinated me. If I were younger and still working I just might find myself working in that situation! Wireless, wings, and stethoscope!

The Royal Flying Doctor Service started in 1928 with one plane. Today, in Alice Springs, they operate with six doctors, six nurses, six pilots, three planes, and three engineers providing free service to the public. Their goal is to do three clinics a day or 1000 a year in the Outback. They all work twelve-hour shifts for two days, have one day off and repeat.

It was shocking to learn 18 percent of their business involves tourists, many at Ayers Rock. The annual budget was $9 million. Planes cost $4.5 million each.

A drug box containing 100 drugs, packaged by number rather than name, is kept at numerous outposts around the country. Much prescribing is done by phone. The service in Alice Springs covers an area 70 kilometers in diameter from the city. The population in this area, excluding the city, is 16,000. The pilots have access to over 150 airstrips.

No other service in the world operates over such a vast territory, providing such a comprehensive health service. They are not merely an aerial ambulance, but a remote area health care provider. The Alice Springs service averages five evacuations a day. They are no longer then two hours away from any location. The entire service covers 2.3 million square kilometers.

Late afternoon we found ourselves at the 1792 overland telegraph station, which was set up in Alice Springs as headquarters for a communication system. The system consisted of 12 relay stations, one located every 250 miles from there to Darwin on the north coast.

Normal annual rainfall in the area is ten inches, however, there was no rain in 1999, the year before, and so far in 2000, the city had received 40 inches! The Todd River is dry most of the time.

The station had several well-preserved buildings. In one of the homes was a piano.

The docent said, "This piano arrived by camel. It was balanced with water, and had to be unloaded each night and reloaded each morning!"

After enjoying a delicious fish dinner, Jacinta of the Walpiri tribe (aborigine), who had a Caucasian father, spoke about her culture. She was a very sweet girl who seemed to be successfully living between two cultures. She was a fascinating speaker and answered lots of questions for us.

The next morning's wake-up call of 3:15 was in the middle of the night and we were all ready to leave the hotel by 3:45. The event? An early morning balloon ride to watch the sun rise over the Outback.

At the end of the sealed road (paved) we continued to travel six miles over a washboard dirt road, the balloon truck following right behind. As daylight appeared we looked down on mobs of kangaroos hopping about, and many wild horses trotting around.

The little mounds of tan we learned were spinifex, a mounded beach grass that covers a lot of the bush and comes in 30 varieties. It survives with little water by developing rolled, sharp blades with cactus tip barbs.

The colors of the sunrise were spectacular. I just knew my camera couldn't capture it, but I tried anyway. However, it remains in my mind forever.

After breakfast it was a 300-mile bus ride to Ayers Rock. This long ride was broken up with a stop at a small museum, and camel rides for all brave enough to go for it.

The camel gets up on his hind legs first, which tends to propel one a bit forward, then up go his front legs. When lying down the front legs go down first! Then the hind legs go down with a plop. There wasn't too much of a jolt as the camel got up, but going down we let out a whoop! We both were propelled forward, but we managed to stay in the saddle! We had plenty of time to ride as long as we wanted.

Australia is the largest producer of camels in the world and exports them all over the globe.

The road, over flat uninteresting bush, was a sealed one in good condition. A road train is three to five big 18-wheelers hooked in tandem and we saw several in the outback. One can see for miles and miles.

By noon we were ready for another break. It was a pleasant stop for lunch at one of the 220 outback stations. The 1881 station was just a little one covering 800,000 acres (1200 square miles)! The property had one natural spring, 40 watering holes, 100 miles of pipeline, and 6000 head of cattle. That countryside can only support 1-2 head of cattle per square kilometer. The normal annual rainfall is seven inches. Neighbors are a long way off! Talk about isolation! Both of the children were students of School of the Air.

The hotel at Ayers Rock was part of a complex housing four hotels from five-star to a backpackers hostel. Built by the Northern Territory government, it recently was sold. The complex had a post office, moderate-sized grocery store, shops, and information and tourist center.

The complex can accommodate 5000 visitors a night. It has its own generating plant and water supply, some of which was solar. The complex employed 4800 people. It is the only facility in the area to serve visitors.

We were booked in the five-star hotel and it was lovely, unfortunately we would have only one night there. We had time to walk around a bit and check out the complex before the short ride to watch the sun set on Uluru (Ayers Rock). Our bus was one of many parked in a very large special viewing area. Although there were a lot of people, crowding was not a problem.

It's traditional to sip champagne while watching the sun set on the rock. While we were gazing at the rock, the driver and guide went about setting up a small table, putting out snack foods, and opening champagne.

We had champagne after the balloon ride that morning, and again that evening, wow, champagne twice in one day!

Sunset there was a pretty fantastic event. I swear the colors of the rock changed about every two minutes! It was really something. It was a beautiful evening, but I suspect it is probably almost always very clear in that area.

We all had decided not to try to climb up to the top of Uluru, as it is sacred ground to the Aborigines and climbing the rock, once a very popular thing to do, is being discouraged.

The next morning I got up early, as I had elected, with a few others, to walk the five and a half miles around the rock. Because of recent rains, including the night before, the path around the rock was wet in places, and many times it was necessary to maneuver around puddles and spongy soil.

In spite of that, plus stopping to read interesting signs along the way, we all finished the walk in two hours. We started just at daybreak and watched the sun rise over the rock. By the time we finished, the temperature was beginning to climb. It was going to be another hot day.

Uluru refers to a water hole near the summit. At 1150 feet, Uluru is the largest sandstone monolith in the world, and like an iceberg has perhaps two-thirds more lying under ground. It is one of the world's great natural wonders. There are many caves in the rock and 75 art sites. The Red Center of the Outback is just about geographically in the center of Australia.

In 1983 the area around Uluru was returned to the native people. However, it was not long before they realized they were not able to handle and manage the park, so a cooperative agreement was reached with the Park Service that now maintains and manages the area.

The native people take spiritual care of Uluru, as they believe gods from Dreamtime passed by there, imbuing formations with their spirits. Caring for the land is how they confirm their humanity.

Twenty-five percent of the park fee plus a $75,000 annual royalty are returned to the Aborigines. About 300 of the Anangu tribe live on one side of the rock.

Kata Tjuta, commonly called the Olgas, has 36 domes. It was named after Queen Olga of a Spanish province. The highest point is 1650 feet. Kata Tjuta means *many heads*. A wooden catwalk takes one to an excellent viewing area. It is 16 miles around the base of the formation. The fine dirt is very red, looking a lot like paprika.

The Visitors' Center has an excellent museum with multiple displays that explain the aboriginal culture and history. Personally I find the culture fascinating.

Immediately after lunch it was off to the airport for a two-and-a-half hour flight to Cairns. It was Qantas' 80th anniversary, so they served everyone on the flight champagne. This champagne business was getting to be a habit!

After landing, we took a two-hour bus ride of 96 miles to our hotel at Cape Tribulation in the Daintree Rainforest.

Cairns, gateway to the tropical north, was settled in 1876. It became a town in 1885, and a city in 1932. Australia is the world's largest producer of sugar. Vegemite is the end product of the sugar process. Many people eat it on toast and children in many parts of the world grow up on it, but I find the taste vile.

We crossed the Daintree River on a cable ferry. The road after crossing was narrow and winding. It seemed like a long ride, as much of it was done in the dark, and the last hour or so in the rain.

What a facility that hotel turned out to be! The cabins were lovely, but it was morning before we could really see where we were situated. During the night we listened to lots of nature noises. It was great! Waking in the morning, I was quiet while I sat with a cup of coffee in our little sitting area. I could see nothing but lush foliage!

Located in the Daintree Rainforest the first part of the facility opened in 1989. Because of its rainforest location, great care was taken to design the resort to blend into its surroundings, and to be ecologically sensitive to that World Heritage Area. Covering 250 acres, it was designed to have minimal impact on the local flora and fauna. The cabins built on high set poles required minimal removal of trees. The use of boardwalks minimizes the impact of pedestrian traffic, preventing damage to the forest floor.

The facility had its own water supply and generated all its electricity. Besides the lovely cabins the facility also had a 40-unit villa, large reception area, long house, pool, bar, in-house accommodations for 70 staff, and an education and adventure lodge. There was also a private beach.

It was only a short ride to another beach where we waded out to a small motorboat that took us out to the waiting *Rum Runner IV*, a 55-foot catamaran. It was an hour and a half ride out to the 1250-mile long reef. The Great Barrier Reef is the largest coral system in the world protecting hundreds of small offshore islands on Australia's east coast from Brisbane north to Cairns.

It was a wet ride, and it didn't take long for us on deck to get soaking wet. It was a misty day, and by the time we anchored and got in the water it was actually raining. The water was warm. The snorkeling was quite good.

The return trip was a lot smoother. The drizzle stopped as we approached the beach. It was an all day outing. This had been a much better experience on the Great Barrier Reef than my first trip when I visited Green Island.

Green Island housed a restaurant, gift shop, dive shop, toilets, design lockers, and a swimming pool. The tropical foliage lent a very relaxing and calm atmosphere. There were sandy beaches for swimming. That day before lunch I walked the two-mile perimeter of the island walking in shallow water. A small boat took us out to the reef to snorkel. The snorkeling was fair, visibility was not the best, and because of the popularity of the area I suspect some of the reef had been killed. Large numbers of people tend to destroy. So I was happy with the better experience six years later.

Captain Cook named the area Cape Tribulation after his ship ran aground on Endeavor Reef. The rain forest, only ten-20 degrees south of the equator, was named in 1832 after Richard Daintree, an explorer and businessman. 130 million years old that wilderness area covers 100 hectares. The Daintree National Park was established in 1979 and designated a World Heritage Site in 1988.

The area protects 70 species of animals and over 200 bird species including the cassowary, plus many flowers and plants. It is the only place in the world where two World Heritage Sites meet —the Daintree Rainforest and the Great Barrier Reef.

The Daintree Rainforest is a coastal rainforest running in pockets for 270 miles. It is an upland rainforest and is the largest rainforest in the Heritage complex. Thirteen of the 19 flowering plants are found only there, 60 percent of Australia's bat species live in that rainforest. There are no monkeys in Australia.

One morning while at Daintree we took a boat ride through Coopers Creek. Thornton Peak (1300+ feet) towers in the background over the estuary. That mountain range collects the rain clouds and then sends the rain to the valley and coast. Normal rainfall is about 60 inches a year. The brackish estuary contains 20 of the 69 known mangrove varieties.

Mangroves protect 70 percent of the tropical shore around the world. Seventy percent of the mangrove roots are above the surface. There is a filter at the bottom of each root, which filters salt out of the water. Mangroves in this area grow 30-50 feet tall.

We spotted both a baby crocodile and a large adult sunning himself on the bank. Crocks prefer temperatures of at least 30 degrees C. Female crocks are territorial. They reach 14 feet long. Males, reach 23-27 feet, can weigh up to two ton, and wander in and out of territories. It is possible for them to live 80-100 years; they can swim 60 miles into the ocean. Crocks eat mud crabs, wallaby, and mud pigs among other things. Capable of slowing their heartbeat, they can stay submerged in the water for an hour.

Crocks breed December to April and lay 30-80 eggs in a nest. The gestation period is six to eight weeks. Mama monitors the nest, then uncovers it removing the ten-inch hatchlings to the water. The temperature of the nest determines the sex of the egg, 85 degrees is good for a female, 90 degrees for a male. While laying her eggs the crock enters a trace-like state, afterward she returns to her vicious self.

These cold-blooded reptiles can move up to 18 miles an hour but cannot zigzag. A crock has no tongue and cannot swallow under water. It has piercing, but no grinding teeth. The growth rate is about three feet every ten years.

It was nice to see the winding road back to Cairns in daylight. After crossing the Daintree River we stopped briefly at the *Big Croc Café, A Place for a Bite* to buy ice cream.

Cairns (pronounced *cans*) is not my favorite place. The motels are like any other. The city is flat, very walkable, and being a seaside community the humidity is usually high.

Older homes were built on stilts in order to catch the sea breezes. It is too hot there for many crops to grow, but sugarcane, macadamia, and pineapple do well and there are many such plantations around.

Sugarcane is cut once a year and then regrows. After the third cutting the fields are burned and the remains plowed under. Beans are planted to replace the nitrogen to the soil, and then the next year sugarcane is planted to start the cycle over again.

The Atherton tableland receives more rain, but is less humid and more conducive to farming pursuits. The tableland is 200 kilometers (120 miles) long and slowly rises from 1000 feet to 2000 feet. We rode a bus up to the town of Kuranda, 1000 feet above sea level. The town can be reached by road, cable car, or train.

The road was well paved, narrow, and contained 116 curves. It cuts through a beautiful rain forest. Where the rainfall is three to four feet a year! The soil is poor and the terrain steep. However it is so dense that it produces an umbrella, making the area ecologically self-sufficient. It is one of the world's oldest rain forests, and is on Australia's heritage list. Pythons in the forest can grow to be 20-30 feet long!

The sky cable ride from Cairns to Kuranda is nearly five miles long, making it the longest in the world. The cables are above the rain forest, and the view spectacular.

Kuranda was a small town full of shops and eateries, with an aboriginal influence.

We rode the train back to Cairns. The track goes through 15 tunnels, the longest being a third of a mile long and passes over 30 bridges. Construction of the railroad was an engineering feat of tremendous magnitude. Many lives were lost during construction.

The first soil was turned in 1886. Built in three sections, the first and third sections were relatively easy. The second section involved steep grades, dense jungle, and the Aborigines defending their territory. Section two contains the tunnels and 93 curves going from nearly 5.5 meters (18 feet) at Redlynch to 327 meters (1,063 feet) at Myola. In 1887 bulldozers and modern equipment were not available. This railroad built with strategy, fortitude, dynamite, hand tools, buckets, and bare hands, opened to the public in 1891.

We saw many marvelous waterfalls. The scenery was certainly gorgeous! What an awesome ride.

The ride was an hour and a half, the last half-hour being in Cairns getting to the railroad station.

Like England some words have different meanings. Down Under, one queues (cues) up, not lines up for whatever. One ticks off, not checks off, one's choice. The freeway is a motorway. A parking lot is a carpark. One gives way to traffic, not yield. One overtakes on the road, not passes.

One's sweater is a jumper. An appetizer is an entrée, as it is the entrance to a meal. And of course a toilet is exactly that, not a restroom, wash room, bathroom, or ladies' room, just simply a toilet.

On the first trip the guide had a party in his room the last night. Upon leaving we decided to use the stairs down to the restaurant for dinner. Our intentions were good, but you can imagine our surprise when we ended up in a locked area near the pool! We had a good laugh, made a bit of noise until someone came to rescue us. Neither of us realized the room key in our pocket would have unlocked the gate. A couple of embarrassed gals then made it to dinner!

It is always sad to leave a place when one has had a good time. On the first trip I flew to New Zealand first, but on the second trip when we left Australia we then flew on to New Zealand.

Australia is a large and fabulous country with lots of contrasts. I'm lucky to have seen so much of it.

Chapter 7

Down Under -- New Zealand

I love the kiwi fruit, had never seen the kiwi bird, and had heard that the Kiwi people were friendly. I was about to find out. One trip started on the North Island, New Zealand, and the other ended on the South Island.

We arrived at 5 AM New Zealand time in Auckland, New Zealand. Our bus driver greeted us with *Kia Ora! Kia Ora (*key aura), a Maori word meaning "hello." In New Zealand it is used like Hawaiians use *aloha.*

The airport is about a thirty-minute drive from downtown, and since we arrived a couple of hours earlier than most groups the driver took us on an extensive city tour before the traffic got heavy, driving on the left side of the road, as they do in England.

Auckland is known as the "City of Sail." In greater Auckland there are an estimated 70,000 boats, both motor and sail. There are a half-dozen marinas in the city, the largest one housing 2000 boats and many boat garages housing up to 200 boats.

New Zealanders are physically active and sport oriented. Obviously sailing is a popular sport, but hiking, running and ball playing are also popular. There are 102 beaches within an hour's drive of the city.

We saw only one billboard, and that was at a harbor. We didn't take long to note the cleanliness of the countryside. Litter was conspicuously absent.

It was also evident that mountain ranges and hilly terrain

dominate the landscape. The Southern Alps, a massive mountain range with 223 named peaks, extends 2300 kilometers.

Mount Eden, 643 feet above sea level, is the city's highest point, giving one a marvelous 360° view of the city. On a clear day Tasmania can be seen on the horizon. Looking down in a fairly deep volcanic crater it was evident the walls were covered with cow patties. It's quite a climb down to that point, so I wonder who the brave soul was who wrote *Happy Anniversary Joann* in cow patties at the bottom?

Until 1863 Manukau Harbor was the main shipping port. When a ship ran aground on a shifting sand bar drowning 160 people, it spurred the development of Auckland Harbor.

In 1959 north shore commuters gained easy access to the city with the completion of the harbor bridge.

In the tenth century Polynesians arrived from Hawaii. They found abundant food supplies and fertile soils, and by the twelfth century there were established settlements in most of the country. The Dutch navigator, Abel Tasman, discovered New Zealand in 1642 giving it its name.

In 1769 Captain James Cook and his crew were the first Europeans to set foot on New Zealand soil, 127 years after Tasman.

Most of the country's 3.5 million people are European. Three fourths of the population live on the North Island with 84 percent of them living in urban areas. Auckland's population is 1.5 million. The largest minority group is Maori making up ten percent of the population, another four percent are Pacific Island Polynesians.

All native trees are evergreens, and there are many varieties providing a lush greenness all year. All deciduous trees have been imported. The native pokutukawa tree is known as the Christmas tree because it has a mass of red color in December.

There are many active volcanic craters in the country and earthquakes of varying degrees are fairly common. Auckland's Orakai Basin is a water filled crater where many water sports are enjoyed.

The last serious quake was in the 1950s near Wellington. The last volcanic eruption was in 1936. There are many geysers in the country and some of them had been acting strange, so it was anybody's guess what was going on deep in the earth's bowels.

(Those geysers were acting strange for a reason. One of the volcanoes did blow in September, the day after we left Rotorua.)

The country has little in the way of natural resources. Strawberries, timber and logs, kiwi fruit, and wool are large export items.

All automobiles are imported, as New Zealand does not manufacture cars. Unwisely many kiwi plants were exported and now the country faces competition for this crop, the largest competition coming from Brazil.

Kiwi grows on a vine similar to a grapevine and needs a windbreak to grow successfully. The vines are trellised so the fruit can be picked from beneath. All of the fruit is picked by hand in May. Actually the kiwi is the Chinese gooseberry, but when New Zealand was ready to market the fruit they knew the original name would be a hindrance, so they renamed it.

Auckland is located between two harbors, Manukau on the west and on the east by Waitemata, a Maori word meaning *sparkling waters*. The narrowest point is only two kilometers wide. Until 1960 a lot of effluent was dumped into the harbor and it was anything but sparkling. Since the dumping has stopped the waters again have become clear.

Auckland, established as a city in 1840, was the capitol of New Zealand until 1865 when the capitol was moved to Wellington.

It was only 600 years ago that Rangitoto Island appeared out of the sea. The perfect cone shape, bush covered island, standing in the Hauraki Gulf, has become a favorite emblem of Waitemata Harbor.

In 1840 Captain William Hobson negotiated with the Ngato-

Whatua tribe for the purchase of what now is Auckland.

When the city awakened on our first day, our first stop was the museum located in a Greek style war memorial.

Since we had eaten at 4 AM we decided to go to the coffee shop first. I wanted to try Pavlova, the dessert that is such a rival between Australia and New Zealand.

Lucky me, they had Pavlova. I guess some people would think it strange to be eating dessert so early in the morning, but I sure enjoyed the baked meringue pie shell filled with whipped cream (the real stuff) and topped with thin slices of kiwi! I've eaten several variations of Pavlova since, but that was a very good one.

Afterward we did a look-see through the varied and interesting museum. The taxidermy exhibit of native birds was of particular interest to me as was the glass exhibit. Several busloads of children arrived, but they quickly disappeared into learning centers.

On my first trip we stayed in lovely large urban hotels in contrast to the second trip when our accommodations were small quaint establishments in residential areas. Each has its advantages and the contrast gave me wonderful variety.

After checking into the hotel at noon, most of us walked to the waterfront where we found a variety of eating establishments. Afterward we took the city bus to Kelly Tarlton's most unusual aquarium. To begin with, the whole aquarium is underground housed in old sewage tanks, the same ones that used to dump effluent into the harbor!

Kelly was an imaginative thinker. He wanted to buy the storage tanks from the city, but the city would not sell them. Everyone thought he was loco. Finally after a time and negotiation the city agreed to lease the tanks to Kelly for a dollar a year. Kelly agreed but said he wanted a thousand-year lease for his $1000.

Kelly designed, planned, and supervised all the building. Tons of junk had to be removed and carted off and extensive cleaning done before construction could even begin. The aquarium opened in 1985. We walked through the new Antarctica exhibit admiring the emperor penguins, the world's largest, in contrast to the fairy penguins, the world's smallest, we saw in Australia.

From that exhibit one can walk through the rest of the aquarium or step on a moving walkway. It was like being in a tunnel with fish all around and on top of you. Absolutely incredible!

I'd never seen the *underside* of a ray before. Several different kinds swam over our heads. Big fish, small fish, all colors and shapes, swam up, over, and down. It was the most amazing thing. Coming to the end of the moving walkway I hadn't had enough and ended up rotating two more times! Then we reluctantly exited.

Kelly died at age 48, just a few weeks after the aquarium opened. New Zealand's Jacques Cousteau, it is said that diving contributed to his premature death.

It was late afternoon when we got on a city bus to return to the hotel. The driver made conversation with us and eventually took us right to the door of our hotel. We were finding New Zealanders very friendly indeed!

The next morning at breakfast we sat at a table next to a couple of Qantas stewardesses. It was a beautiful sunny day. They told us that the west coast was more rugged and the surfing better. The scenery was superb with the dark lush covered hills rising above the coast. The surf was wild and the sunsets over Tasmania glorious.

There were many beautiful gardens easily accessible in the city. At the sunken gardens along the waterfront at the Savage memorial monument, the gardens were spectacular and the view of the harbor marvelous. Michael Savage, New Zealand's first labor prime minister, is credited with pulling New Zealand out of the depression. He died in 1940.

A visit to the Conservatory and Botanical Gardens was fantastic. The flowers were outstanding and I saw many plants I'd never seen before. Oh, to have a yard like that!

Because the kiwi bird is nocturnal, most visitors never see one in the wild. At the gardens there was a special dark room with glassed enclosures housing the kiwi. We stood and watched him for some time.

When I asked the driver about a floral clock, he took us to the park where one was located. That really was above and beyond the call, but that is how our driver was —fabulous! I saw my first floral clock over forty years ago in Canada, and they have fascinated me ever since.

On the way to Rotorua, we stopped for lunch at the Big Apple where we could visit an old-timey saloon. Acres of kiwi were growing nearby so we had a good look at how the vines were staked.

After lunch we stopped at a swinging suspension bridge that was lots of fun to walk. The bridge was pretty much covered with a fine wire on the sides and overhead, but it did *swing*! The only casualty was some one's hat blown off into the ravine.

Driving south, though the rich New Zealand countryside and the fertile Waikato Valley, the driver and guide continued to educate us.

There are no barns, as we know them, in New Zealand. It seemed strange to see grazing horses wearing blankets, but it soon became a familiar sight. The blankets helped to keep the horses warm on cool nights. They also kept the dust off their coats and protected their skin from the sun.

Another odd thing we saw was that the tails of all the cows had been cut off. There is no fly problem, and it's said that the urine of a cow in the eye of the farmer can cause a serious hepatitis-like illness, and that's the primary reason for bobbing the cow's tail. No tail lashing in this country while milking!

New Zealand is a narrow isthmus 1000 miles long. The Waihita River, at 220 miles, is the longest river in the country and is dammed nine times for hydroelectric production. It's the Mississippi of New Zealand.

Cumera, a sweet potato much lighter in color and less

flavorful than our yam, is a staple of the New Zealand diet. Potatoes, vegetables, especially onions and green beans, are grown in the Waikato Valley. Fiji and Indian (from India) laborers do most of the physical work.

New Zealand has no poisonous snakes or spiders.

Cambridge is the horse breeding area of New Zealand, their Kentucky.

A 1936 volcanic eruption in the Rotorua area killed 150 people. In 1990 two earthquakes registered 6 on the Richter scale.

Mid-afternoon we arrived at Waitomo Cave, also known as the glowworm grotto/cave. Waitomo is derived from two Maori words, *wai* meaning "water," and *tomo* meaning "cave." In this area the Waitomo River vanishes into the hillside. A New Zealand Mountie and a British surveyor discovered the cave in 1887. They rafted down the river but could go only half way into the cave. Two weeks later they discovered the present entrance, and in 1889 the first tour took place.

The glowworm is different from a firefly. The light from a glowworm is less than that from a firefly, but when multiplied by thousands the sight is spectacular. The life span of the glowworm is eleven months and there are four stages. First comes the egg which turns to larvae, then to a cocoon, and finally to a fly. The glow comes from the larvae suspended from the ceiling. It snares its prey by dangling filaments of sticky beads. Chemical oxidation creates the glow.

After touring the cave we boarded boats to float quietly though the grotto where thousands of worm larvae hung suspended from the ceiling. What a rainbow of color, like none any man could create. We were all as quiet as church mice, it was the most fantastic sight! Picture taking was not allowed.

We arrived at our hotel about 5:30 after a perfectly delightful and full day. The hotel bordered on a massive thermal area known as Whakarewarewa, one of the most accessible thermal areas in New Zealand.

From our hotel window, the steam rising from the steam vents created a mystical appearance.

In the morning we had a tour of Rotorua. A small Anglican church along the bay with a wall facing the water has a stain glass window of Jesus. When the waves in the bay are just right it appears that Jesus is walking on the water. It was pretty fantastic.

The city wasn't too big, and after getting our bearings we had no trouble getting around during the free afternoon. We chose to visit the Orchid Gardens. The gardens and flowers were lovely, but the water organ/ballet was spectacular.

The gardens, built in 1985, cost 1.3 million dollars. The water organ contained 700 pipes and 14 pumps. The set of pipes, made in Germany cost $250,000, and there are only another four or five sets like them in the world. Water shoots dramatically from the pipes simulating a ballet and the whole performance is set to computerized music. When the water show was over, I wanted to sit through it again. So we did. It really was one of the neatest things I've ever seen.

Walking about town we saw several small steam vents. In a small park we saw a hobo cooking his dinner just like in the old days—steaming a foil pack over the vent.

Walking through the park we stopped and watched some people play lawn balls. The men were dressed in white slacks and shirts and the women in white skirts and blouses. It was all quite proper and rather interesting to watch.

Then we continued on to view the hot springs baths/spa. The Tudor style building, built in 1906 at a cost of 40,000 pounds, had the intention of competing with European spas. It was not quite complete when opened in 1908.

With lessened use and deterioration, the Department of Health, in 1947, declared the baths a danger. Designated for demolition in 1956, there was such a protest that in 1963 the building and two and a half acres were given to the Rotorua City Council with a grant of $120,000.

110

Since then, a restaurant, cabaret, museum and art gallery have made restoration possible. In 1988 it was renamed The Bath House and now the historic building houses the Rotorua Museum of Art and History.

On the walk back to the hotel the street was lined with rhododendrons that were simply gorgeous! They were like a tree and in full bloom.

That evening we enjoyed a Hangi feast and Maori entertainment at the hotel.

On another day we made a visit to New Zealand's forestry experimental station located in a redwood forest. We walked through the lovely cool forest. Redwoods grow so fast there that the wood is too soft and porous for any useful purpose. The trees were only a few years old but the size of a century old tree.

Coming into a clearing we faced the *flying fox*. We stopped so anyone who wanted to ride it could. Several men and a couple of us women climbed a rather tall tower and one at a time stepped into a sling. Stepping off the platform one rode a cable about 400 meters to a sudden jolting halt. It was a neat ride though. The hardest part was climbing out of the sling while hanging suspended in the air. Then one of the fellows would volunteer to run the sling back up to the platform for the next brave sole. It was fun being a kid again!

The first stop of the day on our way back to Auckland was Rainbow Fairy Springs, built as a combination trout farm and visitor attraction. The springs produce 4.5 million liters of water a day. The nursery pond houses trout until they are a year old, then they are released into another pond for another year. At age two they are released into a six-foot deep pond where they can come and go to and from the river. They know food is always available in the pond.

A cable car lift took us to the top of a mountain for a panoramic view of Rotorua. There was also a very nice aviary for native birds, where we were free to wander at our leisure. Rainbow

Springs works closely with the Department of Conservation and other wildlife agencies in the promotion and preservation of New Zealand's flora and fauna and is actively involved in breeding and preservation of endangered species. They also have educational and research programs.

Leaving the springs we rode out to a farm/restaurant for a very good BBQ lunch served at picnic tables in a large building. Afterward, outside we watched a dog round up sheep. This was the first of several sheep dog demonstrations I've seen. It's fascinating how the dog just brings the sheep in.

Down the road we visited the Agrodome, where we saw and learned about 19 different kinds of sheep. An animated MC kept a lively program moving. The show ended with a sheep shearing demonstration, taking only seconds for the sheep to loose all its wool!

There is a great deal of Maori influence in New Zealand, mostly on the North Island. Whakarewarewa is called *Whaka* by the local people, pronounced *Faka*. In Maori the *wh* is pronounced as an *f.* The thermal area is one of the most extraordinary sights in the country. Everywhere you turn, the earth bubbles, boils, and spits. The odor of hydrogen sulfide, much like rotten eggs hangs in the air. After breakfast one morning we had an extensive tour of the village that exists among all the steam vents. A visit to Whaka gives one great insight into the Maori culture.

At the entrance to the village we met a local guide who cautioned us not to stray from the paths, as it could be very dangerous.

The Maori cook in a natural steam oven called a *hangi.* Strategically placed, the Maori never need worry about building a fire. They have steam twenty-four hours a day.

As we passed a hot water pool the guide said, "We also cook vegetables in these pools of boiling water. We wrap the items to be cooked in cloth covered with burlap, tie them, and submerge them in the pool."

Pipes lead from the cooking pool down to large communal bathtubs. The water flows by gravity to the tubs below. The water is always crystal clear. The tubs are filled each morning so that by evening the water has cooled enough for bathing! The tubs are emptied each night, scrubbed and cleaned.

A large volcanic eruption in 1886 wiped out three tribes. The few people who survived made their way here so the inhabitants of this village are descendents of the survivors of that eruption. *Pa* is the name for a walled village and it is always high on a hill with a look out tower.

The twenty-year war, in 1863, really lasted only a year, but guerillas continued to fight the Maori occasionally for twenty years.

We stopped by a geyser called Pohutu meaning "big splash" because this geyser shoots 80 feet into the air. Of late it had been a little erratic, but it performed several times a day. While we stood there we were lucky to see her shoot high into the air. It was quite a sight!

The village cemetery sits above ground, because if you dig very far into the ground, you'll find yourself in hot water. Each of the seven Maori tribes also has a sacred hill cemetery. Why seven tribes? One for each canoe that sailed from Hawaii many years ago. Those people called New Zealand *Aotearoa*, meaning "land of long white cloud," which is what New Zealand looks like on the horizon. The Maori are one race, but several traditional differences exist between the tribes such as language, ritual, arts, crafts, and protocol.

Years ago the totara tree was used to make canoes. Termites don't bother that wood. Today the wood is used for the many woodcarvings seen everywhere. Incidentally, authentic Maori woodcarvings have only three fingers on the hands, as the Maori believe only in birth, fertility, and death. The Ti tree has been used for medicinal purposes for many years, for a dye, and for durable fence posts.

Before exiting the village after a fascinating tour we walked through the "dark pavilion" where we saw another kiwi bird in its natural environment and learned a little more about the national bird. Seldom seen in the wild it hunts by smell, not by sight. Its nostrils are located at the tip of its long curved beak, technically making his beak the shortest of any bird, as a beak is measured from the nostrils to the tip. The kiwi has no wings so cannot fly. He is all fur and feathers over a very small skeleton. It lays the largest egg for its body weight, and the male incubates the egg for 80 days.

The Maori have always had a sacred relationship with the sea and land. Modern environmental concerns reflect the values the Maori have held for centuries.

The North and South Islands have quite different terrains and cultures. On the South Island we visited Christchurch and Queenstown.

Arriving in New Zealand from Australia all wooden objects needed to be claimed. We watched authorities take a didgeridoo from the fellow in front of us. However, our little commercial critters sailed right through inspection.

The temperature was 42 degrees that evening we arrived in Christchurch! It had been a long day with two plane changes and a two-hour layover in Sydney. With the time change it was midnight New Zealand time and 11:00 PM Cairns time. We had boarded the first plane in Cairns at 9:00 AM.

The room had a good radiator which we definitely turned on. We woke to sunshine and a crisp morning.

Christchurch is located in the Cantabury Plain, the flattest area in the country. Christchurch stretches from the ocean to the foothills of the mountains and is completely flat. The city had just celebrated its 125th anniversary.

The Cantabury Region also includes the Southern Alps which are the highest points in the country. The River Avon runs through the city. Christchurch is the largest city on the South Island, and the third largest city in New Zealand, after Auckland and Wellington.

In 1850 the Cantabury Company, a group of leading British churchmen, sent six ships with 1200 settlers (Cantabury Pilgrims) to Christchurch. Four ships sailed, with the other two following a month later. Property was selling for 6 pounds an acre. Churches were the focal point of the whole community, and the center city is dominated by church spires.

Christchurch is perhaps the most English of all cities in New Zealand, and all the streets have English names. The present city, compact and easy to explore, is very walkable. The Victorian homes have lovely English Gardens. A charming city, it was hard to remember that we were in New Zealand and not England.

We climbed 700 meters, over a switch-back paved road into the mountains. Stopping at the summit provided an excellent view of Port Littleton, a deep, active, commerical harbor located in a volcano crator, and on the other side of the road Christchurch stretched to the sea. Hiking tracks were visible everywhere.

A recent storm had blown through the area doing a lot of damage. The road had only reopened recently after weeks of closure. We saw the slow clean up of hundreds of felled pine trees. Everywhere we went we noted school children in school uniforms, the norm for all public schools. The children also wear hats, many of them with neck flaps to guard against the sun. People are very sun conscious.

Because New Zealand experiences constant urban renewal, there are virtually no slum areas in the country. We were surprised at the niceness of the city housing when driving by. Like Melbourne, the streets were wide and the city had free center-city tram and bus service.

Mona Vale, an historic mansion perched on the River Avon, was our lunch stop. The grounds and gardens were beautiful. The weather was warm and quite comfortable. We took a punt ride down the river to the bridge.

A punt is a flat-bottomed-long boat, wide enough to seat two abreast, that is propelled by someone pushing it along with a long pole. Six of us rode at a time. It was fun and I found the mansions and gardens along the river beautiful. At Mona Vale, the rose garden was all in bloom and those roses were so fragrant.

We made the most of a free afternoon by visiting the Canterbury Museum, Art Gallery, Arts and Crafts Center, the Bridge of Remembrance, and Cathedral Park (1864), doing a wee bit of shopping along the way.

In the evening we caught the restaurant tram. What a unique dining experience! We circled the city several times while dining on an excellent lamb meal with first class service.

The next morning we headed for Mount Cook. At 12,346 feet, it is the highest peak in New Zealand, and is called *Aoraki* by the Maori. The mountain wears a permanent crown of snow and ice.

The Southern Alps are bigger than the Swiss, French, and Austrian Alps combined, and run the length of the west coast on the South Island. Eighty percent of the South Island is mountainous, with the rest of the island being plains. New Zealand, 1000 miles north to south, sits half way between the equator and the South Pole.

Leaving Christchurch, we drove through the green-belt which surrounds the city where no commercial building is allowed. It is mostly farmland, with dairy and horse breeding farms.

The rolling hills, much of it pine covered forest mingled with blooming yellow Scottish broom weed, was very picturesque.

Because water is so readily available, most power in the country is hydroelectric. Although we passed over many bridges spanning dry streams, we were told when the snow melts those dry beds became raging rivers.

An interesting and unique potty stop was in Ashburton. The clean public unisex toilets were all push button. A button was pushed to close the door. Another button was pushed to dispense the toilet paper. The toilet flushed only when the sensor activated soap and faucet were in use! A forced cleanliness? Then one must push a button to open the door.

A sign warned that in nine minutes you would be given a warning and at ten minutes the door would automatically open. You'd best finished your business!

In late afternoon we stopped in Mackinze to see and read the dog statue that pays tribute to sheep dogs. We then took a short, brisk walk in the cold wind to the small church that is a memorial to Mackinze County.

The docent inside the interdenominational church told us the Duke of Gloucester laid the foundation for the church in January 1935, and the church was completed in August of that year with the condition that no plant or stone be disturbed. The wood shingle roof was replaced with a slate one in 1957. Cupboards in the vestry were made from wood taken from the old Tekapo Bridge when it was torn down in 1954.

Beautiful lupines in several colors lined the road for miles. The story was that some farmer's wife found the road a boring one, so she threw lupine seeds all along the way as she went to town. Past Mackinze we approached Lake Tekapo, which is the topmost lake. Because of a stiff wind we drove carefully along a canal.

That canal, 18 feet deep, was part of a water system that generated 30 percent of the country's electricity. According to the water engineer on our trip, it was a unique, well-thought-out system using gates and gravity flow. The waters in the glacial lakes were a gorgeous turquoise, even though the sky was overcast.

A few miles from Mount Cook it started to mist, and it began to rain lightly by 4:30 when we arrived at the Hermitage, located in Mount Cook National Park. It was cold and windy.

We went to the main lodge for dinner where we found cozy fires burning in the fireplace of each room. We enjoyed a fantastic full buffet.

This was the first time I've ever run into a wine bar. A glass of wine was $5.50, but all the wine you wanted was $9.00, you just had to help yourself to any one of four or five wines on the bar!

Trivia at dinner included: In 1893, New Zealand was the first country to give women the vote. There are more golf courses per capita than any other country. There are 12 sheep for every person. Velcro was invented in New Zealand.

Tongariro National Park was the second established in the world. Yellowstone was the first. New Zealand also has the only alpine parrot, the kea, and the only flightless parrot, the kakapo. The kiwi is the oldest bird on earth.

One look out the window the next morning and it was obvious it had snowed during the night! It felt more like winter than summer.

That morning we spotted several rainbows over the mountains. We passed by the protected breeding grounds for the endangered stilt that lays its eggs on unprotected beaches where they are nearly always destroyed. Presently there are only 33 known breeding pairs.

After climbing 3000 feet to the scenic Lindis Pass, we descended into an agricultural valley. We saw beehives everywhere.

The Lake Dustan area has the warm days of about 100° and cool nights, down in the 30s that are perfect for growing grapes. There are many vineyards in the area, but because the annual rainfall is only 17 inches, the vineyards are irrigated.

People call Cromwell the fruit bowl of the country because farmers raise apples, apricots, cherries, and pears.

We had lunch at the Taramea Winery. The owner explained they started the small winery in 1987 and only bottle 5000 cases a year. Because the area has proved to be such a good growing area for grapes, 23 wineries have sprung up in the past five years. Though a young industry in that area, their wines were good.

In Queenstown on the way to the hotel, we stopped by the Kawara suspension bridge, where A.J. Hackett introduced bungee jumping in 1988. Queenstown is known as the home of the bungee jump. Because of strong winds no one was jumping that day. The bridge looked awfully high, and the river below looked awfully cold!

Queenstown, 1020 feet above sea level, is located on the shores of Lake Wakatipu. Snaggletooth peaks of the Remarkable Mountain Range surround this 77-kilometer long glacial lake. Queenstown with its breath-taking scenery, wide open spaces, lakes, rivers, alpine water, green valleys, and snow-covered peaks, is a town of all seasons. It has something for everyone and is called "The Playground of the South."

Queenstown was a major stopover for Maoris looking for the green stone. When gold was discovered in the Shotover River, Queenstown became a gold mining settlement, now it is New Zealand's sports capitol. Action and adventure is its trademark, a real paradise for adrenaline junkies!

White water rafting and jet boating on rivers pioneered there. Hang gliding, parachute jumping, mountain biking, take your pick. It's all there. The city is also the base for Fiordland National Park, New Zealand's largest National Park located in some very rugged country.

Downtown, nothing was more than a few minutes walk away, but the area was a bit hilly. The permanent population is 4000, but at any time there are 25-30,000 people in town.

Our hotel, located just a bit away from busy downtown Queenstown, was a lovely small tranquil hotel with fabulous views. Two large lounges, each with a fire burning in the fireplace, opened out onto a large terrace overlooking the Shotover River and the valley below.

Our suite was large, with a sitting room looking out on a small patio and garden and the lovely grounds beyond. The atmosphere was restful and quiet, and at night there were no city lights to illuminate our room. It was lovely, and our stay was most delightful.

The next morning we were the first of several pick-up stops

for the bus, which eventually was nearly full. After making all the hotel stops, we rode for two hours over curvy roads along Lake Wakatipu, the third deepest lake on the South Island. We passed several tiny towns: Kingston with 100 people; Garston, the most inland town in New Zealand; Athol; and Jollie's Pass. Mossburn, a larger town of about 500 people is the deer capital of New Zealand. All residents there derive their income from deer farming and processing. They can process up to 600 deer a day.

The road, built as a single lane in 1940, was widened to two narrow lanes in 1960. The highest point in the Remarkables is 7200 feet.

The green pastures were full of grazing sheep, cattle, some deer and several sheep stations were situated around the lake.

Red deer were introduced into this area in 1902. Thirty years later nearly all the deer had been killed as everyone considered them a pest. In the 1950s a market in Germany was found for venison. Helicopters then started rounding up and capturing live deer, and deer farming began in earnest. Farm raised venison is labeled *sevina* in supermarkets.

At the quiet town of Manapouri we boarded a catamaran for a 45-minute ride across Lake Manapouri. Disembarking we loaded another bus for the trip over Wilmot Pass, which took us through a cool, temperate rainforest, a World Heritage Designated Site. It is the second wettest rainforest (Hawaii has the wettest) in the world with waterfalls everywhere.

After the drive over Wilmot Pass, we descended to Deep Cove over the steepest road in New Zealand. We boarded a large catamaran for a three-hour cruise along Doubtful Sound, which is not a sound but a fiord. Glaciers form fiords, where rivers form sounds.

The east side of the Alps is the dry side, receiving only 13 inches of rain a year. The west side has an annual rainfall of 300 inches!

It was a cold, rainy day so we stayed inside the boat's cabin.

We saw bottlenose dolphins, fur seals, the rare Fiordland crested penguin, and white-fronted terns. The islands in the fiord shoot out of the lake rising to the sky, with no shoreline.

On the return bus ride we drove through the National Park. That temperate rain forest covered 1.2 million hectares, making it the fifth largest rain forest in the world. This 22-mile single lane road passing through the forest was 35 years old.

Waterfalls were everywhere, big, small, wide, narrow, high, and low. They were beautiful, producing oohs and ahs each time we saw one. There are three permanently named waterfalls, and hundreds of temporary ones appear after a rain.

In the forest the first growth to appear are mosses, followed by lichens, and then other plants. That forest's major growths included red, silver, and mountain beech trees. We saw a lot of sphagnum moss growing. It can hold 25 times its weight in water. All bees have been imported, as New Zealand has no native bees.

I was surprised to see snow in a rain forest! I always think of rain forests as tropical, but I learned something new.

The Manapouri Power Station was built in 1963-1970. A new tunnel was nearly complete. When done, it will allow the power plant to run at full capacity. The first tunnel was built by blasting and removing the debris by hand. The new tunnel was dug with a tunnel-boring machine, which takes six men to operate, and the debris is removed as small stones. The two tunnels are 75 meters apart.

There are seven generators located 260 feet under ground. The water drops 692 feet to the turbines, then the water is released another 535 feet into the fiord. The idea for a power plant was suggested in 1904, but it was not until the 1940s that someone figured out a way to do it, and it was the 1960s before it was actually built.

At the bottom of the tunnel, most of us got off the bus and walked down a few steps to a viewing platform overlooking the generating room.

It was a long, 14-hour day and I'm not sure it was worth what we saw. But, that evening we indulged in room service. The hot chili tasted good, and we wondered what our families were eating on that Thanksgiving Day!

The next day remained misty until mid morning when it cleared into a beautiful day. We then took the shuttle into town where we visited the Botanical Gardens before walking around the mall. The hills of Queensland are covered with hotels and homes. Everyone must work in the tourist industry

That evening we went back to the waterfront to catch the *TSS Earnslaw*, a 1912 steam paddle wheeler, for a 45-minute ride across Lake Wakatipu to the Walter Peak Estate. The lovely Victorian mansion sits on beautifully landscaped grounds, part of 170,000 acres where 40,000 sheep roam.

We enjoyed a lovely buffet dinner. On the return boat ride across the lake we wandered to the stern of the boat to join a sing along with the piano player.

Our time on the South Island had come to an end. Auckland still remains my favorite New Zealand city, although it's hard to compare because the North and South Islands are so different. There is no question the human Kiwis are friendly, delightful people.

Chapter 8

Gooneys of Midway

Over a million birds you say, all in one place? No, a million *gooney birds*. That's just part of midway's aviary population. Over fifteen other species, including 43,000 black-footed albatross pairs also call Midway Island home. Talk about an up close and personal wildlife experience. It was incredible!

Part of the Hawaiian archipelago, but not part of the state, Midway lies 1200 miles northwest of Honolulu, and consists of three low coral and sand islands (Eastern, Sand, and Spit) with a total landmass of 1600 acres. Midway is not on most travel company's agendas, so why in 1997 did I travel there? To make a long story short, I did a friend a favor. Our primary purpose for this trip was to participate in a couple of research projects, one on spinner dolphins, and one on the endangered Hawaiian monk seals.

As it turned out that friend did me a favor, because the trip turned out to be a Ten, among my most fun and memorable!

From the very beginning, everyone on the island stressed that Midway is a refuge and not a resort. A resort puts the needs of people first where a refuge puts the needs of wildlife first, those of the people second. That was fine with us!

Midway has such a rich history that I must talk about it a bit before getting to the wonderful gooneys.

Midway, was a treeless, windswept, sand, and sea grass atoll when discovered by Captain N.C. Brooks in 1859. It has a semi-tropical climate with slightly more extremes than Hawaii. January and February are the rainiest months, with an annual rainfall of 12 inches.

Midway was the first offshore island to be annexed by the U.S. in 1867 under the Guano Act. Since there are no bird rookeries on Midway, the collection of guano would have been a tedious, nearly impossible task. However, history would prove this annexation to be a most strategic move.

In the spring of 1903 the Commercial Pacific Cable Company arrived on the island. On July 4, 1903, from that station, President Theodore Roosevelt sent the first around-the-world cable, which took nine minutes to complete.

In 1935 Pan American Airways set up a base for its Clipper Seaplane Service, making Midway a regular fuel stop for their Trans-Pacific air route, which included Honolulu, Wake Island, Guam, and Manila.

The U.S. Naval Air Station Midway was commissioned in August 1941.

Many people do not realize that on December 7, 1941 in addition to the bombing of Pearl Harbor, Midway was also shelled destroying the hospital and half of the hanger. One fuel tank that was hit smoldered for days serving as a beacon for returning U.S. pilots.

The Battle of Midway, June 4-6, 1942, was the turning point of the war in the Pacific and lasted three days. It was the first Japanese naval defeat in 300 years. Most of the battle took place 100 miles from Midway, but the atoll was also bombed. In spite of the Japanese outnumbering the U.S. forces 4:1, The U.S. sank three Japanese aircraft carriers plus numerous other ships with the loss of only one U.S. carrier, the USS Yorktown. Shore artillery hit and damaged two Japanese ships and several aircraft.

During the Korean War, Midway played an important role as a defensive outpost in the Distant Early Warning (DEW) System, and was a port of call and air traffic center during the Vietnam War.

It was hard to imagine 1200-acre Sand Island supporting 3500 people for three decades.

In 1969 President Nixon secretly met with Vietnam's President Thieu there. In 1978 the air station became a Naval Air Facility and dependents started to leave.

In 1988 the atoll was designated Midway Atoll National Wildlife Refuge and is the only remote Pacific Refuge available to the general public. It is managed by the U.S. Fish and Wildlife Service who have set up strict guidelines, that all visitors must obey.

The air facility operationally closed in 1993.

Today, the entire infrastructure is on Sand Island. Spit, the smallest island, is totally a refuge and has been purged of all non-native vegetation. Tiny, it basically has no history. Eastern Island's old abandoned runway has become overgrown and is now a wide boulevard for birds. All of the buildings and structures on Eastern Island have been torn down. Visitation to Eastern Island is restricted to small, guided groups. Sand Island is the largest and the only human inhabited one. The island is 1.8 miles long and 1.2 miles at its widest point. The 250 human inhabitants share the island with an avian population in the millions.

On Sand Island the enlisted barracks have been torn down; only the Bravo and Charlie BOQs remain. Termites ate and destroyed both the chapel and the Cannon school.

Senior Officer housing now houses island staff. The unfriendly bird golf course is no more. Most of the operational structures remain.

The tallest point on the island is the 165-foot water tower. All fresh water is obtained by catchments, stored in three huge tanks, sent through two treatment systems, and then pumped through a system to all faucets. In the era of 3500 residents fresh water had to be barged in to Midway.

There are 43 designated historical sites/buildings on Midway.

Dolphins and Seals:

A long barrier reef creates Midway's large five-mile long lagoon. With the exception of one day, when rather heavy rains and windy conditions created whitecaps in the lagoon, we were able to get out in the research boat every day. We always saw dolphins in schools of a hundred or more. It was great fun to watch them ride the bow wave of the boat. Photographing dolphins in the air is quite a trick as one has to be so quick, but I finally did master that task for personal use. The researcher did all the real photography with much more sophisticated equipment than my handy dandy little camera.

The research information will impact the development of boat usage in the atoll. The aim is to disturb the dolphins as little as possible in order to keep them in the area and not to disturb them enough to leave.

Midway is a perfect place for such a study as the shallow clear waters of the lagoon allow for detailed observation below the water as well as above it.

Spinner dolphins swim mostly in deep waters, but are found in regions where there are shallow platforms or islands where they can rest during the day in lagoons and bays. They typically live in tropical waters, but range into temperate water with a worldwide distribution.

The schools of dolphins on Midway are larger than those around the other Hawaiian Islands, very likely because there are fewer sheltered land and resting areas.

The lagoon provides a safe and quiet place for the dolphins to rest and escape from the area's large shark population.

Although spinner dolphin society is highly promiscuous, family units are apparent. Most interactions are learned associations with possible non-relatives. As with many dolphin species, spinners appear to form a fission-fusion society where group size and composition constantly changes. Some spinner studies have noted some segregation by age and sex. Schools appear to have no single leader and all activity seems to be determined by general consensus of the school

Most dolphins are day feeders but spinners feed on fish, squid, and shrimp in deep waters at night. They have been documented to dive to depths of two to 300 meters while feeding.

The Hawaiian monk seal, seldom seen around the inhabited Hawaiian Islands, is the most Hawaiian of Hawaii's marine animals. The most primitive of all the living seals, they are found mostly in the northwest part of the archipelago. Maybe they're shy of people because in the past, so many have been killed.

They are so named because they are solitary animals, similar to monks. They also have very little fur on the top of their head and the skin folds around the neck resemble a monk's cowl collar.

Monk seals inhabit tropical and temperate waters. The Hawaiian monk has been endangered since 1976 with a total population of only 1200 animals.

The research objective was to monitor the seal population in terms of age, sex, numbers, composition; and identify the beaches to determine if there's a seasonal pattern. It also was to determine reproductive and survival rates, identify birth sites and nursery beaches as well as their diet. Documentation of scars, injuries, entanglements, and other threats were also determined. Potential entangling debris was removed and disposed of, and any seal found entangled was freed. Also included was education to promote the understanding of the seals' plight and to promote the importance of non-disturbance.

The monk seal has a rather sad history. Many seals were clubbed to death for meat, oil, and skins. Disturbance of hauling-out areas forced mothers and babies to go out to sea where sharks further reduced the population. Others drowned accidentally when entangled in lost fishing nets that drifted from the North Pacific.

Adult seals are generally about seven feet long and weigh 350-400 pounds. Their life span may reach 30 years. Generally seals remain close to the island of their birth.

Seals have been known to dive 500 feet and remain under water for as long as 20 minutes when feeding. Feeding on eels, small reef fish, octopus, and lobster, they can eat as much as ten percent of their body weight each day providing a thick layer of blubber as an energy reserve. Although the monks live in warm waters their blubber layer is no less than that of seals in colder climates.

A newborn pup weighs 35-40 pounds and will quadruple his weight during the 40-day nursing period. A pregnant, seven-foot female can weigh 600 pounds and will lose half of that weight during the nursing period, as she does not leave her pup during that time, even to feed. The weaned pup slowly loses weight, as he learns to feed on his own by trial and error. He will feed around his birthplace. Adult females often have a pup every year.

Breeding season is generally spring and summer. Gestation lasts about ten and a half months with most births occurring in March to May, although births have been recorded in every month. Newborn pups have black fuzzy short hair, which falls out during nursing and is replaced with silver-gray fur on the back and creamy white fur on the underside. Subsequent molts occur annually. Only elephant and monk seals molt each year. Each animal has his own molting schedule, the process taking about two weeks. The seal remains on the beach during molting and does not feed during that period.

The monk seal bone structure is quite different from that of other seal species. Its limbs and flippers are very short. On land they are very awkward, unable to haul out on rocks like other species. They kind of wiggle and inch their way along. But in the water they are sleek and graceful.

It is illegal to fish within a fifty-mile radius of a known seal habitat. It is also illegal to harass, capture, or kill a seal.

Gooney Birds:

I did not know that the gooney goes to sea in July for four months. I really would have been disappointed if the birds were at sea during my stay. We couldn't have timed our visit better!

The day after our arrival all the residents got pretty excited when the first gooney flew in. The second day we saw five birds, then 15, and after that they were too numerous to count. We spent a lot of time sitting on the beach watching them come in. It was busier than the busiest airport.

Every morning when I got up, the first thing I would do was look out the window to see how many birds were on the lawn. After ten days the ground everywhere was covered with not only Laysan Albatross but also Blackfooted Albatross. Eventually a half million Laysan mating pairs had returned home. The Inn was full, and one no longer could walk a straight line anywhere!

Seventy percent of the world's population of this beautiful, sometimes comical, gooney bird lives on Midway.

The gooney bird mates for life, with an occasional exception, and every late October/early November returns to the same spot and waits for its mate. The Laysan Albatross, the smallest of the 15 species, has a wingspan of six and a half feet and weighs seven to eight pounds. Unlike other albatross who feed during the day, the Laysan is a night feeder.

They are absolutely beautiful gliding in the air. The underside of their wings is a bright white with black accents and trims. In the air they are most graceful. Landing into the wind, the landing is also graceful and upright, but when they misjudge and land with the wind the result is a nosedive, tumble, or summersault; their antics are beyond description and very funny to watch.

The mating ritual is fascinating to observe and watching became a favorite pastime for all of us. The gooney makes many different noises. The most common are the clacking of their beaks and sky pointing, called sky mooing. They really do sound like a cow.

Albatross are synchronous breeders. Mama lays a single half-pound egg in early December and dad immediately begins to incubate it. Mama goes to sea to feed for a couple of weeks returning to take over the sitting duties while Dad goes to feed. This alternating behavior goes on for 60 days until the chick hatches.

It takes both parents to raise the chick. If one parent dies, the chick will die. Both parents continue to alternate going to sea to feed the chick. A chick will tap the beak of the parent to stimulate regurgitation, then places its beak inside that of the parent catching every single drop. The chick fledges, when five months old. When the chick flies off to sea for the first time, it remains at sea for three to five years before returning to Midway to find a mate.

Twenty percent of the chicks will die before fledging and seven to ten percent of the fledging chicks will be eaten by the tiger sharks that come into the lagoon during fledging season just for that reason. And we think we're the only smart ones on earth!

The oldest known tagged bird is 43 years old. It is unusual for birds to mate in winter, but it is very hot on Midway in the summer, which makes it difficult for the birds to stay cool. Their webbed feet are very vascular and the birds thermo-regulate through them by sitting on the backs of their feet with the webbed toes in the air, off the ground.

During World War II the birds were killed in huge numbers by gunfire and airplanes. The Navy plowed under thousands because they clogged the runways. Discovering the gooney does not like hard surfaces the Navy paved the runway solving that problem! The Navy erected a huge gooney statue to celebrate the endurance of this wonderful bird.

The Blackfooted albatross has a seven-foot wingspan and weighs about a pound more than the Laysan. The 43,000 mating pairs make up the second largest colony of this specie in the world. The Blackfooted is a day feeder. A beautiful bird when erect, but it usually leans forward with head down when walking, giving a very ominous appearance. They can be very aggressive, so it is best to keep one's distance.

They can attack in four ways: by biting, by scratching with tiny claws on their webfeet, by defecating on you, or by vomiting on you. They are capable of five-foot projectile vomiting. Researchers said the odor is so *bad* that one can never get it out of clothes. It makes a skunk smell like a rose!

The mating ritual is similar to that of the Laysan. The Blackfoot prefer sandy nesting areas so are most commonly found on the perimeter of the island, where the Laysan are found inland preferring grassy nesting areas.

For each of three years 10,000 albatross were banded. The current protocol was to band 1500 Laysan and 1500 blackfoot each year, a formidable task, and all the biologists involved had the marks and scars to prove it. Chicks are banded on the right foot, adults on the left.

Seabirds have been programmed for centuries to eat anything floating on the surface of the water, which always used to be fish eggs, squid, or fish. Now tons of plastic are floating on our oceans' surfaces. The birds innocently eat it. When their stomach gets full of plastic they no longer have the urge to feed and die of malnutrition and dehydration. The research office had two huge cartons of Bic lighters that had been collected from the beaches.

It was an appalling sight, and one that sickened us all, when we saw dead birds whose deteriorating bodies revealed a stomach full of plastic.

There is no doubt that the million plus gooneys dominate Midway Atoll, but they share their home with many other birds. Millions of birds migrate through the area and fifteen other species call Midway home.

Midway is an incredible wildlife spectacle, a living laboratory and ecosystem under constant study. I expanded my horizons a great deal in a very relaxed, fun atmosphere. It was an incredible vacation!

Chapter 9

A Swiss Hike

There I was on the top of a mountain, listening to the serenade of tinkling cowbells wafting up from the valley below, with the best cup of coffee $3 could buy. Pure ecstasy!

My first trip to Europe gave me a good preview of where I wanted to return for a more in-depth visit, and Switzerland was at the top of that list. The coffee was so strong in most of Europe that I couldn't drink it, so it had been nearly two weeks since I'd had a cup of coffee.

A cable car and gondola had delivered us 6000 feet to the top of Strasserhorn. As I walked into the chalet café/gift shop I spotted a hot plate with both a pot of coffee and a pot of hot water.

Excited, I blurted out, "Oh, you have hot water!"

Then in the next breath I asked the shocked young man behind the counter to fill a cup half way with coffee and then to fill it with hot water.

"No. No," he said. "This is not strong coffee. We put liquor in it."

I pleaded with him to please do as I asked and he did. I took my precious cup of coffee out into the sun on the deck and thoroughly enjoyed the best cup of coffee ever, and the only cup of coffee I had that whole trip.

Incidentally, I had a marvelous glass of sparkling ice tea one noon in Lucerne, Switzerland. It also was the only glass of ice tea I had that trip.

In Lucerne the lion statue so impressed me that when I returned a few years later in 1998, I wanted my friend to see it. I even remembered how to get there, so on arrival day of our hiking adventure in Switzerland, we walked from the hotel to the monument.

The 39-foot lion was carved out of white sandstone in 1820-21. A symbol of courage and strength, fighting to the death, it commemorates the Swiss guards killed in 1792 in the French Revolution. The arrow that pierced the lion's heart protrudes from his back while his giant paw covers the shield, protecting it even in death. The tear on the lion's cheek says it all. I was just as touched the second time as when I first saw it, and if I'm ever in Lucerne again, I'll go see the lion again.

Located on the shores of Lake Lucerne lying between Mount Rigi and Mount Pilatus, Lucerne, Switzerland is a beautiful city with a population of 62,500. The city, founded in 1178 by Benedictine monks, is the capitol of its canton (state).

The city has a medieval heritage evident in the 14th century walls, parts of which are still standing. Nine of the original twenty plus towers remain today.

The city is full of fine old churches and many old buildings that display marvelous painted facades. The paintings on the Balances Hotel date back to 1893. Though never restored, they remain in good condition.

Cobblestone alleys lined with small shops of every description and small sidewalk cafés abound in the city. Located in the heart of Switzerland, Lucerne is ideal for walkers, but sturdy flat-soled shoes are a must for all the cobblestones.

The Reuss River runs through old town dividing the city into two nearly equal parts. Several footbridges span the river. The most famous, the Kapellbruke Bridge, is the signature of Lucerne. Also known as the chapel bridge, it is the oldest covered bridge in Europe. Built in 1333, the bridge leads to the doorstep of the chapel built in 1178. In 1993 a boat docked nearby, caught fire.

The blaze spread to the bridge and caused major damage. Because the bridge has such symbolic significance to the city, it was rebuilt. The octagonal tower at one end of the bridge was once a navigational light for the river, then a prison, and finally a water tower. Today the tower is available for private parties.

A second wooden footbridge, not as famous as the Kapellbruke, spans the river where in 1856 a dam was built to control water flow. The dam is still used today, as 60 percent of Switzerland's electricity is hydroelectric.

Lake Lucerne is the second largest lake in Switzerland. Measuring 160 square kilometers, it is 214 meters deep. Lake Geneva is bigger but 50 percent of it belongs to France. Some of Switzerland's oldest steam ships sail Lake Lucerne's clear cool waters.

On a sunny warm Sunday we walked to the dock and boarded a steamer going up the lake. We enjoyed the scenery of the many mountain peaks surrounding the calm lake. All of the 34 mountain peaks in Switzerland over 2000 meters (6500 feet) have names.

We disembarked at Hertinstein and walked to Weggis, a picturesque little town nestled between the lakeshore and the mountain peaks, with a population of 2500. Flowers were plentiful and gorgeous everywhere, on porches, on windowsills, and in small pocket gardens and parks. We walked past some beach areas. Weggis is a true resort town with both summer and winter activities.

That evening we walked to the train station for our first train ride. Our destination was in the opposite direction to Hitzkirch where we were met by a van for a ride up a hill to a local farm. Viewing the very steep hill ahead of us I was sure glad we weren't hiking it. At the top we had a lovely view of the valley and surrounding countryside below.

Farms in Switzerland are small, only a few acres. Only six percent of the population is involved in agriculture, 34 percent of the people are involved in industry, and 60 percent are in the service industry i.e.: restaurant, hotel, and the like. Only ten percent of farmers can make a livable wage from farming so 90 percent need to have another job as well. Farming has changed from beef to milk cows, although there are still some beef cows. The Swiss Brown Cow is a distinct and popular breed.

Early in the morning on another day, we found ourselves walking to the ferry pier for an hour and a half boat ride to Alpnachstad. We all were amazed at how clean the ferries were. The water wheel apparatus was clearly visible behind a Plexiglass guardrail in the center of the ship's main deck. The brass shone brightly enough to reflect one's image.

In 1889 it took a year to build the approximately three-mile cog railroad up Mount Pilatus. Built at a 48 percent incline, it is the world's steepest cog railway. It was like going straight up the face of the mountain.

Legend has it that Pilatus was a holy man who slayed the dragon living on the mountain, and that's how the mountain got its name.

Unfortunately for us the heavy mist turned into rain the farther up the mountain we traveled.

The hotel had packed each of us a picnic lunch, which originally was meant to be eaten on the trail down the mountain. On that rainy day, one alternative was to eat in the middle of the foyer of the building at the top of Pilatus. Even though there were very few people about, that alternative was not very appealing to any of us. Our guide, who knew everyone and his brother in the country, went into the restaurant and talked the manager into letting us eat our lunch inside. On this rather nasty weather-wise day, we were the only people in the big room. Most of us ordered a cup of soup and a hot drink. We were especially careful to pick up all our mess and carry it off, as we were grateful for their hospitality.

After lunch we took the gondola down to 1415 feet to Frakmuntegg where we started to hike. Our destination was

Krienseregg at 1026 feet. It was raining pretty hard so it didn't take long for us to get good and wet. A couple of people had packed umbrellas, but they were only minimally useful. Somehow it seemed pretty ludicrous to be hiking sporting an opened umbrella, and the scene tickled my funny bone. At Krienseregg we took a small cable car to the bottom where we boarded a bus for a short ride back to Lucerne, stopping first for a tour of the alphorn factory.

The small company, and only manufacturer, produces two horns a day or about 250 a year. Twenty-five percent of the horns are exported to the United States, 25 percent to Asia, mostly Japan, and the remaining 50 percent stay in Switzerland.

The length of the horn determines the pitch, the longer the horn the deeper the pitch. The horn has no holes or valves, and the average price is about $2000. We were given a chance to try to blow an alphorn. A couple of the fellows had some success, but the rest of us couldn't even make a sound!

On our last day in Lucerne, we caught the 7:45 AM train for Engleberg, the name meaning "mountain of angels." Small gondolas took us half way up the mountain where we transferred to a large standup gondola for the ride to next platform. Finally we transferred into the Rotair, the world's only rotating gondola. It too was a large standup gondola whose floor rotated 360 degrees in minutes. It was pretty impressive, and when we came out of the clouds the gondola was filled with a chorus of oohs and ahs. What a view!

At the top of this glacier, people were playing in the snow. It was very slippery but not as cold as I had expected. At 10,627 feet it was a little misty but not enough to obstruct our view or to get us wet. We were just standing in the clouds!

A 427 foot ice cave was constructed between 1974 and 1978. The long cave, with several rooms, had a constant temperature of 30-31 degrees. It was pretty unusual. We read it takes ten years for one meter of snow to become ice. The ice in this glacier ranged from 48-162 feet.

After being well cooled in the cave, many of us stopped in the café for a hot drink. Once warmed, we took the Rotair down to the next platform called Trubsee, meaning the "lake of sorrows."

While hiking around the relatively small lake we stopped many times to examine and learn the names of the many alpine flowers in bloom. It was an easy hike on a well-maintained gravel path. About three-quarters of the way around, a path to Engleberg headed off to our right. The sign said one hour.

When hiking in Switzerland the signs are always posted in time, not miles. The Swiss don't talk about miles or meters when hiking, only the length of time it takes to get somewhere.

All but two of us decided to take this "short cut," while the guide and the other two finished walking around the lake and taking the gondola back to the bottom. *Big mistake!* This footpath turned out to be a cow path. It was mucky in spots with a lot of slippery rocks. So, we played mountain goat for the next two and a half hours climbing up and down over them!

Several times I was nearly ready to turn back. But it always looked like it got better up ahead, and it did, but not for long. However, by the time it turned mucky again we really had reached the point of no return so we just trudged on.

Over two hours later, when we finally hit level ground, several of us were ready to pay some farmer to give us a ride to the railway station. Since no farmer or motor vehicle of any kind was in sight we continued on. When we rounded the last turn in the road I felt like shouting, "Yes, there's the station. I can't believe we all made it!"

Engleberg is a darling little town with a large Benedictine monastery and a casino, owned by the mayor who gave us an interesting lecture on his little town.

Back in Lucerne we crossed over the Kapellbruke Bridge for the last time heading for the hotel. I soaked my aching body in the deep tub until the water turned cold. Then I tackled the repacking before falling into bed after a long and busy day.

Swiss trains are electric, smooth, and quiet. The country has a very good mass transit system. Trains run frequently and on time. One had better be at the station and paying attention when the schedule says the train is due to depart, or you end up waiting for the next one!

Zurich is a city full of towers and old churches with steeples everywhere. St. Peter's church tower boasts the largest clock face in the world, over 26 feet in diameter!

But the thing I enjoyed most in Zurich was strolling down the famous Bahnhofstrasse, a wide boulevard running from the train station for three-quarters of a mile to the edge of Lake Zurich. The wide sidewalks allowed for lots of window-shopping in the many high priced specialty shops. Sidewalk cafés sat nestled between the shops and dining tables spilled outside onto the sidewalk.

We repeatedly interrupted our leisurely stroll by stopping to view and comment on the over hundred life-size cows standing all along the way. Apparently there had been a contest. Each cow was sponsored by a firm and decorated by a different artist. I just fell in love with the silly, colorful cows, and by the time we reached Lake Zurich I had used a whole roll of film photographing them.

I think it was the following year that Chicago copied this cow idea. And after that I understand New York did a similar thing. However, Zurich was the first with the idea and contest, and I was there.

Since we were leaving Zurich for Davos on the 2 PM train, we thought it prudent to walk back to the train station for lunch. Since I mostly see the inside of European airports, I'm not too familiar with train stations. But, this one was like one I've never seen. Whether it's typical of European train stations or not, I don't know, although a few others we transferred through during the trip were much less complex.

Both the upper and lower levels were lined with shops, cafés, and kiosks. On the lower level was a very clean restroom or WC for water closet. Depositing one and a half francs in the turn-style enabled the traveler to buy any needed toilet article including shampoo. There were nice private showering facilities. The sink faucets produced both cold and hot running water. It was a restroom to be proud of. Also on the lower level were hundreds of lockers in different sizes.

In the center of the upper level stood the equivalent of a farmer's market with just about anything one might desire, vegetables, sausage, cheese, tea, flowers, and the list goes on.

We chose a large restaurant for lunch with outside tables so we could people watch.

The three-hour-ride with one stop requiring a change of trains was pleasant and picturesque with a running commentary from our guide.

Swiss citizenship is not easily obtained. A child born of a Swiss dad is an automatic Swiss citizen; of a Swiss mother and non-Swiss dad requires some simple paperwork. A non-Swiss married to a Swiss must live in the country five years before becoming eligible for citizenship, otherwise a non-Swiss must live in the country eleven years. For foreigners, citizenship is a difficult process. Equally difficult for a non-Swiss is obtaining a work permit.

Davos is the sister city of Aspen, Colorado. At 5117 feet, it is Switzerland's highest town and its largest mountain resort. In winter, skiers overrun this little town of 11,500. In addition to the seventy hotels, local residents rent out another 12,000 beds in their homes.

One day after breakfast we caught the city bus downtown to the gondola that would take us up to Ischalp, where we were to start hiking. It didn't take long for my friend and me to realize we walked at a different pace. As it happened the same thing turned out to be true of another couple of gals, so we just switched partners. Later, this new walking partner and I became friends and later made several other trips together.

By the time we'd made it to the small cheese factory in the mountains, we had climbed up 500 feet. A walk through the cheese factory to the deck outside afforded us a breath taking view of the valley and alpine meadow below. There are 90 farms in the Davos area and farming has changed its focus from beef to milk. Annually the area produces four million liters of milk. We sampled cheese along with a little wine while watching some of the cheese making process.

Leaving the cheese factory, the walk was a 1500-foot decent to Clavadel. We walked over a smooth, well-kept trail until we reached the forest. The path through the forest was a well maintained one, a bit narrow at times, with several switchbacks. But the bonus was passing by the melodious sound of running waterfalls.

We stopped to eat our box lunch by a large waterfall. That is where I lent my old Girl Scout knife to one of the fellows whittling a walking stick. It didn't take him long to break the main blade. He felt bad and so did I as I'd had that knife for over fifty years. But what can one do when accidents happen? I did feel though that he should have at least made the effort to replace my knife.

In Clavadel a bus was available back to Davos, but most of us decided to continue walking. With instructions to just follow the signs we did fine, and after leaving the hiking trail, one of the fellows with a good sense of direction got us over the proper streets straight back to the hotel.

For dinner one evening we took the bus to a well-known restaurant where our guide knew the owner. After a Swiss dinner the owner served us all a small glass of *kirsch or kirschwasser,* a brandy distilled from cherries and a local specialty. The owner was very proud of his kirsch, and it was very nice of him to treat us.

After dinner we took the bus back to the hotel. Although it wasn't but a mile or so, we both had on dress shoes and not walking shoes.

The view of the mountains from our Davos hotel window was

spectacular, but the next morning we woke to mist over the mountains. During breakfast the mist developed into a good downpour, but by hike departure time the rain had slowed to a heavy drizzle. The hike walking around small Lake Davos only took a couple of hours.

By noon the weather cleared and it looked like it might be nice for the afternoon hike. This time we took a funicular, similar to a gondola but on a track, to Schatzalp to visit and hike around the alpine botanical gardens. At the end of the funicular ride we disembarked at the Hotel Berghotel Schatzalp.

Davos originally was known as a health center and spa for people with lung problems. A huge sanatorium was built in 1899. By 1950 the city decided to change its focus and image to a ski and summer resort. The sanatorium, located at the base of the botanical gardens, was converted to a hotel at that time.

The hike around the gardens was hilly and at times quite steep. Paths were very narrow necessitating single file walking. It was an unusual garden with small pockets of flowers in numerous areas. Needless to say the area was very rocky, so to me it really was a rock garden. Many flowers were in bloom, and we saw the famous edelweiss in all its glory.

By the time we were ready for the funicular ride back down to street level it was clouding up over the mountains. Every weekend in July, Davos hosts a music festival, so we walked over to the Post Hotel to see what was going on. We found a seat on the hotel balcony just as it started to rain!

A live band was playing under a tent at the far end of the yard. We had a great spot for both seeing all the activity and for listening to the music. We listened to some good jazz for quite awhile. When it stopped raining we wandered down into the courtyard to check out the vendors. A bit later we decided to take advantage of the break in the weather and walk the mile or so back to the hotel.

Early in the morning we boarded the Glacier Express for the all day ride to Interlaken. Our first stop was six hours away at Brig.

The eight-mile long Furka Tunnel is the world's longest narrow railway tunnel. The stunningly beautiful Rhone Valley produced one oh and ah after another. Most of us had a book for the long ride, but the gorgeous scenery took precedence over reading.

The scenery was breathtaking along the Rhine Gorge to the Overalp Pass. The slow climb up to the pass afforded us a good view of the wildflowers growing in the fields. As always when riding the trains, we had a very nice reserved car. We just had to look for the car with our name on it before boarding. At the track we stuck our Swiss Card in a little machine that cut off a little stub, and marked the station and date on the ticket. A pretty neat and efficient system!

A porter entered our car to tell us when it was time to go to the dining car for lunch. The dining car was the last car on the train requiring us to walk through several wobbly unsteady cars connections. Lunch was good, hot, and plentiful with seconds offered on the rosti and vegetables. There was ample meat in the first serving. Rosti is shredded potatoes with shredded onion, cooked similarly to our hash browns. They most often include cheese that melts during cooking. There are many variations on rosti, a typically Swiss dish.

During lunch the train crept at a snail's pace up a steep incline, and it seemed at times we might actually stop. In several areas train tracks actually hung over the mountainside. The eye-catching view continued. When our time was over in the dining car the waiter came by saying, "Thank you, bye." When he repeated it several times, we all got the hint that our dinner hour was over!

In Brig we had an hour layover so we headed into town to look around. Sidewalk cafés were full. We walked the cobblestone streets and alleyways admiring the many towers and church steeples, no two appearing alike.

Back on the train it wasn't long before we noticed mist over the mountains, and soon it started to rain.

In Spietz, with only minutes to spare, we changed trains again. As we approached Lake Thun it was raining so hard we could hardly see the lake. Thank goodness our centrally located hotel was only a block from the train station. Interlaken has a train station at each end of the city about a mile apart. Trains for different destinations leave from each station.

August 1st is National Day in Switzerland, their equivalent to our 4th of July. After dinner in the hotel, we sat on our room balcony and watched fireworks.

Interlaken meaning "between lakes," is located between 12-mile long Lake Thun and nine-mile long Lake Brienz. The first steam ships sailed the lakes in 1839, and several ships continue to sail the lakes on a regular schedule between the many small villages surrounding the lakes. A depth of 261 meters (848 feet) makes Lake Brienz the deepest lake in Switzerland.

Two years of apprenticeship is required to become a fisherman. Four fishermen make their living from Lake Brienz taking twenty ton of fish annually from the lake, 98 percent of which is perch, the rest is a trout-like fish.

Interlaken, with a population of 15,000, is a huge winter ski area. Hotel Victoria, built in 1869, is the only five-star hotel in the city. Hotel Interlaken, built in 1400, is the oldest hotel in town. A plaque on the hotel front states that Lord Byron stayed there in 1816 and Mendelssohn in 1832.

Interlaken is level and a very easy city to walk. The main street is called Hoheweg and is one straight long shopping and hotel area running between the two train stations. It seemed every store window in the whole country was full of Swiss watches and Swiss Army knives.

The city boasts English, Alpine, and Japanese gardens. The latter being the largest and a symbol of friendship between Japan and Switzerland. Ever since some Japanese fellow won a skiing event, his countrymen have flocked to Switzerland. As many as 250,000 Japanese had visited the previous year.

The horse and buggies on the streets were all owned by seven people, and are only available from Easter to October.

On another day, a train took us to Ballenberg, Switzerland's only outdoor museum, which opened in 1978. Eighty homes of every Swiss style and from every canton are on sixteen of the seventy-acre museum. Many of the restored houses were over a century old. The park has many lovely wooded hiking trails, and all kinds of demonstrations and exhibits. I found the lace making and the herbal medicine of particular interest. The museum is only open from Easter to late October.

Brienz, a small village of 2500, had some neat little shops. Home to the only wood carving school in Switzerland, the school has a four-year apprenticeship program. The famine of the 1800s was a big contributing factor for the beginning of woodcarving. In 1870 there were over 1000 woodcarvers. The school, established in 1884, presently had only 30 carvers.

On a cloudy day, an early train took us to Lauterbrenner where we picked up a nice hiking trail taking us to Murren. While hiking, we passed many of the 72 waterfalls in the area, one of which was 1170 feet high. Halfway through the hike we stopped at a lovely new restaurant for some famous hot chocolate. It amazed me how in the middle of nowhere a café or a restaurant would suddenly appear.

Monks founded Murren, a quaint little village at an altitude of 5390 feet, in 1133. Murren means *many fountains.*

We were all dubious about the weather as we approached the cable car station. What would it be like at 10,000 feet? The station lobby had a TV, relaying pictures from the top of Mount Schilthorn. The TV showed it clear as can be at the top, so we boarded the cable car for the ride up. About two thirds of the way, at 8783 feet, we had to change cars at a platform station.

When we broke through the clouds we feasted on a breathtaking view of the Alps. At the top one can see over 200 peaks. It was so very clear. The TV monitor in the station had been

145

right! We walked around the 360-degree viewing platform, took pictures, and couldn't stop exclaiming about the beauty that lay before our eyes. A windbreaker jacket was sufficient, as it really was not very cold.

Eventually several of us found our way into the Piz Gloria revolving restaurant for lunch. The James Bond movie, *In Her Majesty's Secret Service,* was filmed there in the late 60s. The restaurant, built in 1967, rotates one revolution every hour. We by-passed the gift shop and spent all our time just trying to absorb the incredible beauty before us. Just as we were ready to catch the cable car down to Murren the clouds started to roll in over the mountaintops and by the time we reached the station below the TV showed the entire area to be completely fogged in. Were we lucky!

By mid afternoon we arrived at the many stairs that led us to the ravine tunnel elevator, which took us to the stairway leading up to Trummelbach Falls. The noise of 20,000 liters of water per *second* cascading down the mountain was deafening. It was a damp and slippery hike to the top. These glacier fed falls drain water from Mountains Eiger, Monch, and Jungfrau. The sight was spectacular and very difficult to capture on film. Because of the noise it was nearly impossible to carry on a conversation. When that day was over we had traveled on fourteen modes of transportation and climbed over 200 steps!

The sun was shining brightly and it was another early start when we caught a train for Grindlewald. From there a bus took us on a short ride down into the valley where a ten-minute hike took us to the Mannlichen Gondola Station. This gondola ride is the longest one in Europe. The six kilometer, 300 meter ride took us a half-hour before depositing us at 7317 feet.

We listened to a cowbell serenade from the alpine meadows we were quietly passing over all the way to the top. Clear at the top we looked down at the valley and meadows below. In the alpine meadows "cow rights" are owned by cooperations, and there are only so many. Each farmer has a certain number of "rights," not necessarily equal, and his cows may pasture many miles from his farm. One cow over two years old is equal to one cow right, three calves equal one right, and a nursing mom and her calf are one right. The cows can pasture only 100 days a year. Needless to say a lot of hay is needed to feed them during the cold winter. The hay is stored in small windowless chalet-type buildings seen all over the pastures.

From the lookout we hiked on a good path down to Kleine Scheidegg where we enjoyed a typical Swiss lunch of spaghetti Bolognese and salad.

After lunch we started down hill toward Wengen and encountered some friendly goats. One silly little goat followed me quite a way wanting to eat out of my pocket! But there was nothing in my pocket for him to eat. The good size bell around his neck just kept tinkling away as we walked along.

It was awesome walking in the shadow of the Eiger, Monch, and Jungfrau. Eiger is a Celtic word meaning "big man." Monch is a German word for "horse." Years ago Grindlewald was known for the good quality of its horses. When the horses were ready for sale they would be placed at the foot of the mountain and people from far away would come to buy them. And Jungfrau means "virgin." Years ago nuns wore small, white, pointed caps. The monks said when Jungfrau was covered with snow it looked just like the nun's caps. Of course the nuns were virgins, hence the mountain's name. The Swiss Alps are simply gorgeous. The hiking paths we traveled were in excellent condition.

It was a five-hour train ride, necessitating four train changes, to Lugano. To say we were taking the scenic route is a bit of an understatement as *all* of Switzerland's routes are scenic! Lugano is known as Italian Switzerland.

The center of the 19-kilometer-long Simplon tunnel is the Italian-Swiss border. Part of this privately owned tunnel belongs to Italy. We traveled in enough of Italy that the conductor wanted to see our passports.

This private railroad crosses 83 bridges and goes through 31 tunnels. It also carries 800,000 passengers a year from Domodosola to Lugano. Approaching the southern part of Switzerland was like leaving one country and entering another. The geography changed dramatically. Stone houses replaced the lovely wooden Swiss chalets. High-rise buildings started to appear. The mountains were covered with lush green forests. Palm trees and tropical flora started to emerge.

The narrow road connecting Switzerland with Italy was built in 1907, the railroad in 1923. Today one can enter the city of Lugano via an underground railroad.

Lugano, the largest city in the Italian-speaking canton of Ticino, is built around Lake Lugano. Houses and hotels are built up the mountainsides, as the area is very hilly. Switzerland's southernmost tourist town is the closest Swiss city to Italy. The city is built on several levels. A nearby funicular got us from our hotel level down to lake level. We found traffic heavy, and it appeared there was no such thing as a pedestrian right of way.

The city of only 28,000 has the feel of a large metropolitan area. It is a curious mix of Swiss, Italian, and the tropics. Like the rest of the country, the city is full of cobblestone alleyways lined with shops and sidewalk cafes. Lugano's climate is semi-tropical and very warm most of the year. There is a lovely park and wide pedestrian walkway around the lake, but the beautiful flowers we had come to know had disappeared.

One afternoon we took a boat ride around Lake Lugano. Small villages cluster all around the lake, so the boats also serve as ferries for those living in the more isolated villages. A small part of the lake is in Italy and there is a small amount of Italian coastline.

One day we rode the city bus to Paridiso. From there it was only a short walk to the gondola station for a ride to the top of Mount San Salvadore. The view at the top was spectacular. After a while we took a footpath leading to a small old church. Climbing a couple flights of stairs to the roof and observation deck, we found ourselves up above the tree line with a magnificent 360-degree view of the lake and city.

There was a hiking trail down the mountain but it was very rocky, steep, and looked a bit of a challenge. Since neither of us had our walking sticks with us we decided to ride the gondola down to street level.

Following a map to the post bus stop, we had only a short wait for the bus. As we boarded I showed the driver the business card from the grotto restaurant and asked, "You go here?"

He answered, 'Yes, yes, the last stop."

Little did we know that we were in for a hair-raising ride over a narrow switchback, hairpin turn road up, up, and up. One narrow overpass left the driver no more than an inch to spare on either side of the bus. He was good! When we got off, the driver pointed us in the right direction.

We followed the cobblestone alley for quite a way and I was beginning to wonder if we were in the right place. But a few yards farther, after a curve in the alley the grotto suddenly appeared. We were in the right place after all!

English. Forget it, there was no one around who spoke any English! The menu was in Italian, but at least we could understand pizza and salada. The pizza was good, and we still laugh about the tomato salad we ordered. You can imagine our look of surprise when we were served a large bowl of quartered tomatoes! That was all, just ripe tomatoes.

After an equally hair-raising ride down the mountain we were happy to be back in Paridiso. From there we decided to walk along the waterfront back to Lugano.

The train back to Zurich was a through train taking only three hours.

After two and a half weeks it was tough to say good-bye to that cohesive group. We had hiked up and hiked down in rain, mist, sun, and fair skies. We had taken ferries, trains, post trains, buses, post buses, gondolas, funiculars, cog rails, cable cars, the rotaire, and the Glacier Express to reach our hiking starting points. The temperature had ranged from 70-80 degrees, and we'd had a wonderful time with a delightful Swiss guide named Charlie. It had been great fun to be one of "Charlie's Angels" for this most spectacular vacation. I could do it again!

Chapter 10

Polar Bears and Cold Weather

Tundra buggies, frozen tundra, and polar bears. The thought was fascinating except for one thing, I don't like cold weather, but more important I really don't own any cold weather clothes.

For three years, every time I'd travel with my New Jersey friend, she'd talk about wanting to go to see the polar bears. And I kept telling her I didn't own clothes for such a trip, and besides I liked *warm* weather.

Then one day I was sitting at my desk when a flash of lightning hit me. Immediately I picked up the phone and called her. Yes, if she still wanted to make the trip, I'd go ahead and go with her. My daughter skis, and I could borrow her clothes! Why hadn't I thought of that before?

After a phone call to her organization of choice, I was almost let off the hook. That company said they were completely booked for the following October. Although used to booking a trip several months in advance I could hardly believe they were totally booked a full year in advance!

But now that I had agreed to make the trip, she was not about to give up. There's only about a six-week window that polar bears can be seen in Churchill, Manitoba, Canada. As soon as Hudson Bay freezes over, the bears are gone for their annual feast of seal.

After some research and homework on her part, we ended up on a conference call with another company, and settled on a date in late October 1999 that suited us both.

As the months passed, we agreed to meet in Minneapolis, on Saturday and fly to Winnipeg together. She was not a morning person, so I agreed to an afternoon flight vs. my usual choice of a morning flight. I guess the fact that we each could make compromises is what made us good traveling companions.

The Delta flight left the terminal on time, and was cruising down the runway just about to lift off, when suddenly the pilot slammed on the breaks. What a surprise that was! I didn't know a plane could stop so fast, but seat belts kept us all safely in our seats.

The loud speaker crackled to life, "Ladies and Gentlemen, this is the captain speaking. Some of the lights on the control panel came on showing we don't have enough lift-off speed, so I've had to abort the flight. We will return to the terminal to let the mechanics take a look."

What a way to start the trip! A little later we were informed Atlanta was faxing instructions, and that we would only be on the ground about a half-hour. The flight was nearly full, and everyone was making connections in Atlanta. I had scheduled an hour to change planes. Now it looked doubtful that I would make my connection.

Apparently the problem was a relatively minor one, as we were in the air an hour and fifteen minutes later. Everyone looked at his watch and mentally calculated and wondered about his connecting flight.

I'd already said a silent prayer for a safe flight, now I said another for my gates to be on the same concourse, and to be fairly close together, not on opposite ends of the long concourse.

We landed in Atlanta with my having about 12 minutes to spare, but I swear a beginner was driving the ramp. Anxious passengers filled the aisle as we watched him jockey the ramp in and out of position.

Fortunately, I had an aisle seat, only a few rows back, so I was able to get my bag down quickly, and exit as soon as possible. I was lucky—my gates were in the same concourse, but I still had to make it from gate 32 to 17.

Normally in Atlanta I have to zigzag around people, as I tend to move right along and not meander as many others do. To this day I swear I sent out an aura that said, *stay out of my way, I'm in a hurry and I'm coming through!* I hustled from that gate, doing time and a half, in a straight line right down the center of that concourse. I arrived at the gate, huffing and puffing, with boarding pass in hand, just as they were closing the door. I was the last passenger to board—but I made my connection!

Grateful I did not have to try to contact my friend saying I was delayed, I was waiting at our departure gate in Minneapolis when she arrived. We had decided to spend a couple of days in Winnipeg before going north to Churchill.

Winnipeg is very flat, and the name means "meeting of muddy waters."

One half of Manitoba's population lives in Winnipeg, and with a population of 650,000, Winnipeg, the Provincial capitol of Manitoba, is Canada's seventh largest city. In spite of being geographically isolated, Winnipeg is a center of commerce and culture, which includes a symphony, opera, ballet, theater, and local native artists. Buffalo hunting plains Indians as well as French and English settlers were the first inhabitants.

The east side of the river was settled by the French; the west by the English. There remain two large, distinct areas today. In the French Quarter, signs are in French first, English second.

In 1738 the fur trading company, Northwest Company, established a trading post at the juncture of the Red and Assiniboini Rivers. In 1812, Lord Selkirk, a Scot, brought an agricultural settlement to the area. The city incorporated in 1873, and in 1886 the Canadian Pacific Railroad followed, opening the way for European immigrants. Winnipeg, the principal city in western Canada, is a railroad hub for livestock and grain.

Today at this juncture of the rivers is a 56-acre site called The

Forks. The Forks National Historic Site and Forks Complex, built in 1988, is a crossroads, meeting of the old and the new, meeting of diverse peoples, and a place for people to meet, work, and play. The complex contains markets of all kinds, a public market, shops, eateries and restaurants.

In the adjoining park we walked several of the many bike/hike trails stopping to read the many interpretive displays. A children's museum, and an aboriginal ceremonial pit, with some interesting art surrounding it, are also part of the complex. An old four-story warehouse converted to a shopping plaza, housed unique shops and restaurants.

The city has seen steady growth since the boon days, and the diverse economy includes manufacturing, banking, transportation, and agriculture. Today, distinct ethnic areas in the city include Ukrainian, Jewish, Italian, Polish, Chinese, Mennonite, Hungarian, Portuguese, French, and English neighborhoods.

The Provincial Legislative building, built in 1920, is made of fossilized limestone giving it an unusual texture. Huge bronze buffaloes stand on each side of the grand staircase in the foyer of the building. The buffalo, standing for strength and endurance, is the symbol of Manitoba. An 1883 house, located just behind the legislative building, is the home of the Lieutenant Governor. Appointed for a five-year term, he has the responsibility of handling all royal arrangements and protocol whenever any member of England's royal family visits.

On a ride to Oak Hammock Marsh Interpretive Center, located about 40 miles outside of Winnipeg, the driver told us that Alberta, Manitoba, and Saskatchewan are Canada's three Prairie Provinces. Manitoba, also known as the keystone province, is easternmost, and is nearly in the geographic center of the country. Manitoba is derived from an Indian word meaning *Great Spirit.* In 1870 Manitoba was the fifth province to join the union. In the north stands the sub arctic, the middle section is the Canadian Shield or boreal forest, and in the south lies the lowlands or grasslands.

Arriving at the center, a most informative docent joined us. This center was one of the finest I've ever visited. During a four-month time frame of April-May and September-October 40,000 school children visit the center.

The hands-on activities were inviting. A TV monitor, attached to a remote camera in the marsh, provided an extensive view, way beyond that of the naked eye. Computers gave access to neat information. Metal rubbings, lovely wildlife displays, fish tanks containing marsh fish, various puzzles, and a water tank with sand were among the many offerings as well as a fair sized theater for presentations.

I went outside on the roof to take it the view, but it was windy and chilly! The Interpretive Center contains marsh, meadows, tall grass prairies, lure crops, and aspen and oak bluffs. There are close to 15 miles of hiking trails and dyke walkways in the park. Since 280 species of birds migrate through the area, the marsh is one of the best bird viewing spots in North America.

At the time of my visit, 200,000 water foul were in residence, but by the end of October they all would have flown south. Living in the marsh were 25,000 muskrats that were joined by many insects, reptiles, amphibians, and mammals like rabbits, deer, and beaver. It was an interesting visit!

For me it was a cold, windy day, and the hot lunch of a delicious Irish stew and bannock, an Indian bread, hit the spot. Topped off with apple crumble and ice cream, it was a delight. Lower Fort Garry Historical Site was closed for the season, so we were the only people in their café. They opened the site just for us, and it was wonderful to have the place all to ourselves. After lunch a docent showed us around interpreting displays and answering questions.

After a pleasant, informative couple of days we were off to Churchill, 700 air miles or a 1,000-mile train ride from Winnipeg. The three-hour flight was on a 50 seat Havaland turbo prop plane. A blizzard the night before had deposited a fresh layer of snow for our arrival.

On the short ride to the hotel we were cautioned not to walk around town after dark, or to go out of the perimeters of town. The warning was emphatic!

The first afternoon, I wandered around the small town and stopped at the post office for a unique passport stamp, and made a stop at the bank to exchange a small amount of money.

Churchill lies in the middle of the endless Canadian tundra, and is the same latitude as Stockholm, Sweden and Oslo, Norway. Here, in the *polar bear capitol of the world* the Aurora Borealis are clearly visible at certain times of the year. However, there are no roads connecting Churchill to the outside world; one must arrive by train or plane.

Churchill is the only international harbor on Hudson Bay, and its seaport is 1000 miles closer to Europe than it is to Montreal.

Grain elevators define the skyline, and are a symbol of the town's historic growth. Ships, from all over the world, still visit Churchill to fill their holds with grain. It is not uncommon for ships to stay off shore for several days, before they are able to enter the port.

Building of the railroad commenced in 1911, and in 1929 train service to Churchill began. The railroad was crucial for shipment of grain, from southern Manitoba and Saskatchewan, to grain elevators in Churchill. Even today, Churchill remains the northern most terminus for the railroad.

Three thousand men worked at a frantic pace to complete the 70,000-ton (2.5 million bushels) grain handling facility by 1931. The complex can load 60,000 bushels of grain an hour.

The confluence of four regions, creating four large and distinct habitats, explains the wealth of natural life in the Churchill area. The Churchill River lies to the north, the salty Hudson Bay to the east, and the tree line to the south and west. Since 1980, Churchill has become an internationally renowned center for wildlife research and ecotourism. It is one of the most easily accessible human habitats to view the Northern Lights, beluga whales, arctic and sub-arctic birds, and polar bears in the wild.

Of the world's 3200 mammal species, only 40 live in the Arctic, and nearly half of these are sea mammals. The Arctic seas are richer in nutrients than any other in the world. Salt water freezes at 28-29 degrees. Less then ten species of birds live year round in the Arctic, however, about 100 bird species breed there, but head south for the winter. Of the 30,000 species of fish less than 100 live in the northern seas.

There are no reptiles. By fall all Arctic life prepares for winter. Urged on by special hormones, birds feed incessantly to build fat reserves, for the long flight south. Ground squirrels, who have already doubled their weight, stock dens with a food supply. Arctic foxes also cache a winter's food supply. Caribou have produced one-fifth of their body weight as fat. Plants store lipids in their roots and rhizomes to await spring. Insects produce a glycerol-like anti-freeze, efficient enough to survive temperatures of 70 degrees below, and spend the winter in a suspended animation.

During bear season the live bear traps, placed around the perimeter of town, are checked every few hours. When a bear is caught, he is tranquilized and moved to polar bear jail, located just outside of town. Kept in jail until the bay freezes, he then is transported to the bay and released.

The bear jail is a large Quonset hut left from a SAC base located in Churchill during WW II. Jail can accommodate 27 bears, including several mothers and cubs.

The polar bear, a powerful symbol of the Arctic, is one of the most recognized animals in the world. He is superbly adaptable to one of the world's harshest environments. Its massive size makes a powerful and impressive physical presence.

Mid October each year, 600-1000 hungry polar bears mass along 100 miles of coast, stretching from Nelson to Churchill. It is the largest concentration of polar bears in the world. From 300 to 350 bears make their annual pilgrimage to the Churchill area, waiting for the bay to freeze over for their winter seal hunt.

Excitement was high when we were about to make our first buggy ride out onto the tundra. Both the federal and provincial governments strictly regulate the tundra. Two companies own the seventeen buggy permits to travel over the tundra. And even that is controlled, no running over the tundra like a wild off-road vehicle.

The tundra buggy could be best described as an oblong railroad car mounted on huge all-weather/terrain wheels/tires. Each seat has a large window, which opens easily for better photography. An outside viewing platform is at the rear. The buggy can travel the tundra, in fall and winter, over frozen ground and through snow, and in the summer over soggy terrain. The buggy travels two to three miles per hour on the tundra. The front tires hold six pounds of pressure, the rear nine pounds, and they average six miles per gallon of gasoline. The first tundra buggy was built in 1980.

When loading and unloading the buggy, the bus taking us to the staging area turns around, coming alongside, so its steps are directly opposite the steps of the buggy, requiring only one step on the ground. Transfers are quick. Polar bears can run 25 miles an hour, and who wants to meet one on ground level!

The buggy bounces over rock and the uneven tundra producing a rather rough ride. The buggies are heated, but everything is relative. Granted, a temperature of 40 is warmer than the outside temperature of 0-10, but when animals are spotted, everyone wants to open their window for the photo ops, and the inside temperature plummets rapidly, a minor inconvenience for the fantastic experience. The tundra is totally flat. In some areas scrub bushes grow two to three feet, but of course in winter they are just bare limbs.

The indigenous people, the Inuits, called the polar bear, the world's largest terrestrial carnivore, Nanook. The *King of the Arctic* is a gentle, ever caring mother, with an intense curiosity. Females weigh 500-700 pounds, and males from 1000-1500 pounds. Standing on its hind legs, some bears can reach a height of ten to twelve feet!

Clad in insulating fur and fat, the polar bear is able to sleep through blizzards, or plunge into near freezing arctic waters. The bear's three-layer coat consists of a big layer of fat topped by skin. A thick black under coat of dense fur traps heat. The top layer of fur consists of hollow guard hairs. Acting as a solar collector, these hollow hairs trap the warm rays of the direct sun, passing them onto the heat trapping under coat.

The four-inch outer coat appears from white to yellow, but in effect, its hollow hairs are actually transparent and reflect light. These hairs also add buoyancy when swimming, and the matting ability and oily texture allow the animal to shed water and ice from its body.

The animal's paws, large and rounded, give the bear the capability of flipping a 500-pound seal, from the water, with one swing of its paw! Each paw has five partially webbed claws that assist in swimming. He uses the front legs to propel himself, and his hind legs to stabilize and steer his direction. A strong swimmer, he is able to swim up to 60 miles before needing to rest. The footpads have a heavy fur coat, to protect against frostbite, but are rough enough to add traction on ice. On solid surfaces, the paws spread to distribute weight and act like a snowshoe, making the bear a master at negotiating over ice.

The long, tapered head has small ears and powerful jaws. The 42 teeth include long sharp canines, needed for piercing flesh. Their eyesight is rather poor, except under water, where they can see for 15 feet, when looking for food. They tend to be far sighted, which allows them to search large areas of their environment when feeding. Their hearing, through the small fur lined ears, is nearly equal to that of humans.

The polar bear has a phenomenal sense of smell, and it is said, he can smell a seal buried in a cave, under three feet of snow. The bear is often seen thrusting its nose in the air to utilize its keen sense of smell. The animal not only can smell through three feet of ice, but also for a distance of ten miles! On a clear day, through binoculars, its black nose can be seen from a distance of six miles!

The polar bear's liver, so rich in vitamin A, is toxic to humans. The bears are also susceptible to a parasitic worm that is apparently contracted from eating infected seals. A grown bear's stomach will allow him to consume 150 pounds of food at one time! However, on average, a seal eaten every five days adequately sustains a bear. Summer produces slim pickings for food, and the bear pretty much subsists on its own fat. A polar bear can eat ten percent of its body weight in 30 minutes! The animals have well developed, strong hind leg and neck muscles. In spite of their size, they are agile in the water.

The normal walking gait of the bear is two and a half miles an hour, but it is possible for him to run 25 miles an hour.

We spent the better part of each day out on the tundra. Hot coffee, tea, and cocoa were always available. A favorite drink was tundracinno. Using instant coffee and cocoa the drink is a mixture of three measures coca to one of coffee. It was really tasty and one I occasionally drink at home. The guide toted box lunches, so we could stave off the "hungries" and continue riding over the tundra.

Every day we saw many polar bears, mama with cubs, and big papas. We watched cubs stand on their hind legs and spar—sort of a boxing to strengthen their hind leg and neck muscles and to increase their stamina. It all is in fun for the cubs, but some day as adults could turn into a bloody battle.

The bears came right up to the buggy, sniff around, and often get up on their hind legs for a better look. Up close one realizes just how big these animals are! We never tired of watching them. We saw a few arctic foxes scampering over the tundra.

A pair of polar bears remains together for a week during the mating season of April—May. Courtship and mating takes place on the ice. Polar bears are induced ovulators, meaning that they do not ovulate regularly, but the mating ritual stimulates ovulation.

Gestation is eight months. Mothers normally have twins, but can deliver one or up to four cubs. Mother generally gets pregnant every three years. Mother's milk, thick like condensed milk, is 40 percent fat. Mom can double her weight during pregnancy. Cubs are born between November and February and nurse for five months, during which time mama does not hunt or feed, but stays in the den with her babies.

Cubs look like rats at birth weighing only one to two pounds. They are born hairless, blind, deaf, and helpless. At one month the cubs crawl, at six weeks open their eyes, and by ten weeks, they can keep their balance. By the time they emerge from the den at five months, they generally weigh 29 pounds. They are mature at four to five years. The life span of a polar bear is usually 15-18 years, but can reach 30 years. Mothers with cubs are solitary. Polar bears are very good moms. It is not uncommon for her to run off a male, twice her size to protect her cubs.

The size of the den is approximately 6 x 10 x 4 feet, and the temperature is 40 degrees warmer than the outside air, making it a cozy little home.

The only enemy of an adult polar bear is the human.

Although cold, the weather was clear every day. One evening the sky dropped a few snow flurries on Churchill, and another evening a couple of inches of fresh snow fell. That was my quota of snow for the next ten years!

For the visitor the polar bears are a delight during a desolate winter on the dreary tundra. But after the dark harsh winter comes spring and the tundra turns vibrant with life when colorful wild flowers blanket the ground.

Chapter 11

Poland

Local maps site Warsaw as Warszawa, and that is all the Polish I know. Since it's a difficult language that's all I'll ever know.

Our Hotel, built in 1857, totally refurbished in 1962, was centrally located. Beautiful marble floors, walls, and staircase were in the lobby. Our large room was comfortable.

It was a total surprise to find soap, shampoo, shower caps, and tissues in the bathroom. We were delighted to find the TP was just like ours, not the brown cardboard kind we've lived with in other European countries! The room even had a fully stocked fridge. We were livin'! The hotel, on the edge of central Warsaw, was very quiet.

Advised not to drink the water from the tap, we put off wandering the neighborhood for bottled water until the next day because of rain showers.

We were bused to Old Town for dinner. Because no buses were allowed in Old Town we had a bit of a walk to the restaurant.

Our hotel served an excellent breakfast buffet, but all of our other meals were eaten in various restaurants around town. One morning our tablemate was a fellow from Ukraine, who was in Warsaw for a technological conference. He told us many people stay at the hotel just because of the breakfast buffet.

Our guide knew her spiel well, and we learned quickly that she was rather unresponsive to questions or deviations from her routine. She was like a Drill Sergeant, getting us from here to there, even if we wanted a bit more time somewhere. She was used to handling large tour groups, and although the year was 2000, she was not familiar with the Elderhostel concept or inquisitive seniors.

The first day we went to the art museum for a lecture. In a gorgeous baroque room, Mr. Kindler from the University of Technology told us that Warsaw, located in central Poland on the Wisla (Vistula) River, was the largest city as well as the capitol of Poland. The winged mermaid, Syrena, wields a sword and shield, standing proud as the symbol of Warsaw. Forty million people live in the country, two million in the city.

In 1945, Poland came under U.S.S.R. rule and everything was centralized. By 1949-50 the private sector in Poland totally disappeared. Farms over 100 acres were taken by the state. There were a series of uprisings, and in 1956 when there was much hunger the peasants' uprising resulted in 80 percent of the nation's farms remaining in private hands. Today 27 percent of the labor force works in agriculture, and agriculture remains the biggest hurdle for the country joining the European Union. The unemployment rate was 13 percent.

Poland, about the size of New Mexico, is the largest country in Eastern Europe, both in area and population. However, there are several opinions on what countries make up Eastern Europe. Some think it extends a bit west which would include Ukraine, which certainly is the largest country in the area. Others consider Poland, Czech Republic, and Hungary as being in Eastern Europe, and still others refer to the area as Central/Eastern Europe. In any case, Poland certainly is larger than either the Czech Republic or Hungary.

The country has an extensive and turbulent history. Poland was wiped off the map of Europe for 123 years, in 1795. The Treaty of Versailles in 1918 re-established the Polish State.

The Germans completely overran Poland during WW II.

Between 1950-1989 there was much unrest in the country. 1980 saw the formation of the Solidarity Movement.

A French writer once said, *if you're going to be eaten, at least don't be digestible.* Many years later Stalin remarked that fitting communism into Poland was like putting a saddle on a cow.

In '88-89 there were roundtable talks between the Solidarity and government. In the elections of '89 Solidarity made a clean sweep. The economy was terrible, store shelves were empty, and salaries were low. In 1989 the International Monetary Fund backed the Zloty (Polish currency) to the dollar wiping out the black market. Slowly private industry was reintroduced. Free press, which is essential for success, didn't come to Poland until 1989.

Now 75 percent of industry is in the private sector. The U.S. was one of the first countries to invest in Poland. Communism eliminated any competition so quality was something that had to be learned.

Poland has multi parties now, and a parliamentary democracy with two houses and independent courts. Inflation is down to ten percent from 400 percent! Universal healthcare is not very good, primarily due to budgetary constraints. One-third of the country's general budget goes into pensions that women can collect at 60 and men at 65.

We visited two beautiful palaces while in Warsaw. Both involved long tours with docents who were very knowledgeable, but determined to tell us *every* single detail they knew about each monarch as we stood in a circle in front of his/her portrait.

Beautiful gardens and a landscaped park surrounded the Wilanow Palace. The other palace we visited was the beautiful baroque Royal Castle. In 1596 King Sigismund III Waza chose the castle as the royal residence when the capitol of Poland was moved from Krakow to Warsaw. The Germans deliberately razed the castle during WWII. It has taken many years to painstakingly rebuild.

Warsaw has many parks and lots of tree lined streets. Because

Germans occupied the buildings on Royal Road, that was the only part of the city that escaped bombings and destruction. Now most of these palaces are museums or foreign embassies.

We all gasped when we saw the U.S. embassy. It has got to be the ugliest embassy we have anywhere in the world! (The most beautiful is in Canberra, Australia)

Since eighty-five percent of Warsaw was leveled during WWII, I was amazed at what I saw when we got to Old Town, the historic part of the city. It had all been rebuilt following many of the buildings' original plans.

If I didn't know those buildings were built in the 50s and 60s, I'd have thought that they'd been standing for a couple of centuries. It's positively amazing how the Poles have rebuilt the city!

Late in the afternoon we walked down to a local store to buy bottled water in large containers. We also bought a bottle of wine.

It took both of us to open the wine. I should have packed my other corkscrew. The one on my Swiss Army knife just didn't cut it. I was afraid of ruining the cork.

It was a struggle, but with each of us pulling in a different direction, we eventually popped the cork. And our $2.50 (equivalent U.S.) wine wasn't too bad.

One evening when it wasn't raining we decided to go for a walk. The huge city park was only a block from the hotel. Heading back to the hotel we saw three guards marching. We stopped to watch the changing of the guard at the Tomb of the Unknown Soldier. How lucky!

The highlight of our time in Warsaw was the Chopin piano concert at the Szuster Palace one evening. A private concert just for us, it was excellent. Several of us bought CDs of the artist playing, and I have enjoyed listening to mine many times while I'm working on the computer.

A history professor gave us an excellent history of the country but I won't elaborate on the extensive ancient history.

WWII began with the bombing of the trading town of Danzig (Gdansk). In September, 1939, Warsaw was the recipient of the first German air attack on any *majo*r city. The German army captured the city that same month and the city became the headquarters for the German occupation authorities.

During WW II the Nazis systemically destroyed the city and killed nearly a million residents, including most of the Jews in the infamous Warsaw Ghetto. Warsaw was literally leveled to the ground. The city suffered more devastation and loss of life than any other European city. In spite of this, the Polish underground was centered in the city.

Defies the Storm, the city's motto, reflects the determined and indomitable spirit of the people of Warsaw.

The city was occupied, overrun, and sacked by foreigners over 900 years. The earliest conquerors were the Russians and Swedes, then came Napoleon, and in the 19th century the Prussians.

Five years of Nazi occupation triggered many acts of armed resistance. During the Warsaw Uprising of 1944, more than 250,000 Poles were slaughtered by the Germans in 63 days. After the uprising the Germans killed or deported the remaining population.

Then German demolition teams leveled Warsaw street by street. Six million Poles, a fifth of the population, died during WWII; 85 percent of Warsaw's buildings were destroyed.

Soviet and Polish troops finally liberated the city in January 1945. Only 162,000 people survived the war, mostly living in the western suburbs and east of the river. Soon after the war the new Communist-controlled government established itself in Warsaw.

A series of reforms were introduced in the mid fifties to reduce Soviet domination. A reckless program of industrial expansion left the country bankrupt after ten years. In 1980, strikes over escalating food prices forced out the leader, Gierek, and brought the emergence of Lech Walsea's Solidarity union. In 1981 martial law was declared and Solidarity leaders and activists imprisoned. The courts dissolved Solidarity in 1982 and martial law was lifted in mid 1983. In 1987 Poles cast a vote of no confidence in the communist government and the underground Solidarity movement issued fresh strikes. The sweeping Solidarity victories in 1989 caused the communist coalition to collapse.

In 1990 the government adopted an economic program to switch from a planned to a free-market economy. Price and currency controls were removed. Late that year Walsea was elected president.

The film, *Warsaw Remains*, brought tears to our eyes. The destruction of the city is almost impossible to comprehend. I vowed then to never listen to another Polish joke. It's unbelievable the pain, hardship, loss, and suffering the Poles have suffered.

Over three million Jews lived in Poland before WWII, now there are but 5-12,000 Jews living in the entire country.

At the beginning of WWII the Warsaw Jewish Ghetto was home to 400,000 Jews. In 1941 the Germans built a wall around the Ghetto. Slowly the Jews were removed and sent to concentration camps. The Ghetto Uprising of 1943 totally leveled the Ghetto.

In the 50s and 60s apartment complexes were built in the area and except for the monuments, there is little left to remind one of the horrors that went on there. The wall, except for a few feet by the Ghetto Heroes Monument, is gone.

On the way to Krakow we stopped at Czestochowa to visit the Jasna Gora Monastery where the Black Madonna is housed. Pilgrimages to this area to see the painting, located in the monastery, date back to the 14th century.

Today four to five million people make the pilgrimage each year.

Talk about crowds! Fortunately we had a knowledgeable guide who wound us through back halls to a back entrance to an excellent viewing area.

Krakow, or Cracow, was Poland's capitol until 1596, and

today is a city of 800,000. Poland's third largest city is in the southern part of the country. Founded as a fortress in 700 AD, it became the capitol in the 12th century. In 1815 Krakow was the capitol of the independent republic of Krakow, which was incorporated into Austria in 1846. During WW I the city was the scene of fighting between Austro-German and Russian forces. After the war Krakow was once again a Polish city. Germans occupied the city from 1939-1945 when it was taken by Soviet troops.

This cultural, educational, and industrial city is also located on the Wisla (Vistula) River. This architecturally and historically rich city is compact within an area of Old Town that is only 800 meters by 1200 meters in size.

In January 1945 the Soviet army forced the Germans to evacuate Krakow, thus saving the city from destruction. Much of its old architecture is preserved intact.

Old Town, or the inner city, was surrounded by a wall in medieval times, as were most European cities. The Barbican, built in the 15th century was to protect the walled city, and is one of the largest and oldest remaining in Europe.

Only one of the original seven gates remains. Originally the wall had 47 towers. The moat was twenty meters wide and seven meters deep.

In the 20th century the moat was filled in and now forms a green ring around the inner city.

The 13th century market square measures 200 meters on each side, and is the largest such square in Europe. St. Andrews, an 11th century church, is the oldest in the square. There are 130 churches in Krakow, 75 of them are in Old Town.

St. Mary's gothic church, 1359, the common people's church, sits on one corner of the square, and has two uneven towers. The tallest tower served as a look out tower. Today every hour, on the hour, one can hear a trumpet call from the tower recalling the 13th century trumpeter who was killed by a Tarter arrow in the middle of sounding a warning.

Jagiellonian University, the first university in Poland, founded in 1364, was the alma mater of the astronomer, Copernicus. The building where he studied is still in use, and has a rather pretty inner courtyard.

The royal cathedral and castle sit on Wawel Hill. For centuries, since the first king crowned in 1320, Wawel Cathedral, has been the site of coronations and burials for Polish royalty. A hundred kings are interred in the crypt

Wawel Castle sits behind the cathedral, most famous now for its collection of Flemish tapestries. One hundred thirty-six of the original 156 have been preserved, and is the largest such collection in the world. During WWII the tapestries were sent to Canada for safekeeping and returned in 1961. The work is so fine that it would take a worker one year to complete a square meter! They were specially ordered, and reach from floor to ceiling.

There was little furniture in the castle. The ceilings were beautiful, as were the wall frescos.

The courtyard of the castle had been recently refurbished. The first floor of the castle served as servants' quarters, the second floor as reception rooms, and the third floor was royal living quarters. Originally built as a fortress, it then became a summer home, and now is a museum.

One evening returning to the hotel there was a woman in the lobby with a table of goods. Wandering over for a look-see I spied a gorgeous wool sweater. The weather had been pretty chilly, and besides I couldn't resist the $10-$15 price tag! She accepted U.S. bills. Several of us bought sweaters, and I remarked that now we had warm sweaters, the weather would turn warm. Murphy's law prevailed, and I never did wear that sweater because it did turn warm!

In Krakow we visited the Jewish District, Kazimierz, which before the 1820s was an independent town. In the late 15th century, Jews, after being expelled from Krakow, migrated to the northeast area of the town. A wall separated the Jewish sector from the Christian sector. The Jewish Quarter grew rapidly as Jews fled from all over Europe.

At the outbreak of WWII 70,000 Jews were living there. The current Jewish population is about 100. Six synagogues were in the area. The 15th century Old Synagogue is the oldest Jewish religious building in Poland, and today is a museum. Two other synagogues remain today, but only one is functional.

In 1993 the Center for Jewish Culture and History, opened in the area, and is run by non-Jews. Because it cannot be state run, it is run by a private foundation. Kazimierz is one of the best preserved pre-WWII areas of Jewish religious, learning, and culture, a life no longer possible in Poland because of the lack of facilities.

Prior to the opening of the Center, there was no research or books to teach Jewish culture. In 1986 the U.S. Congress sent two million dollars to help create the project. Those funds paid for 90 percent of the project and the remaining ten percent came from local contributions. The main building needed much repair and restoration. The project is not complete, as they still want to add an office building and build a hotel.

As unbelievable as it seems, we were told that 95 percent of Poles have little knowledge of or interaction with Jews.

Schindler's factory, made famous by the movie *Schindler's List,* is still in existence and functioning as the Telpod Electrical Works. It is a popular tourist stop, and we were no exception.

A visit to Auschwitz was a grim and sobering experience. It was strange indeed to walk under the infamous black arch with the German words *Arbeit Macht Frei* (Work will set you free). All visitors are guided through the concentration camp by a docent.

The majority of people walking under this arch in the early 40s found their freedom in death at the gas chambers.

Auschwitz was the largest Nazi death factory, and actually was a complex of camps where four million Jews were exterminated. The largest unit was Birkenau.

The camp held 13-16,000 people at a time. Women were at Auschwitz for only a few months, then the camp became a work camp for men, and women were housed at Birkenau.

Auschwitz covered 14 acres and had four crematoriums where a million and a half people perished. Seven hundred could be gassed at one time. The record was 20,000 during one 24-hour period. However, the chambers were not used after 1943 as they were considered to be too small!

Birkenau covered 400 acres, had 300 barracks, and held 100,000 prisoners. Three barracks were set aside as latrines that were only long rows of holes, side by side. There was no privacy, soap, or toilet paper. Prisoners were allowed two minutes in the latrine at specified times. Educated and professional people were forced to clean the troughs in the latrines.

Smokestacks of the crematories now stand row after row on the landscape. Of the 200,000 children taken to the camps, only 600 survived, most of them twins who were used for medical experiments. Of the 700 babies born, only 14 survived.

People died at Auschwitz several ways other than the gas chamber. Many died of illness, starvation, suffocation, and many were simply shot in the courtyard between two barracks.

Some of the barracks have been turned into a museum—one like no other. A coldness invades your whole being as you study the many floor to ceiling glass showcases, the length of an entire wall, each with a different display. Mounds of eyeglasses are in one; another is filled with worn shoes; still another is filled with toothbrushes, razors, and shaving brushes that people mistakenly thought they would need.

The huge display of worn suitcases with names and birth dates neatly marked on the front of each put a knot in my stomach. One showcase, the entire length of the wall, was filled with some of the *seven tons* of human hair found when the camp was liberated. I was puzzled that all the hair was gray until the docent explained, that the hair was not cut, until after the visit to the gas chamber, and the gas removed all the color. It was a most sobering visit!

The communists built an industrial suburb around a large steelworks about five miles east of Krakow's historic center. Huge emissions from the steel plant have damaged the city's monuments. A restructuring program is underway to cut pollution, and restoration of historical monuments has begun.

Warsaw is the political capitol of Poland; Krakow, the cultural capitol.

Another day we drove from Krakow to Wieliczka to explore the famous salt mine. We descended nine levels to 1100 feet below ground. Rock salt was discovered here at the end of the 13th century.

The 700-year-old mine has 200 miles of tunnel. An elevator took us down three levels, which left us with only 420 steps to navigate. There are many small rooms holding salt sculptures, but the highlight was the Chapel of the Blessed Kings, which really is a fair sized church measuring 1755 X 55 feet with a 39-foot-high ceiling.

Everything in the room, chandeliers, altarpieces, showcases, and sculptures are carved from salt. 20,000 tons of salts were removed over a 30-year period! (1895-1927). When this masterpiece was completed in 1964, 70 years had lapsed from start to finish. Even the floor looked like flagstone. The salt statue of Pope Paul was a very good likeness.

I had no problem even though claustrophobic, because it was so big. It was an amazing visit!

En route to Lowicz, we stopped in Nieborow to tour the Radziwill family residence. One of the family members, an artist, had many of her paintings on display. We also saw many sculptures displayed throughout the home.

The designer was Dutch, but it still was a surprise to see Delft tiles covering the wall of the curved staircase, and they looked like beautiful wallpaper. The self-guided tour allowed us to tour at our own pace.

The house sat on what appeared to be an isolated area in the rural countryside. The house wasn't all that big in comparison to what we'd been seeing.

Nuns from a Bernardine Monastery served us a delicious soup lunch that day on our way to Lowicz. They prepare and serve lunch to several poor people every day. The nuns were so sweet. When we left they serenaded us with their lovely voices. It was a different and delightful stop.

The next stop was at the Lowicz Castle ruins, where musicians and dancers performed for us. Another delight!

During the performance a woman and a young girl were doing some paper cutting. Later we learned the shears they used were the kind used to shear sheep. What a lot of patience it must take to cut such beautiful delicate patterns and designs. This folk art is unique to that area of Poland. The finished pieces sold for six to ten Zlotys, the equivalent of $2-$3 U.S.

When I arrived home I framed my cutting and every time I pass by it I see the image of that woman and little girl sitting at a table with their big shears cutting colored paper.

The last stop of the day was at Chopin's home, Zelazowa Wola, located on the Utrata River. The home, now a museum, is small and surrounded by a park and gardens. Different countries donated many of the plants in the gardens. After touring the small house we strolled through the lovely gardens.

We had seen a lot of Poland, had excellent lectures, and learned a great deal during our ten days in the country. The country was very clean. It was much more fascinating than we had expected and such a pleasant surprise.

Chapter 12

Prague

Many people think Prague, or locally Praha, is the most beautiful city in the world. I do not find much fault with that. The city is considered a living museum, and an architectural treasure. Prague is a beautiful city full of fairy-tale, castles, manors, and museums. Strolling among the long stone palaces, it felt as though I had stepped back in time

It was nearly an all day trip from Krakow to Prague. Our 35-room hotel was homey and friendly. The friendly atmosphere made it our favorite hotel of the trip. Located in a residential area of Prague, the hotel had no porters so we were glad we had packed light, as there also was no elevator. Not an unusual situation in small European hotels.

The hotel, built in 1910, was once the home of the owner's grandmother. During the Communist regime the house was taken, and she was allowed to remain in a small two-room apartment. When freed from the Communist bloc, the family put in for restitution of the house.

Unfortunately the grandmother died in 1985. The hotel has been restored one floor at a time. In the beginning there were as many employees as there were rooms. That wasn't very profitable, and today there is a much better ratio.

In Prague we quickly learned it stayed light until after 9:00 PM and was light at four in the morning.

Here all our lectures were in the lecture room of the hotel.

Most were three hours with a coffee break halfway. The lecturers were so interesting we had no problem with the length.

The Czech Republic, made up of Bohemia, Moravia, and Silesia, is one of Europe's most historic countries. The 78,864 square kilometers of the Czech Republic are landlocked between Germany, Austria, Slovakia, and Poland. In spite of previous heavy felling of the forest, about one-third of the country is still forested, mostly with spruce trees.

However, the forest of northern Bohemia has been heavily damaged by acid rain, the result of burning low-grade brown coal. Factories and thermal power units expel millions of tons of sulfur dioxide and carbon monoxide into the countryside creating a serious environmental problem.

Our city tour was broken up into four days, with Lenika, our city guide, covering a different section of the city each day.

Lenika was a delightful, animated young woman who mixed historical facts with charming old fables and expressions such as, *Prague is pregnant with history*, and it surely is!

Prague, a city of nearly a million-and-half inhabitants, is built on seven hills and on two banks of the Vltava River. The city's 500 square kilometers is divided into 23 districts.

Prague is the largest city as well as capitol of the Czech Republic. It also is the center of much of the country's cultural and intellectual life. Prague University, established 1348 by Charles IV, is the oldest in Central Europe. Besides being the cultural capitol of the country, Prague also is the main commercial and industrial center enjoying a low unemployment rate.

Often called *the city of one hundred spires,* the town of 'stone and limestone', dating back to 965, is one of the reasons UNESCO put Prague on its World Heritage list. The Gothic architecture dates to the Roman Emperor, Charles IV. The Habsburg era is credited with the baroque designs.

In spite of being occupied by German forces during WW II the Czech capitol escaped major damage.

The river Vltava runs through the center of the city in the general shape of a question mark. Eighteen bridges span the river, separating Mala Strana (Lesser Town) from Stare Mesto (Old Town). Lesser Town, on the west bank, has the baroque homes of aristocrats, while 13th century Gothic Old Town sits on the eastern bank. Lesser Town, established in 1235, was the home of the workers and craftsmen. It burned in the 16th century and was rebuilt in the 17th and 18th centuries.

The crooked streets of 11th century Old Town wind around ancient Bohemian architectural relics.

Old Town Square is the oldest in Europe. Staromestska Radnice, 1338, (Old Town Hall) is now used only for ceremonial purposes. There is a spiral staircase to the top of the tower which one can climb.

On the front of the Old Town Hall is the astronomical clock. The 1410 clock, restored in the 19th century with a new calendar panel, chimes every hour on the hour from 9 AM to 9 PM. At that time a window opens and the apostles move by the window. The miser moves, saying *spend your money, enjoy life, and have fun.* The fellow looking in the mirror (vanity) says *he who spends time before a mirror has a poor life, he who helps others has a rich life.* The skeleton says, *Enjoy life, it is short. Life now is better than under the Turks. I don't have you now, but I will.*

The clock also shows the years, months, days, and hours, the rising and setting of the sun, east and west, the moon and the signs of the Zodiac.

It was worth standing in the huge crowd to watch the clock chime. It was an interesting and fascinating clock.

Cathedral of Our Lady of Tyn dates to the 14th century. By the end of the ninth century, churches were the first buildings to be made of stone. Wood and earth in castles was not replaced with stone until two centuries later!

Charles IV, whose mom was Czech, dominates the city, and is credited with transforming Prague into a modern city.

Tower gateways flank each end of the stone Charles Bridge, which connects Old Town, and Lesser Town. The most famous of the bridges spanning the Vltava River is nearly 1700 feet long, has sixteen arches, and sports thirty sculptures from the 17th century, one on each of its supports.

The present bridge is the third. A flood destroyed the first wooden bridge; the second of 12th century stone (Judith Bridge) was destroyed by a flood. The present bridge was built in 1357, after consulting an astronomer. It has been called Charles Bridge since 1870.

The pedestrian bridge is an art and crafts gallery, and is crowded at all hours of the day. We crossed this bridge many times concentrating on something different each time, one time the art, another time the statues, and then of course just to cross over the river.

One of the statues on the bridge has *Holy, Holy, Holy* written in Hebrew and in gold. It seems a Jew who mocked the Christian church was made to pay for that statue.

On the Old Town end of the bridge is Charles Square with a larger than life statue of Charles IV in the center. Surrounding Charles Square is the Jesuit complex.

New Town, built around Old Town, was founded in 1348. New Town basically is the industrial and commercial section containing public buildings, banks, and museums.

Wallenstein Palace, 1630, now houses the Senate of the Czech Republic. One day while shopping and sight seeing on our own we stopped to walk through the 1623 French Baroque gardens. The cut and trimmed shrubs with statues and fountains proved a pleasant respite from the hubbub of the city. An artificial grotto/cave was typical of such gardens, but I thought the weird wall was a bit strange.

North of Lesser Town is Hradcany Square, the medieval castle district where royalty once lived. It was founded as a *town* in the 870. Bohemia was founded as a *state*.

Prague Castle is visible from almost everywhere in the city. Covering an area of 50 hectares it was under continuous construction for 500 years. Originally built as a fortification with a moat and small church, it has been enlarged each century, and as a result sports five different architectural styles, one for each century.

Now the palace houses an art gallery, and the president has offices on the second floor. Ninth century ruins can be seen from a viewing area in the courtyard.

The moats around the castle were leveled in 1757, under the reign of Maria Theresa, and now are the site of one of the castle squares.

Vladislav Hall, 1501, with a large wooden plank floor has had several uses over the years. Horse shows were once held there. Later, it was a market place. During the Roman era the hall was enhanced, and now concerts are held there.

One of the most striking rooms in the palace was the old parliament room, complete with red velvet chairs.

St. Wenceslas is the patron saint of Czech lands. His chapel, 1344-64, demonstrates Bohemian art, with the lower parts of the walls inlaid with semi-precious stones.

Prince Wenceslas I established St. Vitus Cathedral in 1344 where Bohemian kings were crowned and buried. The structure stands on the site of two previous churches.

The two towers of St. Vitus are 266 feet high. The bronze doors portray the history of the building. The stained glass Rose Window illustrates various days of creation of the world.

According to legend, in the 3rd century the upbringing of a 17-year old boy was delegated to a nanny because his parents were too busy. The nanny accepted Christianity and the boy followed. The angry powers to be had the boy thrown into a pot of boiling oil, but he survived, thus the expression St Vitus dance.

Outside Prague Castle is narrow 16th century Golden Lane. The tiny houses were originally built into the castle walls for gunners' for defense, later for tradesmen and craftsmen. Now, the lane is lined with artists and crafts people hawking their wares. Walking down the steps my friend saw a painting that took her eye, but we did not have time for her to stop and buy it. On another day we returned, and walked up the stairs 'til she found her painting.

Wenceslas Square was a horse market in medieval times, but now is just about in the center of the city, and is comparable to our Times Square in importance. It is a huge pedestrian walkway lined with stores. The center contains statues and gardens as well as crossovers.

In 1918 the square was the site of celebration of the formation of Czechoslovakia. In 1968 Russian tanks roared through the square. In 1969 university student, Jan Palack, set himself on fire in protest. Just before being freed from the Communist Soviet Bloc in 1989, it was the site of many demonstrations.

The Strahov area is a large complex that includes a monastery (1142), Abbey, cloisters and the Church of Our Lady, which has been rebuilt several times. The church has eight bells. The largest palace in the country, built in 1691, and restored in the 19th century also is in the area, and now the home of the foreign minister.

Jews were free until the 13th century, when they were confined to the Ghetto until the 18th century. Men wore a yellow hat, women a yellow scarf, and armbands were worn until the 16th century.

Street paving and general improvements were made to the Ghetto in the 16th century. Six synagogues were in the area.

Maisel Synagogue was a private synagogue built by a wealthy man in 1592. A 1689 fire caused much damage. It was rebuilt in a smaller version in neo-gothic style in 1892-1905. During WWII the synagogue was a storage area for gold and other treasures. Inside what looked like stripped wallpaper turned out to be the names of 80,000 Jews who were exterminated during the holocaust!

Names were in red, those from Prague were designated with a yellow star, and a whole family was printed in black. There was way too much black. It took four years to accomplish the writing of the names. Looking at that wall was sobering!

Behind the synagogue was a small Jewish cemetery which was used until 1787. The oldest stone was dated 1439, and in some areas, there were twelve layers of graves. As bodies disintegrated, the ground sank, and in time dirt was hauled in so another body could be placed on top.

Eventually there were five layers of bodies. As the weather loosened stones, they floated on top of one another. Now the cemetery is just a mass of jumbled stones.

Also in the city is the oldest synagogue, built in 1270, which is orthodox, and The Pinkas Synagogue, 1519-35, now a museum.

Forty thousand Jews were taken from Prague, with only 1000 returning after the war. But instead of returning to the Ghetto, they settled in other neighborhoods. The present Jewish population in Prague is under 2000.

Located in the ghetto is an interesting clock with the numbers in Hebrew, but the hands go counter clockwise. The maker was just following the fact that Hebrew is read from right to left.

In the course of our visit we each bought a couple of bus tickets for 8 Krons with the intent of using them to get back to the hotel after doing the town on our own. However, we always ended up walking and never used the tickets, so the last day we gave the tickets to the floor maid.

Early in the week, we took a private dinner cruise on the Vltava River. We enjoyed a scrumptious buffet style dinner.

The evening started off with a local apéritif. A little fellow played accordion music for us *all* evening long. He never stopped playing, not even to take a break. It was a lovely evening so several of us decided to have after dinner coffee and tea on the upper deck under the canopy.

The lights of the city were glorious as we cruised beneath the beautiful Charles Bridge back to the pier.

Bertramka is a Mozart museum where we had an opportunity

to wander through the museum before attending a private concert by a string quartet. The concert was positively delightful.

Afterward we gathered outside on the manicured lawn to partake of some champagne. I whispered that I'd had better champagne, and then proceeded to water the lawn!

The docent informed us that a rich man from Lesser Town built Bertramka in 1743. The home had gone through many owners, but it always had been a summer home.

Mozart visited in 1787 writing Don Giovanni on the table on the hill behind us. Mozart's last visit was in August 1791. He then returned to Vienna where he died four months later.

The grounds were beautiful. I *had* to climb that hill and touch that table, but it was much more of a hike than it looked to be! Afterward we had a wonderful dinner there in the restaurant.

One day involved an all day excursion to Karlstejn. En route we stopped in Bohemia at Nizbor to visit a glass factory.

The tour was somewhat rushed, but it didn't matter as it was pretty noisy and dusty inside the factory, making it difficult to hear what the docent said.

Beautiful cut crystal was in the factory store. Unfortunately they didn't ship. Buying anything was a bit of a hassle, as there were only two girls and there were throngs of people wanting to buy.

Arriving in Karlstejn about noon we all headed off to have lunch on that beautiful sunny day. We chose a sidewalk restaurant, and during lunch watched a bridal party arrive by horse-drawn carriage.

A Gothic castle, built 1348-1358 and restored at the end of the 16th and 19th centuries, sat on top of the hill.

It was fun wandering through the many shops where we did a wee bit of shopping.

While in Prague we had fun and interesting evenings.
One evening we attended an outdoor performance of La Traviata. It was a rather modern rendition, but very good. We had good seats

and we enjoyed it. It was a lovely warm evening to be outside.

Another evening we went to a marionette show of Don Giovanni. I couldn't imagine how this might be done, but it was quite an interesting performance. The good-sized marionettes were bigger than any I'd ever seen and the evening provided a lot of laughs.

The folkloric show we attended was outstanding. It was fast moving, and the evening was over before we knew it. The dancers were good. It was truly a fun evening.

The *cimbalom,* a copper-stringed dulcimer of Middle Eastern origin, is the center of Moravian folk orchestras. The polka is said to have originated in Bohemia. It became popular worldwide in 1843 when it was introduced in Paris.

Older folks in the Czech Republic understand and speak German. Everyone learned Russian in school during the last century. Russian has now been replaced with English. The Czech language is not easy to learn or to understand.

The Czechs were friendly, and cultured people. Because of their history they are a tolerant people and are not fanatical about much of anything.

The Czechs hated the Communist Regime, but managed to live with it. They were able to feed themselves, not always with a variety of foods, but they were able to eat.

Many learned English on their own, which to me is always an amazing feat.

Prague is a beautiful city, but unfortunately creating graffiti seemed a booming pastime of the young. Sadly, it marred the wonderful views and scenes everywhere. None of us felt any of the graffiti was "art." We tried to keep our eyes skyward to enjoy the "one hundred spires."

Our historian lecturer told us, "We thank *Imperial America* for the broadcasts of Voice of America, Radio Free Europe, and Radio London. In spite of risking punishment of death if we listened to such broadcasts, we did so anyway, and I and my countrymen thank you."

His gratitude sent shivers down my spine. It had been a wonderful, enlightening week in Prague.

Chapter 13

Budapest

Boxes for rabbits, as our Prague guide had called the concrete boxcar apartments, were all we could see as we approached Bratislava, Slovakia's capitol. They certainly are an ugly blight on the landscape, even if they were a quick solution to fill a need when built.

What was once Czechoslovakia is now the two separate countries of Czech Republic and Slovakia. Approaching western Slovakia the terrain flattened considerably.

A few miles out of Budapest the terrain turned hilly again. Passing acres and acres of wild flowers and corn, it was explained that the corn was grown for cow feed. Sunflowers were cultivated as a crop and we saw fields and fields of them.

The hotel in Budapest was on a rather narrow street with cars parked on both sides. The bus driver *backed* down the street with about an inch to spare on each side. I couldn't believe it!

Zsuzsa (shoo sha) welcomed us to Budapest, and it was a tearful good by to our wonderful Prague guide and driver.

This hotel had about five floors and one small elevator. Almost always we walked the four flights up to our room rationalizing the exercise was good for us, and that we could make it as fast as the elevator, which we most often did. After seeing our huge room with a large closet, it was obvious we would be living in comfort. Checking the bathroom we were again in the land of cardboard TP. Literature had suggested packing TP, so since we had not used it to this point, now was the time. I was not carrying home TP that had been all over Eastern Europe!

Entering the dining room we were handed an apéritif glass. Zsuzsa explained, "This is called *puszta*, and is used to greet a friend. Often made at home, it is made with white Tokay wine, apricot brandy, and bitters. Welcome to Budapest." We all raised our glasses. What a delightful way to start the week!

The tables were set with three napkins, in red, white, and green, folded to resemble the Hungarian flag. We were told that while in Hungary, we would be eating typical Hungarian food, in the belief that food is part of the total experience when visiting a country. We agreed!

All lectures were held in a down stairs classroom. Public transportation trams, buses, and subways were all efficient and reasonable and were used when moving about the city.

Tickets were 95 forints each, and for our personal use, tickets were in the classroom for when we might need them. The same ticket was used on any mode of transportation, but a second ticket was needed when transferring from one to another.

In the better stores a credit card could be used for substantial purchases, otherwise it was basically a cash society. With one U.S. dollar equaling 275-280 forints, it was a bit of a challenge coping with the conversion.

A city guide told us Budapest, sometimes called the Pearl of the Danube, sits on a hundred natural hot springs, which bubble up into the city in several areas. In 1873 the three cities of Buda, Pest, and Obuda (old Buda) united as Budapest.

Budapest, the economic center of the country, is an unpretentious city geographically and culturally. The Danube River, a quarter mile wide, runs through the city separating the banks of Buda and Pest.

Most historic sights are at or near the river. Buda is a hilly area, with Janos Hill, 1710 feet, the highest point, whereas Pest is a flat plain. One third of the population lives in Buda, and two-thirds in Pest. With a city population of 2.1 million, twenty percent of the country's 10.5 million people live in Budapest.

The city boasts 237 historical monuments, 223 museums and galleries, 40 theaters, seven concert halls, and 200 places of entertainment with a wide variety of choices.

Our guide continued, "History has not spared the city, but it has not destroyed it."

Pest is the commercial and administrative center for not only Budapest but the entire country.

The 500,000 Gypsies are the largest minority population. Other minorities include Germans, Slovaks, Serbs, Croats, Jews, and Romanians. Because the Hungarian borders have changed often, five million ethnic Hungarians find themselves living in neighboring countries, without ever moving! At various times Hungary included Transylvania, Croatia, part of Slovakia, part of Ukraine, and Romania.

All major highways radiate from Budapest like the spokes of a wheel. Transportation and communication systems in the city are extensive and well developed. 1873-1914 marked an intense period of development in Budapest's history. A national railway system, the three ring boulevards of Pest, as well as a radial road were created. Each ring road connects with a bridge on both the north and south end of the city. Understanding this system makes it easier to find your way around.

During the Communist era, large celebrations were held in Heroes' Square, built 1891-1898. A huge plaza, the square is the entrance to City Park. A 118-foot millennial column, topped with a winged statue towers over the square. Two curved columned walls, with 14 Hungarian equestrian hero statues standing between the columns, are on one end of the plaza. The statues were restored in 1996 in honor of the 1100 anniversary of the Magyar conquest. The tomb of the Unknown Soldier lies just in front of the column, between the curved walls.

Flanking Heroes Square is the Museum of Fine Arts, The

Palace of Arts, and Vajdahunyad Castle. These buildings were built in 1896 in preparation for the world exhibition celebrating 1000 years of Hungarian history.

In City Park is a boating lake, the Museum of Agriculture, Szechenyi Baths, one of Europe's largest bathing complexes, and the zoo and botanical gardens.

St. Stephen's is the largest Catholic Church, taking 50 years to build. The collapse of the dome in 1868 helped delay the project that was finished in 1906.

Parliament House is a neogothic structure with a renaissance dome. It is one of the largest state buildings in Europe. As the largest, most beautiful, and best-known buildings in Budapest, it is one of the symbols of the city.

Resembling Westminster, it was built 1885-1904. Its 691 rooms occupy 17,700 square meters. Measuring 871 feet long and 383 feet wide, it is one of the largest parliaments in the world. The dome is 312 feet high. The building is visible from most anywhere on the riverfront. The *only* time before 1990 that an elective legislature convened in its great hall was in 1945.

Margaret Island, about a mile long and a third of a mile wide, covers 321 acres and sits in the middle of the Danube, instead of the city. The island can be reached from two bridges, but no vehicular traffic is allowed on the island. The majority of the island has been a park since 1906. It was named after King Bela IV's daughter who lived there as a nun. She was later canonized as a saint.

The Szechenyi Chain Bridge built in 1849 was the first permanent bridge over the Danube. At night, under its lights, the Chain Bridge looks like a million burning candles.

In the 1800s Count Szechenyi was living the life of a playboy in London when his father died. He went home for the funeral, but because the Danube was frozen over he could not get across the river to attend his father's funeral.

This event changed his life. He stayed home, and became one

of the leading figures in the city in the last half of the 19th century.
The pontoon bridge prior to the chain bridge had to be removed
when ships passed, and it also was at the mercy of storms. A
Scotsman, Adam Clark, was commissioned to go to Budapest to
oversee the massive construction project. He liked the city so
much, he remained there the rest of his life.

Even though 80 percent of the city was bombed in WWII, the
Nazis blew up all the bridges when they retreated from the city.
The Chain Bridge was the first rebuilt after WWII, and reopened in
November 1949, exactly 100 years after the first opening. Two
years after the war ended, all the bridges in the city across the
Danube had been rebuilt.

Castle Hill was made a city in 1255 and usurped the name
Buda from the town north of the area. Thus the old Buda became
Obuda.

Castle Hill was first settled in the 13th century. Following the
Mongol invasion, King Bela IV moved the survivors in Pest to
Buda fortifying the area with a castle and walls. The first
monastery was built in 1243.

By the 15th century Buda was a booming trading place. Turks
leveled the city in 1526. When Buda was retaken in 1686, there
were no intact houses left. The present baroque appearance is from
the mid 18th century.

Bombing again leveled the city in 1944-45, and it has been
painstakingly rebuilt. Now the restored Castle District is a cultural,
arts, and tourist center.

Strolling through the narrow cobblestone lanes and twisted
alleys of the medieval neighborhood, our guide pointed out a
couple of pretty courtyards, hidden from street view. She also said,
"A coat of arms over the doorway indicated some nobleman lived
in the house. Five points in a crown indicate a baron, seven points
a count, and nine points a prince." Today restricted vehicular
traffic enhances the old world charm of the neighborhood, and it is
a much-coveted area in which to live.

The first palace built was Gothic in style, but was almost completely destroyed by the Turks. A baroque palace was built in 1715, with extensions in 1749 and 1790 when it was finished, and only minor alterations have occurred since. It was a royal residence for some 700 years. The Habsburgs did not live there, but stayed at the palace when visiting Buda. Completely burned out during WW II, it has been restored, and today houses several museums.

Matthias Church, also called the Church of Our Lady or the Coronation Church, is a beautiful turn of the century neo-Gothic structure. King Matthias was known for his fairness and justice, and Hungary flourished under his rule. He was married twice in the church that bares his name. Built in the 13-15th centuries, it is another symbol of Budapest.

In 1541, during the Turk occupation, the church was turned into a mosque, and the frescos whitewashed. After Buda was retaken, the Jesuits were given the church, and made some Baroque alterations.

The church became a parish church in 1773, and was restored in the latter part of the 19th century in a neo-gothic style. Today, inside of the church one wall remains in its Turkish geometric design, while frescos are evident elsewhere. The structure has a beautiful mosaic roof. A memorial plaque on the outside of the church commemorates all who lost their lives under Hitler's and Stalin's rule. Because of the exceptional acoustics, concerts often are held in the church.

Fisherman's Bastion, a neo-Romanesque structure, is perched on the edge of the Castle District behind the Matthias Church. Built at the turn of the century in the location of the old fish market, it provides a panoramic view of the Danube River and Pest.

From the backside of the structure one can view part of a medieval wall that is between it and the Hilton hotel. During the construction of the hotel, when the medieval ruins were discovered, the hotel's design was altered to accommodate, not destroy, the ruins.

The Jewish District of Pest has a long and tragic history. Because Jews were forbidden from living in the town during medieval times, the district sprang up just beyond the city wall. In time the city expanded beyond the walls, and the district became part of the city. Huge synagogues in the area, gives one an idea of the vitality of the district. Under German occupation the area became a walled ghetto.

The Dohany Synagogue, with seating capacity for 3000, is a striking Byzantine structure, and is Europe's largest, and the world's second largest, synagogue.

Built in 1859, it is still used by Budapest's conservative Jewish community. Its two onion domes are 140 feet high. The synagogue has recently been restored. The Jewish Museum is next door.

The Holocaust Memorial, designed by a contemporary Hungarian sculptor, is in the form of a weeping willow tree. Thin metal leaves, purchased by survivors and descendents of relatives are slowly filling the branches.

Mr. Wallenberg, a Swedish diplomat, issued false passports and established safe houses that saved thousands of Jews. Still 600,000 died, most at Auschwitz, with only 35 percent of the Jewish population surviving the war. In 1945 the Soviets arrested Mr. Wallenberg, and he died in one of Stalin's work camps.

Hungarians are great believers in the medicinal powers of thermal bathing. Budapest is famous for its thermal waters and 16th century Turkish baths. The baths have a long and proud history going back to Roman times, but it was under Turkish occupation that the bath culture flourished.

Eighty thermal springs feed twelve spa baths with a daily output of 70 million liters of thermal water. One can visit any of the ten or twelve bathhouses still in operation. One afternoon three others and I decided to visit the Szechenyi Baths in the park.

Employees at the baths did not appear very friendly, and the list of prices for various parts of the bath seemed endless. English translations were non-existent, so we took along a local gal from a travel agency who could translate and show us the routine. The process of actually getting to the pools was not difficult, but rather complicated, and we all agreed that without her we would have been in for a trying and stressful afternoon.

We went in all the pools. The water was clear and odorless, except for the hottest pool that had a yellow tinge and a whiff of sulfur. Inside, having lost our translator and unable to read any of the signs, we just hoped we wouldn't wander into a male only area. But all went well.

Many people go to the baths for the day, just like we go to the beach.

When leaving, I couldn't remember which pocket I'd put the little plastic tag in. After checking all the many pockets in my cargo shorts, I finally found it, but I wonder what would have happened if I *had* lost it. Would they have kept me there forever?

One gal misplaced her admission ticket, so she had to forfeit her refund, which we never would have been aware of, if we'd been unaccompanied. It was a fun and interesting afternoon.

One evening passed very quickly when we attended an excellent folkloric show. The dancers were good in the lively show. The gypsy musicians were also excellent. They played all evening without any sheet music.

Just north of Budapest the Danube makes several sharp turns that alter its west-east direction. About 25 miles north of Budapest the river abruptly turns south and this is the start of the Danube Bend (Duna Kanyar), famous for its lovely scenery, small villages, and historic towns. The Danube enters Hungary from the northwest and flows southeasterly forming the border with its northern neighbor, Slovakia. The river swings sharply north and then again south at Vac where it continues a southerly direction through Budapest on toward Serbia and Croatia.

It was about an hour and a half ride to Esztergom where we

stopped at a restaurant for juice or coffee. Afterward we walked the short distance to the Royal Palace, home of the archbishop when he is in town.

Esztergom, a city of about 100,000, became the capitol of the medieval Hungarian State in the 13th century. It is still the center of the Catholic Church in Hungary where 65 percent of the population is Catholic. St. Stephen, born in Esztergom, was crowned there in the year 1000.

On the third floor of the Royal Palace was a very good Christian art museum, with art dating back to the 14th and 15th century.

The Basilica, high on a hill is the largest church in Hungary. It took twenty years to build the Basilica, and when it was consecrated in 1857, Franz Liszt wrote and played his music for the occasion.

The Turks destroyed the original church and palace. A 1500s chapel that survived the Turks was found while building the Basilica. The chapel was dismantled into 1600 pieces and rebuilt *into* the Basilica. The red marble inside is from the Renaissance period, and it is the only chapel from that era still intact in the country.

The Basilica has undergone a few minor changes. Decoration was added to the altar in the 18th century. Four angels have been added to the top of the organ.

The oil painting over the main altar is the largest single canvas painting in the world. Also the mosaics around the dome are actually paintings, not mosaics.

Before leaving we walked down to the wall behind the Basilica to look across the Danube at Slovakia.

Continuing on, we stopped in Visegrad, a village of 2000 for lunch at a new hotel. The hotel sat perched on a high hill with a fantastic view of the Danube Bend through its huge picture windows. Gypsy musicians serenaded us during our meal.

I was a bit apprehensive when I heard we were having venison for lunch, but it was cooked differently, and was very good.

After lunch we drove to the artist colony of Szentendre, which is about 12 miles north of Budapest. In the 17th century, Serbs fleeing from the Turks, settled in Szentendre. There are few Serbs left today, but their Mediterranean-Baroque buildings remain.

Walking the cobblestone alley to the town square looked like a shopper's paradise, but most of us chose to visit a ceramics museum.

The last stop of the day was at Hungarian Museum, an eco-museum, which are becoming quite popular in Europe. Established in 1967 the museum opened in 1974 as a reconstructed village from the last century.

Stopping by an old cemetery the docent explained the wooden grave markers. The blue marker meant the person was a child, the black marker an adult. The marker for a male was pointed, the marker for females rounded. If a female married more than once she had another rounded mound. The markers were carved of wood, and told a story before people could read or write.

No matter how many times I visit a church, castle, old home, or museum, I always find something I've not seen before or did not know.

It is not easy to undo four decades of stunted economic growth and cultural orthodoxy, but Hungry is rapidly moving forward. One symbolic act was to shed such names as Red Army Square, Lenin Boulevard, and other such names, by reverting streets to their original pre-war names.

Not so long ago Budapest, and the rest of Hungary, was filled with memorials to Lenin, Marx, the Red Army, and other reminders of communist rule. In 1989 most of these statues were torn from their foundations and those not totally destroyed were warehoused to collect dust. Eventually a plan for a Socialist Statue Park came about. The park was in an inconvenient location, far from town, and the number of statues limited, so it has not been a very successful endeavor.

However we passed by it and stopped on our way to Lake Balaton. It was an interesting stop. Even though it was early in the morning and not open, we still could see the statutes and had a chance for a photo op.

Szekesfehervar became an important settlement when King Stephen chose it as a burial place for the royal family. Thirty-eight kings were crowned there, and 18 were buried there. Today it's a lively city with a baroque downtown.

We walked around the town of about 100,000. Turks destroyed all but one of the buildings. The town was rebuilt, then bombings during WW II destroyed the town again, and again it was rebuilt.

King Stephen's father had built a church here. King Stephen built the Basilica.

A statue of a naked man on a horse symbolizes that uniforms change, but bravery does not.

Walking around the pleasant little town was a nice break from the bus ride.

Before long we could see Lake Balaton. We continued on to Tihany for lunch at the Park Hotel where we were served a scrumptious salad and a decadent dessert.

Tihany is a village and also a peninsula that stretches five kilometers into the lake. Except for ferries, no motorboats are allowed on the lake.

After lunch three or four went for a dip in the lake but I chose to walk the lovely landscaped grounds.

Lake Balaton, covering 230 square miles, is the largest fresh water lake in Central/Western Europe. The 43-mile-long lake is rather shallow, about ten feet, making it ideal for swimming, sail boats, and wind surfing.

Later in the afternoon we rode up the hill to the twin towered, 18th century, baroque, Benedictine Abbey. The crypt, 1055, was the original church. Andrew I is buried in the crypt. He founded the Benedictine Abbey in 1055. The high altar is built over the crypt, and is heavily adorned with carved wooden sculptures, painted, and overlaid with gold.

Traveling country roads we stopped for dinner in Csopak. The restaurant was in a vineyard where we also partook of a wine tasting.

Dining on the porch provided us a good view of the vineyards. I was sitting by the rail, which turned out to be a great advantage. The first white wine served was okay, but nothing special. They got worse after that, and by the time we reached what was supposed to be a Merlot, I was watering the vineyard.

We'd had some excellent wines with meals, and that wine maker allegedly had won all kinds of awards for his wines, so his wines were a real surprise and disappointment. Many Hungarian wines are excellent, but as far as I was concerned those were not among them.

Hungary, unlike its neighbors, is not a beer culture, and therefore the beer is not exceptional. However, imported beers are available.

Coffee (kave) is drunk throughout the day. The very strong coffee is unfiltered espresso, generally drunk without cream or sugar, a tradition borrowed from the Turks. Tea, when available, was strong and black.

On our last afternoon in Budapest, having had enough of museums and done enough shopping, we decided to go to the zoo. We rode the subway downtown without difficulty. The zoo map was printed in Hungarian, and no one around seemed to speak English. Opened in 1866, it is one of the oldest zoos in the world.

Covering nearly 11 hectares with 69 buildings, the zoo houses some 500 mammals, nearly 700 birds, and 1500 reptiles, fish, and arthropods. The botanical garden has 1500 species of plants. The elephant house, built in 1908, resembles a Turkish Mosque. It is very elaborate and really very beautiful.

Being half way lost a couple of times we looked for a young man because men learn English more than women, and the young people are the ones who always know English. Both times the fellow we scouted out was able to help us — and in English at that.

We found Hungarian people friendly and generous. We were told they tend to be skeptical and read between the lines. The older generation is a bit pessimistic.

The Hungarian language, similar to Finnish, is unusual and complex. Except for our instructors and tour people, we found very few people anywhere who spoke or understood English other than hello, may I help you, and thank you.

Peasants, when freed, began to emigrate out of the country in the late 1800s. After both WWI and WWII professional people emigrated, creating somewhat of a brain drain for the country.

Dramatic political changes in 1989 altered the state of Hungary's capitol, as Budapest woke from a long slumber behind the iron curtain.

The transition to a full market economy resulted in lowered living standards for most people. The removal of state subsidies in 1991 resulted in a severe recession.

Pollution is a huge and costly problem for Hungary. The use of low-grade coal creates sulfur dioxide and acid rain. The ground water under the plains is contaminated with phosphates from the over use of agricultural nitrate fertilizers.

Inflation and unemployment are high. European, Asian, and North American companies have taken advantage of the country's low wage and skilled labor base to establish factories in Hungary. Most of these jobs are in relatively prosperous Budapest and Transdanubia. European Union countries are the recipients of about two thirds of the country's exports.

Our Budapest farewell dinner consisted of a typical Hungarian goulash, (we'd call it beef stew), and it was very good. Following dinner we went outside to the courtyard for an excellent folkloric dance demonstration. At the end, the girls gave everyone a gift of a large heart shaped gingerbread cookie.

It was a wonderful end to a great trip.

Neither of us could pack the beautiful heavy sweaters we

bought in Krakow, and incidentally never had need to wear, after we'd bought them. So we left them in the lecture room for dear sweet Zsuzsa, knowing she lived in a climate where they would come in handy.

Chapter 14

Biking Denmark

So you want a glass of German white wine with your dinner in Denmark? Forget it. The Germans occupied neutral Denmark during World War II and the Danes have neither forgotten nor forgiven that act of aggression. Even as late as 1996 they imported *no* German wines.

I'm not sure why I chose to go to the Kingdom of Denmark, Scandinavia's *country of islands*. I'd had such a good time biking the Danube the year before that I think I just wanted to do another bike trip.

While I waited for dinner to be served on the plane I mulled over in my mind that I hoped the exercise time spent on the stepper at the gym had been adequate to give my legs the strength to peddle forty miles a day. It had just been too hot to ride my bike on the streets of my neighborhood. I hoped my stamina would be up to par. I told myself I was better prepared for this trip than I was the year before. At least I had biking shorts, heavier sneakers, and my sheepskin seat cover, all packed along with my helmet in my carry-on bag. But I concluded it was too late to worry about it now—I was on my way and what would be would be, and I'd just have to cope.

Our Danish guide, a recently retired SAS pilot, met us at the Copenhagen airport. It was about a 50 mile bus ride to Soro, our starting point.

A friend backed out of this trip because she thought Denmark would be hilly. I was sure it would be relatively flat, but there was no convincing her, so I went alone. Our hotel was situated on a nice little hill, and that should have been a clue for me. Little did I know then that the hotel hill was going to be about the smallest hill we would encounter in the next couple of weeks.

During a safety briefing we learned that in this country there are *no* right turns on red.

At many intersections large white triangles, called shark's teeth, are painted across the street that must yield, and one must yield to *all* traffic. At especially dangerous inter-sections a big red cross is painted on signs, reminding you that not everyone obeys the signs.

Entering a traffic circle one must yield to all traffic already in the circle, and *everyone* must yield to bikers following a blue path painted on the outer edge of the circle. Traffic circle turn offs are particularly dangerous.

Denmark is a land of bikers. Everyone rides them, kids, adults, nuns, couriers, in all sorts of dress including business suits and female business wear. I noticed that biking shorts were seen only on foreigners. Danes didn't seem to wear them.

The very first day we biked some *tough* hills, and they were to get worse before the terrain got better! I took the Texas heat with me as we suffered through *90 degree* temperatures, which were abnormally high in Denmark for that time of year. The combination of heat and hills gave me a terrific headache, and I was more than ready to stop at Vester-Broby Kirke, a church located on the west end of Bridgetown. The high temperatures lasted about five days, and we were all happy to see more normal seasonal temperatures arrive!

We stopped at many churches on this trip. Our rest stops almost always were at a church where we were assured of finding clean rest rooms. On this entire trip we found very *clean* restrooms that were always well equipped with essential TP, soap, and paper towels.

One unique thing in the churches were the ship models hanging from the ceiling. Sometimes it was only one ship model, sometimes several, and the sizes varied with the model.

The King introduced Christianity to his country in 980. Prior to that time Danes worshiped many gods, among them Thor, a well-known deity. However, it was 200 years before Christianity had a good foothold in the country. Many large churches were built between 1100-1150.

One church we visited, built in the late 1000s, is one of the oldest churches in Denmark. The crucifix was 12-1300 years old, and the frescos over the altar were painted in 1120 making them the oldest in the country.

One day we biked to Trelleborg to visit the Viking museum. Erick, the Viking, appeared in full Viking dress to give us a lecture and tour of the museum.

Archeological digs show that Trelleborg was an old Viking fortification and not a village. However, it is estimated that about 5000 people occupied the area. The site was between two rivers and is the best-preserved site in Denmark. That rather desolate treeless place was at one time covered with oak forest.

It was a very *hot* day and the tour of the museum was all outside in the unrelenting sun. Close to the end, I skipped out and returned to the museum building where I went into the restroom, took off my tee shirt, got it soaking wet in the sink, and then put it back on. I didn't care what the wet t-shirt looked like. It sure felt good and may have saved me from heat stroke! By the time we left the museum, several others had followed my lead and were wearing wet t-shirts.

Denmark is a country of islands, actually an archipelago of 450 islands, only 97 of which are inhabited. One long peninsula, Jutland, joins Germany on the south connecting Denmark to Europe. Denmark is the southern most country in Scandinavia.

After three days we lost one fellow as he'd had enough of the hills and heat, so he returned home.

Our first ferry ride was on a huge ferry, carrying big trucks as well as trains. There were four train tracks on the loading dock. The ferry berthed where the land tracks ended at the end of the pier and the trains just rolled onto the ferry. It was an interesting operation to watch.

We lined up our bikes down on the lower deck, then went topside to enjoy the view. The ferry ride was the easy part of the day! We had nothing but hills all day, most of which we all walked the last one-third to reach the top. At the top there was a wonderful down hill ride, but then another big hill loomed right up in your face. The hills were so steep you had to brake nearly all the way down to avoid going 50 miles an hour. Often there was a curve at the bottom of the hill and one never knows what hazard might be on the road.

It was a good aerobic workout as I huffed and puffed all day often gasping for what would seem to be my last breath! And I thought Denmark would be flat. Wrong! I had to admit my friend was right. I understand future Danish trips have been altered and rerouted to eliminate many of those tough hills.

Sweat was running into my eyes, my head was soaking wet under my helmet, I was soaking wet with water running down every crevice of my body, and I sure didn't need the cardiac workout. I'd been in first gear all day. To make matters worse after the rest stop we picked up a headwind. I was thinking 'and I *paid* good money to torture myself like this.'

By lunchtime I was about ready to pack it in and go in the van. One gal did ride the van for a day and a half. She developed severe stomach cramps, probably from dehydration. I was glad I was conscientious about drinking fluids.

Approaching the guide I said, "Be honest with me, is the whole trip going to be like this? Don't give me any rhetoric! Just tell me the truth, because I've about had enough."

He replied, "The worst is just about over. There's not too much left today and tomorrow will be better. You're really a much better biker than you think you are, and I'd like to see you continue on as I really think you can make it."

The van driver also encouraged me to continue. They were right, and I did end up peddling all the way. Last year I was *always* last, no matter where I started. Well, this year I started out in the middle and ended up in the middle every time, so I guess that was an improvement.

This group were good bikers but not as fanatical or fast and competitive as the group the year before. Thank goodness!

We stopped at a lovely beach to have lunch. The area was called the Great Bend because it separated the Baltic Sea from the North Sea. The water was cool and the beach crowded. We observed many topless sunbathers.

No Dane lives more than 50 miles from the ocean, be it the Baltic Sea, the Great Bend or the North Sea.

After lunch the hills did flatten out some, and I could at least get into 2nd gear! The wind tempered the heat and made it feel a little cooler, tolerable anyway. It wasn't too long before we hit a dirt path through a forest. It was very scenic and the tree cover cooled us down a bit more.

Coming out of the woods we rode past a gorgeous large castle. Along the ocean bike path the ocean breeze was at our back offering us welcome relief. It was a treat to bike on relatively level ground!

At the very end of the day two huge steep hills had us all dismounting half way up for a walk to the top, but at the top of the second hill we had a nice, *long, gentle* downhill coast through the forest, and suddenly we were in Svendborg.

After securing our bikes our guide said, "It's been a long hard 38 mile day so I'm going to treat you to some Svendborg bitters." I appreciated the effort, but I'm not much of a drinker. I don't know if bitters all taste alike or not. Anyway it was too much for me, but my roommate gladly finished it off. I'd much rather have had a big glass of really cold ice tea!

The museum's head archeologist told us Svendborg, a city of 43,000, was founded in the 11th century by a Danish king. It is and always has been a maritime city, thus much of the décor reflects that history. One half of all Danish ships were built there. The city was once a major seaport, but today shipping only plays a minor role.

Because of the good clay in that area brick making was introduced in 1160. Nearly all of the buildings in the country are brick or half brick and wood, with the wood making diagonal designs, known everywhere as uniquely Danish.

A major fire in 1749 convinced people in the city that tile roofs were a better choice than the picturesque thatched ones. Thatched roofs are expensive to build and to insure, but it is a tradition many wish to maintain, especially in the countryside's small villages.

The countryside was green and very clean. I never saw even a gum wrapper on the ground. Plastic bags are available but most Danes prefer to carry their own bag as we often did.

The cheeses, breads, beer, and pastries were *wonderful*. Danes are good and imaginative cooks. Eating is an event for them. Smorrebrod, no resemblance to an American smorgasbord, is an open face sandwich with any combination of thinly sliced items you want. They are made to order, usually in a bakery or specialty shop. The only limitation is one's imagination.

Quite different from our farms, Danish farms, including the main house and barns are built U-shaped with a central court. Although the number of farms has decreased, the farms have become larger and three-quarters of the country is farmland. Wheat is a major crop. Kellogg's was everywhere, we peddled by many of their fields. Sugar beets and corn follow wheat as major crops.

It is said there are twice as many pigs in Denmark as there are people. Danish ham is a big export item. Fishing, especially for herring, is also big.

I'm not too crazy about dirt and gravel paths, as it's so easy to hit a rock just right and go flying, It takes extra concentration, so rolling hills and lots of dirt paths through woods were the minor challenge another day. A detour to visit Egeskov castle was a fun respite. The grounds were really beautiful and an interesting eight-foot bamboo maze was both fun and a challenge.

The large parking lot confirmed that the castle is quite an attraction. The grounds are large with many picnic tables scattered about. A lovely rose garden was on the grounds. The senior rate to tour the castle was 32 Krona, and it was an interesting self-guided walk through the many large rooms. The castle itself is built on a small island, the lake providing a natural mote.

After a rather tiring, but fun day, we had dinner in the hotel. After dinner we moved upstairs to a special room for dessert and coffee, a rather unusual maneuver. Suddenly there was a loud knock on the door, and lo and behold in came Hans Christian Anderson dressed in top hat and tails. He began to spin a tale telling us about himself.

"I was born April 2,1805 on the island of Fuen. My parents were poor but happy. I was a rather strange child who preferred playing with my puppets to playing with other children. I wrote in my diary *every* day. My father died when I was young, about 12. I was very close to my grandmother.

"I was very self assured and knew at an early age that I would be famous. When I was 14 I went to Copenhagen to try a theater career. But it failed. However, while on the stage I was seen by a fellow who later became my patron. He sent me to Latin school where I wrote forbidden poetry. I also wrote some novels, but they enjoyed only minimal success.

"When I was 30 I started telling fairy tales to children so I could watch their reaction. Then I would write them down, and these are the stories that made me famous. My stories always had a moral to them and sometimes people didn't like that, thinking I was too moralistic."

For generations children have grown up with *The Ugly*

Duckling, The Emperors New Clothes, The Little Mermaid and more.

This actor apparently had built a successful career impersonating the famous author. He was most entertaining. He continued to tell us that Anderson had fallen in love twice, once with Jenny Lind. However, he never married. Our storyteller concluded with, "I died at the age of 70 in Copenhagen in 1875, and I had three million Krona in the bank!" It was a delightful, entertaining evening.

One misty morning we had an hour-long ferry ride that took us from the island of Fuen to the island Aero. We biked the *entire* length of the island to Marstal.

Along the way we visited old churches, some with old frescos. In Denmark, like in much of Europe, most churchyards also served as cemeteries. Churches were always built on a hill. Church towers were usually added after the church was built, and the tower was always built on the west side of the church. (In Texas we look for water towers, in Denmark one looks for the church tower.)

Lunch on this misty day was in Aeroskobing, a fairy tale looking little town. The season was coming to an end for this little resort town. There were very few cars on the cobblestone streets. The pastel houses and shops were small and close together, almost joining, along the narrow streets. Many of the doors were decorated with brass and plaster motifs. It was like being in a make-believe land.

Leaving this lovely little town we faced a horrific hill. What a nasty thing to do to us right after lunch! Everyone ended up walking part of that one.

Another morning we had an early wake-up call as our ferry departed at 7:45. After an hour's ferry ride we arrived on the island of Langeland. We biked the six miles across the island to catch another ferry at 10:30 for the island of Lolland.

After departing the second ferry we biked to a church for lunch, grateful for the cooler weather. The terrain was less hilly, but certainly not flat. I actually made it into 3rd gear some of the time.

After lunch we picked up a strong headwind. Everyone was tired after that 40-mile day but a lovely country hotel awaited us at the end of the day. Our room's balcony overlooked a small lake.

A visit to Maribo Cathedral, built in 1390, was an interesting one. Originally it was a monastery for 60 nuns and 65 Augustine monks. Maribo means *the place where Mary lives.*

Fire destroyed the entire structure in 1600. When rebuilt it was opened to the public. The large church had many gothic arches, but no frescos or ship models hanging from the ceiling. The altar, pulpit, and chandelier were all quite ornate.

As a docent walked us into a room behind the altar she told us the room housed the original altar and a canvas painting of Mary that dated from 1420. The painting in its original wooden frame was preserved under glass. A 1550 bible and a large carved statue of St. Augustine were also in that room. The original crucifix was hollow. During a difficult time in Danish history a priest hid treasures in the crucifix and it was 300 years before they were rediscovered. Imagine that!

Many large beech and chestnut trees covered the grounds providing welcome shade.

On the way to Nysted we detoured to the estate of one of the many resistance workers during WWII when 10,000 Germans occupied the country. This English lady helped many a downed Allied flyer. Eventually the Germans caught her and sent her to a concentration camp. Because she was English the Germans were reluctant to execute her.

She was told to write a letter requesting amnesty. She refused. But the Germans persisted so she eventually wrote the letter, but in defiance of the Germans she wrote her letter on toilet paper. Unfortunately she died in camp a few months before the war ended, but apparently not from mistreatment. Her elderly daughter wanted nothing to do with the estate, so it was owned by a foundation.

Six thousand Danes, most of them resistance fighters, not Jews, were in concentration camps during WWII, and 600 of them died in the camps.

In 1943 a German officer who had lived and had been schooled in Denmark leaked to the Danish authorities that Germany was about to round up all the Jews in Denmark. Overnight, seven thousand Jews were hidden and a few at a time smuggled to neutral Sweden. It is said that Danes checked the phone books to locate Jews and then went knocking on their doors. Only a few refused to leave.

Elderly King Christian X left his palace everyday during the war to mingle among his people. He said that if the Jews were forced to wear yellow stars on their arm he would wear one too.

After visiting a little village of thatched roof homes we continued on to Nysted, a small beach community. After lunch we walked to the city square to meet the vicar, a pleasant man with a good sense of humor, who took us on a walking tour of the city. We enjoyed his commentary during the walking tour. Nysted's population of 5500 supports 11 medieval churches.

It was a delight to bike through the forest along the Baltic Sea. We stopped at the General's teahouse. A couple of kilometers inland was a manor house. The munitions manufacturer owner had made a lot of money, and built the teahouse so each day he could come and have afternoon tea while gazing out over the Baltic Sea. During a stay here Hans Christian Anderson wrote the *Elephant Story,* which was only marginally successful. The view was lovely.

Our last day biking was a short one as this was the day we had to surrender our bikes, always a sad moment. We had ferried among many islands and biked on the islands of Sealand, Fuen, Areo, Langland, Lolland, and Falster over paved paths, streets, gravel, through forest, through many wheat fields, along the sea, and up and down lots and lots of hills.

Then it was on to Copenhagen via Roskilde where we had an

interesting visit at the Viking Museum. Afterward we visited the 800 years old Roskilde Cathedral which encompasses seven architectural styles. Students from all over come to study them.

The first church, built in 970, was a wooden structure, and two limestone buildings followed. In 1175 the present brick Romanesque structure was started. The building was finally finished in Gothic design.

The chapel gates of fancy wrought iron, are throughout the church. This cathedral holds the tombs of 170 people and is the burial place of 20 kings and 17 queens.

As we approached Copenhagen I was glad we weren't biking. The traffic was horrific, and all the one-way streets make it a bear to drive for one unfamiliar with the area. When Tivoli Gardens, a 20-acre amusement park, was built it was well out of town, now it is in the center of the city, just across from the town hall.

A city guide met us in the hotel lobby at 8:30 the next morning for a walking tour of wonderful, wonderful Copenhagen.

Copenhagen is definitely a city made for walkers. The center of town runs from the harbor (Kongens Nytorv, translated: king's new tower) to the town square (Radhuspladsen). The walking street connecting these two squares is known as the Stroget and is a little over a mile long. Really a wide pedestrian mall, it is crowded with shops of every description with various eateries sandwiched in between. There are many narrow streets and small squares running off the Stroget.

Copenhagen means "merchant market." With a population of something over two-million it is Scandinavia's largest city. There are 160 miles of bike paths and every day 50-60,000 bikers enter the city! There are also 1700 city bikes and 125 stands for them. For 25 Krona one can use the bike all day and when it is returned to any city stand the 25 Krona is returned.

Settlements have been in the area for 6000 years, but it was in 1043 that Copenhagen was recorded as a fishing village. The plentiful herring in the harbor brought prosperity to everyone.

Our walking tour ended at the Amelienborg Palace where a large bronze equestrian statue of King Fredrik stands in the center of the courtyard. The palace was built in 1748 by order of the king originally for four wealthy and influential businessmen. The exterior of all four buildings is the same, however, the interior of each has been individualized. The royal family has occupied the palace sine the late 1700s.

We were fortunate to be winding down our city tour at the palace just minutes before the changing of the guard. It was a pretty impressive ceremony.

After the ceremony we walked the one-third mile to view the famous Little Mermaid statue, a gift to the city in 1913 by brewer Carl Jacobsen. The mermaid is quite small perched on her stone in shallow water a few feet off shore.

Wonderful Copenhagen was a wonderful end to a wonderful trip and biking experience.

Chapter 15

Costa Rica

Ever since we disembarked from the mutinied cruise ship in Costa Rica I had wanted to return, and twelve years later I did.

As we boarded this flight, the ramp was lined with customs agents asking each of us how much money we were taking on the trip. Americans are allowed to take up to $10,000 out of the country. I suspect they were sniffing around for drug money. In all my years of travel and on all of my flights, this was a new experience.

The most frequent question asked by visitors is about the water. I was delighted to learn we could drink the water everywhere, in all of our hotels, except one, and we would be alerted to that well in advance. Ice also was safe. Good news!

Costa Rica is not on daylight saving time and daylight began at 5:30 AM. Being early risers, both my son and I were up early. Our hotel was located in a residential area, so we walked the neighborhood before breakfast.

Neither of us had packed rain gear for this trip so for insurance I bought a folding umbrella. It turned out to be a good investment!

Our transportation while in country was a Toyota mini van, which actually had seat belts. The 19 of us had plenty of room in the 25-passenger van.

Most San Jose streets are narrow, and crowded. Gridlock seems to be a way of life. We were cautioned to be very careful when crossing the streets as often Costa Ricans drive by their own rules. After the oil embargo of 1973-74 large American cars were replaced by small foreign imports.

Only one area of the city had wide streets. Telephone service in that area was easy to get, whereas in some parts of the city it could be up to a year's wait for a phone.

Until 1960 the airport was pretty much in the city. After it was moved outside the city, the old airport area became a nice big park.

We were told both crack cocaine and alcohol are readily available in the city and is somewhat of a problem.

Costa Rica, about the size of New Mexico, with a population of a little over 3.5 million people, lies on the Central American isthmus between Nicaragua on the north and Panama on the south. It is a peaceful Central American oasis of unspoiled natural beauty and spectacular scenery. Sometimes the country is referred to as the Switzerland of Central America because of its political stability.

The army was abolished and replaced with a militia in 1948. Costa Rica, a democracy, has managed to remain an island of stability and peace, amidst much political unrest and turmoil of its neighboring countries.

Nearly a third of the country's population lives in San Jose, the political, social, historical, and cultural center of the country. Founded in 1737, it replaced nearby Cartago as capitol of the country in 1823.

San Jose sits in a fertile bowl, at an elevation of 3000 feet, it enjoys warm days and cool nights. The country has two seasons, the rainy season, May to December, the rest of the year is dry. It's fairly easy to get around the city when you realize that avenues run east and west, and streets run north and south. However, the streets run in odd number numerical order on one side of the city and even numbers on the other. For example, Calle Two does not follow Calle One, as they are on opposite sides of the city.

In 1983 Pope John Paul used San Jose as his headquarters while visiting around in Latin and South America.

After President Oscar Arias won the Nobel Peace Prize in 1987 the world began to notice Costa Rica, and our guide felt that event put the country on the world map.

The National Theater or Opera House is a neoclassical building with a baroque interior. In 1828-30 the president encouraged culture. By 1860 a budget was proposed for a theater, but there actually was no money available until 1890.

Most of the materials for the building came from Europe between 1891 and 1897. Earthquakes in 1904 and 1910 caused major damage to the building, and frequent tremors still keep repairmen busy.

The building is a beauty. We walked up the wide staircase to view the original seats in the theater boxes.

In a reception room upstairs the beautiful floor was made from all the woods grown in Costa Rica.

Sitting on the stairs so we could look at the fresco on the hallway ceiling, a docent explained the picture was on the back of the Costa Rica's old five-cent bill. Given specific instructions of size and content, an Italian artist painted the mural in 1897. However, because he had never been in the tropics he made several errors in the painting.

The first thing one notices is the coffee plants, which do not grow at sea level. Coffee only grows above an elevation of 800 feet. The fellow in the foreground is holding a stalk of bananas upside down. That is how bananas grow, but if you carried a stalk that way, the bananas would all fall off! Ships came to the Caribbean coast not the Pacific Coast, and palm trees do not grow on the Pacific Coast. The women are all dressed European style, not in Costa Rican dress. There is no yoke on the oxen, so how could they pull a cart? But the painting was finished and so it was hung.

The National Museum offered an excellent panoramic view of the city. We wandered through the several buildings at our own pace. As we drove around the city I noticed hardly any graffiti.

Leaving the city, we headed north passing many acres of coffee plants. Coffee grows at elevations between 800-5600 feet. Some areas were shaded by large trees, others were not. Above 5600 feet the crops change from coffee to apples and dairy cows. We saw many waterfalls as we traveled up and over the pass where it was raining.

There is but one tunnel in the country and we passed through, it. We passed over the continental divide. At the narrowest point, it is 75 miles across Costa Rica from the Pacific to the Caribbean.

After lunch at Río Danta we took a hike through the rain forest behind the restaurant. It was suggested that we all take the supplied walking sticks along because there were snakes in the area and the path was a bit uneven. We saw an animal about the size of a small dog that was an agouti, a member of the rat family.

Late afternoon we arrived at our hotel in Sarapiqui. It didn't take us long to find the way to the pool for a swim.

In Costa Rica all of our hotels were quaint small ones in rather isolated areas so all morning and evening meals were at the hotels.

In Sarapiqui we ate in the outdoor dining room while the running water of the river below serenaded us.

We woke to the music of the birds singing. After breakfast we were off to raft the white water of the Sarapiqui River.

After a safety briefing and getting fitted with life vest and helmet, we loaded the rafts for a whitewater adventure. After navigating several class II and III rapids we stopped at a shallow pull out point, where we climbed a small cliff and jumped in the water to float back down stream to our rafts. This was stuff that thrills a kid, but it took me some time to muster the courage to jump off that cliff. I was happy when surfacing to find my prescription sunglasses still on my nose. They really were pretty secure with a back strap under my helmet, but I was still apprehensive about the force of the water on impact knocking them off! The cool water was most refreshing.

After paddling about seven miles down river, we pulled off at a sandy spot for lunch. The friendly guides flipped one of the rafts and set up a lunch sandwich buffet for us. It had been a great morning!

We returned to the hotel to change into dry clothes and something a little more acceptable for street wear before heading off to La Selva Biological Station. The weather looked a bit dubious, so I grabbed the umbrella.

A guide walked us through the rainforest preserve located at the confluence of the Sarapiqui and Puerto Viejo rivers.

The station, bordering a national forest, is run by the Organization of Tropical Studies (OTS). Three quarters of the 4000 acres is prime forest, and there are 35 miles of trails.

Studying everything from the smallest ant to the largest tree, 350 species of ants have been identified as well as 3000 mosses and 1900 plants/trees. The station has an extensive school education program.

It was necessary to cross a rather long swinging bridge to enter the trails. The river below was flowing at a pretty good rate. There were scores of birds flying around and singing. It took quite a while to get across the bridge, as we kept stopping to observe the birds.

We had just touched land on the opposite side of the bridge when we spotted toucans. I couldn't believe it. I'd heard toucans in Belize on the way to the Mayan ruins, and again in Panama when going up the Sambu River, but they were so high up in the canopy I could not see them. Now I was looking at many of them. I was so excited!

A bit later we saw several Collared Peccary (wild pigs), crossing the path ahead of us. We also spotted several agouti, small-dog size rodents.

Before the afternoon was over it started to rain. When it rained hard (I was glad I had bought the umbrella.) we turned around and headed back to the reception area.

It was here that I first spotted the T-shirt with the saying:

Only after the last tree has been cut
Only after the last river has been poisoned
Only after the last fish has been caught
Only then will you find money cannot be eaten.
Cree Indians, Canada

Because of deforestation and rapid colonization, the habitat of the Great Green Macaw has been reduced by more than half, from 12,460 hectares to 529 hectares. The hotel owner belonged to a volunteer organization trying to save the macaw. Five years ago there were only 25 mating pairs, now they have increased to 100 pairs, but the bird is still endangered. On the Black Market, one sells for $3000. That is a great deal of money to someone making $300 a month.

The bird mates for life. They live exclusively in the almond tree in the tall canopy of the forest. The almond tree grows 95 to 160 feet tall. The wood is very hard and is a desirable building material. As the leaves fall from the tree, it creates a natural cavity for the bird. The nut is very hard, but the macaw's very strong beak enables him to crack the nut.

People cut the trees on their property to sell the wood. This organization has started paying property owners an annual sum to not cut but to take care of and nurture their almond trees. She told us it seems to be working.

A macaw reproduces at five years of age and has one to three chicks a year. They can live to be 60 years old. Owls and the African bee are the predators of the macaw chicks.

A thousand trees per hectare is recommended as ideal. Seven years ago, the hotel property was ten acres of pastureland. The hotel owners have planted every plant on the grounds, including many almond trees, and now the past pasture was covered with trees and plants. They hope that macaws someday will live all over that area.

These people had done such a remarkable job and were so

216

passionate about their work that I made a donation to their organization before we left Sarapiqui.

Also on the grounds were a butterfly garden, a frog garden, and an orchid garden. The butterfly garden had many of the beautiful Blue Morpho Butterflies.

A typical Costa Rican breakfast includes rice, black beans, scrambled eggs, and toast or tortillas. It was good and hearty fare, which we were served just about every morning. The national drink is Guaro, a rum made from sugar cane and marketed as Guaro Cacique. One day it was available at lunch for us to try.

During our transit to Chachagua, we stopped for lunch in the country. These ranch people graciously let us have a peek inside their country home. The ceilings and walls were of beautiful paneled wood. All the outside doors were gorgeous solid carved wood. Everyone in the country has a ceramic tile porch floor or entryway. The clean shiny tile indicates that the inside of the house is also clean. This is an important status symbol. The home was lovely.

Since a rodeo was taking place that afternoon, we stayed a couple of hours to watch. This was their first rodeo. We were told that several Texans had gone to Costa Rica to show and teach the people how a rodeo is done. Many local people had gathered and were sitting on the arena fence. Not such a safe thing to do in my estimation, but then again I'm not much of a rodeo fan. In spite of the heat, and loud noise/music in the press box we occupied, we had fun watching the cowboys try to rope the calves and ride the bulls. I suspect that rodeo may become a big thing south of the border.

Eventually we needed to move on and by the time we turned off the main road onto the approach road to our lodge in Chachagua it started to rain. Part way up, the lodge security guard was out in force, the road was blocked by a large number of ducks! This hotel was located in the depths of the rain forest on a private preserve. The cabins were separated by lush growth and could be a

217

bit difficult to find. We crossed the river just below a lovely waterfall and walked the path through thick vegetation to our lovely cabin. The bathroom had large picture windows on two sides and all one could see was the tropical vegetation outside. What a view!

An adequate overhang on the fair size porch on the front of the cabin made it a perfect spot to enjoy morning coffee.

The lodge had a resident green macaw that was a little on the cantankerous side. Its mate died a couple of years before and since they mate for life, more than likely she'll be alone for the rest of her life. She flew about at will, but often perched on the open dining room rail, always watchful for fallen crumbs.

I fell asleep to the sound of running water from the waterfall, not far from our bungalow. This lodge was the best, I could have stayed forever.

It was a fairly long ride to the northern border of Alajuela Province. We previously had been told Costa Rica has seven provinces.

Arriving in Los Chiles, we boarded a boat for a ride down the Rio Frío. The river borders the 24,600-acre Caño Negro Wildlife Refuge, which sits in the migratory flyway of hundreds of thousands of birds--a true birder's delight.

Moving down the river was a slow process as the tree-lined banks were full of birds and monkeys. We saw white face and Howler Monkeys including a couple of Howler babies. Those Howlers sure are noisy, perhaps appropriately named. They are all black and I think have rather ugly faces, although the babies sure were cute.

We learned White Face Monkeys will eat anything, but Howlers are vegetarians and eat early in the day because they need sunlight to digest their food.

The boat driver got us close to a tree where we could see tiny tiny bats spread out on the tree trunk. They looked like part of the bark. Not more than two or three inches long, they were lined up vertically six or seven in a row.

We saw several kinds of lizards. Among the many kinds of birds, we saw the snail kite, osprey, northern jacana, ringed kingfisher, blue-grey tanager, green-black heron, egret, large egret, mangrove swallow, roadside hawk, scarlet sandpiper, Amazon kingfisher, black-bellied whistling duck, anhinga, and many more. Macaws live deep in the forests of Costa Rica. Eventually the river opened up into a shallow lagoon.

I had read, and our guide confirmed, that Costa Rica is one of the most ecologically aware countries in the world. In fact one quarter (26 percent) of its land has been set aside as national park or preserve. 13 percent of the land is National Parkland, and an additional 13 percent of the land is private reserve abiding by government agreements. These nature and biological preserves protect a vast array of animals and their habitats, and insures the survival of over 850 species of birds, 205 species of mammals, 376 kinds of reptiles and amphibians, and more than 9000 species of flowering plants, including 1200 varieties of orchids.

Just three decades ago there was hardly a protected area in the country. The country's conservation efforts are even more remarkable considering that it is not a wealthy country, having limited resources. During the first years of the country's park systems, conservationists raced against rampant deforestation to protect as much of the nation's wild lands as possible. Infrastructure is still lacking, and many of the areas still can only be reached on foot or by horseback.

The long ride was a pretty one. The river trip had been full of wildlife and birds I'd never seen. It had been a beautiful warm day. For dinner one night in Chachagua we had the most delicious tenderloin I've ever eaten. I never order steak out because it is never cooked the way I like it, and it's such an easy meal to prepare at home. When eating out I eat something I don't normally cook. I couldn't believe that I had actually been served a perfect steak.

After dinner I took the guide with me to interpret so I could tell the cook how good her meal was and how much I appreciated it. I think she was dubious at first at being summoned, but when I had finished she broke into a big grin.

Walking back to my bungalow in the evening I heard the weirdest sounds. To me it sounded like a clay pot receiving one gong. It was loud and steady. The next morning the guide told me it was a Ting Frog talking.

Costa Rica can be divided into several regions. In the Northwest cattle graze on dry plains as it is the driest region. But the dry cattle ranches give way to lush river deltas and the coast provides popular beaches. Sometimes referred to as the Gold Coast, the challenge is to not overbuild the area with big resorts that would crowd the beaches. Leatherback turtles come ashore here to lay their eggs, and howler moneys and raccoon-like coatis roam the dry tropical forest.

The southwest has a diverse and varied landscape and ecosystems with cloud forests of the Talamanca Mountains to the lowland rain forest and isolated beaches of the Osa peninsula. The area boasts of one of the best botanical gardens in all of Latin America and contains several private biological reserves.

The Atlantic Lowlands is home to some of the country's densest jungle and wildest places. Separated from the rest of the country by towering mountains and volcanoes, the intense heat and wet climate dictates a slower lifestyle. Most of the blacks in this area claim Jamaican ancestry, while the Indians have more in common with people from western Panama. The area boasts miles of isolated coral-fringed beaches, easygoing small towns and enchanting national parks.

A mountainous chain of volcanoes in north-central Costa Rica provides hot, dry plains west of the mountains and upland and lowland jungles, forests, and plains to the east.

Another day lunch was at the Tabacon Hot Springs Resort. As we entered, an attendant placed a plastic wristband on each of us.

This gave us the privilege, after lunch, of partaking of the thermal pools. Lunch was served in an open covered dining room overlooking the lovely grounds. After changing into bathing suits we were given a locker and towel. There are several man-made pools in the river, and several more pools were among the lush tropical landscape. Pool temperatures ranged from rather cool to almost steamy hot. One even had a waterfall. That warm water falling on the neck and back felt heavenly!

After trying several of the pools, both in the river and among the vegetation we settled by ourselves in the uppermost pool. Because it had two streams running into it there were areas of both warm and cool temperatures in the same pool.

My son and I stayed in the pools as long as possible, and begrudgingly got out when it was time to leave.

Our hotel, only ten minutes away, was directly across from Arenal, one of the world's most active volcanoes.

It was an extremely clear day and whiffs of smoke could be seen puffing from the volcano's top.

Arenal exploded to life in 1968, after 400 years of inactivity, and has been steaming and spitting ever since. Eighty people were killed in that massive eruption.

Much of the time the top part of this presently perfect conical volcano is shrouded in clouds. It is said that only about three percent of the people who venture to see Arenal actually see the top.

The best views are at night when, in darkness, the red-hot lava rolling down the side of the volcano is more of a contrast and more vivid. For us, the sky remained clear all night, and the volcano just kept belching its smoke and lava steadily all night long. We were very lucky!

A dam created the 25-mile long Lake Arenal in 1978.The road around it really requires a four-wheel drive vehicle. Several resorts surround the lake, as it is a popular recreation area.

The transfer from Arenal to Buena Vista was a long one

driving from Alajuela Province to Guanacaste Province.

The Guanacaste, meaning "elephant ear," is the national tree of Costa Rica. The seeds of the tree are big and shaped like an elephant's ear.

By late afternoon it started to rain. The road to Buena Vista Lodge was about 10 miles from the main road. It was a narrow, one-car road that not only was winding, but had a lot of ups and downs. It was fortunate we did not meet a car coming down.

In two places the driver took that van over very narrow wooden bridges with no guardrails. Halfway up the road the water was gushing everywhere. There were two areas where rapid water crossed over the road. Those concerned me, as that Toyota was not that far off the ground, and were similar to situations in Texas where one would never attempt to cross. But we made it safely.

We had left our lovely single cabins behind, as these family run cabins were triplexes.

At five the next morning, the Howler Monkeys woke us with their howling. When they finished, the White Throated Magpie sang to us. We were happy to see it would be a sunny day. Walking across the meadow to the entrance of a dry forest we saw leaf cutter ants. The ants carry the leaves to the nest, chew them up, but do not eat them. The chewed mess is medium for fungus to grow, and they do eat the fungus.

During the hour and a half walk to some steam vents, we saw spotted toucans and heard monkeys but couldn't find them. We saw an agouti, white-throated magpies, and a bat falcon.

The strangler fig tree is interesting because it grows from the top to the bottom. An animal drops the seed at the top of the canopy and then the fig grows down using the original tree as a host, although it doesn't live off the other tree. In about 30 years the strangler fig kills the original tree and in another 30 years the fig tree dies.

We also saw an anise plant, and a rubiaccea plant, which is related to the coffee plant. It grows wild, but the beans are not edible.

A dry forest has palm trees, which grow in the dry season when the bigger trees in the forest lose their leaves giving the palm and smaller plants more light.

Arriving at the mud baths, we all went into the steam room built over a natural seam vent. The steam entered through the spaces between the floorboards. It was pretty hot inside, but our guide kept us all entertained with a story.

Leaving the steam room, we gathered around the mud pots and got covered with warm mud. As we air dried you could feel the pulling of the skin, and I'm sure we were a hilarious sight. The dried mud was not so easy to wash off under the showers, but we helped each other especially on the backs. Then it was into any of the three small thermal pools.

Costa Ricans call themselves Ticos. They would rather be called Costa Ricans than Central or Latin Americans. One often hears the country has more schoolteachers than policemen. The literacy rate is over 90 percent. They are proud of their history, culture, and achievements.

We found the people polite and very friendly. Always warm and hospitable, they were willing to help at any time. The country has a deep respect for human rights. Basically a nation of immigrants, the country is a working man's republic.

The ten-mile ride down from Buena Vista was much better than going up in the rain. It was Independence Day, September 15, and a holiday. We stopped in a small town to watch a parade.

One of the gals stopped to buy a Fanta and the clerk cracked the bottle for her asking if she wanted a bag. She kind of a shrugged an okay. The clerk proceeded to pour the drink into a plastic bag, inserted a straw, and handed her the bag. How lucky she was that the bag didn't leak!

Again late in the day, it started to rain. We were headed for a boat ride at the Carara Biological Reserve, Carara means "river of crocodiles." The boat we boarded was covered, at least with a roof.

The river was a partial tidal estuary. In spite of the rain we saw a lot of birds. Our search for crocodiles was not in vain as we spotted several when they surfaced for air.

Our Pacific Coast destination was a real tourist area where the cabins were weird shaped quadruplexes. Although nice, after all of our lovely quaint facilities, we all agreed it was just too touristy.

On a sunny day it was a short drive to Puntarenas where we were cautioned not to leave anything unattended while we waited for the boat. The catamaran, *Calypso*, took us across the Gulf of Nicoya to Punta Coral. Every few minutes a steward came by with fresh pineapple, papaya, or watermelon during the 90-minute ride. It was a beautiful day, and we roamed the boat at will.

Once ashore, our guide held a short briefing, telling us about the facility and saying we could go swimming in the crescent shaped sandy beach, snorkeling, kayaking, or hiking.

I received a kayak lesson from my son, and then we kayaked all around the area. Later, before lunch we went swimming in the warm water.

Talking to the owners of the little island we learned they were originally from San Francisco. They fell in love with Costa Rica on a visit in 1973, and kept figuring a way they could stay. Finally, the fellow realized there was no boat available to take people to the little islands, so he built one and created the "ferry" service to the small off shore islands. Eventually they bought the small island of Punta Coral.

She had been a chef in a San Francisco restaurant, so you can imagine the fabulous lunch we enjoyed in the covered open dining facility attached to an enclosed kitchen.

After lunch it was up hill on the hiking path to the far side of the island to view the ocean. But the return was all down hill. It was a delightful day, and all too soon *Calypso* returned for us.

Back in San Jose, we had the better part of a day to shop or see anything that was still on our list.

The next day at the airport, our gate was next to the liquor store. I wandered in to see if possibly I could find my Coca 'd Amor. I didn't, but some samples of Britta coffee liquor were available. It was good, so I bought a couple of small bottles to take home. I would have purchased more, but I had no room to pack it or easy way to transport it.

We had plenty of time before boarding, so while I watched the luggage, my son returned to the main part of the terminal. While he was gone I started to clean out my pocket, when I suddenly I realized I had both our boarding passes in my pocket. I was beginning to worry as he was gone for some time.

When he returned he told me he inadvertently got on the other side of immigration, then without a boarding pass he couldn't get back in. Showing the gal his ticket she still wouldn't let him through.

Finally he requested an English-speaking agent. When he arrived he showed him his ticket, but the agent couldn't convince the girl to let him through either. He suggested they accompany him to the gate where I was with the passes, but still no go.

Eventually the fellow went and got an American Airlines agent, and they went through the scenario all over again. The agent said to hold on a minute, disappeared, and returned with another boarding pass, then the gal allowed him through.

All ended well, but what a hassle, the only one on the entire trip!

I enjoyed my Britta for some time that fall, and wished I'd been able to carry more. Every time I drank it I remembered the wonderful fun filled adventure we'd had in Costa Rica!

Chapter 16

Tahiti and the Cook Islands

Who hasn't dreamed of going to romantic Tahiti? After watching Hawaii become so commercialized over the years, I too dreamed of Tahiti. Flower leis, Polynesian dancers, thatched roof huts, beautiful sandy beaches, palm trees swaying in the breeze, all go into making Tahiti a romantic and magical place.

So, in 1997, I made the very long flight. Arriving in Los Angeles, I had a four-hour layover before picking up my Air New Zealand flight for the eight-hour trip to Papeete. Losing four to five hours in flight we arrived in the middle of the night at 2:45 AM.

Leaving the airport a native girl presented me a frangipani (plumeria) lei, bringing back memories of similar arrivals in Hawaii years ago.

Arriving at a hotel at 4:45 in the morning, we found fruit drinks poured and waiting for us at check-in. My weary body found the weather hot, steamy, and humid. I managed to find my room by following the signs out, over, up, and around. I lay down on the bed to rest, knowing that sleep would be elusive. I opened the drapes, hardly able to wait for daylight to see what was outside!

A little past 7:00 AM I was standing at the sliding glass door looking out over my little deck absorbing the incredible beauty outside my room. Beyond the grounds was a walkway inside the seawall. Looking across Moon Bay I could see the outline of Moorea. Beyond the sea wall, the bay was a little over 100 yards away.

Full coconut palms and all kinds of tropical flowers and flowering bushes and trees awaited my investigation. The people, mostly hotel workers, walking about all were speaking French.

The little wooden deck outside my room was the perfect place to have coffee. But first on the agenda—after nearly 30 hours of traveling—was a hot shower and a change of clothes.

Brunch was served at 10:30 in the Tiare (flower) room, just off the lobby. At brunch I determined that apparently I was the only single female on the trip.

I wandered the grounds most of the morning. The flora was beautiful. The swimming pool was just like one you'd see on TV with a thatched roof cabana bar in the center. The pool wasn't very deep and was meant more for cooling off than actually swimming. There were several thatched roof cabanas suspended on pilings over the bay. This little paradise would fulfill anyone's romantic dream!

We left the hotel at one for a bus tour of Papeete. Papeete means "basket of water." Tahiti is 2790 miles from Honolulu and 4000 miles from Los Angles. Tahiti is both the country and an island. Tahiti, meaning "many islands," is part of French Polynesia. Tahiti is the largest of the 118 islands and atolls that make up the Society Islands. The island, 35 miles long, is shaped like an hourglass, with two distinct, extinct volcanoes connected by a narrow isthmus.

Moorea lies 16 miles across the bay. Nine of Tahiti's islands are volcanic and five are atolls. Mount Orohena, Tahiti's highest point, towers 7321 feet above sea level. Mount Tohivea on Moorea stands at 3975 feet.

The island's population is 130,000 and the population of all of French Polynesia is 230,000. Papeete is the main shipping and distribution center in Tahiti. The port facilities were expanded in the 1960's. Between 1962-64, nearly 35 acres of land were reclaimed at the northern end of the harbor and now is an industrial and military area.

Papeete's streets were crowded with sport cars, motorbikes, and the island's cheap, public, picturesque transport, Les Truck.

Polynesia geographically is the largest of the Pacific's culture areas and distances between island groups is great. Polynesia lies mostly below the equator and includes the Hawaiian, Cook, Society, and Easter Islands as well as Samoa, Tonga, the Tuamotus and the Marquesas. Fiji sits between Polynesia and Melanesia.

Many of the Society Islands and Rarotonga in the Cooks are high volcanic islands. Volcanic islands are usually surrounded by fringing reefs varying from a few to several hundred yards from the shoreline. These areas most often offer good fishing, and the fringing reefs are essential for the formation of coral atolls.

Shallow, clear, warm salt water allows both coral and calcareous algae to thrive and eventually build a reef. The coral can reach extreme depths.

Tahiti's islands are divided into two groups; the five windward islands include Tahiti and Moorea, the nine leeward islands include Bora Bora. French Polynesia is the farthest east of all the South Pacific Islands. The climate is warm all year and being consistent makes it an anytime paradise.

Indigenous Polynesians represent 70 percent of the population, those of French extraction 15 percent, mixed Polynesians and French eight percent, and Chinese seven percent.

The main islands of Tahiti, Moorea, and Bora Bora have one road around the perimeter of the island, with no roads over the mountains. Metal roofs are slowly replacing thatched roofs as they last longer than the eight or ten years of a thatched roof. The houses were small and almost always on the mountainside of the road. The road tends to follow the water line and there is very little land between the road and the water. The houses are often strung out side-by-side in a single row, and not clustered together.

Bread boxes, long and looking like little houses with slanted roofs are often mistaken for mail boxes, but they are actually for

French bread, which is delivered daily.

During the rainy season, October to March, the annual rainfall measures about 73 inches! We saw many beautiful waterfalls coming out of and falling down the mountains. I was surprised to see so many streams and small rivers.

All islands currently making up French Polynesia had been annexed by France and governed by her until 1957, then became a territorire d'outré-mer with a governor in Papeete, a council and territorial assembly elected in five constituencies.

In 1977 France granted partial internal self-government. Now French Polynesia is an autonomous Territory of the French Republic having two elected members in the French National Assembly, one in the Senate, and one representative in the European Parliament.

The city tour ended at five that afternoon at the boat harbor where we boarded *The World Discoverer* with accommodations for 138 passengers.

It was a beautiful sunny day as we approached Bora Bora. On deck I was taking pictures just as the sun was peeking over the low part of the island.

Bora Bora means "first born" and in this part of the world is pronounced Pora Pora as there is no B sound in Polynesian. The main island, 6 x 3 miles, is surrounded by coral islets. Two smaller islands are separated on the west by a channel. The east side of the island is barren. The fertile west side's main crops are vanilla and copra. Tourism is also a major industry. The population on Bora Bora is 4500.

The interior of the island has slopes, hills, cliffs, and U-shaped mountains with deep gorges and is covered with native vegetation. Captain Cook named the islands the Society Islands because of their close proximity to each other. It is home to 400 species of native flowering plants including more than a dozen orchid varieties.

The World Discoverer was adamant about us always wearing

life jackets when we were in the zodiacs. By 8:30 AM we were ready for our first zodiac ride to the one pier in the harbor. Then it was our first ride in the colorful Les Truck. The one road around the island is 22 miles long and mostly paved.

Bora Bora is incredibly beautiful. Every turn in the road afforded us a photo op. The flora was abundant and colorful, truly a picture I doubt any artist could ever capture.

The local guide on Les Truck told us the island had one physician, one pharmacy, and one hospital—clinic really, as it was only able to handle minor problems.

We made many stops along the way not only for photos but also to learn about the culture. We ate tiny, thumb-sized bananas, which were very sweet, and sampled fresh taro and poke, an island tapioca and papaya pudding.

Relatives are buried in the yards as there are no public cemeteries, and often times a family will erect a shrine in their yard for their loved one.

Ancient open-air temples were called marae and at one stop we saw many coral slabs from a marae. Another ancient relic we saw was the turtle stone, a petroglyph representing several turtles.

During World War II, Bora Bora hosted 6000 men stationed at naval and air bases there. Near the base was a reef where an abundance of friendly and curious moray eels lived.

The island's hotels are located on the southeast side of the island, famous for its gorgeous long white sand beaches.

At 7:30 on another morning, we were loading the zodiacs for an early morning bird hike on Mopelia, a coral atoll. The atoll, roughly circular, has a diameter of five miles with several outcroppings. The only inhabitants were birds, small lizards, and a few harmless spiders. It is also a nesting area for frigate birds and red-footed boobies. Walking the perimeter of the island we saw thousands of birds flying low overhead. Frigate birds and red-footed boobies were easily identifiable. Brown boobies, terns, and noddings were also flying about.

After our hike we moved on to Maupihea, the largest out cropping, to swim and snorkel in the lagoon. On the beach the boat crew opened coconuts for us so we could have a drink of cold coconut milk. Before we went in the water, the gals from the ship put on a pareu tying demonstration for us.

Part of the atoll was a protected nature preserve for the green turtle that swims hundreds of miles to lay her eggs there.

Snorkeling the lagoon was like looking into a fish nursery. It was a safe environment for many species of baby fish because it was difficult for predators to enter the lagoon.

The deck frequently disappeared from under foot during the 350-mile ride to Atiu in the Cook Islands. The rough seas had me clinging to the bulkhead during the night in order to stay in the bunk.

The Cook Islands, west of Tonga, spread out over 850,000 square miles of Pacific Ocean and consists of 15 islands with a total landmass of 93 square miles. The southern islands are fertile and support the majority of the 18,000 residents. Thirty thousand Cook Islanders live overseas, mostly in New Zealand.

The largest island in the southern group is Rarotonga. The northern group of islands are sea level atolls and lagoons.

The residents of the Cook Islands are New Zealand citizens. The language is English, although Polynesian and Maori dialects are also spoken.

The Cooks, governed by a parliamentary system with three political parties, has a stable government. Members are elected for five-year terms. In 1965 when the Cooks became independent, the three-year term was increased to four, and is now five years.

At Atiu we loaded the zodiacs again, only this time we surfed through the breakwater's narrow opening to the beach where we were greeted by conch blowing and drum beating warriors and friendly gals who gave each of us a fresh flower lei. The whole island had turned out to greet us.

Ushered to their open-air recreation building we were given a feast of fresh island fruit served on woven palm fond plates. The tree-ripened fruit was delicious! Then these very friendly people put on a very good dance demonstration for us.

The only means of transportation on the island is Les Truck. But here it was literally a pick up truck with benches placed in the bed of the truck.

The island had many narrow, sometimes tire track, roads. The vegetation was lush and thick. Atiu's high central plateau at 233 feet is a contrast to its neighboring flat islands. Low swamps and a 66-foot high raised coral reef surround the island. Dense forest grows on the west coast and low growing bird nest ferns provide a thick green ground cover. The cliffs of Makatea contain extensive limestone caves.

Atiu's 900 residents live in five villages in clustered groups inland, different from the Tahitians who live around the perimeter of their islands. In 1777 when Captain Cook discovered this volcanic island he named it Island Enuamanu meaning "land of birds." Coffee, taro, pineapple, papaya, and oranges are grown for export to New Zealand.

Stopping at the rather small Atui Coffee Company we learned there are two types of coffee beans grown in the world: robusta and arabica. Robusta beans are dried in their shells absorbing caffeine and acid in the process. Because this would be too bitter to drink plain, the beans are combined with arabica beans, which are dried without their shells.

Arabica beans are only grown in a few places, Atiu, Kenya, and Costa Rica among them. The beans are separated by size before roasting to produce even roasting. The size of the bean does not determine flavor. Caffeine and acid are lost in the roasting process, so that is why dark roasted coffee has less caffeine. Atiu coffee is 100 percent sun dried.

In the center of the island a local docent told us that many years ago someone paced off the island north to south and east and west and marked that point as the center of the island. More recently surveyors repeated the process with modern instruments and found the original marker off by only two meters!

Close by was an ancient marae. High chiefs would gather there to decide if they would or would not go to war. The three tribes on the island are each ruled by its own chief and leadership is passed on to the oldest son.

Tourism is in its infancy on Atiu. Its one tourist facility accommodates the 600 annual visitors. The owner, an Englishman, told us he met his wife, a Tahitian, in New Zealand more than 25 years ago. After a holiday on Atiu in 1979 they decided to move there and flew in on the first plane to land on the island. He built all four bungalows using native woods. The cabins were lovely and the whole area so quiet and peaceful. What a great honeymoon spot!

Aitutaki is generally referred to as an atoll, but its structure is unique, as the island is actually part coral and part volcanic. Covering only eight square miles, it is the northernmost island of the southern islands in the Cook chain. A low barrier reef protects its triangular shaped lagoon, which has 15 small, uninhabited islands in it with the whitest of white sand beaches and beautiful clear water, all fringed with coconut palms.

Again we maneuvered through a cut in the reef. The flower lei, a symbol of love and peace, was again given to each of us.

We walked up hill to a large recreation hall where we sat on benches to watch a dance demonstration accompanied by a small island band.

The Les Trucks for the island tour were a bit more comfortable than the ones on Atiu. Aitutaki is 155 miles from Roratonga and is referred to as the "almost atoll" because of its lagoon, coral reef, and scattered sand islets and a high volcanic island at the northern end. The rolling hills are lined with banana plantations and coconut palms.

This island was lush with foliage, but there were fewer flowering plants. We saw the large heart shaped "elephant ear" type leaf of the taro plant everywhere.

Coffee, pineapple, breadfruit, papaya, mango, guava, and oranges are grown on the island. Cows, goats, chickens, and wild pigs grazed everywhere. But there were no dogs on the island. Fish is the main protein source of the island diet. A boat with supplies arrives once a month. Nearly everything, except fruit and vegetables, needs to be imported.

Religion, mostly Congregational, is a large part of island life. The island council rules life on the island. Each of the seven villages has one representative to the council. All the land belongs to the people, and the government must lease the land for their buildings. The total island population is 2500.

The island's two hotels and seven guesthouses are able to accommodate the island's 1000 annual visitors.

Most of the road around the island was a tire track road.

However, about two miles before we reached an absolutely gorgeous park we hit a paved road. This park was at the lagoon's edge. Palm trees grew everywhere affording relief from the hot sun. Islanders had laid out the most fantastic feast for our lunch. Local musicians serenaded us for over two hours while we ate. The yellow fin tuna was delicious.

The chef told us the fish is sliced very thin, dipped in a marinade, then cooked quickly. When asked for the marinade ingredients he smiled saying it was a family secret.

The food was served on woven palm fond plates. All the large serving dishes were also woven; it made for a very attractive table. Included in the meal were all kinds of fruits, and salads. It was a feast fit for a king!

After we had digested our lunch we took the small boats out to the sandbars to snorkel the reef. The water was so clear we could see the numerous fish with the naked eye. Venturing into the deep holes revealed an under water spectacle. I swam among the fish until I got chilled, then reluctantly got out of the water, sat on the sand bar, and warmed under the tropical sun.

These friendly sweet people definitely know what's important in life. The pace is slow and relaxed. The people are happy and content living in this lovely island paradise. I truly fell in love with Aitutaki!

It was an all evening and night cruise to Rarotonga. A large cut in the reef allowed ships to enter the harbor.

Rarotonga, the largest of the Cook Islands, is the capitol, and spectacularly beautiful. Shaped like a small round bean it is surrounded by a protective reef, which is broken in five or six places. On the east side of the island there are four atolls in the lagoon. Beautiful white sand beaches, fringed with coconut palms surround the island. The turquoise blue lagoon is full of colorful tropical fish.

Rarotonga is directly south of Hawaii, the same distance south of the equator as Hawaii is north of the equator. Thus the climates are similar except the seasons are reversed. Extremes of humidity and rainfall are not common.

After breakfast we left the ship; our luggage went directly to the hotel.

Small, but real buses were on this island. It is twenty miles around the island. There are two roads. The one on the coast has two lanes, one in each direction except for a short distance downtown, Avarua, where there are four lanes. Two lanes in each direction are divided by a wide, grassy median.

The second road is a half-mile inland and connects with many small side roads that wind through banana plantations and farms. Chief Toi built the inland coral road in the 11th century. The road was later fitted with large hand cut lava rocks and only a few years ago covered with macadam.

Few cars were on Rarotonga's roads but mopeds were everywhere. They were very quiet, and obviously a very common and economical means of transportation. Bicycles were also a popular means of transportation. The yellow public buses ran around the island on a pretty regular basis following a printed schedule. There were two buses, one ran clockwise the other anticlockwise. We say counterclockwise, they anticlockwise. One can flag down a bus anywhere and/or request special stops. After 6 PM only one bus runs every two hours until 11 PM. Friday is party night so the buses run until 1AM. On Sunday, buses run only to church.

There are 11,000 people living on Rarotonga. The island is divided into two districts, each run by a powerful clan chief known as ariki. The only rivalry now between the tribes is on the rugby field.

The main town and capitol of the island is Avarua, which stretches along the waterfront. Avarua, the commercial center for the island, has one main street that is easy to navigate with easy identifiable landmarks. The island is often referred to as Raro and everything is on Raro time. Merchants are open 8-4 weekdays and 8-11 on Saturday.

As pearl farms mature, the black pearl industry is becoming an economic boost to the islands. Rarotonga is known for the high quality of its handcrafts, which include carved figurines, musical instruments, and woven goods.

There is a local restriction that no building can be built taller than the tallest palm tree. This has and will continue to retain the picturesque charm of Rarotonga. (I favor that!)

People were friendly and helpful. English was widely spoken, although everyone was bilingual, speaking their own language as well.

Land ownership was the same as in the rest of the Cook Islands.

Homes were larger here than on the out islands and many were made of concrete block with metal roofs. There were only a few "native huts." Telephone poles were concrete, as no pine trees grow on the island.

My hotel room had sliding glass doors leading out onto a wooden verandah. The view included the beach, lagoon, and the breaking surf over the reef. With an ice machine not far away I was able to make my own ice tea!

Diesel generators provide electrical power 24 hours a day, the smaller out islands turn off all power at 11PM. Two natural springs provide a good amount of the water supply, but islanders are still very dependent on rainfall and all homes/buildings have catchment systems. Water now is piped into homes but is not treated, so filtration systems are necessary.

The island is dependent on many imports, most of which come from New Zealand. The Coco-Net arrived in Rarotonga three months before my visit. Coco means "to wander," thus the name of the cellular phone network!

Restaurants were plentiful with something for every palate. Local delicacies included octopus, ika mata which is raw fish marinated in lime juice, then combined with coconut milk and other ingredients—often vegetables and/or salad greens. Motu roni is the innards of the sea cucumber, which I was told, resembles spaghetti. These are cooked with butter, garlic, and other spices. Many natives eat motu romi raw. In this part of the world, sea cucumbers are called sea slugs, which to me has a very slimy connotation. These slugs grow about a foot long and are plentiful in the lagoons near the reef. After extracting the insides the slug is thrown back in the water where it regenerates its loses and in six to eight weeks is again ready for such punishment. Poke is a paw paw pudding. The paw paw is the same as the papaya. It is mixed with tapioca and coconut cream. Orange in color it has a funny texture and a rather bland taste. Coconut is served with each meal, and since I love coconut, I was a happy camper.

The interior of the island is rugged and mountainous covered with dense lush green growth. The narrow valleys and steep hills make it difficult to populate. The Needle, a rock pinnacle, in the center of the island stands 2000 above the fertile valley. It is the highest point on the island and a vigorous hike over a razorback ridge, one few tourists attempt.

I did trek into the jungle with Pa, the medicine man. Pa was a 58-year-old native Rarotongan sporting blond dreadlocks and wearing a tie-dyed pareu wrapped sort of like a diaper. He was some sight, a real local character! He told the 16 of us who were brave enough to follow him, "I've hiked into the mountain over 1000 times."

On the walk to where the lush vegetation began we saw chestnut trees and wild pumpkin/squash vines.

As we walked through the forest he pointed out the tapioca plant, a candlenut tree and the *no no plant*, telling us the oil from the candlenut was used to light lanterns before the days of kerosene. The fruit of the *no no plant* was used for prostate or kidney problems by taking two nuts, some of the leaves, and mixing them with green coconut milk.

We passed by several old plantation ruins deep in the valleys. Following a stream into the lush greenness, we traveled up and over fallen trees; down on the other side; across the stream; balanced over some rocks; and repeated it all over again. It was a pretty rugged hike. The climb was often steep and we crossed that stream so many times!

I was glad mosquito juice no longer has the pungent odor of years past, because I was all doused up with the stuff. The mosquitoes were thick and pesky.

Pa got us to an ancient marae which I'm guessing, was a couple of miles into the jungle. It is very hard to judge distance on this type of a criss-cross, up and down hike.

When we arrived at the site Pa said, before we could step on the marae he'd have to talk to his ancestors and bless the marae. Because he was a high ariki (kahuna, priest) he could do that. When Pa was finished we stepped on the marae to rest a bit.

When Pa asked if we wanted to continue on, it was a unanimous vote to not continue any further. We had been hiking and swatting mosquitoes for several hours, and enough was enough.

Returning to the stream where we had passed a rather pretty waterfall we stopped for a late lunch surrounded by dinosaur ferns. Pa said those ferns grow in only two other places in the world, Hawaii, and Costa Rica. It was extremely quiet and peaceful with only the sound of the waterfall breaking the silence.

The hike was really tough on the knees and thighs. The next couple of days my legs and body was not very happy with the abuse I had given it. At any rate the jungle was really beautiful and I'm glad I trekked it. The purpose of this trek was to learn about local medicinal plants, and that part of the experience I found lacking.

A New Zealand study termed the island of Rarotonga a natural greenhouse with its year round growing season with relatively low insect population. (The bugs were all in the jungle!) The fertile valleys and wide perimeter produce an abundance of bananas, coconut, papaya, oranges, star fruit, mango, breadfruit, passion fruit, taro, frangipani, hibiscus, oleander and many other flowering plants and trees.

Returning to the hotel, I went swimming in the pool to give my joints a soothing bath. The salt water of the ocean probably would have been better, but I had no one to buddy with, and I just could not break my hard and fast rule of never swimming alone.

Most of one day was spent at the Cultural Center. It was a most informative day. Located on the west side of the island, it had lovely landscaped grounds. There were several huts around telling the history of the island. Many huts had demonstrations. It was an extremely interesting day.

Another day was free to shop or whatever. One evening was a Cook Island luau. After two restful, peaceful weeks, all too soon it was time to pack, and get ready to return home.

Chapter 17

Bordeaux on a Bike

When I used to think of Bordeaux I always thought of wine. Now I remember the frogs croaking in the drainage ditch along side the road and the cuckoos hidden in the trees joining the serenade as I peddled by on my bike!

Much of De Gaulle airport in Paris was under construction in 1998, making it quite a hassle to change terminals for my connecting flight to Bordeaux. Once that flight actually got off the ground, over an hour late, it was only a 55-minute flight to Bordeaux. Then it was about an hour's bus ride south to Sabres where this biking adventure began.

The first day everyone is always pretty tired from the flight and time change, so the biking is usually an easy day. In this case it was only eight miles to Lugion over a flat paved road through a pine and fern forest. In the afternoon we visited a beekeeper who gave us a rather extensive lecture on the life and sex of bees and showed us several different kinds of hives, as well as some experimental hives he was using.

Back in Sabres with bikes secured we caught a train for a short ride to the ecomuseum at Las Landes. This railroad, originally built to carry logs out of the pine forest, has been running since 1887.

At one time this whole area was a sandy desolate area with only some small scrubby growth. Napoleon III gave permission to plant the area with pine trees for erosion control, and it became the largest pine forest in Europe.

During the train ride we noticed many of the trees were tapped. The pitch is collected, refined, and then used in turpentine, resins, cosmetics, pharmacy, and paint cleaners

A museum guide told us the museum was established in 1970 and the area called Las Landes covers 600 square miles. She guided us through the museum, explaining everything along the way. It was a most interesting visit.

That evening we were served the specialty of the area—duck. Although duck is not one of my favorite foods it was very good.

Before I go any further I need to say something about food and the French dinner hour. First, the dinner hour tends to be late—at least 7:00 PM, often later. The French make an *event* out of eating. We never had an evening meal that took less than two hours, and often it would approach three hours.

Normally in Europe, and a lot of other places in the world, drinks, including water, are never included with a meal. So it was a pleasant surprise to have wine served with our duck dinner.

And as it turned out we had plenty of wine every evening. Bottles of wine were placed on the table, after four people filled their glasses the bottle was empty, and the guys were not a bit shy about waving the empty bottle in the air for the waitress. Of course we were in wine country, wines were extremely reasonable, and we also had the big boss with us. I suspect that the hotels were just taking good care of him as a thank you for all the business he brings them —-or else he ended up with a good size bar tab, which I doubt. We never paid for a single drink in the evening on the entire trip!

Service was generally slow, the food was generally good, the company and conversation was pleasant, and the evening meal was a great way to wind down after busy and full days of biking.

France, a country of 58 million people is four-fifths the size of Texas. Neighboring countries sharing the northern border are Germany, Belgium, Switzerland, and Luxembourg. Italy borders on the east, and Spain on the southwest. France has access to the

North Sea, Atlantic Ocean, English Channel, and Mediterranean.

Bordeaux, in the southwest part of the country, was warm and sunny so I was able to leave the raingear packed for the entire trip!

Except for the serenade of the frogs and cuckoos little else disturbed the silence for nearly three days as we biked through lovely pine forest. Sand often covered part of the road and bike paths. If one wandered off the pavement the sand bogged you down quickly. A small low mesquite-like shrub grew along the edge of some of the path. The nasty little thorns were the cause of most of our flat tires.

I escaped a flat until the very end of the trip, but I was glad those repairs were the leader's problem and not mine.

All the bikers on this trip were experienced but relaxed, with only one gal thinking this was a competition and that she always needed to be first.

It was a cloudy overcast day as we continued south bucking a headwind the whole twelve miles to Malconx where we stopped for lunch in the town square. Perched under a tree canopy in the center of the square, I was amazed at how the trees had been trimmed and trained on overhead wires to grow sideways instead of up. Very few shops were open and virtually no one was wandering around town.

We spent all afternoon bucking the wind, so we were all ready to stop when we arrived at Lit et Mixe.

On the way north to Arcachon we traveled some busy roads. The French didn't cut us any slack even though we were hugging the curb. They drove fast on the narrow roads. We hit some steep hills which most of us ended up walking the last third to the top.

Parts of the bike paths were over small rolling hills, which presented no problem. With a decent run, one could make it to the top without gearing down and without gasping for your last breath. Ah, the coast down the backside, often at a pretty good clip, was always a delight. On the really big hills it was tempting to fly down with a child's abandon, but a speed of 40-45 miles an hour with traffic, debris, and sometimes curves is pretty foolhardy. An accident in a foreign country, especially one in which you don't speak the language is not my idea of fun. So, we all tempered those down hill rides with a little break power. Some road construction areas were rather stressful.

Most of the group was sensible. However, we had one gal who abandoned all common sense on one very steep down hill ride. We all were well strung out with at least 100 feet between us because of the heavy traffic. Dressed in a black shirt and black shorts, all of a sudden she came down the middle of the street passing all of us as if we were standing still. Hiked out over her handlebars put her little black tail in the air.

I, as well as everyone else, started to break a little more as we really envisioned an accident. Then a dump truck came down the hill. He was right up behind her before realizing he had a biker in front of him. We all held our breath at the sound of his squealing breaks. It was close!

The driver was so upset he pulled off the road and waited until all of us passed. One of the fellows stopped to speak to him and I suspect to apologize for the biker's behavior. I thanked my New Zealand good luck charm for seeing us all safely through that day. As I passed her entering the hotel, I couldn't resist asking her if she had a secret death wish. Since she had in reality endangered us all, nearly everyone spoke to her, and for the rest of the trip she was quite contrite.

Before reaching Arcachon, we took a detour to see the highest sand dune in Europe. It was pretty much a tourist spot, but we were given an hour to walk to the top of the dune and see the ocean on the other side.

A paved walkway, lined with small kiosks, led us to the dune where 151 steps took us to the top. The view was spectacular and worth the climb. We walked back down but many people, mostly kids, slid and tumbled down the dune.

One evening at a hotel in the country with a nice lawn, we had a Bocci Ball lesson, and then chose teams and played a couple of games.

The next morning we biked on roads in heavy traffic to Arcachon Bay to visit an oyster farm!

Arcachon Bay, consists of 75 square miles, three-quarters of which remains under water at low tide. A research institute, located on the bay, works closely with the oyster farmers. The district owns the land and leases oyster farmers specific plots. So each farmer has and knows his own territory. The bay is environmentally rich. Farmers on the bay produce 15 ton of oysters a year per farm.

Oyster farming started in the 1800s. A virus attacked the oysters in the 1960s. In 1968 the Japanese oyster was introduced to replace the lost diseased oysters. In Arcachon Bay the oysters reproduce, which is not the case in either Normandy or Brittany. Farmers there import Arcachon oysters as they grow well when introduced into new areas; they just don't reproduce.

An oyster filters ten liters of water an hour siphoning off food. They spawn in summer and only one to two percent of the larvae survive. Oysters can change sex each season if it is necessary to reproduce.

Red ceramic roof tiles are coated with a limestone mixture and dried. When conditions are right, thousands of tiles, secured together, are put in the water. The larvae attach to the tiles and eight or nine months later the tiles are removed, the oysters are scraped off, and sorted by size. They are then placed in mesh bags, either plastic or steel, and returned to the bay for a year. During that year the bags need to be turned every two weeks. After a year the bags are removed and again the oysters sized, replaced in bags and returned to the bay for another nine months.

It takes three to four years for an oyster to grow to eating size. The oysters from this bay are sent all over France, but are not exported outside of the country.

Winter Garden was built to give visitors to Arcachon

something to do. It was built on 300 acres high on a hill and until 1977 had a large plush casino. A fire destroyed the casino that year and it has never been rebuilt. Instead the area has been replanted with gardens and trees.

When we reached the Garden, our guide wouldn't let us ride the elevator, but insisted we walk up the steep switchback path. It was a climb! The view of the city from the top was magnificent.

Arcachon was established in 1840, and later in 1867, two brothers built a railroad. The mild winter climate and clean air soon turned the area into a center for patients with TB. After Napoleon visited in 1862 the publicity promoted the area even more.

I found crossing Arcachon Bay an interesting experience. The fellows formed a chain handing the bikes down several steps for loading onto a small boat. The crew lashed bikes everywhere!

Fortunately we loaded a bigger boat for the twenty-minute crossing. We unloaded on the other side of the bay at the end of a very long pier in a howling wind.

The wind was steady but somewhat moderated on land. It wasn't too long before we hit the bike path with its small rolling hills and numerous road crossings. It was lovely as it wound through the forest and sand dunes. (We would be heading north along the ocean for a couple of days until we reached Royan.)

Here the bike path was littered with sand, pine needles, pinecones, and lots of those nasty thorny bushes.

About mid afternoon it was my turn to get a flat tire. We pumped up the tire, and I kept going as long as I could to get as close to the guide as possible, so he'd have less back tracking to do.

We pumped the tire a second time before riding into a large rest area where several of the group were gathered debating which way to go. Finally I was off up the hill following several others. We peddled and peddled. When I came up behind one of the fellows, I asked if he thought we were going in the right direction.

"That's why I'm going so slow, I don't think we are."

Before too much longer we came to a large round-a-bout or traffic circle. We all instinctively knew when there was no corner posted that we had taken a wrong turn. We gathered in the little park in the center and after a while a couple of the men stationed themselves at each side so that when someone did come along they would see us. The sixteen of us lost in the middle of France waited nearly two hours. Meanwhile we watched all the families out biking amid the heavy bike traffic.

Eventually the van appeared. The driver pulled over and said he'd had a call at the hotel that half of the group was lost. We were instructed not to move while he went to tell the others where we were. When the rest of the group arrived minutes later, we all started off for the hotel. Since my tire was really flat at that point I was given the option of riding in the van or using the spare bike in the van. Not wanting to peddle an unfamiliar bike that was not fitted to me, I opted to ride the last few miles.

The next day was a short 22-mile day. We started out in a little drizzle, but it soon cleared. As we rode into a little beach town for lunch I again had a flat tire, which was fixed while we ate.

The next morning we had a tailwind that made for easy biking and I must point out a bit unusual, as it seems if there is a wind, you're always bucking it.

We detoured into Soulac to visit a 12th century church. The interesting thing about that church was that it had been buried under the sand for 200 years! Eventually it was uncovered, only to learn that it had been built on top of another church.

The streets of this beach town were narrow and crowded, as it was a holiday. We opted to eat lunch at the beach, but the wind was so strong we had to keep everything covered or capped to keep out the blowing sand. It was a beautiful spot with the roaring surf pounding the beach. The water was so blue and looked clear and clean.

When we left the beach, we experienced a strong tail wind.

We just had to balance ourselves on the bike as the wind literally blew us along without having to peddle! That was a once in a lifetime experience! It was great.

This day we were under some time restraints, as we needed to catch the ferry at Verdan. The ferries crossing the Gironde River are big. We had a fair distance to cover and if this strong wind had been a headwind it would have been a real struggle. We were lucky!

We waited about a half-hour in line with a lot of motor vehicles to load the ferry. The Gironde is a large river. The crossing from Verdan to Royan took a half-hour. These big ferries had one neat feature—the sides of the stern vehicle area dropped onto the pier creating a ramp.

When off-loading the ferry in Royan, via special lanes, we were happy to learn our hotel was only a few blocks from the pier. My room had a nice view of the harbor.

The day in Royan was a bike-free one. Early in the morning we had an interesting lecture on wine. The French talk a lot about "terroir" for which there is no English equivalent. Terroir includes soil, slope, and exposure. The soil of the Medoc is rocky. Medoc means "between waters" and the area known by that name lies between the Atlantic Ocean and the Gironde River.

In the 1700s the swampy area was drained and the wine industry stared in those pockets of gravel. The vine roots can extend down thirty feet. The stones hold the heat of the day and draws water up from the depth in the coolness of night so irrigation is not a necessity. The grapes are completely dependent on nature. The amount of rain and sunshine in the spring determine what kind of a wine year it will be.

Grape vines can live to be 100 years old but usually are pulled at about fifty years. The quality of the grape does not diminish with age but the number of grape clusters declines and fifty years seems to be the break-even point. The vines are at their peak at twenty years of age.

The year on the bottle is the year the grapes were grown, not the year the wine was bottled. The date is permitted on the label *only* when one year's grapes are used, and not permitted if the wine is blended with grapes of more than one year. Although the lecture was nearly three hours long, I found it extremely interesting.

It was a nice sunny day so we chose a sidewalk café for lunch. We leisurely walked back to the hotel admiring the many flower gardens on the way. Back at the designated time, we boarded a bus for a ride to Cognac to visit the Remy Martin facility.

It was a good hour's ride through the French countryside. The bus moved along at a pretty good clip so I estimate it was about 60 miles.

Remy Martin is not the only Cognac facility in Cognac, but without a doubt is the largest. The tour of the facility was done in a Disney-type tram, ending in a large auditorium for further information. There were several bilingual tour guides who conducted tours in language groups.

The Martin facility, established in 1724, is so large that it has its own coppery on the grounds. The coopers make 70,000 barrels a year making it the largest coppery in the world.

Only oak is used to make the barrels. The logs are split and the centers cut into staves that are stacked and dried for three years. It takes 32-36 one-meter long staves to make a barrel.

The facility can bottle 100,000 bottles a day! One aging room contained 6000 barrels 20-25 years old; the next room held 12,000 barrels four years old.

Everything was exceptionally clean. The aromas were delightful. The taste—well I guess you'd just have to like the stuff.

Leaving Royan we rode the 8:00AM ferry across the Gironde River, then we biked south, but inland toward Bordeaux. Everyone was happy the wind had died down, as we knew we had a long day of biking ahead of us. Biking south through the Medoc we encountered gently rolling hills.

There are 8000 grape growers in the Medoc. All grape growers' homes are called chateaus. Many are small, some are very large and castle-like, but most are modest somewhere in between. The chateaux offered us many photo opportunities.

We stopped at one five-star chateau and our guide talked the owner into giving us a mini tour.

We biked to the Chateau Mouton Rothschild for a tour and lecture. This chateau is 45 feet above sea level and has 50 hectares of planted vineyards.

Rothschild bottles 250,000 bottles of wine a year. This was one of three Rothschild chateaus, but this is the one that bottles the premier wines.

Mouton means "small hill." In 1922 Phillipe Rothschild bought the chateau, which at that time, was pretty much in a state of disrepair. In 1924 he decided to bottle his own wine on the chateau grounds, an unheard of activity at that time, as all the growers sent their wine to a wine merchant for bottling. Today the bottling process takes three weeks. In 1923 the wines moved from second growth to first growth, and in 1973 to the premiere wine class where it remains today.

When we reached Paulliac we had to surrender our bikes. This is always an emotional moment. My #2 had carried me safely a good 250 miles, the only mishap being a couple of flat tires.

We had to leave Paulliac early in the morning as a city tour guide was meeting us at the hotel in Bordeaux for a walking tour of the city.

Air France pilots went on strike about half way through our trip, and it appeared they were not going back to work soon. Arriving at the hotel there was a fax waiting with all of our flights rescheduled on other airlines.

Our city guide, a very French flamboyant little guy, spoke English with a heavy accent making it very difficult to understand him. He walked us all over Bordeaux for three hours. Every time we had to cross a street he would run out into the street, stop the traffic by madly waving and yelling at us to "Hurry! Hurry!" Watching him was a show in itself!

We did learn Bordeaux, meaning "port of the moon," is the capitol of the Aquitane region. The Gironde River is moon shaped in that area, thus the name Bordeaux. In 1453 it was the last area to become French again after the Roman Empire.

Bordeaux was a walled city until the 1800s when the walls were torn down and the ditches filled in. Several ports to the city remain. We walked through a couple of them on our tour and through one in the pedestrian mall on the way back to the hotel. The city has a population of 650,000.

The city is full of cobblestone alleys and sidewalk cafés. During the lunch hour the cafés are full with people enjoying food and conversation. Most shops close during the lunch hour. We were to learn that by 2:30 most sidewalk cafés close; even the tables and chairs are taken inside.

This presented a bit of a problem for us, but after finding several cafés closed we finally found one willing to serve us even though they were about to close too. I guess they took pity on the innocent Americans. We had a delightful lunch.

It was a beautiful, sunny day, with no biking so I decided to have a glass of wine. After all, I was in France eating lunch at a sidewalk café on a picturesque cobblestone alley and the picture needed a glass of wine to make it complete!

One does not visit France and expect to find low fat anything, skim milk, cold coke, ice tea, or many of the other things we take for granted. Diet? Forget it! You can expect to give your arteries a good jolt with butter-rich flaky pastries, wonderful cheeses, real cream, whole milk, good French bread, strong coffee, all kinds of fish, and hope that good extremely reasonable wines will counteract any adverse effects. My motto was to relax and enjoy.

It seems everyone in France owns a dog, usually a small one. The dogs go everywhere. It is strange for an American to see a dog in a store, market, or restaurant. I was amazed at how well the dogs behaved. Even when not on a leash, the dogs stuck close to their owner. I never heard a dog bark except out in the country from backyards as we biked by. However, they do drop their business everywhere and anywhere outside so when walking the alleyways you'd better pay attention where you step. The French wouldn't think of carrying a plastic bag. Never mind a super duper pooper-scooper!

It was early to bed the last night, as we were scheduled to board a bus for the airport at 5:30 AM.

The bus was a few minutes late, which made us all a little nervous as the Air France strike had all transportation in the country in chaos. Even at that early hour, with very little traffic, it took nearly 45 minutes to get to the airport.

During the bus ride I reflected on some of the things I had seen and experienced the past two weeks.

The produce we bought in the open-air markets, was vine-ripened and tasted wonderful. But I would not like to shop daily as the French do. The local people carry their own container, usually a basket, to market. Plastic is available now though. It was a sight to watch a squawking hen as she was being weighed for a customer's dinner. The variety of seafood products was amazing in some places, and it was all fresh.

In the countryside where we spent most of our time, the houses and yards were small, but flowers grew everywhere. Window boxes were very popular. The climate must be perfect for roses as everyone grew them. They were often planted at the end of the grapevine rows in the vineyards. It seems that disease will attack the roses first and alert the grower that his grapes may be in danger. The roses were in bloom for us to enjoy.

Besides all the cultivated flowers, wildflowers were in bloom in the countryside. Bright red poppies were a marked contrast to the white queen Ann's lace in the fields.

We saw young people in jeans but the older women always wore a skirt or dress. Even in the fields or garden.

We were told the last two digits on the long license plates designated the province or region.

The water was drinkable everywhere.

However there was one thing that was scarce throughout our travels —toilets! When we did find them they were not always clean and almost always lacked the essential toilet paper. We encountered a couple of male/female water closets equipped with both male and female urinals. We learned early that female urinals are very common. After a couple of uses one learns the best flushing technique—like moving away before pushing the button.

Most of the bike paths were about a meter wide making it a little hairy to meet an oncoming biker or to pass the biker in front.

We never saw a McDonald's until the last day in Bordeaux.

People outside the big cities involved in the tourist industry spoke enough English to get by, but others spoke little or none. Generally the French we met were pleasant, helpful, and honest. Often they were talkative with a desire to improve their English language skills.

The airport was full of anxious travelers. Security was extremely tight due to some kind of a threat. It took forever to get through security, but I got by without having to open my bags, as many others had to do.

I had been rebooked on British Air through Heathrow in London. My flight schedule was just about the same as my original Air France one.

This third, and probably last, bike trip had been fun and enjoyable. The biking was easy, the weather had been good, the group had been a nice one, and the guide had been terrific, what else could anyone ask for!

Chapter 18

Galapagos

The days of sailing into the Galapagos Islands, dropping an anchor and going wherever one wanted are over. Fortunately for the ecosystem, no one can do that any more.

One can still follow in Darwin's footsteps, but with a guide. Yacht owners must check in with authorities on Santa Cruz Island, register, pay the park fee, pick up a guide, and then they can sail about the islands. The guide stays with the yacht all the time it is in the islands and tells them where they can and cannot sail. However, most people visiting the islands today do so through a tour company, as the number of people and boats at any one time in the islands is strictly controlled and regulated.

All the guides are trained at the Darwin Research Center on the island of Santa Cruz. All life is protected and habitats are off limits.

Many trips include either Machu Picchu or the Amazon on the same itinerary as the Galapagos. There are a couple of bigger ships carrying up to 60 passengers sailing the islands, but most trips use small boats carrying eight to 20 passengers.

In 1993 I chose a trip that did Quito, Ecuador and then the Galapagos in detail. It seems the flight schedules always put one's arrival in South America in the evening. The driver who took us to our modern hotel cautioned us to watch our wallets whenever walking the streets anywhere in the city.

Early the following morning in Quito our personal escort

arrived. He took us on an extensive tour of the city saying that anytime we wanted to stop to just let him know.

The Spanish founded the old capitol city of Quito in 1534. I found colonial Quito very hilly reminding me a great deal of San Francisco. The cobblestone streets were very narrow. The buildings had a Moorish influence and were very close together with many of the stucco buildings having inner courtyards.

Street vendors were everywhere. Old men carried heavy loads in baskets, held in place with fabric straps, on their backs. The old men were all bent over, life had to be tough.

The new modern hotels and shops, located in 'new Quito', were in an area less then two decades old. Building codes are earthquake codes requiring steel to reinforce all concrete. The streets in the new part of town were wide, the traffic heavy, and traffic lights and stop signs very few in number.

Ecuador has twelve hours of daylight and twelve hours of darkness every day all year. Mornings are sunny with rain showers arriving nearly every afternoon and the country has eight active volcanoes.

Ecuador was a dictatorship until 1979 when the country became a democracy. There are 16 political parties. Provincial senators and the president are elected for one four year term.

The Andes Mountains run through Ecuador generally from north to south. A few hundred feet above the city, at 10,000 feet, is the site of the Dancing Virgin or Madonna of Quito. Standing a 100 feet tall, she was erected in the early 1980s. Made of cast aluminum, she was manufactured in France, brought to Ecuador in pieces, and reassembled. She is the only winged virgin in the Catholic Church. The virgin standing on a dragon perched on top of the world holds a chain in her hand that extends down and around the dragon's neck, showing good triumphs over evil. It's an impressive statue. Below the statue is a small chapel.

It was twelve miles out of the city over a toll road to the Equatorial Monument. As we descended the 1200 feet from Quito to the monument we noted a dramatic change in the climate. At the monument it was very hot, arid, and dry with cactus growing everywhere.

The monument was fascinating. The only way to the top was via elevator. A walkway around the top provided a 360-degree view of the grounds and countryside below.

To get back to ground level one must use a stairway, every few steps ends on a floor which houses part of the museum. The displays offered a simple, easily understood history of the area and its people. This diversion made the descent easy and interesting.

A well-defined line in the concrete separates the two hemispheres. And before we left the site of course we had to stand with one foot in the northern hemisphere and the other foot in the southern hemisphere.

High altitude tends to slow the digestive process, so Ecuadorians eat their major meal at noon.

Our guide was a pleasant conversationalist and we had a most informative and interesting day and a very enjoyable evening.

For some reason at the Quito airport there was a very long wait to obtain our boarding passes. We were grateful for Diego who was Spanish speaking and took care of this matter for us while we sat in the smoke filled waiting room. Many overseas airports do not measure up to American standards!

Three gates opened out onto the tarmac. Diego escorted us to the proper gate, but it's blinking neon sign said "Cuenca." We were headed to the Galapagos via Guayaquil.

However, everyone else in the area was headed for our destination so we stood firm. Later we found out that the sign had not been changed for three years. So much for relying on accurate signs!

We stood in line at the gate for a long time as there seemed to be a problem with the plane and no reserve plane was in sight. A toilet seat appeared in the forward doorway for a good while, then suddenly disappeared back inside the plane.

Eventually the gate opened, and we walked out over the tarmac to board the plane. The front steps looked pretty crowded, so we headed for the steps in the rear of the aircraft.

We landed in Quayaquil (why-a-keel) for a rather strange maneuver. Retrieving our luggage, we walked a couple hundred yards and boarded another plane. For what reason is anyone's guess!

By late morning we landed in a light rain on Baltra Island, Galapagos. Talk about nostalgia! That lovely open-air airport was so much like the Honolulu airport was in 1955 when I landed there the first time. The lei stands were the only thing missing.

It was a long hour wait to get through customs where one could pay the $80 park fee in either American dollars or Ecuadorian Sucre. Knowing the park would not accept traveler's checks, I had exchanged money the day before at the hotel in anticipation of this expense.

You can imagine the fistful of money I had to equal $160 when 1800 Sucre equaled one dollar! I just handed the stack of bills to the park ranger and asked him to count it.

An old school bus took us on a short ride to the boat harbor. There were no piers in the harbor so we ferried out to our boat in a zodiac.

We were informed that the zodiacs were the *Reina Sylvia's* pangas, and that we would load them many times in the coming days as we always anchored off shore. Panga is a common name in many parts of the world for what we call a dinghy.

The *Reina Sylvia* was a luxury yacht with a capacity of 18 passengers. Air-conditioned throughout, she made all of her own water, so it was safe to drink it. I mistakenly figured we'd have an orientation in the afternoon and really start this adventure in the morning. Wrong. While we were eating lunch and getting acquainted with our traveling companions the engines turned over and we were underway!

About 3:00 PM we dropped anchor for an excursion ashore on

South Plaza Island.

It was exciting to see our first iguanas! Cameras clicked frantically when our guide told us to calm down we'd be seeing lots of Iguanas. He was so right!

Land iguanas wandered everywhere. Red, green, and black/brown, they blend into the terrain unless they are walking on the sandy beach. We needed to watch where we stepped, and amazingly we could get within three or four feet of them. Often they would pose and be still as if saying, okay—snap away.

I've seen a lot of cactus in my day, but I'd never seen prickly pear that grew as big and looked like a tree. The cactus was huge, some nine or ten feet tall and with stalks a good foot in diameter.

Our Ecuadorian guide was in his late twenties with a degree in oceanography. He had been a guide in the islands for several years, was well informed, and able to answer any questions we asked. He taught us a lot and had the patience of a saint. He never rushed my photographer son who often would wait for just the right composition for his picture.

Early morning we loaded the pangas for a ferry ride into Espanola/Hood Island. Loading the pangas was often a challenge, but the crew always lent a firm, helping hand. Espanola provided a sandy beach for landing, but we were warned before leaving that it would be a wet landing. The main inhabitants on the island are marine iguanas.

The rocks were pretty slippery. Iguanas were everywhere. Smaller than land iguanas, they have a different body configuration. Being all black, they blended in with the black lava rocks. One needed to be very careful where one stepped! The marine iguana is a vegetarian living on the algae found in the shallow waters.

About to take our first long hike, we were told that we'd have the opportunity to see lots of masked boobies, blue footed boobies, Galapagos doves, and albatross. The quieter we were the more we'd see. Strict instruction was given to pay attention and *stay* on the paths.

Espanola is flat with high cliffs. The albatross use it for a runway. They literally step off the cliff, catching the wind currents to fly away. When they return they land like an airplane on a runway. These waved albatross have a seven-foot wingspan.

Albatross mate for life. They return to Espanola each spring, find their mate and bare their young. In December they fly off in all different directions. Babies do not return for five years at which time they return to Espanola to find a mate.

Returning to the boat just before lunch we enjoyed a short swim in the warm water. In the afternoon the captain moved the boat to the other side of the island where there was a beautiful white sandy beach for swimming.

We were awakened each morning to the sound of gentle melodious music and the smell of fresh coffee. This was the life!

The Island of Floreana was probably so named because of its abundant flora.

While hiking the guide told us because there is only one variety of bee to do the pollinating, all the flowers on the island are either white or yellow.

The sandy path through lush vegetation led us to a brackish lagoon that was home to over 1000 flamingos. The birds were on the far side of the lagoon. Not liking anything taller than they are we spent a lot of time squatting while watching them.

Leaving the lagoon the hike was over some pretty rough terrain to Flour Beach. One look at the fine white powder-like sand and we knew the beach was appropriately named. It was quite a contrast to the brown sandy beach we'd come ashore on. Unfortunately we couldn't swim there, as the beach is a turtle breeding ground. The beach was also home to thousands of hermit crabs. It was a lot of fun watching the little crabs scamper about and then disappear into a hole.

At Sea Lion Island we moved slowly among hundreds of sea lions that had great fun showing off for us.

We went ashore at Post Office bay. Years ago sailors would leave addressed letters there in a special mailbox. They also would remove any letters addressed to their destination, and when they arrived in port would stamp and mail the letters. The custom continues today.

It was only a short walk to the Darwin Research Center on Santa Cruz Island. We visited a museum and walked around the grounds. We saw many giant tortoises in all stages of growth including babies in pens. When they got a little bigger they were placed in large enclosures. The adults lumbered around the grounds everywhere.

It was pretty hard to get lost in this little town, so just before noon we met at the park on the waterfront. An old bus arrived which took us over a rough narrow dirt road up into the highlands. We had a marvelous lunch at a restaurant with the most magnificent view of the lowlands. After lunch, before we departed, I could not resist walking about the lush landscape. It was just like being in a rain forest, cooler and absolutely beautiful!

On the way down from the highlands we stopped to walk the rim of a sinkhole. Sitting quietly for awhile we listened to the songs of Galapagos doves and watched vermilion flycatchers. The bird's songs were the *only* sound that broke the absolute silence of this quiet place.

Farther down the trail we stopped at a large lava tunnel. Some of the younger people descended the rough terrain to explore its depths.

It was an all night cruise to Tower Island. When retiring we were told there'd be a surprise for us the next morning. When I walked out on deck with my first cup of morning coffee I suddenly stopped short, mesmerized by the sight of two red-footed boobies perched on the bowsprit!

They sat there in all their splendor for a very long time posing as if they thought we expected them to. Red footed boobies feed in deep waters far out to sea. They usually hitch a ride back to shore on the boats that sail the islands.

Tower Island is nicknamed the *Island of Birds* or *Bird Island* for the millions of birds who call it home. We were lucky because it was mating season for the masked boobies, blue footed boobies, and frigate birds.

We spent a great deal of time watching the frigate birds, as their mating ritual is quite spectacular. To attract his mate the male inflates a pouch below his neck, which when inflated looks like a huge red heart. The female can sometimes be pretty choosy and dance around the male for sometime before deciding if this is the love of her life.

Later in the day we hiked up Phillip Steps to a plateau. Glad I was in pretty good shape, as it was a really rugged climb up those steep steps. The terrain on the top was rocky. Boobies were mating all over the place. In addition storm petrels and swallowtail gulls were flying about. I sat a long time watching a pair of boobies doing their mating dance.

It was another all night cruise to Fernandina Island. Hundreds of sea lions, marine iguanas, pelicans, sand crabs, wingless cormorants, sea turtles, and lava lizards inhabit Fernandina. Moving about was an all sense activity. What an experience!

We loaded the pangas for a cruise around the shore looking for penguins, which we found with little difficulty. The penguins are small, and it was great fun to swim with them. Under water they'd sail by our legs close enough to touch. We climbed the 150 steps to the summit for a spectacular view of Darwin Lake and the harbor on the north side of the island. It was dusk when we returned to the boat.

The northern part of the island chain is the youngest, and this was quite evident when visiting Santiago Island, a lava island with very sparse vegetation. We were ashore on Santiago at 8:00AM.

We hiked from the sandy beach across the island to the lava coast. We slowly walked around the point of the island back to the sandy beach where we went swimming.

In the afternoon the boat moved across Sullivan Bay to Bartolome Island. Here we swam with the sea lions and penguins in the warm clear water. The sea lions were completely unafraid and loved to play. I received several nudges from these creatures that are so graceful in the water, yet so cumbersome on land. A facemask revealed all kinds of colorful tropical fish and coral.

The last evening it was with great reluctance that we left the lounge late for our cabins. No one wanted this wonderful vacation to end. Our guide was such a nice young man and had done a terrific job.

We stayed at anchor all night. At 7:00 AM the anchor was winched in, and we were underway for Baltra Island where we must disembark for our flight back to Quito.

On the bus ride back from the harbor to the airport everyone was unusually quiet. No one minded that our flight was a little over an hour late. It gave us some extra time to sit and reflect in the quaint open-air airport while visiting with newfound friends.

This was definitely a vacation for the physically fit as every day involved hiking, some of which were short, but many of which were pretty long and rugged. The terrain was often uneven. Loading the pangas sometimes took a bit of agility. And then there were the steps.

There is no question it was a fabulous vacation—one I shall remember for a very long time.

Chapter 19

From a Haunted Hotel to a Brothel

Among my many varied sleeping arrangements, I had never stayed or slept in a haunted hotel —-until my second trip to Sydney, Australia.

Darling Harbor is the center of the city in an area known as The Rocks and is where all the activity takes place. Our hotel was just a block or two above the harbor.

The story of the 150 year old hotel was framed and on the wall in our room. The second part of the building was built as six terrace houses, and known as Scarlett's Cottages. Scarlett was a well-known lady of the night who lived and died in the area. She also was Eric's one true love, but although in a moment of thoughtlessness she declared her love for him, she did not mean it.

However, Eric died before learning of Scarlett's lie. They say that to this day Eric wanders the halls and rooms of the cottages searching and calling for Scarlett, who had met an untimely tragic death. It is said that on occasion Eric has appeared in front of unknowing hotel staff members inquiring of Scarlett's whereabouts.

Each night at bedtime my roommate and I would wonder if that was the night we might see Eric. However, during our stay none of us saw or heard him wandering about the hotel.

Over the years, I've stayed in all sorts of accommodations. Big, luxury hotels to quaint small family run hotels and everything in between. Also B and Bs, military barracks and BOQs. I've slept in large ship cabins, and in small boat bunks, in tents, trains, college dorms, and once even in a brothel.

Returning home from a winter trip, one of the first things I said, with a big grin, to my daughter at the airport was, "I spent a couple of nights in a brothel."

Stopping in her tracks, she looked at me aghast and said, "You what!" Then I explained.

It happened in Churchill, Manitoba, Canada when I went to see the polar bears. My friend and I chose that particular trip because it included a couple of days at the White Whale Lodge, where mothers and bear cubs are most often seen.

The lodge is located across Hudson Bay so we were transported, a few at a time, by helicopter. The rustic bunkhouse was built in the early 1900s. At that time a large grain facility was being built, 3000 men were living in Churchill, and the lodge was used as a brothel.

The lodge contained a large main room, several small rooms, each with two bunk beds, a dining room, and a kitchen. It was great to be so close to the bears, even though we were the ones inside with bars on the windows and doors, and the bears were the ones who were free. I've gotten a lot of mileage out of the story of staying in a brothel. It's fun to watch the expressions on people's faces before I reveal the whole story!

Incidentally getting to the lodge was an adventure in itself. It was a short helicopter ride across the bay, which on that day looked very cold as we looked down on three to four-foot waves capped with white foam. Landing in the front yard of the lodge, we were cautioned to keep our heads down under the rotating blades of the helicopter, and then we were to hustle into the lodge. Meanwhile there was a fellow standing guard, shooting blanks out of his gun to keep the bears at bay.

As soon as we were in the building, those waiting to leave moved quickly to the waiting helicopter. Then the iron bar gate was closed and locked. It was kind of a strange feeling to be locked inside a barred building. We soon learned the necessity of the bars though when the bears came right up to the windows as well as the barred porch/patio. Even though they were never fed human food, they particularly liked to nose around the often-open kitchen window.

But, I have another story that is even better, and it's much older. It was back in 1970. My husband's ship was going to Hong Kong, and I couldn't pass up that opportunity to see another part of the world.

We had a wonderful time. We stayed at the plush Hong Kong Hilton. The day before the ship was to leave, I put all the stuff we'd bought on the ship to be sent home. That morning after checking out of the hotel I sent my suitcase to the ship, as I was flying home late that afternoon and I couldn't see being bothered with luggage when I didn't have to be. My dirty laundry could wait a couple of weeks to be laundered.

But when we got to the ship, we learned that one of the engines was down, delaying the ship's departure. The long and short of it was that I changed my flight to the next day. My husband went aboard his ship late afternoon, and I went back to the hotel to check back in.

Would you believe that they didn't want to give me a room? I explained that I had paid my bill and checked out that morning. But that didn't seem to make any difference.

With visions of sleeping in the hotel lobby I requested to see the manager. I again explained the situation. I told him if he looked out the window, he could see the ship still along side the pier. I even ended up showing him my airline ticket for the next day. He eventually pulled the records of that morning and finally gave me a room.

What was his problem, you ask.

Because I didn't have any luggage, they thought I was a hooker! And I was not going to conduct any business on their premises!

Chapter 20

England: Lake District and Yorkshire

Ah, sandwich. Actually the Earl of Sandwich —can I relate to him! He was always so busy, and not wanting to take the time to eat he'd put nearly everything between bread. Since I can and very often do the same thing, I was thrilled to drive through Sandwich on my way to London from Dover many years ago.

My first arrival in England was via hovercraft from Calais, France to Dover, England. I clearly remember that I was glad that noisy bumpy ride didn't last any longer than it did. For 55 minutes my brain shook and rattled around in my head!

London, wonderful big London. But first I want to relive a fabulous walking trip in England's Lake District. There was a time I wasn't sure whether I'd be making this trip, as I broke my foot only a few weeks before. The metatarsal was pretty easy to heal, but the joint break on the top of my foot above the arch was another story. The cast came off only a couple of weeks before departure.

While the cast was on my foot I lost a lot of muscle on the inside of my leg. I couldn't believe how quickly that had happened! After the cast came off a friend was helpful in making me do some exercises, and walked with me so I would be in fairly good shape for the miles ahead of me.

From the Manchester Airport to Grasmere, our home base, the driver talked a steady stream telling us many things. Romans came to that area 2000 years ago and the Vikings 1000 years later. The old Roman road is 2480 feet high and one can still walk the path the Romans used to pull carts. Fell is a Viking word meaning "mountain."

Windermere, a large lake, 10.5 x 1 mile, and 276 feet deep has fast flowing water, so the surface water changes every three days. Three steamboats sail the lake. Only three lakes in the district allow motors, two have 10 mph speed limits, and Windermere is the only lake with unlimited motor rules. However, because of erosion and pollution a study of this was underway.

There are 247 bodies of water in the area and only one is called a lake. Mere, water, and tarn all designate a lake. To say Lake Grasmere would be redundant. Tarn is a Viking word meaning "tear" and refers to a small body of water.

Sheep are the predominate farm animals but there are a few ostrich, llamas, and other animals. There are red tail deer and roe deer in the area. On wealthy estates one may see fallow deer that are the largest and were imported from China.

All buildings are made of native stone, blue or green slate. Strict building codes forbid the importation of non-native rock. Historic preservation dictates that if a building is torn down it must be replaced the same size in the same spot.

Our hotel was right on the Grasmere, a beautiful small lake. Years ago many reeds grew in the lake and were used for thatching roofs. Reeds still grow, but not in such abundance as years past.

By the time I got to the hotel my foot was pretty swollen giving me pause to wonder what in the world I was into. But for the immediate solution, I went to the reception desk and asked for a plastic bag of ice.

Our lead guide was the absolute best. We all fell in love with him. Tall and slender with a great sense of humor, he was a world of information, and above all was always kind and considerate. We learned right away that a "few undulations" meant there would probably be nearly a full day of ups and downs, and that little or slight could mean 500 feet straight up!

The first morning, Peter said most Americans determine English walks are really hikes. It did not take us long to absolutely agree! In spite of the fact that hiking boots and walking sticks are difficult to pack in limited luggage I was most grateful for both. And with my foot, I was really glad my boots were well broken in!

Toodling was a slow walk and *cracking on* meant to walk smartly or move quickly. In reality toodle (rhymes with noodle) meant a pace of about three and a half miles an hour and to crack on meant to walk as fast as your legs would go. Everything was so well planned that we seldom had to crack on.

England's National Park history is much shorter than ours, and there are marked differences of how English parks are run compared to U.S. National Parks. The National Park and Access to Countryside Act of 1949 was the beginning of England's eleven National Parks. The major portion of funding comes from the central government with the remainder of the monies coming from local rates, car parks, and fees for guided walks etc.

The main functions of the English National Parks are to preserve and enhance the area's natural beauty, to promote enjoyment of the area, and to look after the needs of the local people.

English National Parks are all living landscapes as people live and work in them. The government does not own the parks. The parks are privately owned and landowners vary from small homes and farms to major landowners who control thousands of acres. Many of the major landowners can trace their history back many generations.

The 880 square miles of the Lake District makes it England's largest National Park and the second so designated, in 1951. (The first park was the Peak District.) The park is a rough circle 35 miles in diameter with 40,000 people living within the park boundaries.

The first day walking along some lovely peaceful green scenery I noted a variety of trees. We noticed many ferns growing in large areas but were to learn that bracken is a very aggressive fern-like plant that grows about hip high. It varies from ferns because instead of a single stem bracken grows additional stems from the main one.

After World War II bracken started taking over some of the fells. It's very pretty but kills all other vegetation. Sheep don't eat bracken so it grows in non-grazing areas. Cut stems are very sharp. Bracken is very difficult to eradicate. It is a common belief that sheep farming must be kept alive to save the fells from the bracken.

The first day was a warm up hike, but still five to six miles to Rydal Mount and eventually around to Dove Cottage. William Wordsworth, a well-known English poet, lived in both of these homes.

The hotel packed us huge sack lunches that we enjoyed on a small beach along the lake. Of course, as usual, I took the Texas heat with me, and for three days the temperature and humidity were way above normal, in fact the humidity was so bad that although I kept drinking my water my skin just kept crying tears!

Rydal Mount sits on four and a half acres on a hilltop, which meant walking up a pretty steep cobblestone street, but the reward was the lovely view.

William Wordsworth lived in several homes before moving to Rydal Mount in 1813 at age 43. He did not own Rydal Mount, because a Mr. Fleming would not sell. However, it was his home for 37 years and his rent of only 35 pounds a year was never increased.

Wordsworth was quite a landscape gardener, and actually landscaped many homes in the area. The grounds at Rydal Mount have remained pretty much as he designed them.

The original two-story house, built in 1574, was added on to in 1750. Having lost two children at their previous home, Wordsworth and his wife, Mary Hutchinson, were ready for a change of scenery when moving to Rydal Mount with three children, ages 10, 9, and 3. Wordsworth died there in 1850.

After touring the home and grounds, it was pretty much down hill to Dove Cottage.

Wordsworth brought his bride to Dove Cottage in 1802 where they remained until 1808 when the family and their many visitors simply outgrew the house

Built in 1600 Dove Cottage was originally a pub. The paneling was very dark—to hide the smoke and alcohol stains. The calling card basket on the entry table, instead of the traditional silver tray, was evidence of Wordsworth's preferred simple life style.

Rooms were very small. The large block slate floors showed the wear of centuries of walking. Houses used to be taxed on the number of windows over seven.

Candles were made by melting either sheep or pig fat. Most often the wax was poured into molds, although another common practice was to run a reed through a candle horizontally. Lighting the candle at both ends of the reed gave off the light of three candles, thus the expression *burning the candle at both ends.*

Most days of hiking meant it would be a green room day, which I think is a delightful expression for "back to nature." England has adequate, clean toilets in freestanding buildings at many of their car parks (parking lots), which I think is such a good idea.

As if we didn't have enough walking during the day, we often later walked into Grasmere village, a delightful little town. Our quaint hotel was once a mansion, so the rooms wound up, over, and down, and there were several public areas/lounges with comfortable furniture. The yard was large, with many old trees providing ample shade. Nearly every evening several of us would sit out on the lawn with a glass of wine and visit before dinner.

It became a habit after dinner, sometimes before, for me to seek out ice to ice down my swollen foot. There were two days when I questioned whether I would be hiking the following day. But each morning I woke with a normal foot and off I went. I had no pain, just a swelling at the end of the day. Weeks later that completely subsided.

Nights were short, as it stayed light until 10 PM and was light again around 4:30 AM, not that it bothered our sleeping any!

It was a nice clear day when we went to Tilberwaite (waite=clearing) and Little Langsdale valley. We had rather a good education about rocks, slate, shale, and landscape.

In the 18th century slate quarrying was a thriving industry. Most of the buildings in the area date from the early 17th century onward, before that construction was mud, straw and pebbles with thatched roofing. Today nearly all buildings are of slate or stone with slate roofs.

The Lake District has very strict building codes and historic preservation program. All proposed building has to go before a board for approval.

Copper, lead, and iron mining were active industries until the early 1900s. The deciduous woodland provided active charcoal burning, tanning, and bobbin industries.

Slate is not good for roads because it does not crush well, but a craft industry using slate has evolved.

The normal rainfall in the Lake District is 60 inches, but in a couple places it can measure as much as 130 inches.

The fells and meadows are dotted with a patchwork of shoulder high slate fences. Some of these fences go right up over the fells disappearing into the sky. The walls are dry set in a double line, 12-18 inches apart. The space between is filled with rubble. A stabilizing stone is placed periodically going all the way through both walls. It is quite a knack to successfully build these walls. No mortar here, and most of the fences are now in as good a shape as when they were built 250-300 years ago!

The Lake District is picturesque with many low mountains, abundant trees and flora. Sheep are seen everywhere and we were to learn a great deal about them, as well as transit through many of their pastures.

Many of the right of ways pass through farmers' lands which meant that at times we climbed occasional fences, ancient wall turnstiles, opened gates, and passed through many kissing gates. Over 2200 miles of public right of way are within the park.

Years ago when there was no church in town, coffins were carried over a coffin road to the nearest cemetery. At one point we walked over a coffin road that now was no more than a hiking path.

Walking through the forest or lush vegetation, we often stopped for an explanation of something or other. The English seem to know so many original expressions. Oak bark was soaked to produce tannin and is the foundation of the expression "I'll tan your hide."

We walked over the 400-year-old Slaters packhorse bridge. There are many of those old bridges around. To get to this bridge we had to climb over an old stile built into the wall. The ancient stile used cantilevered stones as steps, a one-foot wide hole in the top of the wall, and down the other side on more cantilevered stones. The first time maneuvering the stiles was a bit of a challenge, but we quickly got the hang of it.

Those beautifully arched stone bridges over the becks (small streams) are very narrow. Many picturesque bridges as well as the old packhorse bridges are still standing in good condition after almost 400 years.

Every village needed arable land for crops, pasture land for sheep and cattle, and woodlands for carts, wagons, housing, furniture, and charcoal. The arable land is called *in-by-land* because it is in by the farm.

Walking along a narrow lane (alley really) Peter spotted some wild raspberries growing. We all stopped and I, for one, had a ball picking and eating my favorite berry. Before long a couple of cars came along who wanted to pass. One of the fellows quipped we'd created a raspberry jam. A pretty quick wit.

Stopping at a farm, we learned that barns in that part of the country are quite different from those in other parts. Called *bankbarns*, they are literally built into the side of the bank. The top level is easily driven into as it is level with the hill and the hay and feed are stored on the upper floor. The cattle are kept on the lower level. These barns almost always have a winnowing door, which really is a window with three or four horizontal slats, opposite the doublewide barn door. When the big barn doors are open these winnowing doors allow the air to circulate.

Sunday morning was free for those wanting to attend church. At noon we headed to Hawkshead for lunch at the Queen's Head Pub. Afterward it was a visit to St. Michael's, then a walk around Hawkshead. We passed the oldest building used as a Methodist church in the world.

Hanging baskets around the village were gorgeous.

We took a short walk into Tarn Haws, and then it was on to Near Sawrey meaning "boggy." Late in the afternoon we arrived at Beatrix Potter's home, Hill Top, knowing a whole lot more about Peter Rabbit's author from the lecture the previous night, then we knew before leaving home.

Beatrix Potter, born in July 1866, was the first born to a wealthy barrister who made his money from cotton. Beatrix was very close to her father.

Mrs. Potter's job was to take care of five servants and to host teas and dinner parties. Beatrix found her mother cold and domineering.

As a child Beatrix had little contact with the family as she stayed on the third floor of the family home, Bolton Gardens, with a governess. She was excited when at age six a brother was born, for now she would have a playmate. She was in her mid teens before she joined the family for dinner.

She kept a journal written in code from the age of 15 until she was about 30. When the journal was discovered in 1950 it took nine years to decode. The journal revealed her early years. Why a code? Some speculate that her mother was nosey and intrusive.

At age 16 she met and became friends with Vicar Roonsly who encouraged her to write and draw. She and her brother kept all kinds of critters in their third floor abode. Beatrix named them all and created stories about them. She was a naturalist at an early age.

At 24 Beatrix started drawing greeting cards, receiving six pounds for the first batch, making it a profitable business for her for some time.

She also became an expert on fungi, an interest, which was sparked on vacations to Scotland. She conducted extensive experiments and, at age 31, presented a paper on spore formation and other theories. The paper was presented under a pseudonym and by a male friend, as women did not do such things or attend "male conventions" in those days.

Her last governess, Annie Carter, left to marry. When she had children Beatrix sent picture letters to the children—this was the beginning of her books. However, she submitted Peter Rabbit to six publishers, only to receive six rejections, so she self published 150 copies, sold them to friends, then ordered 200 more copies. Peter, Flopsie, Mopsie, and Cottontail have been famous ever since. She illustrated all of her books.

Beatrix was very much dominated by her parents. She met and fell in love with Norman, and of course her parents did not approve. They did not marry, Norman died shortly afterward unexpectedly of pernicious anemia. Devastated by Norman's death Beatrix moved to the Lake District in 1905 buying Hill Top and its 34 acres for a sum of 2800 pounds.

When 46, she met and fell in love with William Heelis. Again her parents disapproved as they were getting older and wanted her to be around to take care of them. Fortunately, her brother returned home at this time and informed his parents that he had been secretly married for six years and that they should let go of Beatrix.

In 1913, at age 47, Beatrix and William were married, and there after she was known as Beatrix Potter Heelis. She became a sheep farmer's wife only writing four books after her marriage.

But Beatrix was no lady of leisure. She often was thought to be a bit eccentric. She dressed as a farmer's wife not as the wealthy person she was. She often wore hats to cover bald spots left from a bout of rheumatic fever she suffered in her 20s. Beatrix shunned publicity and was a bit of a recluse. She put electricity into the barns before the house because she thought the animals would appreciate it more.

Saving the Herdwick sheep from extinction to a now thriving population is accredited to Beatrix Potter Heelis. She became the first woman to serve as president of the Herdwick Sheep Association.

Her farther died a year after her marriage. After being widowed, her mother moved in with Beatrix, but five years later Beatrix bought her mother a farm and moved her into it. Thereafter, she visited her mother for one hour each Wednesday afternoon. A stroke caused the death of her brother at age 46.

Beatrix died of bronchitis on December 22, 1943. She donated 15 farms and over 4000 acres to the National Trust. Hill Top has been open to the public since 1946.

We toured the house at our own pace.

A brief stop in Ambleside gave us a chance to see the bridge house, England's smallest house. The stone structure spans the river and is only a few feet wide. Originally built to store apples, the water running in the river below kept the structure cool.

We walked a rather hilly forest of pine and oak trees. Grizedale was one of the first forests opened to the public. The big undulation that day was at the beginning and it was 500 feet straight up a rocky eroded path, but the view when one reached the top was magnificent!

In the mid 1970s sculptures were allowed and encouraged. They could be made of wood, stone, or metal. There is a special sculpture map of the park. It was great fun looking around for the sculptures as we hiked, making it sort of a treasure hunt. Some were really neat; some were really weird. It was a fun day. A small but nice museum was at the park entrance along with a colorful and unique playground.

One of the most urgent and biggest problems of the Park System is the impact of tourism. The area needs tourist income, but how to control the impact of many people using and enjoying the landscape. Then there is the need for tourist facilities, control of new construction, and types of structures that also impact growth.

The need of the residents is always present. Modern farming methods and commercial forestry also are needs.

Erosion is a constant problem, often caused by destroyed vegetation when people stray off the paths. Repair of paths is a constant manpower and financial problem. Leveling walkways, providing disabled access, identifying drainage problems, replanting and protecting such from sheep and deer are just some of the problems facing the area. It might be said that the area has been loved to death. Trying to find a quiet balance is a challenge.

We drove to Glenridding where we boarded a ferry for a ride to Howtown. The seven-mile plus hike around Ullswater turned out to be no picnic!

Our first stop was at St. Peter's Victorian church. Built in 1880, it replaced a circa 1200 church in the valley of Martindale. Sitting on a hill surrounded by old yew trees, the acre of land was donated by two benefactors. The stain glass windows were new dating from 1975 and were modern.

Much of the rocky path was badly eroded and the undulations were pretty steep and a constant up and down. Occasionally we went through a pasture. We climbed several stiles and went through many gates. One gate had these instructions painted on it, "Go to the left to the beck and follow the river."

Passing through one pasture we were being scolded by loud blatting from the rear. We all stopped to see what was going on. Suddenly the sheep saw a clear passageway and kicked in the afterburners. When he arrived on the other side of us he wandered over to another sheep. It was pretty cute.

If a footpath has been used for seven years it cannot be changed, no matter what the farmer wants to do. At one point we had a view of the only deer sanctuary in the park.

The one day of rain we had in the Lake District was the day we were scheduled for an all day coach ride to play tourist.

Almost immediately we learned one of the mountain passes was closed because a lorry (truck) towing a trailer had overturned.

One expression I really like is the definition of mushroom management—being kept in the dark with stuff coming down on you.

Each farmer brands his sheep with a smit mark, a colored grease mark. The mark may be round dot-like or a stripe, and may be on the shoulder, or flank. We saw smit marks in every color.

England has about twenty breeds of sheep. The ones we saw most were the Herdwick, Blackface, and Swaledale. Sheep and agriculture have long been the major industries in northern England. Lamb is not my favorite food, but I ate some very good lamb in Scarborough and the best I have ever eaten in Grasmere.

The mountain pass remained closed all day, creating a change of plans for us. It was decided that we would take the narrow gauge railway ride in reverse of the original plan. But on arriving at Irton Road the train was full. Peter was beginning to get his knickers in a twist (frustrated). I love that expression! We went to lunch and then caught the train in Boot.

It was raining pretty hard when we arrived at the Burnmoor Inn in Boot. Unable to eat outside on the lovely grounds we all sandwiched (no pun intended) onto small low stools around 18-20" tables in the bar area. It was cozy, and the hot leek soup was delicious and the sandwiches tasty!

The Ravenglass and Eskdale railroad runs through seven miles of the valley and is affectionately known as "La al Ratty." The railroad opened in 1875 to transport iron. It has an unsettled history. In 1913 the three-foot gauge train was closed. The following year the track was narrowed to 15 inches and reopened by a famous model maker.

The train carried passengers and goods into and out of the granite quarries until the quarries closed in 1953. The tourist industry was not big enough to support the railroad at that time, so it was sold at auction in 1960. Now it is a well-known tourist attraction.

The guides drove the mini buses along the parallel road until the road veered off away from the track. We all broke into wild laughter when we saw Peter holding an American flag out the window of his van as he drove along. He had such a great personality and sense of humor!

Later cows were standing grazing in the pastures. We took this as a good sign as some say cows tend to lie down when it is raining, and sure enough when we arrived at Wastwater it was clear.

Gosford means goose ford. The architecture changed some there to pastel sandstone buildings. The Vikings met the Christian English there and mixed well with them. Approaching the west coast of the country and close to the Lake District's northern boundary we saw our first stoplight. Whitehaven was a typical industrial town with a population of 30,000. Since the iron and coal mining industries died the nuclear and chemical plants have helped replace the lost jobs. The city reminded me of any New England industrial city.

We stopped at the Beacon for scones and tea. Afterward we had plenty of time to wander through a rather nice museum.

Whitehaven, located on the Irish Sea, houses a lot of Georgian architecture. Many of the large Georgian mansions originally belonged to rich merchants. Today many of those lovely homes were empty and deteriorating. Many row houses were built up the hillsides.

The demand for coal transformed Whitehaven into a port for transport of coal to Ireland via the Irish Sea. This demand gave way to a ship building industry lasting 200 years.

In 1675 the tobacco trade started and lasted until 1790. The demand for coal and iron continued. By 1634 the population of the hamlet was 250. By the 18th century plots were laid down and Whitehaven became the first planned town since medieval times, remaining essentially unchanged today.

Approaching Keswick we detoured to see Castlerigg, an ancient stone circle.

All too soon our week in the wonderful Lake District was over and we moved on to the Yorkshire moors. En route to Scarborough on England's east coast (North Sea), we left the Lake District at Kendal which was named for the River Kent, meaning "sacred." The slate houses and fences turned to stone and the hills flattened out. The motto of Kendal used to be 'wool is my bread'. Now most of the wool industry is gone and the K and Clark shoe industry has greatly downsized. Snuff is one of the new industries.

The driver stayed pretty much on small rural roads, hitting a motorway (freeway) just outside Scarborough. We stopped in Hawes mid morning for tea. It was very windy, but we warmed with hot tea and scones at Laburnam, a delightful teahouse. On the way back to the bus we strolled through a small rope factory where all the workings were displayed behind large picture windows.

In the small village of Bainbridge we saw the old Roman road and remains of a Roman fort. The Yorkshire Dales National Park has only one natural lake and its highest point is 2000 feet. We saw fewer trees, and because there is a lot of limestone in the area houses were built of it rather than slate, or wood.

And then we were in James Herriot country! Thirsk was where the real Alf Wight practiced for many years as a vet, and was the setting of Herriot's fictional town of Darrowby. The doctor's office is now The World of James Herriot visitor center. Thirst has no village center so that was a figment of Herriot's imagination. In reality Dr. Wight also had an outreach office in Leyburn. The Herriot movie was actually filmed in the village of Askrigg.

Bankbarns were replaced with 17th century field barns, still good size, still double story, with the cattle on the ground level, and feed on the second. Many of the barns no longer used for livestock are being converted into 'stone tents' for back packers.

While we were riding along Peter explained a little about the Mountain Rescue Teams of the Lake District, of which he was a member. The thirteen rescue teams number more than any other area, but the area also has the mountains (fells). All rescue team members must be first class mountaineers to be eligible and they must pass the advanced first-aid requirement. As a result, many go on to be paramedics. There usually is a doctor on each team.

The three main teams each average 80 calls a year. In 1950 there were 14 casualty calls; in 1993 there were 400, a massive increase! Most calls are on weekends and occur all year. In summer there is the influx of people, in winter harsher conditions. Helicopter rescues average 20 percent of the time and mostly involve spinal and head injuries. Heart attack victims are no longer air lifted as dangling in the air by a rope caused greater anxiety and problems.

We passed fields of wheat, barley, corn, and linseed, an occasional market town, and then the construction changed to red brick with red tile roofs. We stopped for a picnic lunch at the Sutton Bank Information Center where there was a nice picnic area.

Although this was a transfer day we still needed to get a hike in, even if a short one, about two miles. The first stop was in a field of heather to explain a ditch and mound dyke, and to point one out that was 1000 years old. We continued walking on a level well-maintained path past a glider take-off area to see the Kilburn white horse.

England has several large white horses carved into mountainsides, but most are in the chalky, southern part of the country. A schoolteacher carved the first horse in 1856. The Kilburn horse, 206'x 320', is carved out of granite and periodically has to be painted white by men hanging by rope over the cliff using long paint rollers.

The population of the North York Moors National Park is 18,000. The National Trust only owns 1.5 percent of this park compared to 25 percent of the Lake District Park. The medieval cross is the North York Moors symbol. These crosses are named and were used as guideposts across the moors. One dates to 600 AD. The tradition was to leave coins on top of the cross if one was able; if one was in need he could take what he needed. The tradition continues today.

The 553 square mile North York Moors National Park is the most easterly of all the parks and has only 12 million visitors a year. Established in 1952 the park has dales and wolds, as we left the fells in the Lake District. 20 percent of the park is forested.

The Park has the most extensive track of heather in all of England and Wales. In late summer a sea of purple covers 160 square miles sweeping the undulating treeless ridges, 33 percent of the park is open moorland. Rare and beautiful wildlife live in the moors.

Farms were located part way up the dales to hook into water supplies from streams and springs.

Our hotel, built as a 19th century four-bedroom home, was converted to a hotel late in the century. During WWII the hotel was used to billet the military. Located on the ocean cliffs, our room had a spectacular view of the city, beach, and North Sea. Located in a residential area it was peaceful and quiet.

A large spa was built below the cliffs in 1640 and for years people flocked to the baths. Pollution shut down the spa years ago and now it is used as a convention center. Concerts are offered frequently, in fact we listened to part of one on a Sunday morning. Scarborough, located just outside the National Park, is not on American tourist agendas, but the British holiday in the typical seaside community.

Many arched packhorse bridges in the area date back to the

17th century.

Some famous people are associated with the area including Captain James Cook who was born near the moors and fulfilled a seafaring apprenticeship in Whitby. Bram Stoker got his inspiration for Dracula while visiting the eerie graveyard at St. Mary's, and Ann Bronte spent many holidays in Scarborough, died and is buried there.

The first day in Yorkshire we woke to cloudy skies and considerably cooler temperatures. I decided that perhaps it would be a good idea to put on my silk long johns since the trousers I was wearing were pretty lightweight.

I was looking forward to our first moor hike just because of the literary romance of the area. We started the day in Rosedale with a walk around the village. The River Seven, so named because of the seven springs that feed it, runs through the village. A small Priory accommodating twelve nuns was in existence from 1158 until Henry VIII dissolved it in 1535, when there were still ten nuns living in the Priory. The nuns' wealth was in wool.

Rosedale's population of about 20 swelled to 3000 in 1847 when iron oar was discovered. Mining was dangerous, and the mines were shut down after World War II.

We were to hike over the Spaunton Moor to Lastingham, finishing at Hutton le Hole.

What a start! The first and really only undulation that day was straight up — 1000 feet to the top of the moor. The cloudy and cool day didn't tame the steady climb upward over a narrow switchback footpath.

Many of us did a fair amount of huffing and puffing, and I, for one, thought we might never make it to the top. But about two hours and two miles later we all made it, only to find it so windy I thought it might blow a couple of the little people over! My mantra had been: I think I can, I think I can, I did!

We stood in the cold wind near the old railroad tracks for an explanation of the old iron kilns where iron oar was decalcified to make it lighter for transport. Some of us thought the kilns would be a nice sheltered place for lunch, but we were assured it was sheltered and much cleaner behind them. It was, and we really enjoyed our picnic on what had now turned into a sunny day. After lunch we had a lesson on how to play cricket, which was pretty funny.

The afternoon was all downhill on a wide reasonably good path. A couple of days later I learned that most groups were taken up the moor over that gentle uphill route, but our group was deemed fit enough to make the climb up the moor through the pastures!

We saw our first ancient cross. It was six foot tall and sat on a 30-inch high base. The Celtics placed large crosses all over the moors to mark their way. It is very easy to lose one's direction on the flat moors, which are often shrouded in mist. Personally I think the Celtic crosses are beautiful. The bell heather, one of three varieties of heather, was in bloom in fairly large patches. Heather is the lifeblood of the red grouse, which is indigenous to the area. The grouse eats the young shoots. When the heather is six or seven inches tall it provides nesting areas, and at its full height of 12-15 inches, it provides protection. Grouse hunting season is in August. There are controlled burns of the heather every 12 years from September to April so there are patches of different stages of growth all the time. Before the roots are burned the fires are put out so only the top growth is burned. We actually were lucky enough to see three grouse!

When the wind blows, and I think that is most of the time on the moors, the heather sways in undulating waves in a sea of color.

It got warmer and warmer as the afternoon wore on. Coming down off the moor a stop in Lastingham provided a visit to the old crypt church. Built in 1078 this church is unique to England. Built on the site of a Celtic monastery, it is a shrine to St. Cedd who brought Christianity to this part of England. He is buried within.

By the time we reached Lastingham I was more than ready to

shed those long johns under my cargo pants.

I decided that the church might not be quite the appropriate place to disrobe, but the deserted church cemetery served nicely. In the blink of an eye, my hiking boots were back on, the silkies in my pocket, no one knew what I'd been up to, and I certainly was more comfortable.

Great ice cream awaited us in the quaint little village of Hutton le Hole.

One evening we walked down off the cliff to go for a look at the Grand Hotel. We had a great view of the Grand's outside from our hotel window, so we wanted to see what it looked like inside. Walking into the Grand lobby, we made a right turn and had only taken a few steps when we were approached and asked if we were staying at the hotel.

Answering no we were informed that only residents were allowed after 6:00 PM and escorted to the door! I'd never been thrown out of a hotel before, but we'd seen what we had come to see, and confirmed what we had heard, 'that the Grand wasn't so grand anymore', so we left peacefully, chuckling to ourselves.

The next day we woke to sunshine and I think everyone's muscles and blisters were happy to be spending a day playing tourist, although the day did include a considerable amount of walking.

We visited castles and Rievaulx Abbey. We had lunch in the community center where the community ladies had hot tea, coffee and short bread for us in addition to lunch.

Excavation of the abbey started in 1920. It must have been exquisite in its day because 800 years later, I found the ruins most impressive. Many of its graceful gothic arches remain standing.

In Whitby, "gem of the northeast coast," a large whalebone archway, near the harbor, greets visitors. At one time there were three shipbuilding yards in Whitby. In fact, Captain Cook's *Endeavor* was built there.

A swing bridge over the Esk River provided passage from the

populated side of the city to the abbey side.

After wandering around the town we crossed the swing bridge and tackled the 199 steps up to St. Hilde, a 7th century abbey and near-by St. Mary's church. The Abbey dominated Whitby, and although much smaller than Rievaulx, it was a gorgeous gothic structure.

I'm thoroughly confused about our Sunday afternoon coastal walk. We drove to Cloughton, ten to 12 miles away to start our walk. We continued walking north, away from Scarborough, then turned east toward the ocean before we headed back south, and this was suppose to be only six miles back to Scarborough!

Along the old railroad we again found ripe raspberries. They were so good! The footpath followed pretty close to the edge of the cliffs. It was a beautiful sunny day and the picnic overlooking the North Sea was a delight. We'd climbed about 600 feet. A wold is a high, treeless area that is farmed.

Several times at low points in the terrain we had to climb down rather steep long steps, then cross over and climb up steps to get back on the top of the cliffs. The steps certainly were preferable to a footpath, but the steps were too wide to take in a normal fashion, as one extra step was required in between, which meant that the same foot was always going up or down. That is pretty hard on the knee and hip of the affected leg. The paths were pretty narrow requiring single file and some times walking with one foot in the ditch unless one is really good at walking with one foot in front of the other, like walking a rail.

Our final moors walk, over Lyke Dyke Walk, an ancient route for transporting the dead on horseback, started at the Flyingdales Early Warning Station, on a windy cloudy day. The last person had just climbed over the fence when it started to rain. We all donned rain gear and fortunately we were close to some big scrubby trees which provided a bit of shelter from what turned out to be only a shower.

We encountered a lot of erosion making for a lot of

maneuvering around many of the really bad places. Ancient burial grounds, called hawes, were seen all over on top of the moors.

The sun was shining by lunchtime. We had reached the summit over a gentle steady climb. After lunch it was all down hill to the village of Goathland. We elected to extend another mile and a half to the beck, then follow it to a waterfall. It was a bit slippery to the waterfall, but the rocks were large boulders so the walking was fairly easy. Reaching the waterfall was well worth the walk! The sound of that rippling water was like music! What a treat!

We could have stayed there a good while but preferring to toodle to Goathland and not crack on we planned accordingly. The shade of a tree-lined path was welcome while it lasted. After passing through several gates we lost our forest canopy and were out in the open sun and pastures. The beck was a mile down from the village so it was a steady fairly steep climb uphill all the way! The footing was good, but the sun was hot.

We couldn't be so close to York and not visit it, so we spent a delightful day in the city. First on the agenda was a three-hour city tour with a local guide, and the first thing we learned was that the ancient gates to the city are called bars because they bar anyone from entering the walled city.

York's streets are called gates from the Viking word. So gates are bars and streets are gates. Confusing.

We walked a good part of the three-mile ancient wall surrounding the inner city. The population inside the walled city is 2000, the city's population reaches 60,000 and greater York approaches 150,000.

York was a city with seven abbeys, fourteen churches and the Minster (the center of Christian teaching and ministering). It took the city 100 years to recover from the destruction wrought by William the Conqueror.

In 1539 King Manor was added to the abbey. Long ago people traveling would stop and stay with the monks at abbeys and monasteries, as there were no travelers' inns. The Manor is now part of the University of York.

The rivers Foss and Ouse flow through the city. William the Conqueror took the River Foss for his private fishing pond. Quirky as it may seem, use of the river still belongs to the Queen, and the city of York pays three pounds fifty annually to the crown for the use of the river. This amount has never been increased, but the Queen keeps the money, which today equals approximately $6.

The city's medieval wall was built on top of the old Roman wall using it as a foundation, a fairly common practice, in those days throughout Europe. Everything remained inside the walled city—garbage, bodies, everything. Eventually the ground level with in the city became elevated. Although the wall was level we could see areas where its height was shorter on the inside due to the inside ground level.

The ancient wall was in need of repair years ago, and the city wanted to simply tear it down. Some wise and concerned conservationists said NO, the end result being the wall was saved and repaired.

The Shambles, now a tourist section of the city, was once a market area. Shambles referred to a meat shelf, then it came to mean a meat store or butchery. As time went on the non-edible parts of the meat trade were thrown into the street (alley) to rot and thus shambles now means a mess.

Stonegate, the ancient throughway alley, is a pedestrian mall where visitors can shop and enjoy a rich medley of medieval and Georgian architecture.

We agreed we wanted to spend as much time sightseeing as possible, so decided to café it for a quick lunch. We did have delicious fish and chips.

York is full of museums, some very specialized for specific interests. The Castle Museum had been recommended so we decided to give it a try. It was a good choice and although we toodled through the three huge multi story buildings we could have easily spent the better part of a week there.

Afterward we did crack on to Yorkminster Cathedral to get a look inside. We knew where it was located because of the morning tour plus the spires could be seen all over town. Docents in such places are always so very knowledgeable.

The Minster, built in 1220, is the fourth building on the site. Built in stages until its completion in 1472, it is the largest medieval structure in England and the largest gothic church north of the Alps.

The Minster contains 128 stain glass windows and one half of all the stain glass in England. John Thornton created the east window in 1405-08. It is the largest stain glass window in the world. The 117 square panes represent 1680 square feet, the equivalent size of a tennis court! It is truly a gorgeous window! Thornton's work surely was a labor of love as his payment was 50 pounds. The five sisters' window, done in 1260, is the oldest window in the Minster.

The Chapel house, built in 1280-90, contains fine carvings and medieval glass.

The ceiling wood in the nave is painted to resemble stone, and it sure fooled me. On one wall, 400-year-old oak figures strike a clock every fifteen minutes. The charming clock movements date to 1749. The 15th century screen is decorated with statues of fifteen kings from William I to Henry VI. There are many points of interest within the Minster. What a magnificent building!

On our transfer from Yorkshire to Manchester we stopped at Saltaire, one of the first planned cities since medieval times.

The 25 acres near the Aire River encompasses 22 streets, 850 homes and many public buildings. Built by Sir Titus Salt in 1853 the woolen mill contained 1200 looms that produced 30,000 yards of fabric a day! The mill employed 3000 workers.

The mill shut down operations in 1892 when Salt was nearly 90. Although the mill is no longer active, Saltaire continues to be a thriving community.

Lunch on this last day was at a delightful tearoom in Haworth where we occupied the entire small establishment. It was a cold, windy, misty day, and the hot soup, as a starter, hit the spot.

We were still touring the Bronte parsonage when five hardy souls decided on a short walk on the moor. They estimated the temperature was about 40, proof that the moors can be harsh and foreboding on a gloomy day. But the moor landscape can also be glorious on a fine day when there is a feeling of spaciousness and a freedom from the pressures of the world. We had experienced both.

The Bronte history is very sad and rather depressing. The mother died young of cancer, and her sister moved to Haworth to care for the children. The father, a minister, died at age 84 having outlived all of his children. The girls all died young.

During the two weeks we had hiked through many pastures where sheep talked to us, and at other times simply ignored our presence as we intruded into their territory. During our visit we walked up fells and down into valleys, walked over moors, climbed a few fences. We had seen and learned a lot, had great accommodations, and good food.

Farewells are always hard for me when a trip has been as wonderful as this one. The guides had all been the greatest, but Peter was so exceptional. It was time for the Kleenex! As the English would say it had been a smashing two weeks. And for me the best part was that my foot held up so I could do it all.

Chapter 21

England: Stratford-upon-Avon — Cotswolds

Mad cow disease and hoof and mouth disease were raging through England in 2001 at the time of this trip. Many people cancelled trips overseas because of the outbreak. I did not, and just decided that I would not eat any beef. Actually this worked to my advantage as the group finalized at only ten. I definitely prefer small groups.

On the eve of my departure I went to bed hearing the TV announce that ten inches of rain had been dumped on Houston. Would I be able to get in and out of the Houston airport the next morning? Was this trip doomed before it even began?

The next morning the TV reported the airport in Houston was clear, but that the storm was moving on to Chicago, my transfer point! I did get out of Houston on time and without difficulty, and I arrived in Chicago after the storm had passed. When all was said and done I arrived in London on schedule, but not everyone in the group was as lucky, as some were diverted and delayed.

In our small hotel in Wilmcote all the rooms were named after a Shakespearean play. I was sleeping with *The Merchant of Venice!*

Our first visit was the Tudor style Mary Arden House, which was only a half block away, and our first encounter with hoof and mouth. There was no way anyone or any vehicle was going to enter the premises without driving over or walking through the chemically treated hay which extended all across the entrance.

That was pretty simple and painless!

Some mushroom shaped stones under the Arden house barn were called stadle stones, not saddle, but stadle. They provided air circulation for the barn, as well as kept out water, and any varmints that might want to get inside.

As we entered the home, an informative docent kept us interested with her stories. Mary Arden, Shakespeare's mother, was the youngest of eight girls. It had always been believed that she lived in that house as a girl until she married. However, a recent survey had revealed that the oldest timber in the home dated only to 1569, and she and John Shakespeare were married in 1557. Now, it's believed that she lived on the Glebe farm just across the way. Glebe in a name meant that the church owned it. Timber was valuable and extra timber on a house was a status symbol showing that one was well off. The house was occupied until 1930.

The original floor of the home would have been earthen, and it is believed that the blue limestone floor was put in afterward. The stone came from a quarry only a quarter mile away. The stones were simply laid on the ground, not set in sand, as they would be today,

When the man in the family returned home from working in the fields, he sat in his armchair to relax and do no more work that day. He was the "chair man."

Before the word table was used, a table was referred to as a board. Of course the man of the house headed the board, thus he became "chairman of the board." The board had a rough side used for eating on, and a smooth side for company show. From this came the expressions "aboveboard," and "good" and "bad side." A child generally stood at the table to eat until about the age of twelve.

With no refrigeration, salt was a precious commodity for curing meat. A man was sometimes paid in salt, thus the expression "worth his salt." Because of the lack of yeast, bread was pretty flat and was sliced through a round loaf, producing a piece not too unlike a tortilla. The bottom part was the least desirable because it usually was a bit overdone having been closest to the fire. Of course the "upper crust" went to the chairman of the board!

Windows in the 1700s were only open wooden framed spaces in the walls. They tended to be small and few in number. Being open left the home exposed in bad weather. When it rained, a cloth covered wooden frame was placed over the window opening. The cloth was smeared with fat from cooking — the original storm window.

I was amazed to hear that the horns from the 'long horn' cattle, if boiled about 48 hours in vinegar, became soft and pliable. After compressing the soft horns flat, they could be peeled into thin layers resembling mica or the modern day capiz shell. Eventually thin layers of horns replaced the fat smeared cloth on the storm windows. I wonder how long the vinegar aroma hung in the air!

Stratford-upon-Avon was only three and a half to four miles from Wilmcote. Avon is a Celtic word meaning "river," strat is Saxon for "soft road," and forde means "over a river." Over time, the final e has been dropped from Stratford. In England it is the River Avon, not the Avon River.

Richard I, known as Richard the Lion Hearted, granted Stratford-upon-Avon a charter in 1196. A charter was necessary to become a market town. Markets in Stratford still exist today. Thursday is a cattle market, and Friday a produce market.

First on the agenda was a canal boat ride on the River Avon. After brief safety instructions the captain told us the canal locks are only seven feet wide, manual, and are operated by of the boat crew. The same winch, which comes with the rental of the boat, operates all the locks.

We found it rather strenuous work to open and close the locks. The canal system was first built in the 1700s. Mr. Wedgwood, of Wedgwood China Company, helped finance the system because too much of his merchandise was being broken via horse and wagon. One can travel a long way on the 2000 miles of canals. Birmingham has more canals than Venice and is known as the Venice of England. The railroad effectively put the canals out of business until the 1960s when the canals and locks were refurbished. All along the river white swans were permanent residents.

After leaving the canal boat at noon it was only a short walk to the manual winch ferry, which took us to the other side of the river.

Holy Trinity Church, Shakespeare's burial ground, was a short distance from the boat stop. Buried with him were his wife Anne, daughter Susanna and her husband John Hall, and granddaughter Elizabeth and her husband Thomas Nash. The Shakespeare Birthplace Trust was established in 1849 when P.T. Barnum wanted to buy the birthplace with the intention of moving it to the U.S. Many prominent citizens formed a group, and collectively outbid Barnum while he was in Spain and unable to counter-bid. The Trust owns and manages several properties.

The twelve lime trees on one side of the church walkway represent the twelve disciples, and the trees on the other side represent the Ten Commandments.

The inner door of the church entrance was a sanctuary knocker. Not all churches had sanctuary knockers, but if they did and one reached it, he was automatically granted 37 days of sanctuary. After that he was on his own.

A Mr. Crofton built the bridge across the River Avon in 1492, and has a family chapel and burial ground in the church. The plague killed one of his daughters then three weeks later killed another. When the tomb was opened for the second daughter, it was evident the first little girl was not dead when she was buried.

Shakespeare's birthplace, built in the 1500s, has seen many alterations and redecorations over the years. But in 500 years that's not a surprise.

The front parlor contained a *first best bed*, which was a bed used only for guests, and was a sign of wealth. Family members never sat on or used the first best bed. The four-posted canopy bed came into use during the Elizabethan era to protect sleepers from anything dropping from the thatched roof where mice and other varmints often would nest! Let your imagination work here!

Shakespeare's dad, John, first rented the house when he moved to Stratford after leaving farming to become a glove maker, merchant, and moneylender. Shakespeare completed grammar school, but was not college educated, which really turned out to be an advantage for him. Since he wrote for the masses, most of whom were illiterate, some scholars felt that a university education might have elevated him to write for a different audience. It was his success that made him one of the few artisans to become wealthy and well known during his lifetime. At his death he owned many properties. It is generally believed that he acquired his entrepreneurial skills from his father.

William, one of eight children, born in 1564, was the third child, but the oldest son. Two girls died before he was born. He and Anne Hathaway had eight children of their own, four boys and four girls. Eight seemed to be the magic number.

The house, once in a rural area, is now surrounded by shops on busy Henley Street. A Trust museum was next door, and in the back of the house was a large garden where pathways were lined with herbs.

The city's almshouses, built in the 1400s for the poor, have been renovated and modernized and are still lived in today.

Halls Croft was the residence of John Hall, husband of Shakespeare's oldest daughter, Suzanne. Although Dr. Hall was Cambridge educated, he was not a medical doctor. However, he ran a thriving dispensary/clinic, and people came from afar to visit him. He kept meticulous records, which showed his most offered treatment for most any ailment was a mixture of gunpowder and pebbles! It must have been effective, but makes one wonder.

If one complained of a sore throat, the doctor would dangle a live frog over the patient's open mouth, convinced that frog spittle would be beneficial for the sore throat. Remember the expression, *a frog in my throat.*

Shakespeare bought New Place in 1597 for sixty pounds, and it is here that he died in 1616 at age 52. The home, built in 1483 for a Lord Mayor of London, was Stratford's grandest piece of real estate when Shakespeare bought it. Unfortunately in 1759 it was torn down by a disgruntled Reverend Gastrell who was most annoyed by the hordes of sightseers, but destroying the house didn't stop them. A lovely garden now occupies the area and sits next to the Nash House.

Six of us decided to walk back to Wilmcote on the footpath beside the canal.

Cotswold is a Saxon word; cots meaning "sheep fold," and wold meaning "upland common." The English Cotswolds is an area of limestone hills where herds of cattle and sheep cover lush green pastures separated by stone walls. Picturesque thatched roof, stone villages are nestled in between.

Small rivers run through most villages, where flower bedecked cottages and expansive manor houses add to the charm of the sleepy little villages. Low stone bridges span the rivers and streams.

Cester or chester, Roman meaning "camp," usually is found at the end of a name indicating Roman origins such as Worchester and Cirencester.

A prime sheep grazing area for centuries, wealthy wool merchants built the churches, whose towers beckon the visitor.

Honey colored Cotswold stone is the building material used almost entirely in the area. Roof thatching is very time consuming and expensive, and like other crafts the art is a dying one. Slate tile roofs are becoming common, and most homes are surrounded with a dry set stone wall about three feet high. We saw flower gardens everywhere.

Buses often cannot make it on the narrow roads of many villages. In spite of the Cotswolds being a prime tourist area, it has maintained its historic appearance and charm. Many of the old homes have been turned into quaint little shops, especially on the main streets.

The Romans built roads, forts, and villas. Fosse is a Roman word meaning "ditch" and the famous Fosse Way is in that area. A ditch on each side of the "roadway" provided protection for its users. The Saxons were farmers, who developed fleece, laying the foundation for the prosperity of medieval merchants, who in turn built the churches and alms houses, many of which are still occupied even though centuries old!

Nearly every little village claims it is the prettiest village in the Cotswolds and it certainly would be difficult to judge any kind of contest!

Chipping Campden, a town of the 14th and 15th centuries, was the most important wool-trading center in the north Cotswolds. Bishop Hicks and William Gravel, two wool merchants, provided for the wool church and market hall. The view from the church overlooking the countryside was picturesque. On the church foyer ceiling were some handsome wooden bosses, ornaments, often of carved wood, but can be plaster, that overlays the joints of wood or plaster beams on decorative ceilings. They are most unique.

Chipping, an Old English word meaning "market," is found in many village names.

In Blockley, we visited Mill Dene Garden. The owner took us on a tour of the lovely three-acre garden she created and had landscaped over the past 25 years. A stream ran through the gardens. The waterwheel of an old mill was silent on the property. The gardens were exquisite.

On a sunny afternoon we enjoyed quite a good birds-of-prey show and demonstration at the Falconry Center in Batsford. Falcons can fly only two minutes. They mostly ride the air currents. When they are full, they are "fed-up." Hawks have very good eyesight, thus the expression *eyes of a hawk.*

It was demonstrated how hawks can fly through narrow spaces when a bird flew between two people or under a seat. Falcons dive 150-200 mph to catch their prey. All birds of prey are carnivorous, and none of them fly just for fun. Owls have excellent hearing, and hunt by sound, not eyesight. These birds do not have a lot of fat on their bodies, if they did, they wouldn't be able to fly, so the bird's bones are lazy and they sit to rest, which gave us the expression "lazy bones."

Bibury was a small village we accessed over a rather steep footpath, after crossing over the trout filled River Coln via the stone footbridge. The colorful English gardens always lift my spirits and make me want to try to duplicate them at home.

Upper and Lower Slaughter are separated by the mile long Warden's Way along the River Eye. Spanned by several footbridges, the river runs down the center of the street in Lower Slaughter. Actually the street consists of two, narrow, paved lanes with the river, walled like a canal, in the center of them. An old mill sits in the center of Lower Slaughter. Both areas are upscale with large homes, many of which are summer residences. Each village has a couple of large, upscale hotels.

We went onto the grounds of one of the hotels and walked the paths, which led through a wooded area and then opened onto lovely gardens on the other side of the hotel. It was a pleasant respite on a warm and sunny day.

Slaughter, by the way, refers to nothing bloody, but is a Saxon word meaning "place of many pools."

Upper Slaughter is one of only twelve villages fortunate enough to have all their boys return from World War I. Therefore the village has no war memorial and on November 11 celebrates with a Thanksgiving program vs. a Memorial Day service.

Our hotel was located in Bourton-on-the-Water, a darling little town on the eastern edge of the Cotswolds. The hotel with 15 rooms was built in 1748 for a Baptist pastor during the time of wealth from the wool trade. The church owned the property until 1938. In 1963 the building was extended and transformed into a hotel. The hotel overlooked the village green where the River Windrush flowed through. It was a sweet hotel in a lovely little village.

A stop at Hailes Abbey ruins, built in 1246, was interesting. Consecrated in 1251 the abbey housed 20 monks and ten lay brothers. Richard, Earl of Cornwall, and brother to Henry III, was caught in a storm at sea in 1242. He vowed that if he survived the storm, he would build a religious house.

Hailes Abbey was the fulfillment of that promise. The first cloister was built of wood, but was replaced with stone at the end of the 15th century. The abbey was destroyed, like nearly all others, during Henry VIII's reign. All churches were Catholic until that time. Henry just ravished England with his destruction of churches. Excavation of Hailes Abbey started in 1890.

Across the carpark stood an old Saxon church built before the Abbey as a 12th century parish church. Recent restoration had revealed ancient medieval paintings that had been whitewashed over for centuries!

Warwick Castle, dominating the city of Warwick, is generally believed to be the finest medieval castle in England. Built on a cliff, its 60 acres were meticulously manicured grounds and gardens.

Built by William the Conqueror in the 12th century, the castle had two uneven towers. The Caesar Tower, built in 1356, was 147 feet tall, while Guy's tower, 1380, was only 128 feet. The intentional irregular design allowed defenders numerous points of defense.

Of all of the castles I've visited over the years, I believe Warwick Castle is one of the finest. Proud, colorful peacocks were permanent residents of the grounds. Rhododendrons were in full bloom. And the blooms were huge! The rose garden was covered with buds and when they burst into bloom it would be a spectacular sight.

There was a fine collection of medieval armor and weaponry. Historic furniture and old master paintings were housed throughout the castle.

The living quarters were occupied as late as the 1970s. The citizens of Warwick were aghast a few years ago when Madam Tussand purchased the castle. Their fear that the castle would be turned into a garish tourist attraction had not materialized. In fact, just the opposite had happened.

Her magnificent, life-sized wax figures in the living quarters were exquisite. They added personality and a great deal of reality to the twelve-room exhibit. My favorite was the maid in the bathroom drawing water for her lady. Bending over the tub of running water, she was so life-like that nearly everyone did a double take, even though we knew the figures were not real.

Many of the woodcarvings left us gasping at the fine workmanship and intricacy.

Children delighted in the ghost tower. The queues (lines) were long, so we decided to skip that exhibit but availed ourselves of the many medieval demonstrations taking place on the grounds. After spending most of the day at the castle, a walking tour of the small town followed.

Lord Leycester's Hospital, built in the 14th century as a home for single army veterans who had completed 22 years of service, has been in continuous service since! Later it was opened to all veterans, and now there are a few who reside there with their wives. Twelve Brethren and their master continue to reside there.

In the back we found a gorgeous restored 500-year-old garden. Within the garden, in front of an ancient Norman arch, stood a large 2000-year-old stone vase.

Before touring the Broughton Castle we enjoyed a ploughman's lunch. Traditionally the ploughman (plow) took his lunch to the field with him in the morning. It consisted of cheese and hard bread or roll. I'm not sure what the drink of the day would have been then, probably ale. Today restaurants add a small salad to the Ploughman lunch.

Walking through the gate at Broughton Castle, I was overwhelmed by the massive size of the yellow stone building. I don't know how many acres it sits on, but once inside the gate you could see nothing but grounds!

Broughton Castle, originally built in the 1300s, consisted of a great hall, two other rooms, and a chapel. Soon after, the three-acre moat was built around the property and the gate added. Today the water in the moat is six-feet deep.

William of Wykeham owned the castle for 70 years after building it. The Fiennes (pronounced Fine) family purchased the castle, and it has been in this family now for over 600 years. The title Lord Saye was bestowed in 1451, and a Lord and Lady Saye still live in the castle living quarters. A major Tudor addition was added to this medieval castle in 1550.

The huge fireplace in the great room took five-foot long logs! Thirty-six leather sand buckets with the family crest lined the shelves in the hall, and no doubt many were located throughout the castle at one time.

We saw period furniture and a fine china collection on display in its many rooms. The walls in the "king" room were covered with the most magnificent Chinese wall paper. It actually consisted of many oblong canvas panels about 40 x 24 inches, floor to ceiling. No two full-length panels were the same. The design depicted all seasons, except winter, with trees, flowers, and birds. About two feet from the floor on each panel was a different decorative vase/jar. Birds were all done in pairs, but no two pairs were the same.

Centuries ago wallpaper was precious, and if one moved they took their wallpaper with them, therefore the paper was not glued to the walls. The designs matched perfectly at the seams. All I could think of was what a job it would be to move and reassemble all those panels —like a Chinese puzzle.

Several movies have been filmed at the castle; *The Madness of King George*, *Henry VIII*, and most recently, *Shakespeare in Love*. The long carpet runner in the upstairs hallway was made for the last picture, and then was left at the castle, as the movie company had no use for it. The docent made the remark, that movies help pay the upkeep of the castle.

From the Cotswolds we moved on to Cornwall. Although geographically close to the Cotswolds, it is a world of its own with spectacular landscapes and stunning rugged coastline. Hedgerows climb the hills defining and dividing the rolling green pastures. The River Tamar separates Cornwall from the rest of the country making Cornwall almost an island. No place is Cornwall is more than 20 miles from the coast and the ocean.

Small quaint fishing villages are found in sheltered coves along the rugged coast. The mild climate is conducive to sunning on the many beaches, and there are many good surfing areas.

Cottages and churches were made of a gray stone, and English gardens continued to abound adding color. We often passed under natural green arches over the roads where the trees and vines on each side had grown over the road and entangled with those on the opposite side.

The land of legendary shipwrecks, it has over 3000 recorded shipwrecks along the rugged coastline.

One rainy afternoon we visited the Shipwreck Museum in Charlestown. It was quite well done, with video narration of several famous shipwrecks. It was full of shipwreck relics. When we had finished walking through the museum we headed upstairs to the Bosun's Diner for tea.

There is a large Celtic influence in Cornwall, and names of Celtic saints are evident. The prefix Tre in a place name means "village" or "field," such as Trelowth, Tregonick, or Treven. The prefix Tor means "hill."

Cornwall has been the home of writers and artists for decades. King Arthur resided in north Cornwall. Daphne du Maurier and

Agatha Christie are but two writers who lived in Cornwall.

Prince Charles has an estate in Cornwall. The eldest royal son has been the Duke of Cornwall for ages. If produce or a product is labeled "duchy," it means the tax goes to the Duke's trust. Prince Charles' trust makes loans/grants to small business enterprises.

Narrow two-lane roads were generally the norm in Cornwall. Some roads were no wider than a one-car lane and it got real interesting sometimes when we met a vehicle going in the opposite direction!

Mevagissey, a small quaint fishing village, has a history of smuggling. In fact smuggling was a common enterprise years ago all along the Cornwall coast. One evening we had fish and chips in a 15th century pub where even today the bar, oak beams, and slate floor were the original. The meaning of history certainly comes alive!

George Bernard Shaw wrote "The Doctor's Dilemma" in 1906 while living in Mevagissey.

Buckfast Abbey, started in 1884, took 32 years for four French monks to build. The leader of a Benedictine Abbey is called an Abbot. The Benedictine premise is prayer, study, and work.

Presently 44 monks live in the Abbey. One is a novice for two years, taking his first vows at 12 months. After four years one can leave, but if he elects to stay he must have the vote of the entire community. Each monk must show stability, obedience, and conversion of life. They are not called brother, unless a priest.

The Parish church was founded over a hundred years ago. It must be self-supporting. The Abbey has the largest and most famous bee business with 800 hives and 16 million bees specially bred to be disease resistant. Farming, stained glass production, and a "toxic" wine all provide income. I'm not sure what "toxic" means, but probably meant intoxicating. The Abbey started a Catholic school in the community, and also has a private school on the premises. The Abbey was beautiful, and it was nice to learn that the monks lived long enough to see the fruition of their dream.

One day we decided to spend the day hiking. Leaving the hotel we walked down a narrow canopy covered lane until we found a footpath. Following it we arrived at Maenporth Beach just as a shower passed overhead.

We took shelter in a still under construction ice cream kiosk at the beach. When the shower abated we found another footpath that led us through a wooded area to the tiny village of Mowensmith. After learning the footpath to some gardens was closed our driver came for us. It was only the second path we ran into that hoof and mouth had closed.

Driving over narrow country lanes was delightful. The hedgerow-lined meadows became part of panoramic views as the bushes and flowers along the roads thinned. Wild flowers bloomed everywhere. Every once in awhile we'd find a small village or a thatched roof house, but we saw no tourists, bus, or fast food restaurants.

We made our way to the village of Gweek where we found a rather extensive seal sanctuary on the Helford River. Two-thirds of the world's Grey Seal population lives off the coast of the British Isles, mostly off Scotland. Pups, born August-September, often get separated from mom by a storm and are bashed against the rocky coast. Many rescues are made of such pups. They are held at the sanctuary and released the following spring. The sanctuary has a hospital, plus several tanks where we found several varieties of seals.

After a hearty lunch at the local pub we headed to Trebah Gardens. The introduction in their flyer says, "This is no pampered, pristine, prissy garden with rows of clipped hedges, close mown striped lawns, and daily raked paths. Instead it is a magnificent old, wild, and magical Cornish garden—the product of 100 years of inspired and dedicated creation followed by 40 years of mellowing and ten years of love and restoration."

And magnificent it was! Even the light rain showers didn't keep us from walking and enjoying the garden. Trebah stands at the head of a 25-acre ravine, 1625 feet long and dropping to 225 feet to the Helford River. Under an umbrella I walked the whole length twice on two different paths plus zigzagging between paths on occasion. The paths were well marked and at the end of the loop stood a memorial to the men of the 29th Division who headed off from there to Normandy for D-Day.

Our hotel in Cornwall was a 27-room 1872 Victorian manor house sitting on six acres. Since there were no restaurants within easy walking distance we ate dinner at the hotel. They employed a fantastic chef!

Penzance is a seaside community. Our hotel across the street from the ocean promenade offered us a delightful view of Mount's Bay and St. Michael's Mount. In the 16th century Spanish raiders destroyed most of the town, so most buildings date from the 18th century. However, one evening we did find the Turks Head Pub where we learned the 14th century inn was the oldest in town. The extensive menu was very reasonable and the generous meal was extremely good.

One of Cornwall's most famous landmarks is St. Michael's Mount. It sits 200 feet above the bay on the highest point of the granite and slate island rising out of the water. Built over the site of a Benedictine chapel, it has been a church, fortress, and private residence. It was one huffing hike over a very rough cobblestone path to the top, but the views were spectacular, the castle was lovely, and it certainly was worth the climb!

One can walk the causeway, built in 1425, only at very low tide, otherwise it's a pound fare for the ferry ride, which is just a motorized, open rowboat that held twelve people. Eight boats run continuously. At the top of one of the pair of stairs at the island loading piers is a gold footprint marked VC in commemoration of Queen Victoria's visit in 1846. I wonder if she made the climb to the top.

The castle was a defense in 1585 when the Spanish tried to invade, and for any significant disturbance since. St. Michael's

Mount was built by the same French monks who created Normandy's Mont St. Michel.

The organ in the present chapel dates from around 1791. The castle housed period furniture and old maps. Lovely wooden floors were throughout, and the castle was bright inside because of its rather large windows for its day.

St. Ives has been known as an artist colony since the 1880s. A darling quaint little seaside village, it is easy to see why Whistler went there to paint, and Daphne de Maurier and Virginia Wolfe to write.

No vehicle larger than the shuttles can make it into the village, so a large carpark was located high above town. The streets were only lanes and the area was very hilly.

The Cornwall landscape was dotted with the stacks of tin mines. Once the tin center of Europe, tin mining supplied the lifeblood of many small communities.

A visit to the Geevor Tin Mine was an interesting one. I went on the mine tour, but this claustrophobic old lady was very happy to see daylight!

This mine with 160 miles of tunnel continued to operate longer than most, but closed in 1990. At that time it employed 370 men, 130 of whom worked under ground. All the workers lived within a seven to ten-mile radius of the mine. In 1991 they started flooding the under-ocean mine. It took three and a half years to bring the water to sea level! In 1993 part of the mine reopened as a museum.

Mining was men's work. No women were allowed in the mines. Years ago boys as young as eight were sent into the mines. Often a mine was a family enterprise. It is totally dark in the mines, with candles providing the only light! A miner had to supply all his own tools, candles, gunpowder etc. One was paid only on what he produced. All miners were contract labor; no hourly wage in those days. The men would stay in the mines ten to 12 hours in cramped positions from dawn to nightfall. The life span of a miner was only about 40 years. They suffered poor eyesight, as they worked long hours six days a week. Many died of TB. Mining was rock, darkness, and water. It was one hard life!

Minack Theater was the most fantastic outdoor theater I've ever seen. In the early 1920s a young girl named Rowena Cade had a vision of a theater by the bay to be built into the granite cliffside. She set out to accomplish just that. With the help of two men she did create and build a perfectly gorgeous theater in the most spectacular setting. The theater, with nearly perfect acoustics, seats 750, and is truly magnificent!

Ms. Cade never married. This was her life's work. Fortunately she lived until 1983 so she could enjoy the fruits of her labors. There were interruptions, like WWII, and hardships along the way, but her dogged determination produced a positively lovely theater. Flowers grew everywhere among the rocks in the theater forming one huge rock garden. The ocean, many hundreds of feet below, made a wonderful backdrop for the theater.

We watched part of a rehearsal for an upcoming play. Seated halfway down in the theater we could hear everything going on without the use of any microphones. The summer theater season runs 17 weeks and performs mostly Shakespearean plays.

Now what can I say about the Eden Project, Bath, Salisbury, Stonehenge, or London? There are whole tour books written on London, as there is so much history there and so much to see and do. So what I'm going to say in view of space limitations is, maybe, another day. For now I'm going on to Land's End.

Approaching Land's End we lost the trees as the landscape became quite barren. Land's End is the most westerly point in England. The area has been turned into sort of an amusement area, which was a bit of a disappointment.

The rugged rocky coast reminded me of the Maine coast. The lighthouse stood alone on a large protruding rock base as a steady warning to all who sailed and dared to get too close to the shoreline. The choppy seas continually washed over the rocks.

Having been in England several times I've picked up some English expressions, some appropriate and some really cute. Getting my knickers in a twist (frustrated) is one of my favorites. A hole in the wall refers to an ATM. Brits don't phone, they ring up. Wick refers to a dairy farm. If you've been ear wigging you've been eavesdropping. If you want a specific kind of beer it's best to find a free house where a variety of brands are sold vs the only one a company makes if you visit a company owned pub. Along the beck (small stream) you may pass a weir (small dam). Maybe on the trail you're carrying a nip and tattie pie for lunch (turnip and potato).

Dale is a Viking word for valley, Grizedale means pig valley. We never saw a tatty (scruffy) person or a silent policeman (speed bump). Swaite is a clearing. Cobbles are small dinghy-type fishing boats. Coppice is wood that is cut every 15 years. Smalls are one's delicate washables. And these days I don't need to worry about blotting my copybook because I'm using a computer and not the pen with ink wells many of us grew up with.

About the Author

After taking 16 years off from her nursing career, Winnie Bowen returned to school to update her skills. In the 1980s she opened a Home Health Agency, acting as administrator until her retirement in 1992.

During those years she remained an active volunteer in Scouts, Brownies, PTA, and in water safety and first-aid programs. Her mid-life crisis hit at age 55 with her children educated and gone from the nest. She volunteered her time to the Texas Lions Camp for Crippled Children and AARP tax and 55 Alive programs.

She often speaks to civic groups. At the annual meeting in 2002, she left the Board of Senior University Georgetown, having served four years. She continues on the program committee. Presently she volunteers in the hospital gift shop and teaches geography and related topics to her granddaughter's elementary class.

Between travels, she is an avid gardener and maintains a totally landscaped back yard. She walks several times a week, bikes, reads as much as time permits, and of course writes. Having written travel pieces for newspapers for ten years, writing a book about her travels seemed like the natural next step for her.

She always has time to visit with friends who are welcome any time of the day. She is one busy senior citizen who thrives on the activity and thinks her life is nothing but normal.

To order additional copies of
Wish You Were Here

Name _____

Address _____

_____

$19.95 x _____ copies =   _____

Sales Tax   _____
(Texas residents add 7.75% sales tax)

Please add $3.50 postage and handling per book   _____

Total amount due: _____

WINNBOW@JUNO.COM

Please send check or money order for books to:

Winnie Bowen
~~**P.O. Box 1785**~~ 204 Tallwood Dr.
Georgetown, TX 78628

For a complete catalog of our books, visit our site at
http://www.WordWright.biz

313

Printed in the United States
861200003B